OXFORD WORLD'S CLASSICS

WILLA CATHER

The Song of the Lark

Edited with an Introduction and Notes by
JANET SHARISTANIAN

OXFORD
UNIVERSITY PRESS

OXFORD
UNIVERSITY PRESS

Great Clarendon Street, Oxford OX2 6DP

Oxford University Press is a department of the University of Oxford.
It furthers the University's objective of excellence in research, scholarship,
and education by publishing worldwide in

Oxford New York

Athens Auckland Bangkok Bogotá Buenos Aires Calcutta
Cape Town Chennai Dar es Salaam Delhi Florence Hong Kong Istanbul
Karachi Kuala Lumpur Madrid Melbourne Mexico City Mumbai
Nairobi Paris São Paulo Singapore Taipei Tokyo Toronto Warsaw

with associated companies in Berlin Ibadan

Oxford is a registered trade mark of Oxford University Press
in the UK and in certain other countries

Published in the United States
by Oxford University Press Inc., New York

Editorial matter © Janet Sharistanian 2000

First published as an Oxford World's Classics paperback 2000

British Library Cataloguing in Publication Data

Data available

Library of Congress Cataloging in Publication Data

Data available

ISBN 0-19-283201-8

3 5 7 9 10 8 6 4 2

Typeset in Ehrhardt
by RefineCatch Limited, Bungay, Suffolk
Printed in Great Britain by
Cox and Wyman Ltd., Reading, Berks.

CONTENTS

ACKNOWLEDGEMENTS

I would like to thank Danny J. Anderson, Victor Cardell, Teresa Fernandez, Clinton N. Howard, Stanley Lombardo, Daniel T. Politoske, Carl J. Strikwerda, Vicky Unruh, and Sarah Young for their assistance with various aspects of the Explanatory Notes.

INTRODUCTION

In *The Song of the Lark* (1915) Willa Cather wrote a most unusual novel: the narrative of a female artist's growth, development, and achievement set in the context of an American epic. Cather's novel falls into the category of the *Künstlerroman* or 'artist novel', a subset of the *Bildungsroman* or novel of formation, which traces the growth and development of an individual and generally concludes with an assessment of his or her place in society. As many readers have noticed, when the protagonist of the *Bildungsroman* is a woman her choices in adulthood are frequently limited to marriage on the one hand and privation or death on the other, particularly in novels of the nineteenth and early twentieth centuries. *The House of Mirth* (1905), a modified *Bildungsroman* by Cather's near-contemporary Edith Wharton, provides a graphic example. Wharton's protagonist, Lily Bart, who is restricted by both gender and class, is raised to be the decorative possession of a wealthy man, exhibiting his status through her beauty and refinement. Though set adrift by her father's financial ruin and the deaths of her parents, Lily refuses to auction herself off to the highest bidder in a marriage of convenience. As a result, after a series of painful crises that both cause and result from downward mobility, Lily ends as a beautiful corpse. Cather's Thea Kronborg is Lily Bart's opposite: the independent artist moving along a trajectory of accomplishments that ultimately leads to success and fame, not the dependent *objet d'art* tracing a spiral of social decline.

Even among female *Künstlerromane*, *The Song of the Lark* is exceptional. Elizabeth Ammons has pointed out that American women writers from the mid-nineteenth to the early twentieth centuries wrote and rewrote the figure of the woman as artist.[1] This is true; however, accomplishment and recognition generally elude these characters. Kate Chopin, Virginia Woolf, and Edith

---

[1] Elizabeth Ammons, *Conflicting Stories: American Women Writers at the Turn into the Twentieth Century* (New York, 1991), 121.

Wharton—all of them, like Cather, important white women writers of the middle and upper-middle classes in the United States and England around the turn of the century—chose female artists as protagonists, but the fates of these women are very different from that of Thea Kronborg. In *The Awakening* (1899) and *To the Lighthouse* (1927) the heroines must choose between the domestic sphere, which society rewards with approval, and the artistic realm, in which the female artist is maginalized even when she achieves her creative goals. In Wharton's novella *The Touchstone* (1900) the famous woman author, dead before the narrative begins, is reduced to a commodity when her lawyer 'friend' sells her letters to finance his marriage.

In effect, then, Chopin, Woolf, and Wharton expressed their anxieties about female authorship through their handling of women artists. Though male writers have often felt themselves to be at odds with their societies—James Joyce's autobiographical *Portrait of the Artist as a Young Man* (1916) is the classic example—the *Künstlerroman* of the male artist has flourished, often in first or early novels. By contrast, even women writers who have been productive, widely read, and critically acclaimed have typically been too reserved about their ambitions or too convinced of their anomalousness as women to inscribe themselves as successful artists in the protagonists of their texts. Cather's protagonist is not different from these other characters because she eludes conflict. On the contrary: Thea faces both external and internal struggle at each point along her path. She is different from these other female artists because her creator allows her to make a decisive choice for art and rewards her with success.

The Song of the Lark is also unusual among Cather's fictions in this respect. Cather's twenty-year apprenticeship (1892–1913) in newspaper and magazine journalism in Lincoln, Pittsburgh, and New York included a good deal of drama and music criticism, and her fiction about artists extends from her first collection of short stories, *The Troll Garden* (1905), to almost her last novel, *Lucy Gayheart* (1935). However, among Cather's fictional artists only

Thea Kronborg has a great talent that is both fulfilled and socially recognized rather than being stifled, ignored, or corrupted.

So far as structure is concerned, Cather's best-known novels, such as *My Ántonia* (1918), *The Professor's House* (1925), and *Death Comes for the Archbishop* (1927), comprise radical experiments with narrative form marked by shifts in point of view, interruptions in continuity, and limited exposition. But in *Song*, by far her longest work, Cather came as close as she ever would to full-blown realistic narration. Finally, though Cather drew upon personal experience as well as memories of specific individuals and places throughout her writing, only in *The Song of the Lark*, her most overtly autobiographical novel, did she explicitly trace her own slow and gradual development from provincial midwesterner to cosmopolitan artist.

In order to effect such a transformation, Cather had to come to terms with the vast Nebraska landscape and the small town of Red Cloud to which she had been abruptly transferred as a nine-year-old. Doing so meant leaving the plains and the small town— but also locating in these seemingly provincial materials a central source for sophisticated writing. Similarly, Thea Kronborg's odyssey from small-town preacher's daughter to leading soprano at the Metropolitan Opera necessitates a dramatic break with her family and community. But they also provide her with the means to leave and the values, experiences, and memories that she will draw on to express her art.

In Cather's life and in her novel, the female artist has to secede from home, family, and everyday society in order to bring her talents to fruition. At the same time, her talents are nurtured by and expressive of the world that she has left behind. Unlike Cather, who visited Nebraska frequently until both of her parents died, Kronborg does not literally return to the scenes of her childhood. Metaphorically speaking, though, both author and protagonist continually return to the past, to their childhoods in wide-open landscapes, because these are essential components of their make-up as individuals and as artists.

Cather's *Künstlerroman* occupies a distinctive position in the sequence of her novels, which also helps to explain its uniqueness. She could not have written such a narrative, in which the protagonist achieves inseparable identities as a person and as a performer, until she had fully committed herself to the writer's vocation and uncovered her own material after years of working in imitative modes. These modes derived primarily from male writers or Europeanized examples. Cather modelled her early stories about artists and their followers upon fiction with similar subject matter by the American writer Henry James (1843–1916). James, born in New York City, had been partly educated in Europe and moved permanently to England in 1876, convinced that the American scene was hostile towards creative talent and offered no adequate subject matter for his writing. Though she eventually rejected his bias against America as a source for creativity, Cather was indebted to James as the leading exponent of fiction as an art form rather than as entertainment or reportage. Similarly, when Cather began contemplating the possibility that pioneer experience in the American West was her central subject matter, she had to address the fact that this experience was almost uniformly expressed through a masculine discourse organized around a lone male hero who turns his back on social forms and asserts his will against the forces of nature. If Cather were to write out of her own experience and point of view, she would have to find some other way of representing human interaction with the wilderness.

Cather published *O Pioneers!*, both her first fully distinctive narrative and her first publication to elicit substantial interest and praise, in 1913. Once she had produced this breakthrough text, in which the protagonist, Alexandra Bergson, achieves heroic status as a midwestern pioneer not by subduing but by nurturing the land, Cather was free to speak with some authority about the developmental processes, labours, conflicts, satisfactions, and sacrifices involved in becoming a woman artist—whom she saw as another kind of pioneer. This she did in her next novel, *The Song of the Lark*.

How Cather got to this point is a convoluted story that begins in the rural South after the Civil War. Born in 1873, she was the eldest child in a large family descended from Welsh, English, and Protestant Irish settlers who had emigrated to the United States in the mid-eighteenth century. Cather spent her early years in a well-established rural area near Winchester, Virginia, where there was something to look at besides space and where social institutions and amenities were in place. Though the family income was modest, especially in the wake of the Civil War, Back Creek Valley provided comfort, order, and tradition as well as important roles in local society for several members of the family.

In 1883, when Cather was nine, her family moved from their farm Willow Shade, whose enormous sheep barn had burned down, to the great plains of Webster County in southeast-central Nebraska, where several relatives, including her paternal grandparents, had already settled in order to escape consumption (tuberculosis), which was widespread in the Shenandoah Valley. Like other white settlers from Europe and the eastern United States they were encouraged by the completion of the transcontinental railroad, the passage of the Homestead Act, and declining threats from native Americans, who had already been forced westward. However, a year and a half of farming on the raw prairie was more than enough for Charles Cather, who took up real estate and moved his wife and children into the small town of Red Cloud (named after Chief Red Cloud of the Oglala Sioux), a fast-growing division point on the Burlington–Missouri railroad where the majority of settlers were newly arrived European immigrants.

Cather experienced removal from established eastern society to the seemingly endless land as a disruption not only of her existence but of her very consciousness. She later represented her earliest reactions to the prairie—in the middle of nowhere, at the apparent end of the world—in Jim Burden, the Virginia-born narrator of *My Ántonia*, who 'felt erased, blotted out' between the shaggy grass and 'the complete dome of heaven' when he arrived in Nebraska.[2] Similarly Red Cloud, where the first homestead claims had been made only thirteen years before, was an

---

[2] *My Ántonia*, Book I, ch. I.

embryonic social formation compared to the community the Cathers had left behind. Nevertheless, despite (or perhaps because of) her fear of obliteration, the shock these new experiences dealt to the developing consciousness of the child probably constituted the single most important factor in Cather's formation as an artist.

Cather gained many other things from this abrupt transition that eventually fed into her vocation and her portrait of Thea: a strong sense of the power and beauty of nature; familiarity with various European cultures, several of whose representatives became her informal teachers; friendships with immigrant women storytellers who, like her grandmother Boak, were living examples of women as artists; a great deal of freedom; and an understanding of the necessity for self-reliance.

Nevertheless, Cather's artistic development, like that of her protagonist in *Song*, was neither rapid nor smooth. On the contrary, Cather was nearly forty before she published *O Pioneers!* As Sharon O'Brien and others have shown, before Cather could take a chance on herself as an artist or bring a new kind of subject matter to serious American fiction by drawing on the pioneer materials to which she was connected through experience, memory, and emotion, she had to face a series of interrelated developmental tasks that were both personal and vocational.[3]

Cather was part of the first generation of American women writers who aimed to meet the highest and most 'universal' artistic standards. For these women, it was not enough simply to pay the bills or to achieve popularity with a limited segment of the reading public, as had the domestic novelists of the nineteenth century. But how were they to accomplish their higher objectives when 'universal' and 'masculine' were interchangeable terms and artistic authority lay in the hands of male writers and critics? In addition, in order to become even a professional journalist and editor, much less a creative artist, Cather had to challenge the conventional gender expectations of late Victorian culture, which defined women's province as nurturing others in the domestic

---

[3] Sharon O'Brien, *Willa Cather: The Emerging Voice* (New York, 1987), esp. Part I.

sphere, not dedication to one's own talents or a quest for public recognition. Selflessness was women's socially mandated calling; for a woman to nurture her own self was equivalent to selfishness. For Cather these gender expectations were most vividly represented by her mother, Virginia Boak Cather, whom Hermione Lee describes as 'a well-bred, imperious, handsome Southern belle, fussy about dress and social graces in the old genteel tradition',[4] who dominated her family and possessed a strength of will matched only by that of her eldest daughter.

Although in her earliest writings Cather firmly identified with the prestige accorded to male authors and with 'masculine' subject matter, throughout life her deepest emotional attachments were to other women. Cather did not label herself a lesbian, and we do not know whether her relationships with these women were sexual. In addition, some of her attractions were to men—among them the young Mexican Julio, whom she met during a crucial 1912 trip to the Southwest that helped free her to write *O Pioneers!* and fed directly into *The Song of the Lark*. Moreover, it is anachronistic to assume that if Cather's historical context had been different, she would have chosen to write overtly about homoerotic love. The value she places on privacy in her novels reflects a reaction to growing up in a small town and a repudiation of the loss of individuality that she associated with modernization as well as a necessity to conceal her emotions from public view. Nevertheless, conflicting needs to express and to suppress her emotional experience inevitably had an impact on Cather's development of identity and vocation. In sum, in order to achieve a clear sense of herself as an artist, Cather had to resolve the riddle of identity; in order to achieve a clear sense of identity, she had both to confront society's limited expectations for women and acknowledge her own affinity with them.

Cather faced other tasks as well. One of these was the necessity to support herself, which Chopin and Wharton, both married women of the upper classes, did not encounter. Cather's journalistic years in Pittsburgh and New York (1896–1911) enhanced her

---

[4] Hermione Lee, *Willa Cather: Double Lives* (New York, 1989), 28.

skills and self-confidence as a writer and an independent woman, provided a route out of the provinces—about which she could not have written if she had not left them—as well as a widened frame of reference and opportunities and funds for travel, and brought her Isabelle McClung, the strongest attachment of her life, and Edith Lewis, her companion for nearly forty years, both of whom provided her with emotional and intellectual support and surroundings in which to write. Moreover, during her tenure at *McClure's Magazine* (1906–11), where she eventually became managing editor, Cather enjoyed the prestige of working on one of the nation's leading magazines under a publisher, S. S. McClure, who had great faith in her abilities. Nevertheless, Cather gradually felt trapped by her arduous and time-consuming work, which soaked up her energies like a giant sponge but failed to nourish her as an imaginative writer.

As has frequently been noted, the regional writer Sarah Orne Jewett, whom Cather fortuitously met when McClure sent his editor to Boston on assignment, played a crucial role in resolving this crisis. Jewett, reaching out to a younger artist near the end of her own life, diagnosed Cather's creative malaise, provided her with a model of a woman who had made lasting art out of purely local materials (in Jewett's case, rural Maine), and challenged Cather to leave the magazine and dedicate herself to her own work.

A similar intervention occurs in *The Song of the Lark* when Andor Harsanyi, Thea's Chicago piano teacher, discovers by chance that his student's real talent is vocal. However, after a period of study with voice teacher Madison Bowers, a cynical man who depresses Thea as much as he teaches her, Thea becomes exhausted by her long years of effort, study, and aspiration. She leaves Chicago for a period of respite in the Southwest. There her energies are renewed, and she finally gains a clear understanding of art's purposes and its origins in natural and human life. She then moves decisively into a final phase of professional training, which is followed by success as an opera singer.

Although there are numerous connections between Cather and Thea Kronborg, the most fundamental parallel between author and protagonist is expressed in the underlying dynamic of the novel. In this pattern, individual development is equated with geographical movement—to *grow* is to *go*. From its beginning the narrative moves away from the confines of Moonstone, whose 'social classifications' conform so precisely to 'certain topographical boundaries' that 'every child understood them perfectly' (p. 30). Gradually building to an epic sweep, it encompasses broader and broader reaches of both geography and history as it travels back to prehistoric indigenous culture in the Southwest and out to European geography and culture.

Thea's curiosity about other ethnic groups—unusual among Moonstone children—is fed by frequent visits to the German Kohlers and the Mexicans, who live, literally, on the other side of the railroad tracks. Formative events in childhood and adolescence that teach Thea about the larger world and pull her away from home include trips to the sand hills, to Denver, and to 'a reunion of old frontiersmen, up in Wyoming' (p. 50). Despite her drive and talent, without the extended periods of study in Chicago made possible by Ray Kennedy's life-insurance money Thea would have fulfilled Wunsch's sarcastic prophecy by '"marry-[ing] some *Jacob* here and keep[ing] the house for him", (p. 68) or exhausting herself in the 'dull and exacting' (p. 96) labour of teaching piano to students with '"no ambition"' (p. 94). Though Thea's little attic room 'had always been her refuge', at the end of the summer in Moonstone that she spends between her two winters in Chicago she knows that 'its services were over; its time was done' (p. 205). She and her siblings have grown up to be two different kinds of people: 'Nothing that she would ever do in the world would seem important to them, and nothing they would ever do would seem important to her' (p. 206). The narrator comments, 'That Sunday in July was the turning-point . . . She found it hard even to practice at home' (p. 211).

After her experiences among the Cliff-Dweller ruins of Panther Canyon, both 'Moonstone and Chicago had become vague'. 'She had never been alone for so long before, or thought so much' (p. 260). Only in 'this abstracted state', in which Thea merges, mind and body, with her surroundings, does she 'at last

[make] up her mind what she [is] going to try to do in the world' (p. 261). Immediately, she decides to study in Germany. Five years later, when Mrs Kronborg is slowly dying, Thea begs her to hang on for a few more months because complications at the Dresden opera house have provided an 'unhoped-for opportunity to go on in a big part . . . It was not that [Thea] chose to stay; she had to stay—or lose everything' (p. 342). In response, Mrs Kronborg, though disappointed, is 'serene and fateful'. To Dr Archie she says, ' "The children you don't especially need, you have always with you, like the poor. But the bright ones get away from you. They have their own way to make in the world" ' (p. 343).

Thea eventually returns to the United States to perform with the Metropolitan Opera, her literal journeyings having brought her to the destination of her personal odyssey: the world of art. The younger daughter of the Methodist minister in Moonstone, Colorado has metamorphosed into 'Kronborg', and to her old friend Dr Archie, who is in the audience at a performance of *Lohengrin*, 'She seemed much, much farther away . . . than she had seemed all those years when she was in Germany' (p. 349).

Although Cather firmly separates Thea from her origins, the writer also indicates her protagonist's dependence upon them. This tension between autonomy and connectedness is reflected in the structure of the novel. On its most immediate level the narrative is progressive and linear, moving in synchrony with the protagonist's phases of existence. The slow peregrination through Thea's childhood is followed by the intensifying pace of adolescence and early adulthood, the opening out of time into eternity in Panther Canyon, and eventually by the recovery of antiquity through Wagnerian opera, with its basis in Scandinavian legends of human and divine life. Always, the movement is away from Moonstone and all that it admires.

On another level, however, the text is cyclical rather than linear. The disproportionate length of Part I, 'Friends of Childhood', indicates the centrality of childhood to the adult artist. The novel ends back in Moonstone with an Epilogue told from Aunt Tillie's point of view, not with Part VI, 'Kronborg', in which Thea per-

forms to applause 'almost savage in its fierceness' (p. 402). In Panther Canyon (Part IV, 'The Ancient People') Thea 'is getting back
to the earliest sources of gladness that she could remember . . . the
sun, . . . the brilliant solitudes of sand' (p. 252). Through her
absorption in the remains of Cliff-Dweller civilization, she is also
returning to 'a continuity of life that reached back into the old time'
(p. 258): 'The Cliff-Dwellers had lengthened her past' (p. 261).

Moreover, the older Thea becomes and the greater her
accomplishments, the more she and others recognize the degree
to which she was formed by her origins and how dependent upon
them she is for her interpretations. Even when Thea is preparing
to leave for Germany, she wonders 'Why . . . she [was] called
upon to take such chances' when, 'After all, she was a Moonstone
girl, one of the preacher's children' (p. 322). But Fred Ottenburg
considers it advantageous to Thea that '"Her scale of values will
always be the Moonstone scale"' because this will prevent her
from '"getting off the track"' both artistically and '"generally"'
(p. 311). (Appropriately, this comment occurs after Thea has
refused to be his mistress.) Ten years later Thea explains the
break-up of her love affair with the singer Nordquist in
Moonstone terms. First his wife demanded a hundred thousand
marks, then fifty thousand marks, to consent to a divorce. Thea
refused to pay any sum because, as she explains, '"I can't be
careless with money. I began the world on six hundred dollars,
and it was the price of a man's life . . . I always measure things by
that six hundred dollars"' (p. 386).

Similarly, the world that she has left behind is critical to Thea's
art. Partly because of the character of her voice, partly because of
her roots, Thea's talent is '"a natural development"'. According
to Fred, those who speak of Kronborg as '"a great actress"' don't
understand that her effectiveness results not from '"inventing a
lot of business"' but rather from '"simplif[ying] a character
down to the musical idea it's built on and mak[ing] everything
conform to that"' (p. 357).

Oliver Landry, her friend and accompanist, believes that nothing
is more important to a singer than having '"a rich personality"'.
When he describes how Thea worked on the part of Elizabeth

while her mother was dying, Thea's '"anxiety and grief getting more and more into the part"' until the last act was '"as homely as a country prayer meeting: might be any lonely woman getting ready to die"' (p. 379), it becomes clear that this particular rich personality is traceable to Mrs Kronborg and to the simplicity and expansiveness of Thea's upbringing. Moreover, at bitter or difficult moments Thea is saved by memories of '"the old things, things like the Kohlers' garden"' (p. 388). She bases her interpretation of '"heroic parts"' on her understanding of '"the dead people"' of Panther Canyon, who, she imagines, must have been '"a reserved, somber people . . . they taught me the inevitable hardness of human life"' (p. 391). And her unusual interpretation of Fricka, typically played as a '"Fat German woman scolding her husband"' (p. 375), is centred on memories of her mother, to the point that Thea dresses her hair as her mother did, '"so you got the shape of her head . . . such a calm, white forehead"' (p. 375). It is no surprise that in her triumphant performance of Sieglinde that ends the narrative proper, Thea 'merely came into full possession of things she had been refining and perfecting for so long' (p. 403).

The movement away from and back to origins is not the only paradoxical element in *The Song of the Lark*. The novel is permeated by apparent contradictions. Though Cather organized *Song* around contrasting polarities—past and present, old world and new world, childhood and adulthood, country and city, life and art, obscurity and fame—she also made each element dependent upon its opposite.

Cather insists upon her protagonist's exceptional nature from the beginning of the novel, but she also surrounds Thea with a stream of mentors and supporters. Before Thea's piano studies are even mentioned, the reader is told that she is set aside, different, destined for something special. Technically the novel begins with the birth of Thor, the Kronborgs' seventh child, but the real event in Part I, Chapter I is the metaphorical rebirth (the first among many) of eleven-year-old Thea, their fourth child. Her pneumonia catches the attention of Dr Archie, though her father has forgotten all about it. Dr Archie considers the Reverend to be '"an ass . . . about the seventh! . . . The baby would have got into the world somehow; they always do. But a nice little girl like that—she's worth the whole litter"' (pp. 11–12). During her recovery Archie makes sure that Thea enjoys the privacy of the parlour, 'where nobody but company . . . ever slept', and brings her rare Malaga grapes to eat, though in other Moonstone households they are reserved for display (pp. 12–15).

The opening chapters of the novel assemble a veritable chorus to tell the reader how distinctive Thea is. Professor Wunsch goes to the homes of his other piano students to instruct them, but because 'Thea had talent' (p. 25) he arranges to teach her at the Kohlers' house, where he boards and can be more at ease. Mrs Kronborg, the only other individual in Moonstone who comprehends the word 'talent', knows that Thea 'must practice four hours a day' for 'A child with talent must be kept at the piano, just as a child with measles must be kept under the blankets' (p. 25). Any other Moonstone mother would react to the announcement that her daughter was gifted by keeping the child's hair curled and making sure that she played frequently in public. The 'shallowness and complacency' of the young women whom Wunsch taught in St Louis and Kansas City 'maddened' him, for—like most people, it is implied—their only ambition 'was to get something for nothing'. Consequently he is even more impressed by 'his pupil's power of application, her rugged will' (p. 30) than by her native ability.

Freight conductor Ray Kennedy, who is thirty but has been on his own since he was Thea's age, missed his opportunity to 'strike it rich' on the Bridal Chamber silver mine (p. 48). He aims to make up for all his disappointments by marrying Thea 'as soon as she should be old enough' (p. 43), because although he 'had no very clear idea of what might be going on in Thea's head, . . . he knew that something was' (p. 54).

Mr Kronborg considers all his offspring to be remarkable, but Mrs Kronborg finds Thea 'more interesting than her other children, and . . . [takes] her more seriously'. This involves protecting Thea's privacy, defending her unorthodoxies, and letting her follow 'her own routine' whereas the other children need guidance and direction (p. 60). And Thea's 'addle-pated aunt',

Tillie Kronborg, who serves as Thea's first and final fan, finds an outlet for her 'romantic imagination' in her niece, whose '"wonderfulness"' she speaks of to the neighbours as 'an accepted fact' (p. 61).

These examples do not cover a seventh of the novel, nor do they include Thea's supporters outside Moonstone or passages in which the protagonist thinks about herself or is described in specifically musical terms. But here is another paradox: though Thea's story takes the form of growth, movement, development, her status as one set apart actually rests on a deterministic foundation. Cather represents Thea's uniqueness as predestined and inevitable, a given that antedates the working out of the plot. Her fate parallels the nation's 'manifest destiny', which the narrator invokes at the end of Part IV, Chapter VI as Thea springs to her feet at the sight of 'an eagle' in 'strong, tawny flight' (p. 272).

Thea's long list of indispensable mentors and friends includes characters who assist in her development as individual or artist and sometimes as both. In effect, there are three levels of characterization: those who—like her sister Anna—attempt to hold Thea back; those who move her forward; and the central figure, around whom the text revolves.

Though Dr Archie's musical knowledge is limited, he saves Thea from pneumonia, persuades the Kronborgs that she must be allowed to study in Chicago, lends her money to train in Germany, and reappears at the end of the novel to observe her onstage and offstage lives. Treating the thirteen-year-old as if she were an adult, he introduces her to Balzac, Scott, and Burns. When the incident of the tramp challenges Thea with the problem of evil, she takes her confusion not to her ministerial father but to Dr Archie, a man of science, whose distinctly American response is that since evil is unavoidable, one must aim for success: '"The people who forge ahead and do something, they really count. . . . We all like people who do things, even if we only see their faces on a cigar-box lid"' (p. 123).

Ray Kennedy's legacy is not limited to life insurance: the railroad man also brings the larger natural and human world into Thea's frame of reference. The Mexican community, whose musicality Thea respects, is in Moonstone because of Ray (p. 48). Ray tells Thea tales of his adventures in Mexico and the South- west, takes her to the sand hills and to Denver, and long before she goes to Arizona communicates his admiration for the Cliff- Dweller ruins at Canyon de Chelly, where he ' "learned more . . . about what makes history . . than in all the books I've ever read" ' (p. 105). Ray does not understand Thea's ambitions, but their last moment of contact is 'the first time she had seen her face in that kindest mirror a woman can ever find' (p. 130).

Herr Wunsch discovers and nurtures Thea's talent, and when he leaves she is proficient enough to take over his pupils. More- over, the talent that he encourages is vocal, not just instrumental. Though it is Harsanyi who recognizes that Thea's vocation should be her voice, Wunsch prepares the way for this discovery. Having overheard Thea singing in the church choir, he encour- ages her to use her 'beautiful child's voice' (p. 29) and to read poetry aloud, for then she drops 'the speech of Moonstone' and speaks in 'a soft, rich contralto', a 'nature-voice' (p. 70). Thea gravitates towards hard work—to her, a problem is an enemy— but Wunsch encourages even greater discipline, treating mile- stones such as Christmas or a birthday merely as opportunities to assign more practice. However, Wunsch is an idealist as well as a disciplinarian. When he insists that only one woman could sing Gluck's *Orpheus*, he is also teaching Thea the difference between conventional female beauty (such as that of Lily Fisher) and beauty created by a woman artist with a voice and with ' "some- thing in there, behind the eyes" ' (p. 66). Most importantly, Wunsch, whose name means desire, insists that ' "Nothing is far and nothing is near, if one desires. The world is little, people are little, human life is little. There is only one big thing—desire" ' (p. 69). The fact that Wunsch has lost such desire himself only reinforces his understanding of its importance.

If Herr Wunsch and Mrs Kronborg mirror each other, Ray Kennedy parallels Mr Kronborg. Thea's perception that Ray 'never, by any chance, for a single instant, understood her!' (p. 97)—that is, did not sense the 'second self' that will ultimately be expressed in her music—applies equally to her father.

Unlike his wife, whose father was a professional musician in Sweden and who received enough training to learn the difference between acquired skill and aptitude, Mr Kronborg understands music only as an accompaniment to religious services or a source of family income. However, even he recognizes that Thea is not made for marriage: ' "A girl with all that energy has got to do something, same as a boy, to keep herself out of mischief. . . . let her do something to make herself independent" ' (pp. 91–2).

Critical response to these supporters has been divided. Some critics take their cue from a conversation in which Ray counters Thea's insistence that ' "Everybody's up against it for himself" ' by pointing out that ' "there are a lot of halfway people in this world who help the winners win, and the failers fail" ' (p. 109). They argue that Cather sets up Thea's mentors as inferior creatures who exist to bring the superior being to fruition. Others note that all the characters who help or serve her, including the Indian women potters as Thea imagines them, are persons with second selves—a social self that participates in the group and a secret self that goes beyond or improves upon or deviates from the average or norm. Another view is that her mentors and admirers are individuals with some internal need which Thea helps them fill, as they help her fill her internal need, which is to become herself. Of note is the fact that many of these supporters—Dr Archie, Andor Harsanyi, even Tillie Kronborg—eventually get what they want. Even Fred marries Thea at the end of the novel—after she has achieved her artistic goals.

This brings us to a further inconsistency, this time between Cather behind the text and Thea within it. Having undergone the experience of actually becoming a creative artist, Cather deviated in *The Song of the Lark* from the emphatic pronouncements about isolated artists that she had expressed in her earliest prose. Critics who claim that she adhered faithfully to these pronouncements throughout her career are ignoring subtle shifts in her views that occurred over the passage of time.

The best-known of the early writings is a college essay, 'The

Personal Characteristics of Thomas Carlyle' (1891).[5] In flam-
boyant diction, young Willa (she was seventeen) compared
Carlyle to 'the lone survivor of some extinct species, . . . this
great Titan, . . . [who] rushed off into the desert to suffer alone'.[6]
Discussing Mrs Carlyle, Cather declared that 'The wife of an
artist, if he continues to be an artist, must always be a secondary
consideration with him'.[7] Similarly, in 'Shakespeare and Hamlet'
(also published in 1891), she proclaimed that 'If an artist does any
good work he must do it alone. No number of encouraging or
admiring friends can assist him, they retard him rather'.[8]

At this stage Cather saw artists as separated from and thoroughly at odds with their society. Such isolationism is logical
given her age and gender, her distance from urban centres where
artists gathered in significant numbers, self-consciousness about
her differences from more conventional young people, and the
romantic conception of the artist that she inherited from her
reading. Undoubtedly, creativity and artistry were Cather's central drives. But the girl from Red Cloud, Nebraska, who enjoyed
plentiful assistance from others in the process of becoming Willa
Cather, American author, was ready by the time she wrote *The
Song of the Lark* to acknowledge the paradox that without social
context one cannot achieve artistic independence.

Female aspiration, and the qualities that are required to
achieve a challenging goal, are more readily accepted today than
in the early twentieth century. Nevertheless, contemporary
readers sometimes find it difficult to accept Thea's wholehearted
focus on her work. They take their cue from Thea's response to
Dr Archie's worry about whether she has enough personal life:
'"My dear doctor, I don't have any. Your work becomes your
personal life. . . . It's like being woven into a big web. You can't
pull away, because all your little tendrils are woven into the picture"' (p. 385). Since this is followed by the information that Thea

[5] When her University of Nebraska English professor secretly had this composition
published in a Lincoln Sunday paper, Cather, smitten by the sight of her words in print,
changed her professional ambitions from medicine to literature.
[6] Willa Cather, *The Kingdom of Art: Willa Cather's First Principles and Critical Statements 1893–1896*, ed. Bernice Slote (Lincoln, Nebr., 1966), 424–25.
[7] Ibid. 423.   [8] Ibid. 434–5.

did not marry Nordquist, they conclude that Thea has sacrificed personal happiness for her art. Perhaps as a result, some readers also overlook the exposition of Thea's later marriage to Fred Ottenburg that is provided in the Epilogue.

Fred is of course a highly suitable mate for Thea: devoted to music yet not a performer, and self-confident enough to concede that he will never be ' "the whole target" ' (p. 268). Cather probably provided her protagonist with a husband in order to appease the expectations of 1915, when a woman's happiness—indeed, her legitimacy—was equated with her marriageability. None the less, it is clear that Thea's fulfilment lies outside the traditional domain. She and her art are interchangeable. As the narrator tells us, singing is her 'one way of being really kind, from the core of her heart out; . . . [the] one way in which she [can] give herself to people largely and gladly' (p. 373). Thea achieves what she has always wanted, which is to be a fine artist; she is successful and admired; that she also has Fred for a husband is clearly an afterthought.

At this stage of her career Cather's respect went to women who were generative in some way: stalwart mothers like Mrs Kronborg, pioneering singers like Olive Fremstad, upon whom she based the details of Thea's professional life,[9] or writers such as Sarah Orne Jewett. For women such as the wives of Dr Archie and Fred Ottenburg, who give nothing to the world but are absorbed in self or social trivia, she exhibits utter contempt. The irony is that Thea—like her creator—pours her devotion into her work in the same way that women of the early twentieth century were expected to pour their devotion into their families. But Thea's mentors are her real family, and the 'child' she gives birth to is herself as artist. As Susan Rosowski points out, the conversation in which Thea tells Dr Archie that her work and her personal life are one and the same describes 'the artist *as* woman', not 'the sacrifice of the woman to the artist'.[10]

[9] R. Giannone, *Music in Willa Cather's Fiction* (Lincoln, Nebr., 1968), H. Lee, *Willa Cather* (New York, 1989), S. O'Brien, *Willa Cather: The Emerging Voice* (New York, 1987), J. Woodress, *Willa Cather: A Literary Life* (Lincoln, Nebr., 1987).

[10] Susan J. Rosowski, 'Writing against Silences: Female Adolescent Development in the Novels of Willa Cather', *Studies in the Novel*, 21.1 (1989), 67.

In her preface to the revised edition of *The Song of the Lark* (see Appendix), Cather suggested that the novel would have been better minus the last two sections. However, without them readers would not have visible evidence of Thea's success. In addition, if either section, but especially 'Kronborg', were eliminated, so too would the issue of Thea's separation from traditional female affiliative roles and the acknowledgement that her nurturing side goes into her voice and art rather than into others. This in turn would limit the complexity of the text. As it stands, *The Song of the Lark* challenges readers to recognize the incongruity of applauding an unconventional female protagonist only if she manages to live up to all the conventional standards for women. For Thea Kronborg, whom Cather constructs as an individual, not as Everywoman, selfhood and song are synonymous.

NOTE ON THE TEXT

The Song of the Lark, Cather's third and longest novel, was published by Houghton Mifflin in October 1915 in a first printing of 3,000 copies. The first edition went through nineteen impressions before Cather extensively revised the text for Volume II of the Autograph Edition in 1937, in the process cutting about 6,900 words or about 4.7 per cent of the 1915 edition, primarily in the last two sections and the Epilogue. In the sixteenth printing, January 1932, the poem was removed from the dedication page. The author's preface to the Autograph Edition, which discusses the formulation and structure of the novel, first appeared in the English Travellers Library Edition (London, 1937). It is provided here in an Appendix to the text. The 1932 revisions represent Cather's attempt to make the novel conform as much as possible to her later theory of fiction. The 1915 edition, which represents her original conception, is printed here.

SELECT BIBLIOGRAPHY

Journalism

The Kingdom of Art: Willa Cather's First Principles and Critical Statements 1893–1896, ed. Bernice Slote (Lincoln, Nebr., 1966).

Biography

Lee, Hermione, *Willa Cather* (New York, 1989).

O'Brien, Sharon, *Willa Cather: The Emerging Voice* (New York, 1987).

Woodress, James, *Willa Cather: A Literary Life* (Lincoln, Nebr., 1987).

Criticism

Ammons, Elizabeth, *Conflicting Stories: American Women Writers at the Turn into the Twentieth Century* (New York, 1991).

Baker, Bruce, 'Portrait of the Artist by a Young Woman', *Willa Cather Pioneer Memorial Newsletter*, 37.3–4 (1994), 40–2.

Donovan, Josephine, *After the Fall: The Demeter-Persephone Myth in Wharton, Cather, and Glasgow* (University Park, Pa., 1989).

Dubek, Laura, 'Rewriting Male Scripts: Willa Cather and *The Song of the Lark*', *Women's Studies: An Interdisciplinary Journal*, 23 (1994), 293–306.

Fetterley, Judith, 'Willa Cather and the Fiction of Female Development', in Carol J. Singley and Susan Elizabeth Sweeney (eds.), *Anxious Power: Reading, Writing, and Ambivalence in Narrative by Women* (Albany, NY, 1993), 221–34.

Flannigan, John H., 'Thea Kronborg's Vocal Transvestism: Willa Cather and the "Voz Contralto"', *Modern Fiction Studies*, 40 (1994), 737–64.

Fryer, Judith, 'Desert, Rock, Shelter, Legend: Willa Cather's Novels of the Southwest', in Vera Norwood and Janice Monk (eds.), *The Desert Is No Lady: Southwestern Landscapes in Women's Writing and Art* (New Haven, 1987), 27–46.

Giannone, Richard, *Music in Willa Cather's Fiction* (Lincoln, Nebr., 1968).

Harvey, Sally Peltier, *Redefining the American Dream: The Novels of Willa Cather* (Rutherford, NJ, 1995).

Henigan, Robert, 'Kronborg as Orpheus: A Tragic Dimension of *The Song of the Lark*', *Willa Cather Pioneer Memorial Newsletter*, 32 (1988), 28–33.

Heycock, Robin and Woodress, James, 'Willa Cather's Cuts and Revisions in *The Song of the Lark*', *Modern Fiction Studies*, 25 (1979/80), 651–8.

Hoover, Sharon, 'The "Wonderfulness" of Thea Kronborg's Voice', *Western American Literature*, 30.3 (1995), 257–74.

Huf, Linda, *A Portrait of the Artist as a Young Woman* (New York, 1983).

Leonardi, Susan J., 'To Have a Voice: The Politics of the Diva', *Perspectives on Contemporary Literature*, 13 (1987), 65–72.

Moseley, Ann, 'The Dual Nature of Art in *The Song of the Lark*', *Western American Literature*, 14 (1979), 19–32.

—— 'A New World Symphony: Cultural Pluralism in *The Song of the Lark* and *My Ántonia*', *Willa Cather Pioneer Memorial Newsletter*, 39 (1995), 7–12.

Murphy, John, Adams-Hunter, Linda, and Rawlins, Paul (eds.), *Willa Cather: Family, Community, and History* (Provo, Ut., 1990).

Nealon, Christopher, 'Affect-Genealogy: Feeling and Affiliation in Willa Cather', *American Literature*, 69.1 (1997), 5–37.

Nettels, Elsa, 'Tradition and the Woman Artist: James's *The Tragic Muse* and Cather's *The Song of the Lark*', *Willa Cather Pioneer Memorial Newsletter*, 36 (1992), 27–31.

Peck, Demaree, *The Imaginative Claims of the Artist in Willa Cather's Fiction* (Selingsgrove, Pa., 1996).

Rosowski, Susan J., *The Voyage Perilous: Willa Cather's Romanticism* (Lincoln, Nebr., 1986).

—— 'Writing against Silences: Female Adolescent Development in the Novels of Willa Cather', *Studies in the Novel*, 21.1 (1989), 60–77.

—— 'Willa Cather's Female Landscapes: *The Song of the Lark* and *Lucy Gayheart*', *Women's Studies*, 11 (1984), 233–46.

Roulston, Robert, 'The Contrapuntal Complexity of Willa Cather's *The Song of the Lark*', *Midwest Quarterly*, 17.4 (1976), 350–68.

Schwind, Jean, 'Fine and Folk Art in *The Song of the Lark*', *Cather Studies*, 1 (1990), 89–102.

Tatum, Stephen, 'Word Music in "The Ancient People", Part IV of *The Song of the Lark*', *Willa Cather Pioneer Memorial Newsletter*, 31 (1987), 25–31.

Titus, Mary, 'Cather's Creative Women and DuMaurier's Cozy Men: *The Song of the Lark* and *Trilby*', *Modern Language Studies*, 24.2 (1994), 27–37.

Wasserman, Loretta, 'The Lovely Storm: Sexual Initiation in Two Early Willa Cather Novels', *Studies in the Novel*, 14 (1982), 348–57.

Further Reading in Oxford World's Classics

Cather, Willa, *Alexander's Bridge*, ed. Marilee Lindemann.
——*O Pioneers!*, ed. Marilee Lindemann.
Chopin, Kate, *The Awakening and Other Stories*, ed. Pamela Knights.
Wharton, Edith, *The House of Mirth*, ed. Martha Banta.
Woolf, Virginia, *To the Lighthouse*, ed. Margaret Drabble.

A CHRONOLOGY OF WILLA CATHER

1873 Born 7 December in Back Creek Valley, near Winchester, Virginia, first child of Charles Fectigue Cather (b. 1848) and Mary Virginia Boak Cather (b. 1850). Named Wilella for deceased aunt; family nickname 'Willie'.

1874 Family moves to grandfather William Cather's nearby sheep farm, Willow Shade, accompanied by maternal grandmother Rachel Boak.

1877 Grandparents William and Caroline Cather emigrate with three daughters to Webster County, Nebraska, where son George and his wife, Frances, are successful farmers. Brother Roscoe born.

1880 Brother Douglass born.

1881 Sister Jessica born.

1882 Begins calling herself 'Willa Love Cather', after an uncle who died in the Civil War and the doctor who delivered her.

1883 Willow Shade is sold after sheep farm burns down. Family, including Rachel Boak and several cousins and dependants, moves to grandparents' farm in south-central Nebraska. Cather visits immigrant settlers' homesteads, making friends with pioneer farm women and listening to their stories.

1884 Father gives up farming, moves family into small frame house in prairie town of Red Cloud, where he opens a real estate and loan office.

1888 Brother James born. Cather crops hair and adopts male dress (until 1892); calls herself 'William Cather, M.D.' and 'William Cather, Jr.'; announces plans to become a surgeon.

1890 June, graduates with two classmates from Red Cloud High School, delivers speech defending scientific inquiry. September, moves to Lincoln, enrols in Latin School, preparatory school of University of Nebraska. Sister Elsie born.

1891 March, first published essay, 'Concerning Thos. Carlyle', appears in *Nebraska State Journal* (submitted by her English teacher). September, enters University of Nebraska, where her interests shift to literatures and languages; active in student publications and societies. Relationship with Louise Pound dominates her emotional life until 1894.

1892 First short story (submitted by another teacher) and poem published locally. Begins to abandon masculine dress and appearance.

1893 Grandmother Boak dies. November, begins contributing regularly to *Nebraska State Journal* (until 1900); becomes known for biting theatre criticism.

1895 Graduates from University of Nebraska; remains in Lincoln as associate editor for Lincoln *Courier*.

1896 Returns to Red Cloud, where she is bored and unhappy; publishes 'On the Divide', first story in national magazine. June, leaves for Pittsburgh and editorship of *Home Monthly*, a new women's magazine. Continues publishing fiction, poetry, and criticism in addition to doing her 'regular' work, a pattern that continues until 1911.

1897 Resigns from *Home Monthly*; begins work as staff writer for Pittsburgh *Leader*.

1899 Introduced to Isabelle McClung, daughter of wealthy and prominent Pittsburgh judge Samuel McClung and wife Fannie, with whom she begins an intense and lifelong friendship based partly on mutual interests in the arts.

1900 Resigns from *Leader*; moves temporarily to Washington, DC to work as translator.

1901 Returns to Pittsburgh to live with Isabelle McClung and her family in their Murray Hill Avenue mansion, where she is given her own study (remains until 1906). Begins teaching at Central High School.

1902 June, first trip to Europe, with Isabelle McClung.

1903 April, collection of poetry entitled *April Twilights* published by Richard G. Badger. Submits short fiction to S. S. McClure, who invites her to New York. On summer visit to Nebraska meets Lincoln native Edith Lewis. Autumn, begins teaching English at Allegheny High School in Pittsburgh.

1905 March, collection of short fiction, *The Troll Garden*, published by McClure, Phillips & Co. Spends summer in the west with Isabelle McClung.

1906 Spring, leaves Pittsburgh when S. S. McClure offers her a job at *McClure's Magazine* in New York, where she lives in Greenwich Village.

1907 Moves to Boston on assignment for *McClure's*, where she rewrites Georgine Milmine's *The Life of Mary Baker G. Eddy and the History of Christian Science* and meets various prominent Bostonians.

1908 Develops close friendships with Annie Fields, widow of Boston publisher James T. Fields, and her companion, Maine novelist and short-story writer Sarah Orne Jewett. Spring, travels to Europe with Isabelle McClung. Autumn, returns to New York, moving into a Greenwich Village apartment with Edith Lewis; becomes managing editor of *McClure's*; Jewett, in correspondence with Cather, tells her that her own writing will continue to suffer as long as it is pursued in the margins of her busy professional life.

1909 Greatly saddened by death of Sarah Orne Jewett. Assumes full editorial responsibility for *McClure's* when S. S. McClure leaves for Europe.

1911 Writes novel, *Alexander's Bridge*; takes brief leave from *McClure's*, which she spends with Isabelle McClung; upon returning to New York, decides not to return to the magazine.

1912 *Alexander's Bridge* published as *Alexander's Masquerade* in instalments in *McClure's* (she may have submitted it under a pseudonym). May, Houghton Mifflin publishes *Alexander's Bridge* in book form. March–May, visits brother Douglass in Arizona and explores the Southwest; beginnings of a permanent love for the region. Spends autumn writing in Pittsburgh, where she stays with the McClungs.

1913 Moves with Edith Lewis into a large apartment at 5 Bank Street in Greenwich Village. June, *O Pioneers!*, dedicated to Sarah Orne Jewett, published by Houghton Mifflin; excellent critical response. Ghost-writes S. S. McClure's autobiography, which begins running (autumn) in *McClure's Magazine* as *My Autobiography*, by S. S. McClure (published in book form, 1914). Begins writing *The Song of the Lark*; meets Wagnerian soprano Olive Fremstad in New York.

1914 Works on *The Song of the Lark*.

1915 Finishes *The Song of the Lark*, which is published in October by Houghton Mifflin; reviews are good. Summer, visits Mesa Verde, Taos, and Santa Fe with Edith Lewis. Autumn, Judge McClung dies, and Cather stays with Isabelle McClung for the rest of the year.

1916 April, Isabelle McClung marries violinist Jan Hambourg; Cather is shocked and depressed. Returns to Santa Fe and Taos with Edith Lewis. Visits brother Roscoe in Wyoming. Begins work on *My Ántonia*.

1917 Awarded first honorary degree, Doctor of Letters, from University of Nebraska in June. Summer and autumn, works on *My Ántonia* while visiting the Hambourgs in New Hampshire.

1918 George and Frances Cather's son, G. P. Cather, a soldier in the American Expeditionary Force, killed on the Western Front; Cather begins planning novel based on his life. September, Houghton Mifflin publishes *My Ántonia*; reviews are good.

1919 Continues work on World War I novel, tentatively entitled *Claude*.

1920 Travels to France to do research for *Claude*. *Youth and the Bright Medusa*, collection of eight short stories, published in September by Alfred A. Knopf, her new publisher.

1921 Finishes *Claude*, now titled *One of Ours*.

1922 Begins writing *A Lost Lady*. September, *One of Ours* published by Knopf; sales are good, but not the reviews. December, Cather and her parents are confirmed in the Episcopal Church.

1923 April–June, *Century Magazine* serializes *A Lost Lady*, which Knopf publishes in book form in September. April, Knopf publishes expanded edition of *April Twilights*. Awarded Pulitzer Prize for *One of Ours*.

1924 June, awarded honorary degree from University of Michigan. Begins editing two-volume edition of Sarah Orne Jewett's fiction for Houghton Mifflin. Begins writing *The Professor's House*. Meets D. H. Lawrence in New York.

1925 *The Best Short Stories of Sarah Orne Jewett* published. Begins writing *My Mortal Enemy*. June, *Collier's Magazine* begins serializing *The Professor's House*, which Knopf publishes in September. Begins working on *Death Comes for the Archbishop*. Travels to the Southwest with Edith Lewis during the summer, and has cottage built on Grand Manan Island, New Brunswick, Canada.

1926 New edition of *My Ántonia*, with revised introduction, published by Houghton Mifflin. October, Knopf publishes *My Mortal Enemy*. Finishes *Death Comes for the Archbishop*.

1927 *The Forum* serializes *Death Comes for the Archbishop*, which Knopf publishes in September. Bank Street apartment torn down; Cather and Lewis move to a residential hotel.

1928 March, father dies. June, receives honorary degree from Columbia University. Autumn, begins *Shadows on the Rock*. December, mother suffers paralytic stroke while visiting family members in California.

1929   Spends spring in California with her mother. Elected to National Institute of Arts and Letters. June, receives honorary degree from Yale University.

1930   Spends spring in California with her mother. Receives honorary degrees from University of California at Berkeley and Princeton University. August, mother dies. August, Knopf publishes *Shadows on the Rock*. Last visit to Nebraska, for Christmas family reunion.

1932   *Obscure Destinies*, collection of short fiction ('Neighbor Rosicky', 'Old Mrs Harris', 'Two Friends') published by Knopf in August. December, Cather and Edith Lewis move to new apartment on Park Avenue.

1933   Receives Prix Fémina Américain, prestigious French literary prize, for *Shadows on the Rock*. Begins writing *Lucy Gayheart*. June, receives honorary degree from Smith College. Develops chronic inflammatory wrist and hand injuries that interfere with her writing.

1934   Finishes *Lucy Gayheart*.

1935   *Women's Home Companion* serializes *Lucy Gayheart*, which Knopf publishes in August. Isabelle Hambourg falls ill.

1936   Collection of essays, *Not Under Forty*, published by Knopf in November.

1937   Spends year helping Houghton Mifflin prepare Library Edition of her collected works, which appears in 1937–8. Begins writing *Sapphira and the Slave Girl*, based on her Virginia background.

1938   Elected to American Academy of Arts and Letters. Brother Douglass and Isabelle Hambourg both die.

1939   September, finishes *Sapphira and the Slave Girl*, which Knopf publishes in December.

1941   Spring, visits brother Roscoe in San Francisco. Begins novel set in Avignon, France, never completed.

1942   July, undergoes surgery; never recovers full health.

1944   Receives Gold Medal of the National Institute of Arts and Letters.

1945   Brother Roscoe dies.

1947   Dies in New York, 24 April; buried in Jaffrey, New Hampshire.

1948   Collection of short fiction, *The Old Beauty and Others*, published by Knopf.

THE SONG OF THE LARK*

"It was a wond'rous lovely storm that drove me!"
LENAU'S "Don Juan"*

TO

ISABELLE MCCLUNG*

> On uplands,
> At morning,
> The world was young, the winds were free;
> A garden fair,
> In that blue desert air,
> Its guest invited me to be.*

CONTENTS

PART I

FRIENDS OF CHILDHOOD

PART I

FRIENDS OF CHILDHOOD

I

DR. HOWARD ARCHIE had just come up from a game of pool with the Jewish clothier and two traveling men who happened to be staying overnight in Moonstone. His offices were in the Duke Block, over the drug store. Larry, the doctor's man, had lit the overhead light in the waiting-room and the double student's lamp on the desk in the study. The isinglass sides of the hard-coal burner were aglow, and the air in the study was so hot that as he came in the doctor opened the door into his little operating-room, where there was no stove. The waiting-room was carpeted and stiffly furnished, something like a country parlor. The study had worn, unpainted floors, but there was a look of winter comfort about it. The doctor's flat-top desk was large and well made; the papers were in orderly piles, under glass weights. Behind the stove a wide bookcase, with double glass doors, reached from the floor to the ceiling. It was filled with medical books of every thickness and color. On the top shelf stood a long row of thirty or forty volumes, bound all alike in dark mottled board covers, with imitation leather backs.

As the doctor in New England villages is proverbially old, so the doctor in small Colorado towns twenty-five years ago was generally young. Dr. Archie was barely thirty. He was tall, with massive shoulders which he held stiffly, and a large, well-shaped head. He was a distinguished-looking man, for that part of the world, at least. There was something individual in the way in which his reddish-brown hair, parted cleanly at the side, bushed over his high forehead. His nose was straight and thick, and his eyes were intelligent. He wore a curly, reddish moustache and an imperial, cut trimly, which made him look a little like the pictures of Napoleon III.* His hands were large and well kept, but ruggedly formed, and the backs were shaded with crinkly reddish hair. He wore a blue suit of woolly, wide-waled serge; the traveling men had known at a glance that it was made by a Denver tailor. The doctor was always well dressed.

Dr. Archie turned up the student's lamp and sat down in the swivel chair before his desk. He sat uneasily, beating a tattoo on his knees with his fingers, and looked about him as if he were bored. He glanced at his watch, then absently took from his pocket a bunch of small keys, selected one and looked at it. A contemptuous smile, barely perceptible, played on his lips, but his eyes remained meditative. Behind the door that led into the hall, under his buffalo-skin driving-coat, was a locked cupboard. This the doctor opened mechanically, kicking aside a pile of muddy overshoes. Inside, on the shelves, were whiskey glasses and decanters, lemons, sugar, and bitters. Hearing a step in the empty, echoing hall without, the doctor closed the cupboard again, snapping the Yale lock. The door of the waiting-room opened, a man entered and came on into the consulting-room.

"Good-evening, Mr. Kronborg," said the doctor carelessly. "Sit down."

His visitor was a tall, loosely built man, with a thin brown beard, streaked with gray. He wore a frock coat, a broad-brimmed black hat, a white lawn necktie, and steel-rimmed spectacles. Altogether there was a pretentious and important air about him, as he lifted the skirts of his coat and sat down.

"Good-evening, doctor. Can you step around to the house with me? I think Mrs. Kronborg will need you this evening." This was said with profound gravity and, curiously enough, with a slight embarrassment.

"Any hurry?" the doctor asked over his shoulder as he went into his operating-room.

Mr. Kronborg coughed behind his hand, and contracted his brows. His face threatened at every moment to break into a smile of foolish excitement. He controlled it only by calling upon his habitual pulpit manner. "Well, I think it would be as well to go immediately. Mrs. Kronborg will be more comfortable if you are there. She has been suffering for some time."

The doctor came back and threw a black bag upon his desk. He wrote some instructions for his man on a prescription pad and then drew on his overcoat. "All ready," he announced, putting out his lamp. Mr. Kronborg rose and they tramped through the empty hall and down the stairway to the street. The drug store below was dark, and the saloon next door was just closing. Every other light on Main Street was out

On either side of the road and at the outer edge of the board sidewalk, the snow had been shoveled into breastworks. The town looked small and black, flattened down in the snow, muffled and all but extinguished. Overhead the stars shone gloriously. It was impossible not to notice them. The air was so clear that the white sand hills to the east of Moonstone gleamed softly. Following the Reverend Mr. Kronborg along the narrow walk, past the little dark, sleeping houses, the doctor looked up at the flashing night and whistled softly. It did seem that people were stupider than they need be; as if on a night like this there ought to be something better to do than to sleep nine hours, or to assist Mrs. Kronborg in functions which she could have performed so admirably unaided. He wished he had gone down to Denver to hear Fay Templeton* sing "See-Saw." Then he remembered that he had a personal interest in this family, after all. They turned into another street and saw before them lighted windows; a low story-and-a-half house, with a wing built on at the right and a kitchen addition at the back, everything a little on the slant— roofs, windows, and doors. As they approached the gate, Peter Kronborg's pace grew brisker. His nervous, ministerial cough annoyed the doctor. "Exactly as if he were going to give out a text," he thought. He drew off his glove and felt in his vest pocket. "Have a troche,* Kronborg," he said, producing some. "Sent me for samples. Very good for a rough throat."

"Ah, thank you, thank you. I was in something of a hurry. I neglected to put on my overshoes. Here we are, doctor." Kronborg opened his front door—seemed delighted to be at home again.

The front hall was dark and cold; the hatrack was hung with an astonishing number of children's hats and caps and cloaks. They were even piled on the table beneath the hatrack. Under the table was a heap of rubbers and overshoes. While the doctor hung up his coat and hat, Peter Kronborg opened the door into the living-room. A glare of light greeted them, and a rush of hot, stale air, smelling of warming flannels.

At three o'clock in the morning Dr. Archie was in the parlor putting on his cuffs and coat—there was no spare bedroom in that house. Peter Kronborg's seventh child, a boy, was being soothed and cosseted by his aunt, Mrs. Kronborg was asleep, and the doctor was going home. But he wanted first to speak to Kronborg, who, coatless and fluttery, was pouring coal into the kitchen stove. As the doctor crossed the dining-room he paused and listened. From one of the wing rooms, off to the left, he heard rapid, distressed breathing. He went to the kitchen door.

"One of the children sick in there?" he asked, nodding toward the partition.

Kronborg hung up the stove-lifter and dusted his fingers. "It must be, Thea.* I meant to ask you to look at her. She has a croupy cold. But in my excitement—Mrs. Kronborg is doing finely, eh, doctor? Not many of your patients with such a constitution, I expect."

"Oh, yes. She's a fine mother." The doctor took up the lamp from the kitchen table and unceremoniously went into the wing room. Two chubby little boys were asleep in a double bed, with the coverlids over their noses and their feet drawn up. In a single bed, next to theirs, lay a little girl of eleven, wide awake, two yellow braids sticking up on the pillow behind her. Her face was scarlet and her eyes were blazing.

The doctor shut the door behind him. "Feel pretty sick, Thea?" he asked as he took out his thermometer. "Why didn't you call somebody?"

She looked at him with greedy affection. "I thought you were here," she spoke between quick breaths. "There is a new baby, isn't there? Which?"

"Which?" repeated the doctor.

"Brother or sister?"

He smiled and sat down on the edge of the bed. "Brother," he said, taking her hand. "Open."

"Good. Brothers are better," she murmured as he put the glass tube under her tongue.

"Now, be still, I want to count." Dr. Archie reached for her hand and took out his watch. When he put her hand back under the quilt he went over to one of the windows—they were both tight shut—and lifted it a little way. He reached up and ran his hand along the cold, unpapered wall. "Keep under the covers; I'll come back to you in a moment," he said, bending over the glass lamp with his thermometer. He winked at her from the door before he shut it.

Peter Kronborg was sitting in his wife's room, holding the bundle which contained his son. His air of cheerful importance, his beard and glasses, even his shirt-sleeves, annoyed the doctor. He beckoned Kronborg into the living-room and said sternly:—

"You've got a very sick child in there. Why didn't you call me before? It's pneumonia, and she must have been sick for several days. Put the baby down somewhere, please, and help me make up the bed-lounge here in the parlor. She's got to be in a warm room, and she's got to be quiet. You must keep the other children out. Here, this thing opens up, I see," swinging back the top of the carpet lounge. "We can lift her mattress and carry her in just as she is. I don't want to disturb her more than is necessary."

Kronborg was all concern immediately. The two men took up the mattress and carried the sick child into the parlor. "I'll have to go down to my office to get some medicine, Kronborg. The drug store won't be open. Keep the covers on her. I won't be gone long. Shake down the stove and put on a little coal, but not too much; so it'll catch quickly, I mean. Find an old sheet for me, and put it there to warm."

The doctor caught his coat and hurried out into the dark street. Nobody was stirring yet, and the cold was bitter. He was tired and hungry and in no mild humor. "The idea!" he muttered; "to be such an ass at his age, about the seventh! And to feel no responsibility about the little girl. Silly old goat! The baby would have got into the world somehow; they always do. But a nice little girl like that—she's worth the whole litter. Where she ever got it from—" He turned into the Duke Block and ran up the stairs to his office.

Thea Kronborg, meanwhile, was wondering why she happened to be in the parlor, where nobody but company—usually visiting preachers—ever slept. She had moments of stupor when she did not see anything, and moments of excitement when she felt that something unusual and pleasant was about to happen, when she saw everything clearly in the red light from the isinglass sides of the hard-coal burner—the nickel trimmings on the stove itself, the pictures on the wall which she thought very beautiful, the flowers on the Brussels carpet,* Czerny's "Daily Studies"* which stood open on the upright piano. She forgot, for the time being, all about the new baby.

When she heard the front door open, it occurred to her that the pleasant thing which was going to happen was Dr. Archie himself. He came in and warmed his hands at the stove. As he turned to her, she threw herself wearily toward him, half out of her bed. She would have tumbled to the floor had he not caught her. He gave her some medicine and went to the kitchen for something he needed. She drowsed and lost the sense of his being there. When she opened her eyes again, he was kneeling before the stove, spreading something dark and sticky on a white cloth, with a big spoon; batter, perhaps. Presently she felt him taking off her nightgown. He wrapped the hot plaster about her chest. There seemed to be straps which he pinned over her shoulders. Then he took out a thread and needle and began to sew her up in it. That, she felt, was too strange; she must be dreaming anyhow, so she succumbed to her drowsiness.

Thea had been moaning with every breath since the doctor came back, but she did not know it. She did not realize that she was suffering pain. When she was conscious at all, she seemed to be separated from her body; to be perched on top of the piano, or on the hanging lamp, watching the doctor sew her up. It was perplexing and unsatisfactory, like dreaming. She wished she could waken up and see what was going on.

The doctor thanked God that he had persuaded Peter Kronborg to keep out of the way. He could do better by the child if he had her to himself. He had no children of his own. His marriage was a very unhappy one. As he lifted and undressed Thea, he thought to himself what a beautiful thing a little girl's body was,—like a flower. It was so neatly and delicately fashioned, so soft, and so milky white. Thea must have got her hair and her silky skin from her mother. She was a little Swede, through and through. Dr. Archie could not help thinking how he would cherish a little creature like this if she were his. Her hands, so little and hot, so clever, too,—he glanced at the open exercise book on the piano. When he had stitched up the flax-seed jacket, he wiped it neatly about the edges, where the paste had worked out on the skin. He put on her the clean nightgown he had warmed before the fire, and tucked the blankets about her. As he pushed back the hair that had fuzzed down over her eyebrows, he felt her head thoughtfully with the tips of his fingers. No, he couldn't say that it was different from any other child's head, though he believed that there was something very different about her. He looked intently at her wide, flushed face, freckled nose, fierce little mouth, and her delicate, tender chin—the one soft touch in her hard little Scandinavian face, as if some fairy godmother had caressed her there and left a cryptic promise. Her brows were usually drawn together defiantly, but never when she was with Dr. Archie. Her affection for him was prettier than most of the things that went to make up the doctor's life in Moonstone.

The windows grew gray. He heard a tramping on the attic floor, on the back stairs, then cries: "Give me my shirt!" "Where's my other stocking?"

"I'll have to stay till they get off to school," he reflected, "or they'll be in here tormenting her, the whole lot of them."

II

For the next four days it seemed to Dr. Archie that his patient might slip through his hands, do what he might. But she did not. On the contrary, after that she recovered very rapidly. As her father remarked, she must have inherited the "constitution" which he was never tired of admiring in her mother.

One afternoon, when her new brother was a week old, the doctor found Thea very comfortable and happy in her bed in the parlor. The sunlight was pouring in over her shoulders, the baby was asleep on a pillow in a big rocking-chair beside her. Whenever he stirred she put out her hand and rocked him. Nothing of him was visible but a flushed, puffy forehead and an uncompromisingly big, bald cranium. The door into her mother's room stood open, and Mrs. Kronborg was sitting up in bed darning stockings. She was a short, stalwart woman, with a short neck and a determined-looking head. Her skin was very fair, her face calm and unwrinkled, and her yellow hair, braided down her back as she lay in bed, still looked like a girl's. She was a woman whom Dr. Archie respected; active, practical, unruffled; good-humored, but determined. Exactly the sort of woman to take care of a flighty preacher. She had brought her husband some property, too,—one fourth of her father's broad acres in Nebraska,—but this she kept in her own name. She had profound respect for her husband's erudition and eloquence. She sat under his preaching with deep humility, and was as much taken in by his stiff shirt and white neckties as if she had not ironed them herself by lamplight the night before they appeared correct and spotless in the pulpit. But for all this, she had no confidence in his administration of worldly affairs. She looked to him for morning prayers and grace at table; she expected him to name the babies and to supply whatever parental sentiment there was in the house, to remember birthdays and anniversaries, to point the children to moral and patriotic ideals. It was her work to keep their bodies, their clothes, and their conduct in some sort of order, and this she accomplished with a success that was a source of wonder to her neighbors. As she used to remark, and her husband admiringly to echo, she "had never lost one." With all his flightiness, Peter Kronborg appreciated the matter-of-fact, punctual way in which his wife got her children into the world and along in it. He believed, and he was right in believing, that the sovereign State of Colorado* was much indebted to Mrs. Kronborg and women like her.

Mrs. Kronborg believed that the size of every family was decided in heaven. More modern views would not have startled her; they would simply have seemed foolish—thin chatter, like the boasts of the men who built the tower of Babel,* or like Axel's plan to breed ostriches in the chicken yard. From what evidence Mrs. Kronborg formed her opinions on this and other matters, it would have been difficult to say, but once formed, they were unchangeable. She would no more have questioned her convictions than she would have questioned revelation. Calm and even-tempered, naturally kind, she was capable of strong prejudice, and she never forgave.

When the doctor came in to see Thea, Mrs. Kronborg was reflecting that the washing was a week behind, and deciding what she had better do about it. The arrival of a new baby meant a revision of her entire domestic schedule, and as she drove her needle along she had been working out new sleeping arrangements and cleaning days. The doctor had entered the house without knocking, after making noise enough in the hall to prepare, his patients. Thea was reading, her book propped up before her in the sunlight.

"Mustn't do that; bad for your eyes," he said, as Thea shut the book quickly and slipped it under the covers.

Mrs. Kronborg called from her bed: "Bring the baby here, doctor, and have that chair. She wanted him in there for company."

Before the doctor picked up the baby, he put a yellow paper bag down on Thea's coverlid and winked at her. They had a code of winks and grimaces. When he went in to chat with her mother, Thea opened the bag cautiously, trying to keep it from crackling. She drew out a long bunch of white grapes, with a little of the sawdust in which they had been packed still clinging to them.

They were called Malaga grapes* in Moonstone, and once or twice during the winter the leading grocer got a keg of them. They were used mainly for table decoration, about Christmas-time. Thea had never had more than one grape at a time before. When the doctor came back she was holding the almost transparent fruit up in the sunlight, feeling the pale-green skins softly with the tips of her fingers. She did not thank him; she only snapped her eyes at him in a special way which he understood, and, when he gave her his hand, put it quickly and shyly under her cheek, as if she were trying to do so without knowing it—and without his knowing it.

Dr. Archie sat down in the rocking-chair. "And how's Thea feeling to-day?"

He was quite as shy as his patient, especially when a third person overheard his conversation. Big and handsome and superior to his fellow townsmen as Dr. Archie was, he was seldom at his ease, and like Peter Kronborg he often dodged behind a professional manner. There was sometimes a contraction of embarrassment and self-consciousness all over his big body, which made him awkward—likely to stumble, to kick up rugs, or to knock over chairs. If any one was very sick, he forgot himself, but he had a clumsy touch in convalescent gossip.

Thea curled up on her side and looked at him with pleasure. "All right. I like to be sick. I have more fun then than other times."

"How's that?"

"I don't have to go to school, and I don't have to practice. I can read all I want to, and have good things,"—she patted the grapes. "I had lots of fun that time I mashed my finger and you wouldn't let Professor Wunsch* make me practice. Only I had to do left hand, even then. I think that was mean."

The doctor took her hand and examined the forefinger, where the nail had grown back a little crooked. "You mustn't trim it down close at the corner there, and then it will grow straight. You won't want it crooked when you're a big girl and wear rings and have sweethearts."

She made a mocking little face at him and looked at his new

scarf-pin. "That's the prettiest one you ev-*er* had. I wish you'd stay a long while and let me look at it. What is it?"

Dr. Archie laughed. "It's an opal. Spanish Johnny brought it up for me from Chihuahua* in his shoe. I had it set in Denver, and I wore it to-day for your benefit."

Thea had a curious passion for jewelry. She wanted every shining stone she saw, and in summer she was always going off into the sand hills to hunt for crystals and agates and bits of pink chalcedony. She had two cigar boxes full of stones that she had found or traded for, and she imagined that they were of enormous value. She was always planning how she would have them set.

"What are you reading?" The doctor reached under the covers and pulled out a book of Byron's poems. "Do you like this?"

She looked confused, turned over a few pages rapidly, and pointed to "My native land, good-night."* "That," she said sheepishly.

"How about 'Maid of Athens'?"

She blushed and looked at him suspiciously. "I like 'There was a sound of revelry,' "* she muttered.

The doctor laughed and closed the book. It was clumsily bound in padded leather and had been presented to the Reverend Peter Kronborg by his Sunday-School class as an ornament for his parlor table.

"Come into the office some day, and I'll lend you a nice book. You can skip the parts you don't understand. You can read it in vacation. Perhaps you'll be able to understand all of it by then."

Thea frowned and looked fretfully toward the piano. "In vacation I have to practice four hours every day, and then there'll be Thor* to take care of." She pronounced it "Tor."

"Thor? Oh, you've named the baby Thor?" exclaimed the doctor.

Thea frowned again, still more fiercely, and said quickly, "That's a nice name, only maybe it's a little—old-fashioned." She was very sensitive about being thought a foreigner, and was proud of the fact that, in town, her father always preached in English; very bookish English, at that, one might add.

Born in an old Scandinavian colony in Minnesota, Peter

Kronborg had been sent to a small divinity school in Indiana by the women of a Swedish evangelical mission, who were convinced of his gifts and who skimped and begged and gave church suppers to get the long, lazy youth through the seminary. He could still speak enough Swedish to exhort and to bury the members of his country church out at Copper Hole, and he wielded in his Moonstone pulpit a somewhat pompous English vocabulary he had learned out of books at college. He always spoke of "the infant Saviour," "our Heavenly Father," etc. The poor man had no natural, spontaneous human speech. If he had his sincere moments, they were perforce inarticulate. Probably a good deal of his pretentiousness was due to the fact that he habitually expressed himself in a book-learned language, wholly remote from anything personal, native, or homely. Mrs. Kronborg spoke Swedish to her own sisters and to her sister-in-law Tillie, and colloquial English to her neighbors. Thea, who had a rather sensitive ear, until she went to school never spoke at all, except in monosyllables, and her mother was convinced that she was tongue-tied. She was still inept in speech for a child so intelligent. Her ideas were usually clear, but she seldom attempted to explain them, even at school, where she excelled in "written work" and never did more than mutter a reply.

"Your music professor stopped me on the street to-day and asked me how you were," said the doctor, rising. "He'll be sick himself, trotting around in this slush with no overcoat or overshoes."

"He's poor," said Thea simply.

The doctor sighed. "I'm afraid he's worse than that. Is he always all right when you take your lessons? Never acts as if he'd been drinking?"

Thea looked angry and spoke excitedly. "He knows a lot. More than anybody. I don't care if he does drink; he's old and poor." Her voice shook a little.

Mrs. Kronborg spoke up from the next room. "He's a good teacher, doctor. It's good for us he does drink. He'd never be in a little place like this if he didn't have some weakness. These women that teach music around here don't know nothing. I wouldn't have my child wasting time with them. If Professor Wunsch goes away, Thea'll have nobody to take from. He's careful with his scholars; he don't use bad language. Mrs. Kohler is always present when Thea takes her lesson. It's all right." Mrs. Kronborg spoke calmly and judicially. One could see that she had thought the matter out before.

"I'm glad to hear that, Mrs. Kronborg. I wish we could get the old man off his bottle and keep him tidy. Do you suppose if I gave you an old overcoat you could get him to wear it?" The doctor went to the bedroom door and Mrs. Kronborg looked up from her darning.

"Why, yes, I guess he'd be glad of it. He'll take most anything from me. He won't buy clothes, but I guess he'd wear 'em if he had 'em. I've never had any clothes to give him, having so many to make over for."

"I'll have Larry bring the coat around to-night. You aren't cross with me, Thea?" taking her hand.

Thea grinned warmly. "Not if you give Professor Wunsch a coat—and things," she tapped the grapes significantly. The doctor bent over and kissed her.

III

BEING sick was all very well, but Thea knew from experience that starting back to school again was attended by depressing difficulties. One Monday morning she got up early with Axel and Gunner, who shared her wing room, and hurried into the back living-room, between the dining-room and the kitchen. There, beside a soft-coal stove, the younger children of the family undressed at night and dressed in the morning. The older daughter, Anna, and the two big boys slept upstairs, where the rooms were theoretically warmed by stovepipes from below. The first (and the worst!) thing that confronted Thea was a suit of clean, prickly red flannel, fresh from the wash. Usually the torment of breaking in a clean suit of flannel came on Sunday, but yesterday, as she was staying in the house, she had begged off.

Their winter underwear was a trial to all the children, but it was bitterest to Thea because she happened to have the most sensitive skin. While she was tugging it on, her Aunt Tillie brought in warm water from the boiler and filled the tin pitcher. Thea washed her face, brushed and braided her hair, and got into her blue cashmere dress. Over this she buttoned a long apron, with sleeves, which would not be removed until she put on her cloak to go to school. Gunner and Axel, on the soap box behind the stove, had their usual quarrel about which should wear the tightest stockings, but they exchanged reproaches in low tones, for they were wholesomely afraid of Mrs. Kronborg's rawhide whip. She did not chastise her children often, but she did it thoroughly. Only a somewhat stern system of discipline could have kept any degree of order and quiet in that overcrowded house.

Mrs. Kronborg's children were all trained to dress themselves at the earliest possible age, to make their own beds,—the boys as well as the girls,—to take care of their clothes, to eat what was given them, and to keep out of the way. Mrs. Kronborg would have made a good chess-player; she had a head for moves and positions.

Anna, the elder daughter was her mother's lieutenant. All the children knew that they must obey Anna, who was an obstinate contender for proprieties and not always fair-minded. To see the young Kronborgs headed for Sunday-School was like watching a military drill. Mrs. Kronborg let her children's minds alone. She did not pry into their thoughts or nag them. She respected them as individuals, and outside of the house they had a great deal of liberty. But their communal life was definitely ordered.

In the winter the children breakfasted in the kitchen; Gus and Charley and Anna first, while the younger children were dressing. Gus was nineteen and was a clerk in a dry-goods store. Charley, eighteen months younger, worked in a feed store. They left the house by the kitchen door at seven o'clock, and then Anna helped her Aunt Tillie get the breakfast for the younger ones. Without the help of this sister-in-law, Tillie Kronborg, Mrs. Kronborg's life would have been a hard one. Mrs. Kronborg often reminded

Anna that "no hired help would ever have taken the same interest."

Mr. Kronborg came of a poorer stock than his wife; from a lowly, ignorant family that had lived in a poor part of Sweden. His great-grandfather had gone to Norway to work as a farm laborer and had married a Norwegian girl. This strain of Norwegian blood came out somewhere in each generation of the Kronborgs. The intemperance of one of Peter Kronborg's uncles, and the religious mania of another, had been alike charged to the Norwegian grandmother. Both Peter Kronborg and his sister Tillie were more like the Norwegian root of the family than like the Swedish, and this same Norwegian strain was strong in Thea, though in her it took a very different character.

Tillie was a queer, addle-pated thing, as flighty as a girl at thirty-five, and overweeningly fond of gay clothes—which taste, as Mrs. Kronborg philosophically said, did nobody any harm. Tillie was always cheerful, and her tongue was still for scarcely a minute during the day. She had been cruelly overworked on her father's Minnesota farm when she was a young girl, and she had never been so happy as she was now; had never before, as she said, had such social advantages. She thought her brother the most important man in Moonstone. She never missed a church service, and, much to the embarrassment of the children, she always "spoke a piece" at the Sunday-School concerts. She had a complete set of "Standard Recitations," which she conned on Sundays. This morning, when Thea and her two younger brothers sat down to breakfast, Tillie was remonstrating with Gunner because he had not learned a recitation assigned to him for George Washington Day at school. The unmemorized text lay heavily on Gunner's conscience as he attacked his buckwheat cakes and sausage. He knew that Tillie was in the right, and that "when the day came he would be ashamed of himself."

"I don't care," he muttered, stirring his coffee; "they oughtn't to make boys speak. It's all right for girls. They like to show off."

"No showing off about it. Boys ought to like to speak up for their country. And what was the use of your father buying you a new suit, if you're not going to take part in anything?"

"That was for Sunday-School. I'd rather wear my old one, anyhow. Why didn't they give the piece to Thea?" Gunner grumbled.

Tillie was turning buckwheat cakes at the griddle. "Thea can play and sing, she don't need to speak. But you've got to know how to do something, Gunner, that you have. What are you going to do when you git big and want to git into society, if you can't do nothing? Everybody'll say, 'Can you sing? Can you play? Can you speak? Then git right out of society.' An' that's what they'll say to you, Mr. Gunner."

Gunner and Alex grinned at Anna, who was preparing her mother's breakfast. They never made fun of Tillie, but they understood well enough that there were subjects upon which her ideas were rather foolish. When Tillie struck the shallows, Thea was usually prompt in turning the conversation.

"Will you and Axel let me have your sled at recess?" she asked.

"All the time?" asked Gunner dubiously.

"I'll work your examples for you to-night, if you do."

"Oh, all right. There'll be a lot of 'em."

"I don't mind, I can work 'em fast. How about yours, Axel?"

Axel was a fat little boy of seven, with pretty, lazy blue eyes. "I don't care," he murmured, buttering his last buckwheat cake without ambition; "too much trouble to copy 'em down. Jenny Smiley 'll let me have hers."

The boys were to pull Thea to school on their sled, as the snow was deep. The three set off together. Anna was now in the high school, and she no longer went with the family party, but walked to school with some of the older girls who were her friends, and wore a hat, not a hood like Thea.

IV

"AND it was Summer, beautiful Summer!" Those were closing words of Thea's favorite fairy tale,* and she thought of them as she ran out into the world one Saturday morning in May, her music book under her arm. She was going to the Kohlers' to take her lesson, but she was in no hurry.

It was in the summer that one really lived. Then all the little overcrowded houses were opened wide, and the wind blew through them with sweet, earthy smells of garden-planting. The town looked as if it had just been washed. People were out painting their fences. The cotton wood trees were a-flicker with sticky, yellow little leaves, and the feathery tamarisks were in pink bud. With the warm weather came freedom for everybody. People were dug up, as it were. The very old people, whom one had not seen all winter, came out and sunned themselves in the yard. The double windows were taken off the houses, the tormenting flannels in which children had been encased all winter were put away in boxes, and the youngsters felt a pleasure in the cool cotton things next their skin.

Thea had to walk more than a mile to reach the Kohlers' house, a very pleasant mile out of town toward the glittering sand hills,—yellow this morning, with lines of deep violet where the clefts and valleys were. She followed the sidewalk to the depot at the south end of the town; then took the road east to the little group of adobe houses where the Mexicans lived, then dropped into a deep ravine; a dry sand creek, across which the railroad track ran on a trestle. Beyond that gulch, on a little rise of ground that faced the open sandy plain, was the Kohlers' house, where Professor Wunsch lived. Fritz Kohler was the town tailor, one of the first settlers. He had moved there, built a little house and made a garden, when Moonstone was first marked down on the map. He had three sons, but they now worked on the railroad and were stationed in distant cities. One of them had gone to work for the Santa Fé, and lived in New Mexico.

Mrs. Kohler seldom crossed the ravine and went into the town except at Christmas-time, when she had to buy presents and Christmas cards to send to her old friends in Freeport, Illinois. As she did not go to church, she did not possess such a thing as a hat. Year after year she wore the same red hood in winter and a black sunbonnet in summer. She made her own dresses; the skirts came barely to her shoe-tops, and were gathered as full as they could possibly be to the waistband. She preferred men's shoes, and usually wore the cast-offs of one of her sons. She had never learned much English, and her plants and shrubs were her companions. She lived for her men and her garden. Beside that sand gulch, she had tried to reproduce a bit of her own village in the Rhine Valley. She hid herself behind the growth she had fostered, lived under the shade of what she had planted and watered and pruned. In the blaze of the open plain she was stupid and blind like an owl. Shade, shade; that was what she was always planning and making. Behind the high tamarisk hedge, her garden was a jungle of verdure in summer. Above the cherry trees and peach trees and golden plums stood the windmill, with its tank on stilts, which kept all this verdure alive. Outside, the sage-brush grew up to the very edge of the garden, and the sand was always drifting up to the tamarisks.

Every one in Moonstone was astonished when the Kohlers took the wandering music-teacher to live with them. In seventeen years old Fritz had never had a crony, except the harness-maker and Spanish Johnny. This Wunsch came from God knew where,—followed Spanish Johnny into town when that wanderer came back from one of his tramps. Wunsch played in the dance orchestra, tuned pianos, and gave lessons. When Mrs. Kohler rescued him, he was sleeping in a dirty, unfurnished room over one of the saloons, and he had only two shirts in the world. Once he was under her roof, the old woman went at him as she did at her garden. She sewed and washed and mended for him, and made him so clean and respectable that he was able to get a large class of pupils and to rent a piano. As soon as he had money ahead, he sent to the Narrow Gauge lodging-house, in Denver, for a trunkful of music which had been held there for unpaid board. With tears in his eyes the old man—he was not over fifty, but sadly battered—told Mrs. Kohler that he asked nothing better of God than to end his days with her, and to be buried in the garden, under her linden trees. They were not American basswood, but the European linden, which has honey-colored blooms in summer, with a fragrance that surpasses all trees and flowers and drives young people wild with joy.

Thea was reflecting as she walked along that had it not been for Professor Wunsch she might have lived on for years in Moonstone without ever knowing the Kohlers, without ever seeing their garden or the inside of their house. Besides the cuckoo clock,—which was wonderful enough, and which Mrs. Kohler said she kept for "company when she was lonesome,"—the Kohlers had in their house the most wonderful thing Thea had ever seen—but of that later.

Professor Wunsch went to the houses of his other pupils to give them their lessons, but one morning he told Mrs. Kronborg that Thea had talent, and that if she came to him he could teach her in his slippers, and that would be better. Mrs. Kronborg was a strange woman. That word "talent," which no one else in Moonstone, not even Dr. Archie, would have understood, she comprehended perfectly. To any other woman there, it would have meant that a child must have her hair curled every day and must play in public. Mrs. Kronborg knew it meant that Thea must practice four hours a day. A child with talent must be kept at the piano, just as a child with measles must be kept under the blankets. Mrs. Kronborg and her three sisters had all studied piano, and all sang well, but none of them had talent. Their father had played the oboe in an orchestra in Sweden, before he came to America to better his fortunes. He had even known Jenny Lind.* A child with talent had to be kept at the piano; so twice a week in summer and once a week in winter Thea went over the gulch to the Kohlers', though the Ladies' Aid Society thought it was not proper for their preacher's daughter to go "where there was so much drinking." Not that the Kohler sons ever so much as looked at a glass of beer. They were ashamed of their old folks and got out into the world as fast as possible; had their clothes made by a Denver tailor and their necks shaved up under their hair and forgot the past. Old Fritz and Wunsch, however, indulged in a friendly bottle pretty often. The two men were like comrades; perhaps the bond between them was the glass wherein lost hopes are found; perhaps it was common memories of another country; perhaps it was the grapevine in the garden—knotty, fibrous shrub, full of homesickness and sentiment, which the Germans have carried around the world with them.

As Thea approached the house she peeped between the pink sprays of the tamarisk hedge and saw the Professor and Mrs. Kohler in the garden, spading and raking. The garden looked like a relief-map now, and gave no indication of what it would be in August; such a jungle! Pole beans and potatoes and corn and leeks and kale and red cabbage—there would even be vegetables for which there is no American name. Mrs. Kohler was always getting by mail packages of seeds from Freeport and from the old country. Then the flowers! There were big sunflowers for the canary bird, tiger lilies and phlox and zinnias and lady's-slippers and portulaca and hollyhocks,—giant hollyhocks. Beside the fruit trees there was a great umbrella-shaped catalpa, and a balm-of-Gilead, two lindens, and even a ginka,—a rigid, pointed tree with leaves shaped like butterflies, which shivered, but never bent to the wind.

This morning Thea saw to her delight that the two oleander trees, one white and one red, had been brought up from their winter quarters in the cellar. There is hardly a German family in the most arid parts of Utah, New Mexico, Arizona, but has its oleander trees. However loutish the American-born sons of the family may be, there was never one who refused to give his muscle to the back-breaking task of getting those tubbed trees down into the cellar in the fall and up into the sunlight in the spring. They may strive to avert the day, but they grapple with the tub at last.

When Thea entered the gate, her professor leaned his spade against the white post that supported the turreted dove-house, and wiped his face with his shirt-sleeve; someway he never managed to have a handkerchief about him. Wunsch was short and stocky, with something rough and bear-like about his shoulders. His face was a dark, bricky red, deeply creased rather than wrinkled, and the skin was like loose leather over his neck band—he wore a brass collar button but no collar. His hair was cropped close; iron-gray bristles on a bullet-like head. His eyes were always suffused and bloodshot. He had a coarse, scornful mouth, and irregular, yellow teeth, much worn at the edges. His hands were square and red, seldom clean, but always alive, impatient, even sympathetic.

"*Morgen*,"* he greeted his pupil in a businesslike way, put on a black alpaca coat, and conducted her at once to the piano in Mrs. Kohler's sitting-room. He twirled the stool to the proper height, pointed to it, and sat down in a wooden chair beside Thea.

"The scale of B flat major," he directed, and then fell into an attitude of deep attention. Without a word his pupil set to work.

To Mrs. Kohler, in the garden, came the cheerful sound of effort, of vigorous striving. Unconsciously she wielded her rake more lightly. Occasionally she heard the teacher's voice. "Scale of E minor. . . . *Weiter, weiter!* . . . *Immer* I hear the thumb, like a lame foot. *Weiter . . . weiter*, once; . . .*Schön!** The chords, quick!"

The pupil did not open her mouth until they began the second movement of the Clementi sonata, when she remonstrated in low tones about the way he had marked the fingering of a passage.

"It makes no matter what you think," replied her teacher coldly. "There is only one right way. The thumb there. *Ein, zwei, drei, vier*,"* etc. Then for an hour there was no further interruption.

At the end of the lesson Thea turned on her stool and leaned her arm on the keyboard. They usually had a little talk after the lesson.

Herr Wunsch grinned. "How soon is it you are free from school? Then we make ahead faster, eh?"

"First week in June. Then will you give me the 'Invitation to the Dance'?"*

He shrugged his shoulders. "It makes no matter. If you want him, you play him out of lesson hours."

"All right." Thea fumbled in her pocket and brought out a crumpled slip of paper. "What does this mean, please? I guess it's Latin."

Wunsch blinked at the line penciled on the paper. "Wherefrom you get this?" he asked gruffly.

"Out of a book Dr. Archie gave me to read. It's all English but that. Did you ever see it before?" she asked, watching his face.

"Yes. A long time ago," he muttered, scowling. "Ovidius!" He

took a stub of lead pencil from his vest pocket, steadied his hand
by a visible effort, and under the words

> "*Lente currite, lente currite, noctis equi*,"*

he wrote in a clear, elegant Gothic hand,—

> "Go slowly, go slowly, ye steeds of the night."

He put the pencil back in his pocket and continued to stare at the
Latin. It recalled the poem, which he had read as a student, and
thought very fine. There were treasures of memory which no
lodging-house keeper could attach. One carried things about in
one's head, long after one's linen could be smuggled out in a
tuning-bag. He handed the paper back to Thea. "There is the
English, quite elegant," he said, rising.

Mrs. Kohler stuck her head in at the door, and Thea slid off
the stool. "Come in, Mrs. Kohler," she called, "and show me the
piece-picture."

The old woman laughed, pulled off her big gardening-gloves,
and pushed Thea to the lounge before the object of her delight.
The "piece-picture," which hung on the wall and nearly covered
one whole end of the room, was the handiwork of Fritz Kohler. He
had learned his trade under an old-fashioned tailor in Magdeburg
who required from each of his apprentices a thesis: that is, before
they left his shop, each apprentice had to copy in cloth some well-
known German painting, stitching bits of colored stuff together
on a linen background; a kind of mosaic. The pupil was allowed
to select his subject, and Fritz Kohler had chosen a popular painting of Napoleon's retreat from Moscow.* The gloomy Emperor
and his staff were represented as crossing a stone bridge, and
behind them was the blazing city, the walls and fortresses done in
gray cloth with orange tongues of flame darting about the domes
and minarets. Napoleon rode his white horse; Murat,* in Oriental
dress, a bay charger. Thea was never tired of examining this work,
of hearing how long it had taken Fritz to make it, how much it
had been admired, and what narrow escapes it had had from
moths and fire. Silk, Mrs. Kohler explained, would have been
much easier to manage than woolen cloth, in which it was often

hard to get the right shades. The reins of the horses, the wheels of the spurs, the brooding eyebrows of the Emperor, Murat's fierce mustaches, the great shakos of the Guard, were all worked out with the minutest fidelity. Thea's admiration for this picture had endeared her to Mrs. Kohler. It was now many years since she used to point out its wonders to her own little boys. As Mrs. Kohler did not go to church, she never heard any singing, except the songs that floated over from Mexican Town, and Thea often sang for her after the lesson was over. This morning Wunsch pointed to the piano.

"On Sunday, when I go by the church, I hear you sing something."

Thea obediently sat down on the stool again and began, "*Come, ye Disconsolate.*"* Wunsch listened thoughtfully, his hands on his knees. Such a beautiful child's voice! Old Mrs. Kohler's face relaxed in a smile of happiness; she half closed her eyes. A big fly was darting in and out of the window; the sunlight made a golden pool on the rag carpet and bathed the faded cretonne pillows on the lounge, under the piece-picture. "Earth has no sorrow that Heaven cannot heal," the song died away.

"That is a good thing to remember," Wunsch shook himself. "You believe that?" looking quizzically at Thea.

She became confused and pecked nervously at a black key with her middle finger. "I don't know. I guess so," she murmured.

Her teacher rose abruptly. "Remember, for next time, thirds. You ought to get up earlier."

That night the air was so warm that Fritz and Herr Wunsch had their after-supper pipe in the grape arbor, smoking in silence while the sound of fiddles and guitars came across the ravine from Mexican Town. Long after Fritz and his old Paulina had gone to bed, Wunsch sat motionless in the arbor, looking up through the woolly vine leaves at the glittering machinery of heaven.

"Lente currite, noctis equi."

That line awoke many memories. He was thinking of youth; of his own, so long gone by, and of his pupil's, just beginning. He would even have cherished hopes for her, except that he had become

superstitious. He believed that whatever he hoped for was destined not to be; that his affection brought ill-fortune, especially to
the young; that if he held anything in his thoughts, he harmed it.
He had taught in music schools in St. Louis and Kansas City,
where the shallowness and complacency of the young misses had
maddened him. He had encountered bad manners and bad faith,
had been the victim of sharpers of all kinds, was dogged by bad
luck. He had played in orchestras that were never paid and wandering opera troupes which disbanded penniless. And there was
always the old enemy, more relentless than the others. It was long
since he had wished anything or desired anything beyond the
necessities of the body. Now that he was tempted to hope for
another, he felt alarmed and shook his head.

It was his pupil's power of application, her rugged will, that
interested him. He had lived for so long among people whose sole
ambition was to get something for nothing that he had learned
not to look for seriousness in anything. Now that he by chance
encountered it, it recalled standards, ambitions, a society long
forgot. What was it she reminded him of? A yellow flower, full of
sunlight, perhaps. No; a thin glass full of sweet-smelling, sparkling Moselle wine. He seemed to see such a glass before him in
the arbor, to watch the bubbles rising and breaking, like the silent
discharge of energy in the nerves and brain, the rapid florescence
in young blood—Wunsch felt ashamed and dragged his slippers
along the path to the kitchen, his eyes on the ground.

V

THE children in the primary grades were sometimes required to
make relief maps of Moonstone in sand. Had they used colored
sands, as the Navajo medicine men do in their sand mosaics, they
could easily have indicated the social classifications of Moonstone, since these conformed to certain topographical boundaries,
and every child understood them perfectly.

The main business street ran, of course, through the center of
the town. To the west of this street lived all the people who were,

as Tillie Kronborg said, "in society." Sylvester Street, the third parallel with Main Street on the west, was the longest in town, and the best dwellings were built along it. Far out at the north end, nearly a mile from the court-house and its cottonwood grove, was Dr. Archie's house, its big yard and garden surrounded by a white paling fence. The Methodist Church was in the center of the town, facing the court-house square. The Kronborgs lived half a mile south of the church, on the long street that stretched out like an arm to the depot settlement. This was the first street west of Main, and was built up only on one side. The preacher's house faced the backs of the brick and frame store buildings and a draw full of sunflowers and scraps of old iron. The sidewalk which ran in front of the Kronborgs' house was the one continuous sidewalk to the depot, and all the train men and roundhouse employees passed the front gate every time they came uptown. Thea and Mrs. Kronborg had many friends among the railroad men, who often paused to chat across the fence, and of one of these we shall have more to say.

In the part of Moonstone that lay east of Main Street, toward the deep ravine which, farther south, wound by Mexican Town, lived all the humbler citizens, the people who voted but did not run for office. The houses were little story-and-a-half cottages, with none of the fussy architectural efforts that marked those on Sylvester Street. They nestled modestly behind their cottonwoods and Virginia creeper; their occupants had no social pretensions to keep up. There were no half-glass front doors with doorbells, or formidable parlors behind closed shutters. Here the old women washed in the back yard, and the men sat in the front doorway and smoked their pipes. The people on Sylvester Street scarcely knew that this part of the town existed. Thea liked to take Thor and her express wagon and explore these quiet, shady streets, where the people never tried to have lawns or to grow elms and pine trees, but let the native timber have its way and spread in luxuriance. She had many friends there, old women who gave her a yellow rose or a spray of trumpet vine and appeased Thor with a cooky or a doughnut. They called Thea "that preacher's girl," but the demonstrative was misplaced, for when they spoke of Mr. Kronborg they called him "the Methodist preacher."

Dr. Archie was very proud of his yard and garden, which he worked himself. He was the only man in Moonstone who was successful at growing rambler roses, and his strawberries were famous. One morning when Thea was downtown on an errand, the doctor stopped her, took her hand and went over her with a quizzical eye, as he nearly always did when they met.

"You haven't been up to my place to get any strawberries yet, Thea. They're at their best just now. Mrs. Archie doesn't know what to do with them all. Come up this afternoon. Just tell Mrs. Archie I sent you. Bring a big basket and pick till you are tired."

When she got home Thea told her mother that she didn't want to go, because she didn't like Mrs. Archie.

"She is certainly one queer woman," Mrs. Kronborg assented, "but he's asked you so often, I guess you'll have to go this time. She won't bite you."

After dinner Thea took a basket, put Thor in his baby-buggy, and set out for Dr. Archie's house at the other end of town. As soon as she came within sight of the house, she slackened her pace. She approached it very slowly, stopping often to pick dandelions and sand-peas for Thor to crush up in his fist.

It was his wife's custom, as soon as Dr. Archie left the house in the morning, to shut all the doors and windows to keep the dust out, and to pull down the shades to keep the sun from fading the carpets. She thought, too, that neighbors were less likely to drop in if the house was closed up. She was one of those people who are stingy without motive or reason, even when they can gain nothing by it. She must have known that skimping the doctor in heat and food made him more extravagant than he would have been had she made him comfortable. He never came home for lunch, because she gave him such miserable scraps and shreds of food. No matter how much milk he bought, he could never get thick cream for his strawberries. Even when he watched his wife lift it from the milk in smooth, ivory-colored blankets, she managed, by some sleight-of-hand, to dilute it before it got to the breakfast table. The butcher's favorite joke was about the kind of meat he sold Mrs. Archie. She felt no interest in food herself, and she hated to prepare it. She liked nothing better than to have Dr. Archie go to Denver for a few days—he often went chiefly because he was hungry—and to be left alone to eat canned salmon and to keep the house shut up from morning until night.

Mrs. Archie would not have a servant because, she said, "they ate too much and broke too much"; she even said they knew too much. She used what mind she had in devising shifts to minimize her housework. She used to tell her neighbors that if there were no men, there would be no housework. When Mrs. Archie was first married, she had been always in a panic for fear she would have children. Now that her apprehensions on that score had grown paler, she was almost as much afraid of having dust in the house as she had once been of having children in it. If dust did not get in, it did not have to be got out, she said. She would take any amount of trouble to avoid trouble. Why, nobody knew. Certainly her husband had never been able to make her out. Such little, mean natures are among the darkest and most baffling of created things. There is no law by which they can be explained. The ordinary incentives of pain and pleasure do not account for their behavior. They live like insects, absorbed in petty activities that seem to have nothing to do with any genial aspect of human life.

Mrs. Archie, as Mrs. Kronborg said, "liked to gad." She liked to have her house clean, empty, dark, locked, and to be out of it—anywhere. A church social, a prayer meeting, a ten-cent show; she seemed to have no preference. When there was nowhere else to go, she used to sit for hours in Mrs. Smiley's millinery and notion store, listening to the talk of the women who came in, watching them while they tried on hats, blinking at them from her corner with her sharp, restless little eyes. She never talked much herself, but she knew all the gossip of the town and she had a sharp ear for racy anecdotes—"traveling men's stories," they used to be called in Moonstone. Her clicking laugh sounded like a typewriting machine in action, and, for very pointed stories, she had a little screech.

Mrs. Archie had been Mrs. Archie for only six years, and when she was Belle White she was one of the "pretty" girls in Lansing, Michigan. She had then a train of suitors. She could truly remind Archie that "the boys hung around her." They did. They thought her very spirited and were always saying, "Oh, that Belle White, she's a case!" She used to play heavy practical jokes which the young men thought very clever. Archie was considered the most promising young man in "the young crowd," so Belle selected him. She let him see, made him fully aware, that she had selected him, and Archie was the sort of boy who could not withstand such enlightenment. Belle's family were sorry for him. On his wedding day her sisters looked at the big, handsome boy—he was twenty-four—as he walked down the aisle with his bride, and then they looked at each other. His besotted confidence, his sober, radiant face, his gentle, protecting arm, made them uncomfortable. Well, they were glad that he was going West at once, to fulfill his doom where they would not be onlookers. Anyhow, they consoled themselves, they had got Belle off their hands.

More than that, Belle seemed to have got herself off her hands. Her reputed prettiness must have been entirely the result of determination, of a fierce little ambition. Once she had married, fastened herself on some one, come to port,—it vanished like the ornamental plumage which drops away from some birds after the mating season. The one aggressive action of her life was over. She began to shrink in face and stature. Of her harum-scarum spirit there was nothing left but the little screech. Within a few years she looked as small and mean as she was.

Thor's chariot crept along. Thea approached the house unwillingly. She didn't care about the strawberries, anyhow. She had come only because she did not want to hurt Dr. Archie's feelings. She not only disliked Mrs. Archie, she was a little afraid of her. While Thea was getting the heavy baby-buggy through the iron gate she heard some one call, "Wait a minute!" and Mrs. Archie came running around the house from the back door, her apron over her head. She came to help with the buggy, because she was afraid the wheels might scratch the paint off the gate-posts. She was a skinny little woman with a great pile of frizzy light hair on a small head.

"Dr. Archie told me to come up and pick some strawberries," Thea muttered, wishing she had stayed at home.

Mrs. Archie led the way to the back door, squinting and shading her eyes with her hand. "Wait a minute," she said again, when Thea explained why she had come.

She went into her kitchen and Thea sat down on the porch step. When Mrs. Archie reappeared she carried in her hand a little wooden butter-basket trimmed with fringed tissue paper, which she must have brought home from some church supper. "You'll have to have something to put them in," she said, ignoring the yawning willow basket which stood empty on Thor's feet. "You can have this, and you needn't mind about returning it. You know about not trampling the vines, don't you?"

Mrs. Archie went back into the house and Thea leaned over in the sand and picked a few strawberries. As soon as she was sure that she was not going to cry, she tossed the little basket into the big one and ran Thor's buggy along the gravel walk and out of the gate as fast as she could push it. She was angry, and she was ashamed for Dr. Archie. She could not help thinking how uncomfortable he would be if he ever found out about it. Little things like that were the ones that cut him most. She slunk home by the back way, and again almost cried when she told her mother about it.

Mrs. Kronborg was frying doughnuts for her husband's supper. She laughed as she dropped a new lot into the hot grease. "It's wonderful, the way some people are made," she declared. "But I wouldn't let that upset me if I was you. Think what it would be to live with it all the time. You look in the black pocketbook inside my handbag and take a dime and go downtown and get an ice-cream soda. That'll make you feel better. Thor can have a little of the ice-cream if you feed it to him with a spoon. He likes it, don't you, son?" She stooped to wipe his chin. Thor was only six months old and inarticulate, but it was quite true that he liked ice-cream.

VI

SEEN from a balloon, Moonstone would have looked like a Noah's ark town set out in the sand and lightly shaded by gray-green tamarisks and cottonwoods. A few people were trying to make soft maples grow in their turfed lawns, but the fashion of planting incongruous trees from the North Atlantic States had not become general then, and the frail, brightly painted desert town was shaded by the light-reflecting, wind-loving trees of the desert, whose roots are always seeking water and whose leaves are always talking about it, making the sound of rain. The long, porous roots of the cottonwood are irrepressible. They break into the wells as rats do into granaries, and thieve the water.

The long street which connected Moonstone with the depot settlement traversed in its course a considerable stretch of rough open country, staked out in lots but not built up at all, a weedy hiatus between the town and the railroad. When you set out along this street to go to the station, you noticed that the houses became smaller and farther apart, until they ceased altogether, and the board sidewalk continued its uneven course through sunflower patches, until you reached the solitary, new brick Catholic Church. The church stood there because the land was given to the parish by the man who owned the adjoining waste lots, in the hope of making them more salable—"Farrier's Addition," this patch of prairie was called in the clerk's office. An eighth of a mile beyond the church was a washout, a deep sand-gully, where the board sidewalk became a bridge for perhaps fifty feet. Just beyond the gully was old Uncle Billy Beemer's grove,—twelve town lots set out in fine, well-grown cottonwood trees, delightful to look upon, or to listen to, as they swayed and rippled in the wind. Uncle Billy had been one of the most worthless old drunkards who ever sat on a store box and told filthy stories. One night he played hide-and-seek with a switch engine and got his sodden brains knocked out. But his grove, the one creditable thing he had ever done in his life, rustled on. Beyond this grove the houses of the depot settlement began, and the naked board walk, that had run in out of the sunflowers, again became a link between human dwellings.

One afternoon, late in the summer, Dr. Howard Archie was fighting his way back to town along this walk through a blinding sandstorm, a silk handkerchief tied over his mouth. He had been to see a sick woman down in the depot settlement, and he was walking because his ponies had been out for a hard drive that morning.

As he passed the Catholic Church he came upon Thea and Thor. Thea was sitting in a child's express wagon, her feet out behind, kicking the wagon along and steering by the tongue. Thor was on her lap and she held him with one arm. He had grown to be a big cub of a baby, with a constitutional grievance, and he had to be continually amused. Thea took him philosophically, and tugged and pulled him about, getting as much fun as she could under her encumbrance. Her hair was blowing about her face, and her eyes were squinting so intently at the uneven board sidewalk in front of her that she did not see the doctor until he spoke to her.

"Look out, Thea. You'll steer that youngster into the ditch."

The wagon stopped. Thea released the tongue, wiped her hot, sandy face, and pushed back her hair. "Oh, no, I won't! I never ran off but once, and then he didn't get anything but a bump. He likes this better than a baby-buggy, and so do I."

"Are you going to kick that cart all the way home?"

"Of course. We take long trips; wherever there is a sidewalk. It's no good on the road."

"Looks to me like working pretty hard for your fun. Are you going to be busy to-night? Want to make a call with me? Spanish Johnny's come home again, all used up. His wife sent me word this morning, and I said I'd go over to see him to-night. He's an old chum of yours, isn't he?"

"Oh, I'm glad. She's been crying her eyes out. When did he come?"

"Last night, on Number Six. Paid his fare, they tell me. Too sick to beat it. There'll come a time when that boy won't get back,

I'm afraid. Come around to my office about eight o'clock,—and you needn't bring that!"

Thor seemed to understand that he had been insulted, for he scowled and began to kick the side of the wagon, shouting, "Go-go, go-go!" Thea leaned forward and grabbed the wagon tongue. Dr. Archie stepped in front of her and blocked the way. "Why don't you make him wait? What do you let him boss you like that for?"

"If he gets mad he throws himself, and then I can't do anything with him. When he's mad he's lots stronger than me, aren't you, Thor?" Thea spoke with pride, and the idol was appeased. He grunted approvingly as his sister began to kick rapidly behind her, and the wagon rattled off and soon disappeared in the flying currents of sand.

That evening Dr. Archie was seated in his office, his desk chair tilted back, reading by the light of a hot coal-oil lamp. All the windows were open, but the night was breathless after the sand-storm, and his hair was moist where it hung over his forehead. He was deeply engrossed in his book and sometimes smiled thought-fully as he read. When Thea Kronborg entered quietly and slipped into a seat, he nodded, finished his paragraph, inserted a bookmark, and rose to put the book back into the case. It was one out of the long row of uniform volumes on the top shelf.

"Nearly every time I come in, when you're alone, you're reading one of those books," Thea remarked thoughtfully. "They must be very nice."

The doctor dropped back into his swivel chair, the mottled volume still in his hand. "They aren't exactly books, Thea," he said seriously. "They're a city."

"A history, you mean?"

"Yes, and no. They're a history of a live city, not a dead one. A Frenchman undertook to write about a whole cityful of people, all the kinds he knew. And he got them nearly all in, I guess. Yes, it's very interesting. You'll like to read it some day, when you're grown up."

Thea leaned forward and made out the title on the back, "A Distinguished Provincial in Paris."*

"It doesn't sound very interesting."

"Perhaps not, but it is." The doctor scrutinized her broad face, low enough to be in the direct light from under the green lamp shade. "Yes," he went on with some satisfaction, "I think you'll like them some day. You're always curious about people, and I expect this man knew more about people than anybody that ever lived."

"City people or country people?"

"Both. People are pretty much the same everywhere."

"Oh, no, they're not. The people who go through in the dining-car aren't like us."

"What makes you think they aren't, my girl? Their clothes?"

Thea shook her head. "No, it's something else. I don't know." Her eyes shifted under the doctor's searching gaze and she glanced up at the row of books. "How soon will I be old enough to read them?"

"Soon enough, soon enough, little girl." The doctor patted her hand and looked at her index finger. "The nail's coming all right, isn't it? But I think that man makes you practice too much. You have it on your mind all the time." He had noticed that when she talked to him she was always opening and shutting her hands. "It makes you nervous."

"No, he don't," Thea replied stubbornly, watching Dr. Archie return the book to its niche.

He took up a black leather case, put on his hat, and they went down the dark stairs into the street. The summer moon hung full in the sky. For the time being, it was the great fact in the world. Beyond the edge of the town the plain was so white that every clump of sage stood out distinct from the sand, and the dunes looked like a shining lake. The doctor took off his straw hat and carried it in his hand as they walked toward Mexican Town, across the sand.

North of Pueblo, Mexican settlements were rare in Colorado then. This one had come about accidentally. Spanish Johnny was the first Mexican who came to Moonstone. He was a painter and decorator, and had been working in Trinidad, when Ray Kennedy told him there was a "boom" on in Moonstone, and a good many

new buildings were going up. A year after Johnny settled in
Moonstone, his cousin, Famos Serreños, came to work in the
brickyard; then Serreños' cousins came to help him. During the
strike, the master mechanic put a gang of Mexicans to work in
the roundhouse. The Mexicans had arrived so quietly, with their
blankets and musical instruments, that before Moonstone was
awake to the fact, there was a Mexican quarter; a dozen families
or more.

As Thea and the doctor approached the 'dobe houses, they
heard a guitar, and a rich barytone voice—that of Famos
Serreños—singing "La Golandrina."* All the Mexican houses had
neat little yards, with tamarisk hedges and flowers, and walks
bordered with shells or whitewashed stones. Johnny's house was
dark. His wife, Mrs. Tellamantez, was sitting on the doorstep,
combing her long, blue-black hair. (Mexican women are like
the Spartans; when they are in trouble, in love, under stress of
any kind, they comb and comb their hair.) She rose without
embarrassment or apology, comb in hand, and greeted the
doctor.

"Good-evening; will you go in?" she asked in a low, musical
voice. "He is in the back room. I will make a light." She followed
them indoors, lit a candle and handed it to the doctor, pointing
toward the bedroom. Then she went back and sat down on her
doorstep.

Dr. Archie and Thea went into the bedroom, which was dark
and quiet. There was a bed in the corner, and a man was lying on
the clean sheets. On the table beside him was a glass pitcher, half-
full of water. Spanish Johnny looked younger than his wife, and
when he was in health he was very handsome: slender, gold-
colored, with wavy black hair, a round, smooth throat, white
teeth, and burning black eyes. His profile was strong and severe,
like an Indian's. What was termed his "wildness" showed itself
only in his feverish eyes and in the color that burned on his tawny
cheeks. That night he was a coppery green, and his eyes were like
black holes. He opened them when the doctor held the candle
before his face.

"*Mi testa!*" he muttered, "*mi testa*, doctor. *La fiebre!*" Seeing the doctor's companion at the foot of the bed, he attempted a smile. "*Muchacha!*"* he exclaimed deprecatingly.

Dr. Archie stuck a thermometer into his mouth. "Now Thea, you can run outside and wait for me."

Thea slipped noiselessly through the dark house and joined Mrs. Tellamantez. The somber Mexican woman did not seem inclined to talk, but her nod was friendly. Thea sat down on the warm sand, her back to the moon, facing Mrs. Tellamantez on her doorstep, and began to count the moonflowers on the vine that ran over the house. Mrs. Tellamantez was always considered a very homely woman. Her face was of a strongly marked type not sympathetic to Americans. Such long, oval faces, with a full chin, a large, mobile mouth, a high nose are not uncommon in Spain. Mrs. Tellamantez could not write her name, and could read but little. Her strong nature lived upon itself. She was chiefly known in Moonstone for her forbearance with her incorrigible husband.

Nobody knew exactly what was the matter with Johnny, and everybody liked him. His popularity would have been unusual for a white man, for a Mexican it was unprecedented. His talents were his undoing. He had a high, uncertain tenor voice, and he played the mandolin with exceptional skill. Periodically he went crazy. There was no other way to explain his behavior. He was a clever workman, and, when he worked, as regular and faithful as a burro. Then some night he would fall in with a crowd at the saloon and begin to sing. He would go on until he had no voice left, until he wheezed and rasped. Then he would play his mandolin furiously, and drink until his eyes sank back into his head. At last, when he was put out of the saloon at closing time, and could get nobody to listen to him, he would run away—along the railroad track, straight across the desert. He always managed to get aboard a freight somewhere. Once beyond Denver, he played his way southward from saloon to saloon until he got across the border. He never wrote to his wife; but she would soon begin to get newspapers from La Junta, Albuquerque, Chihuahua,* with marked paragraphs announcing that Juan Tellamantez and his wonderful mandolin could be heard at the Jack Rabbit Grill, or the Pearl of Cadiz Saloon. Mrs. Tellamantez waited and wept and combed her hair. When he was completely wrung out and burned up,—all but destroyed,—her Juan always came back to her to be taken care of,—once with an ugly knife wound in the neck, once with a finger missing from his right hand,—but he played just as well with three fingers as he had with four.

Public sentiment was lenient toward Johnny, but everybody was disgusted with Mrs. Tellamantez for putting up with him. She ought to discipline him, people said; she ought to leave him; she had no self-respect. In short, Mrs. Tellamantez got all the blame. Even Thea thought she was much too humble. Tonight, as she sat with her back to the moon, looking at the moonflowers and Mrs. Tellamantez's somber face, she was thinking that there is nothing so sad in the world as that kind of patience and resignation. It was much worse than Johnny's craziness. She even wondered whether it did not help to make Johnny crazy. People had no right to be so passive and resigned. She would like to roll over and over in the sand and screech at Mrs. Tellamantez. She was glad when the doctor came out.

The Mexican woman rose and stood respectful and expectant. The doctor held his hat in his hand and looked kindly at her.

"Same old thing, Mrs. Tellamantez. He's no worse than he's been before. I've left some medicine. Don't give him anything but toast water until I see him again. You're a good nurse; you'll get him out." Dr. Archie smiled encouragingly. He glanced about the little garden and wrinkled his brows. "I can't see what makes him behave so. He's killing himself, and he's not a rowdy sort of fellow. Can't you tie him up someway? Can't you tell when these fits are coming on?"

Mrs. Tellamantez put her hand to her forehead. "The saloon, doctor, the excitement; that is what makes him. People listen to him, and it excites him."

The doctor shook his head. "Maybe. He's too much for my calculations. I don't see what he gets out of it."

"He is always fooled,"—the Mexican woman spoke rapidly and tremulously, her long under lip quivering. "He is good at heart, but he has no head. He fools himself. You do not understand in this country, you are progressive. But he has no judgment, and he is fooled." She stooped quickly, took up one of the white conch-shells that bordered the walk, and, with an apologetic inclination of her head, held it to Dr. Archie's ear. "Listen, doctor. You hear something in there? You hear the sea; and yet the sea is very far from here. You have judgment, and you know that. But he is fooled. To him, it is the sea itself. A little thing is big to him." She bent and placed the shell in the white row, with its fellows. Thea took it up softly and pressed it to her own ear. The sound in it startled her; it was like something calling one. So that was why Johnny ran away. There was something awe-inspiring about Mrs. Tellamantez and her shell.

Thea caught Dr. Archie's hand and squeezed it hard as she skipped along beside him back toward Moonstone. She went home, and the doctor went back to his lamp and his book. He never left his office until after midnight. If he did not play whist or pool in the evening, he read. It had become a habit with him to lose himself.

VII

THEA'S twelfth birthday had passed a few weeks before her memorable call upon Mrs. Tellamantez. There was a worthy man in Moonstone who was already planning to marry Thea as soon as she should be old enough. His name was Ray Kennedy, his age was thirty, and he was conductor on a freight train, his run being from Moonstone to Denver. Ray was a big fellow, with a square, open American face, a rock chin, and features that one would never happen to remember. He was an aggressive idealist, a free-thinker, and, like most railroad men, deeply sentimental. Thea liked him for reasons that had to do with the adventurous life he had led in Mexico and the Southwest, rather than for anything very personal. She liked him, too, because he was the only one of her friends who ever took her to the sand hills. The sand hills were a constant tantalization; she loved them better than anything near Moonstone, and yet she could so seldom get to them. The first dunes were accessible enough; they were only a few miles beyond the Kohlers', and she could run out there any day when she could do her practicing in the morning and get Thor off her hands for an afternoon. But the real hills—the Turquoise Hills, the Mexicans called them—were ten good miles away, and one reached them by a heavy, sandy road. Dr. Archie sometimes took Thea on his long drives, but as nobody lived in the sand hills, he never had calls to make in that direction. Ray Kennedy was her only hope of getting there.

This summer Thea had not been to the hills once, though Ray had planned several Sunday expeditions. Once Thor was sick, and once the organist in her father's church was away and Thea had to play the organ for the three Sunday services. But on the first Sunday in September, Ray drove up to the Kronborgs' front gate at nine o'clock in the morning and the party actually set off. Gunner and Axel went with Thea, and Ray had asked Spanish Johnny to come and to bring Mrs. Tellamantez and his mandolin. Ray was artlessly fond of music, especially of Mexican music. He and Mrs. Tellamantez had got up the lunch between them, and they were to make coffee in the desert.

When they left Mexican Town, Thea was on the front seat with Ray and Johnny, and Gunner and Axel sat behind with Mrs. Tellamantez. They objected to this, of course, but there were some things about which Thea would have her own way. "As stubborn as a Finn," Mrs. Kronborg sometimes said of her, quoting an old Swedish saying. When they passed the Kohlers', old Fritz and Wunsch were cutting grapes at the arbor. Thea gave them a businesslike nod. Wunsch came to the gate and looked after them. He divined Ray Kennedy's hopes, and he distrusted every expedition that led away from the piano. Unconsciously he made Thea pay for frivolousness of this sort.

As Ray Kennedy's party followed the faint road across the sagebrush, they heard behind them the sound of church bells, which gave them a sense of escape and boundless freedom. Every rabbit that shot across the path, every sage hen that flew up by the trail, was like a runaway thought, a message that one sent into the desert. As they went farther, the illusion of the mirage became more instead of less convincing; a shallow silver lake that spread for many miles, a little misty in the sunlight. Here and there one saw reflected the image of a heifer, turned loose to live upon the sparse sand-grass. They were magnified to a preposterous height and looked like mammoths, prehistoric beasts standing solitary in the waters that for many thousands of years actually washed over that desert;—the mirage itself may be the ghost of that long-vanished sea. Beyond the phantom lake lay the line of many-colored hills; rich, sun-baked yellow, glowing turquoise, lavender, purple; all the open, pastel colors of the desert.

After the first five miles the road grew heavier. The horses had to slow down to a walk and the wheels sank deep into the sand, which now lay in long ridges, like waves, where the last high wind had drifted it. Two hours brought the party to Pedro's Cup, named for a Mexican desperado who had once held the sheriff at bay there. The Cup was a great amphitheater, cut out in the hills, its floor smooth and packed hard, dotted with sagebrush and greasewood.

On either side of the Cup the yellow hills ran north and south, with winding ravines between them, full of soft sand which drained down from the crumbling banks. On the surface of this fluid sand, one could find bits of brilliant stone, crystals and agates and onyx, and petrified wood as red as blood. Dried toads and lizards were to be found there, too. Birds, decomposing more rapidly, left only feathered skeletons.

After a little reconnoitering, Mrs. Tellamantez declared that it was time for lunch, and Ray took his hatchet and began to cut greasewood, which burns fiercely in its green state. The little boys dragged the bushes to the spot that Mrs. Tellamantez had chosen for her fire. Mexican women like to cook out of doors.

After lunch Thea sent Gunner and Axel to hunt for agates. "If you see a rattlesnake, run. Don't try to kill it," she enjoined.

Gunner hesitated. "If Ray would let me take the hatchet, I could kill one all right."

Mrs. Tellamantez smiled and said something to Johnny in Spanish.

"Yes," her husband replied, translating, "they say in Mexico, kill a snake but never hurt his feelings. Down in the hot country, *muchacha*," turning to Thea, "people keep a pet snake in the house to kill rats and mice. They call him the house snake. They keep a little mat for him by the fire, and at night he curl up there and sit with the family, just as friendly!"

Gunner sniffed with disgust. "Well, I think that's a dirty Mexican way to keep house; so there!"

Johnny shrugged his shoulders. "Perhaps," he muttered. A Mexican learns to dive below insults or soar above them, after he crosses the border.

By this time the south wall of the amphitheater cast a narrow shelf of shadow, and the party withdrew to this refuge. Ray and Johnny began to talk about the Grand Canyon and Death Valley, two places much shrouded in mystery in those days, and Thea listened intently. Mrs. Tellamantez took out her drawn-work and pinned it to her knee. Ray could talk well about the large part of the continent over which he had been knocked about, and Johnny was appreciative.

"You been all over, pretty near. Like a Spanish boy," he commented respectfully.

Ray, who had taken off his coat, whetted his pocket-knife thoughtfully on the sole of his shoe. "I began to browse around early. I had a mind to see something of this world, and I ran away from home before I was twelve. Rustled for myself ever since."

"Ran away?" Johnny looked hopeful. "What for?"

"Couldn't make it go with my old man, and didn't take to farming. There were plenty of boys at home. I wasn't missed."

Thea wriggled down in the hot sand and rested her chin on her arm. "Tell Johnny about the melons, Ray, please do!"

Ray's solid, sunburned cheeks grew a shade redder, and he looked reproachfully at Thea. "You're stuck on that story, kid. You like to get the laugh on me, don't you? That was the finishing split I had with my old man, John. He had a claim along the creek, not far from Denver, and raised a little garden stuff for market. One day he had a load of melons and he decided to take 'em to town and sell 'em along the street, and he made me go along and drive for him. Denver wasn't the queen city it is now, by any means, but it seemed a terrible big place to me; and when we got there, if he didn't make me drive right up Capitol Hill! Pap got out and stopped at folkses houses to ask if they didn't want to buy any melons, and I was to drive along slow. The farther I went the madder I got, but I was trying to look unconscious, when the end-gate came loose and one of the melons fell out and squashed. Just then a swell girl, all dressed up, comes out of one of the big houses and calls out, 'Hello, boy, you're losing your melons!' Some dudes on the other side of the street took their hats off to her and began to laugh. I couldn't stand it any longer. I grabbed the whip and lit into that team, and they tore up the hill like jack-rabbits, them damned melons bouncing out the back every jump, the old man cussin' an yellin' behind and everybody laughin'. I never looked behind, but the whole of Capitol Hill must have been a mess with them squashed melons. I didn't stop the team till I got out of sight of town. Then I pulled up an' left 'em with a rancher I was acquainted with, and I never went home to get the lickin' that was waitin' for me. I expect it's waitin' for me yet."

Thea rolled over in the sand. "Oh, I wish I could have seen those melons fly, Ray! I'll never see anything as funny as that. Now, tell Johnny about your first job."

Ray had a collection of good stories. He was observant, truthful, and kindly—perhaps the chief requisites in a good story-teller. Occasionally he used newspaper phrases, conscientiously learned in his efforts at self-instruction, but when he talked naturally he was always worth listening to. Never having had any schooling to speak of, he had, almost from the time he first ran away, tried to make good his loss. As a sheep-herder he had worried an old grammar to tatters, and read instructive books with the help of a pocket dictionary. By the light of many camp-fires he had pondered upon Prescott's histories, and the works of Washington Irving, which he bought at a high price from a book-agent. Mathematics and physics were easy for him, but general culture came hard, and he was determined to get it. Ray was a freethinker, and inconsistently believed himself damned for being one. When he was braking, down on the Santa Fé, at the end of his run he used to climb into the upper bunk of the caboose, while a noisy gang played poker about the stove below him, and by the roof-lamp read Robert Ingersoll's* speeches and "The Age of Reason."*

Ray was a loyal-hearted fellow, and it had cost him a great deal to give up his God. He was one of the step-children of Fortune, and he had very little to show for all his hard work; the other fellow always got the best of it. He had come in too late, or too early, on several schemes that had made money. He brought with him from all his wanderings a good deal of information (more or less correct in itself, but unrelated, and therefore misleading), a high standard of personal honor, a sentimental veneration for all women, bad as well as good, and a bitter hatred of Englishmen. Thea often thought that the nicest thing about Ray was his love for Mexico and the Mexicans, who had been kind to him when he drifted, a homeless boy, over the border. In Mexico, Ray was Señor Ken-áy-dy, and when he answered to that name he was somehow a different fellow. He spoke Spanish fluently, and the sunny warmth of that tongue kept him from being quite as hard as his chin, or as narrow as his popular science.

While Ray was smoking his cigar, he and Johnny fell to talking about the great fortunes that had been made in the Southwest, and about fellows they knew who had "struck it rich."

"I guess you been in on some big deals down there?" Johnny asked trustfully.

Ray smiled and shook his head. "I've been out on some, John. I've never been exactly in on any. So far, I've either held on too long or let go too soon. But mine's coming to me, all right." Ray looked reflective. He leaned back in the shadow and dug out a rest for his elbow in the sand. "The narrowest escape I ever had, was in the Bridal Chamber. If I hadn't let go there, it would have made me rich. That was a close call."

Johnny looked delighted. "You don' say! She was silver mine, I guess?"

"I guess she was! Down at Lake Valley. I put up a few hundred for the prospector, and he gave me a bunch of stock. Before we'd got anything out of it, my brother-in-law died of the fever in Cuba. My sister was beside herself to get his body back to Colorado to bury him. Seemed foolish to me, but she's the only sister I got. It's expensive for dead folks to travel, and I had to sell my stock in the mine to raise the money to get Elmer on the move. Two months afterward, the boys struck that big pocket in the rock, full of virgin silver. They named her the Bridal Chamber. It wasn't ore, you remember. It was pure, soft metal you could have melted right down into dollars. The boys cut it out with chisels. If old Elmer hadn't played that trick on me, I'd have been in for about fifty thousand. That was a close call, Spanish."

"I recollec'. When the pocket gone, the town go bust."

"You bet. Higher'n a kite. There was no vein, just a pocket in the rock that had sometime or another got filled up with molten silver. You'd think there would be more somewhere about, but *nada*.* There's fools digging holes in that mountain yet."

When Ray had finished his cigar, Johnny took his mandolin and began Kennedy's favorite, "Ultimo Amor." It was now three o'clock in the afternoon, the hottest hour in the day. The narrow shelf of shadow had widened until the floor of the amphitheater was marked off in two halves, one glittering yellow, and one purple. The little boys had come back and were making a robbers' cave to enact the bold deeds of Pedro the bandit. Johnny, stretched gracefully on the sand, passed from "Ultimo Amor"* to "Fluvia de Oro,"* and then to "Noches de Algeria,"* playing languidly.

Every one was busy with his own thoughts. Mrs. Tellamantez was thinking of the square in the little town in which she was born; of the white churchsteps, with people genuflecting as they passed, and the round-topped acacia trees, and the band playing in the plaza. Ray Kennedy was thinking of the future, dreaming the large Western dream of easy money, of a fortune kicked up somewhere in the hills,—an oil well, a gold mine, a ledge of copper. He always told himself, when he accepted a cigar from a newly married railroad man, that he knew enough not to marry until he had found his ideal, and could keep her like a queen. He believed that in the yellow head over there in the sand he had found his ideal, and that by the time she was old enough to marry, he would be able to keep her like a queen. He would kick it up from somewhere, when he got loose from the railroad.

Thea, stirred by tales of adventure, of the Grand Canyon and
Death Valley, was recalling a great adventure of her own. Early in
the summer her father had been invited to conduct a reunion of
old frontiersmen, up in Wyoming, near Laramie, and he took
Thea along with him to play the organ and sing patriotic songs.
There they stayed at the house of an old ranchman who told them
about a ridge up in the hills called Laramie Plain, where the
wagon-trails of the Forty-niners* and the Mormons* were still visible. The old man even volunteered to take Mr. Kronborg up into
the hills to see this place, though it was a very long drive to make
in one day. Thea had begged frantically to go along, and the old
rancher, flattered by her rapt attention to his stories, had inter-
ceded for her. They set out from Laramie before daylight, behind
a strong team of mules. All the way there was much talk of the
Forty-niners. The old rancher had been a teamster in a freight
train that used to crawl back and forth across the plains between
Omaha and Cherry Creek, as Denver was then called, and he had
met many a wagon train bound for California. He told of Indians
and buffalo, thirst and slaughter, wanderings in snowstorms, and
lonely graves in the desert.

The road they followed was a wild and beautiful one. It led up
and up, by granite rocks and stunted pines, around deep ravines
and echoing gorges. The top of the ridge, when they reached it,
was a great flat plain, strewn with white boulders, with the wind
howling over it. There was not one trail, as Thea had expected;
there were a score; deep furrows, cut in the earth by heavy
wagon wheels, and now grown over with dry, whitish grass. The
furrows ran side by side; when one trail had been worn too deep,
the next party had abandoned it and made a new trail to the right
or left. They were, indeed, only old wagon ruts, running east and
west, and grown over with grass. But as Thea ran about among
the white stones, her skirts blowing this way and that, the wind
brought to her eyes tears that might have come anyway. The old
rancher picked up an iron ox-shoe from one of the furrows and
gave it to her for a keepsake. To the west one could see range after
range of blue mountains, and at last the snowy range, with its
white, windy peaks, the clouds caught here and there on their

spurs. Again and again Thea had to hide her face from the cold for a moment. The wind never slept on this plain, the old man said. Every little while eagles flew over.

Coming up from Laramie, the old man had told them that he was in Brownsville, Nebraska, when the first telegraph wires were put across the Missouri River, and that the first message that ever crossed the river was "Westward the course of Empire takes its way."* He had been in the room when the instrument began to click, and all the men there had, without thinking what they were doing, taken off their hats, waiting bareheaded to hear the message translated. Thea remembered that message when she sighted down the wagon tracks toward the blue mountains. She told herself she would never, never forget it. The spirit of human courage seemed to live up there with the eagles. For long after, when she was moved by a Fourth-of-July oration, or a band, or a circus parade, she was apt to remember that windy ridge.

To-day she went to sleep while she was thinking about it. When Ray wakened her, the horses were hitched to the wagon and Gunner and Axel were begging for a place on the front seat. The air had cooled, the sun was setting, and the desert was on fire. Thea contentedly took the back seat with Mrs. Tellamantez. As they drove homeward the stars began to come out, pale yellow in a yellow sky, and Ray and Johnny began to sing one of those railroad ditties that are usually born on the Southern Pacific and run the length of the Santa Fé and the "Q" system before they die to give place to a new one. This was a song about a Greaser* dance, the refrain being something like this:—

> "Pedró, Pedró, swing high, swing low,
> And it's allamand left again;
> For there's boys that's bold and there's some that's cold,
> But the góld boys come from Spain,
> Oh, the góld boys come from Spain!"

VIII

WINTER was long in coming that year. Throughout October the days were bathed in sunlight and the air was clear as crystal. The town kept its cheerful summer aspect, the desert glistened with light, the sand hills every day went through magical changes of color. The scarlet sage bloomed late in the front yards, the cottonwood leaves were bright gold long before they fell, and it was not until November that the green on the tamarisks began to cloud and fade. There was a flurry of snow about Thanksgiving, and then December came on warm and clear.

Thea had three music pupils now, little girls whose mothers declared that Professor Wunsch was "much too severe." They took their lessons on Saturday, and this, of course, cut down her time for play. She did not really mind this because she was allowed to use the money—her pupils paid her twenty-five cents a lesson—to fit up a little room for herself upstairs in the half-story. It was the end room of the wing, and was not plastered, but was snugly lined with soft pine. The ceiling was so low that a grown person could reach it with the palm of the hand, and it sloped down on either side. There was only one window, but it was a double one and went to the floor. In October, while the days were still warm, Thea and Tillie papered the room, walls and ceiling in the same paper, small red and brown roses on a yellowish ground. Thea bought a brown cotton carpet, and her big brother, Gus, put it down for her one Sunday. She made white cheesecloth curtains and hung them on a tape. Her mother gave her an old walnut dresser with a broken mirror, and she had her own dumpy walnut single bed, and a blue washbowl and pitcher which she had drawn at a church fair lottery. At the head of her bed she had a tall round wooden hat-crate, from the clothing store. This, standing on end and draped with cretonne, made a fairly steady table for her lantern. She was not allowed to take a lamp upstairs, so Ray Kennedy gave her a railroad lantern by which she could read at night.

In winter this loft room of Thea's was bitterly cold, but against her mother's advice—and Tillie's—she always left her window open a little way. Mrs. Kronborg declared that she "had no patience with American physiology," though the lessons about the injurious effects of alcohol and tobacco were well enough for the boys. Thea asked Dr. Archie about the window, and he told her that a girl who sang must always have plenty of fresh air, or her voice would get husky, and that the cold would harden her throat. The important thing, he said, was to keep your feet warm. On very cold nights Thea always put a brick in the oven after supper, and when she went upstairs she wrapped it in an old flannel petticoat and put it in her bed. The boys, who would never heat bricks for themselves, sometimes carried off Thea's, and thought it a good joke to get ahead of her.

When Thea first plunged in between her red blankets, the cold sometimes kept her awake for a good while, and she comforted herself by remembering all she could of "Polar Explorations," a fat, calf-bound volume her father, had bought from a book-agent, and by thinking about the members of Greely's party:* how they lay in their frozen sleeping-bags, each man hoarding the warmth of his own body and trying to make it last as long as possible against the on-coming cold that would be everlasting. After half an hour or so, a warm wave crept over her body and round, sturdy legs; she glowed like a little stove with the warmth of her own blood, and the heavy quilts and red blankets grew warm wherever they touched her, though her breath sometimes froze on the cover-lid. Before daylight, her internal fires went down a little, and she often wakened to find herself drawn up into a tight ball, somewhat stiff in the legs. But that made it all the easier to get up.

The acquisition of this room was the beginning of a new era in Thea's life. It was one of the most important things that ever happened to her. Hitherto, except in summer, when she could be out of doors, she had lived in constant turmoil; the family, the day school, the Sunday-School. The clamor about her drowned the voice within herself. In the end of the wing, separated from the other upstairs sleeping-rooms by a long, cold, unfinished lumber room, her mind worked better. She thought things out more clearly. Pleasant plans and ideas occurred to her which had never come before. She had certain thoughts which were like companions, ideas which were like older and wiser friends. She left them there in the morning, when she finished dressing in the cold, and at night, when she came up with her lantern and shut the door after a busy day, she found them awaiting her. There was no possible way of heating the room, but that was fortunate, for otherwise it would have been occupied by one of her older brothers.

From the time when she moved up into the wing, Thea began to live a double life. During the day, when the hours were full of tasks, she was one of the Kronborg children, but at night she was a different person. On Friday and Saturday nights she always read for a long while after she was in bed. She had no clock, and there was no one to nag her.

Ray Kennedy, on his way from the depot to his boarding-house, often looked up and saw Thea's light burning when the rest of the house was dark, and felt cheered as by a friendly greeting. He was a faithful soul, and many disappointments had not changed his nature. He was still, at heart, the same boy who, when he was sixteen, had settled down to freeze with his sheep in a Wyoming blizzard, and had been rescued only to play the losing game of fidelity to other charges.

Ray had no very clear idea of what might be going on in Thea's head, but he knew that something was. He used to remark to Spanish Johnny, "That girl is developing something fine." Thea was patient with Ray, even in regard to the liberties he took with her name. Outside the family, every one in Moonstone, except Wunsch and Dr. Archie, called her "Thee-a," but this seemed cold and distant to Ray, so he called her "Thee." Once, in a moment of exasperation, Thea asked him why he did this, and he explained that he once had a chum, Theodore, whose name was always abbreviated thus, and that since he was killed down on the Santa Fé, it seemed natural to call somebody "Thee." Thea sighed and submitted. She was always helpless before homely sentiment and usually changed the subject.

It was the custom for each of the different Sunday-Schools in Moonstone to give a concert on Christmas Eve. But this year all the churches were to unite and give, as was announced from the pulpits, "a semi-sacred concert of picked talent" at the opera house. The Moonstone Orchestra, under the direction of Professor Wunsch, was to play, and the most talented members of each Sunday-School were to take part in the programme. Thea was put down by the committee "for instrumental." This made her indignant, for the vocal numbers were always more popular. Thea went to the president of the committee and demanded hotly if her rival, Lily Fisher, were going to sing. The president was a big, florid, powdered woman, a fierce W.C.T.U.* worker, one of Thea's natural enemies. Her name was Johnson; her husband kept the livery stable, and she was called Mrs. Livery Johnson, to distinguish her from other families of the same surname. Mrs. Johnson was a prominent Baptist, and Lily Fisher was the Baptist prodigy. There was a not very Christian rivalry between the Baptist Church and Mr. Kronborg's church.

When Thea asked Mrs. Johnson whether her rival was to be allowed to sing, Mrs. Johnson, with an eagerness which told how she had waited for this moment, replied that "Lily was going to recite to be obliging, and to give other children a chance to sing." As she delivered this thrust, her eyes glittered more than the Ancient Mariner's,* Thea thought. Mrs. Johnson disapproved of the way in which Thea was being brought up, of a child whose chosen associates were Mexicans and sinners, and who was, as she pointedly put it, "bold with men." She so enjoyed an opportunity to rebuke Thea, that, tightly corseted as she was, she could scarcely control her breathing, and her lace and her gold watch chain rose and fell "with short, uneasy motion."* Frowning, Thea turned away and walked slowly homeward. She suspected guile. Lily Fisher was the most stuck-up doll in the world, and it was certainly not like her to recite to be obliging. Nobody who could sing ever recited, because the warmest applause always went to the singers.

However, when the programme was printed in the Moonstone *Gleam,* there it was: "Instrumental solo, Thea Kronborg. Recitation, Lily Fisher."

Because his orchestra was to play for the concert, Mr. Wunsch imagined that he had been put in charge of the music, and he became arrogant. He insisted that Thea should play a "Ballade" by Reinecke.* When Thea consulted her mother, Mrs. Kronborg agreed with her that the "Ballade" would "never take" with a Moonstone audience. She advised Thea to play "something with variations," or, at least, "The Invitation to the Dance."

"It makes no matter what they like," Wunsch replied to Thea's entreaties. "It is time already that they learn something."

Thea's fighting powers had been impaired by an ulcerated tooth and consequent loss of sleep, so she gave in. She finally had the molar pulled, though it was a second tooth and should have been saved. The dentist was a clumsy, ignorant country boy, and Mr. Kronborg would not hear of Dr. Archie's taking Thea to a dentist in Denver, though Ray Kennedy said he could get a pass for her. What with the pain of the tooth, and family discussions about it, with trying to make Christmas presents and to keep up her school work and practicing, and giving lessons on Saturdays, Thea was fairly worn out.

On Christmas Eve she was nervous and excited. It was the first time she had ever played in the opera house, and she had never before had to face so many people. Wunsch would not let her play with her notes, and she was afraid of forgetting. Before the concert began, all the participants had to assemble on the stage and sit there to be looked at. Thea wore her white summer dress and a blue sash, but Lily Fisher had a new pink silk, trimmed with white swansdown.

The hall was packed. It seemed as if every one in Moonstone was there, even Mrs. Kohler, in her hood, and old Fritz. The seats were wooden kitchen chairs, numbered, and nailed to long planks which held them together in rows. As the floor was not raised, the chairs were all on the same level. The more interested persons in the audience peered over the heads of the people in front of them to get a good view of the stage. From the platform Thea picked out many friendly faces. There was Dr. Archie, who never went to church entertainments; there was the friendly jeweler who ordered her music for her,—he sold accordions and guitars as well as watches,—and the druggist who often lent her books, and her favorite teacher from the school. There was Ray Kennedy, with a party of freshly barbered railroad men he had brought along with him. There was Mrs. Kronborg with all the children, even Thor, who had been brought out in a new white plush coat. At the back of the hall sat a little group of Mexicans, and among them Thea caught the gleam of Spanish Johnny's white teeth, and of Mrs. Tellamantez's lustrous, smoothly coiled black hair.

After the orchestra played "Selections from Erminie,"* and the Baptist preacher made a long prayer, Tillie Kronborg came on with a highly colored recitation, "The Polish Boy."* When it was over every one breathed more freely. No committee had the courage to leave Tillie off a programme. She was accepted as a trying feature of every entertainment. The Progressive Euchre Club* was the only social organization in the town that entirely escaped Tillie. After Tillie sat down, the Ladies' Quartette sang, "Beloved, it is Night,"* and then it was Thea's turn.

The "Ballade" took ten minutes, which was five minutes too long. The audience grew restive and fell to whispering. Thea could hear Mrs. Livery Johnson's bracelets jangling as she fanned herself, and she could hear her father's nervous, ministerial cough. Thor behaved better than any one else. When Thea bowed and returned to her seat at the back of the stage there was the usual applause, but it was vigorous only from the back of the house where the Mexicans sat, and from Ray Kennedy's *claqueurs.** Any one could see that a good-natured audience had been bored.

Because Mr. Kronborg's sister was on the programme, it had also been necessary to ask the Baptist preacher's wife's cousin to sing. She was a "deep alto" from McCook,* and she sang, "Thy Sentinel Am I."* After her came Lily Fisher. Thea's rival was also a blonde, but her hair was much heavier than Thea's, and fell in long round curls over her shoulders. She was the angel-child of the Baptists, and looked exactly like the beautiful children on soap calendars. Her pink-and-white face, her set smile of innocence, were surely born of a color-press. She had long, drooping eyelashes, a little pursed-up mouth, and narrow, pointed teeth, like a squirrel's.

Lily began:—

"*Rock of Ages, cleft for me*,* carelessly the maiden sang."

Thea drew a long breath. That was the game; it was a recitation and a song in one. Lily trailed the hymn through half a dozen verses with great effect. The Baptist preacher had announced at the beginning of the concert that "owing to the length of the programme, there would be no encores." But the applause which followed Lily to her seat was such an unmistakable expression of enthusiasm that Thea had to admit Lily was justified in going back. She was attended this time by Mrs. Livery Johnson herself, crimson with triumph and gleaming-eyed, nervously rolling and unrolling a sheet of music. She took off her bracelets and played Lily's accompaniment. Lily had the effrontery to come out with, "She sang the song of Home, Sweet Home, the song that touched my heart."* But this did not surprise Thea; as Ray said later in the evening, "the cards had been stacked against her from the beginning." The next issue of the *Gleam* correctly stated that "unquestionably the honors of the evening must be accorded to Miss Lily Fisher." The Baptists had everything their own way.

After the concert Ray Kennedy joined the Kronborgs' party and walked home with them. Thea was grateful for his silent sympathy, even while it irritated her. She inwardly vowed that she would never take another lesson from old Wunsch. She wished that her father would not keep cheerfully singing, "When Shepherds Watched,"* as he marched ahead, carrying Thor. She felt that silence would become the Kronborgs for a while. As a family, they somehow seemed a little ridiculous, trooping along in the starlight. There were so many of them, for one thing. Then Tillie was so absurd. She was giggling and talking to Anna just as if she had not made, as even Mrs. Kronborg admitted, an exhibition of herself.

When they got home, Ray took a box from his overcoat pocket and slipped it into Thea's hand as he said goodnight. They all hurried in to the glowing stove in the parlor. The sleepy children were sent to bed. Mrs. Kronberg and Anna stayed up to fill the stockings.

"I guess you're tired, Thea. You needn't stay up." Mrs. Kronborg's clear and seemingly indifferent eye usually measured Thea pretty accurately.

Thea hesitated. She glanced at the presents laid out on the dining-room table, but they looked unattractive. Even the brown plush monkey she had bought for Thor with such enthusiasm seemed to have lost his wise and humorous expression. She murmured, "All right," to her mother, lit her lantern, and went upstairs.

Ray's box contained a hand-painted white satin fan, with pond lilies—an unfortunate reminder. Thea smiled grimly and tossed it into her upper drawer. She was not to be consoled by toys. She undressed quickly and stood for some time in the cold, frowning in the broken looking-glass at her flaxen pig-tails, at her white neck and arms. Her own broad, resolute face set its chin at her, her eyes flashed into her own defiantly. Lily Fisher was pretty, and she was willing to be just as big a fool as people wanted her to be. Very well; Thea Kronborg wasn't. She would rather be hated than be stupid, any day. She popped into bed and read stubbornly at a queer paper book the drug-store man had given her because he couldn't sell it. She had trained herself to put her mind on what she was doing, otherwise she would have come to grief with her complicated daily schedule. She read, as intently as if she had not been flushed with anger, the strange "Musical Memories" of the Reverend H. R. Haweis.* At last she blew out the lantern and went to sleep. She had many curious dreams that night. In one of them Mrs. Tellamantez held her shell to Thea's ear, and she heard the roaring, as before, and distant voices calling, "Lily Fisher! Lily Fisher!"

IX

MR. KRONBORG considered Thea a remarkable child; but so were all his children remarkable. If one of the business men downtown remarked to him that he "had a mighty bright little girl, there," he admitted it, and at once began to explain what a "long head for business" his son Gus had, or that Charley was "a natural electrician," and had put in a telephone from the house to the preacher's study behind the church.

Mrs. Kronborg watched her daughter thoughtfully. She found her more interesting than her other children, and she took her more seriously, without thinking much about why she did so. The other children had to be guided, directed, kept from conflicting with one another. Charley and Gus were likely to want the same thing, and to quarrel about it. Anna often demanded unreasonable service from her older brothers; that they should sit up until after midnight to bring her home from parties when she did not like the youth who had offered himself as her escort; or that they should drive twelve miles into the country, on a winter night, to take her to a ranch dance, after they had been working hard all day. Gunner often got bored with his own clothes or stilts or sled, and wanted Axel's. But Thea, from the time she was a little thing, had her own routine. She kept out of every one's way, and was hard to manage only when the other children interfered with her. Then there was trouble indeed: bursts of temper which used to alarm Mrs. Kronborg. "You ought to know enough to let Thea alone. She lets you alone," she often said to the other children.

One may have staunch friends in one's own family, but one seldom has admirers. Thea, however, had one in the person of her addle-pated aunt, Tillie Kronborg. In older countries, where dress and opinions and manners are not so thoroughly standardized as in our own West, there is a belief that people who are foolish about the more obvious things of life are apt to have peculiar insight into what lies beyond the obvious. The old woman who can never learn not to put the kerosene can on the stove, may yet be able to tell fortunes, to persuade a backward child to grow, to cure warts, or to tell people what to do with a young girl who has gone melancholy. Tillie's mind was a curious machine; when she was awake it went round like a wheel when the belt has slipped off, and when she was asleep she dreamed follies. But she had intuitions. She knew, for instance, that Thea was different from the other Kronborgs, worthy though they all were. Her romantic imagination found possibilities in her niece. When she was sweeping or ironing, or turning the ice-cream freezer at a furious rate, she often built up brilliant futures for Thea, adapting freely the latest novel she had read.

Tillie made enemies for her niece among the church people because, at sewing societies and church suppers, she sometimes spoke vauntingly, with a toss of her head, just as if Thea's "wonderfulness" were an accepted fact in Moonstone, like Mrs. Archie's stinginess, or Mrs. Livery Johnson's duplicity. People declared that, on this subject, Tillie made them tired.

Tillie belonged to a dramatic club that once a year performed in the Moonstone Opera House such plays as "Among the Breakers,"* and "The Veteran of 1812."* Tillie played character parts, the flirtatious old maid or the spiteful *intrigante*.* She used to study her parts up in the attic at home. While she was committing the lines, she got Gunner or Anna to hold the book for her, but when she began "to bring out the expression," as she said, she used, very timorously, to ask Thea to hold the book. Thea was usually—not always—agreeable about it. Her mother had told her that, since she had some influence with Tillie, it would be a good thing for them all if she could tone her down a shade and "keep her from taking on any worse than need be." Thea would sit on the foot of Tillie's bed, her feet tucked under her, and stare at the silly text. "I wouldn't make so much fuss, there, Tillie," she would remark occasionally; "I don't see the point in it"; or, "What do you pitch your voice so high for? It don't carry half as well."

"I don't see how it comes Thea is so patient with Tillie," Mrs. Kronborg more than once remarked to her husband. "She ain't patient with most people, but it seems like she's got a peculiar patience for Tillie."

Tillie always coaxed Thea to go "behind the scenes" with her when the club presented a play, and help her with her make-up. Thea hated it, but she always went. She felt as if she had to do it. There was something in Tillie's adoration of her that compelled her. There was no family impropriety that Thea was so much ashamed of as Tillie's "acting" and yet she was always being dragged in to assist her. Tillie simply had her, there. She didn't know why, but it was so. There was a string in her somewhere that Tillie could pull; a sense of obligation to Tillie's misguided aspirations. The saloon-keepers had some such feeling of responsibility toward Spanish Johnny.

The dramatic club was the pride of Tillie's heart, and her enthusiasm was the principal factor in keeping it together. Sick or well, Tillie always attended rehearsals, and was always urging the young people, who took rehearsals lightly, to "stop fooling and begin now." The young men—bank clerks, grocery clerks, insurance agents—played tricks, laughed at Tillie, and "put it up on each other" about seeing her home; but they often went to tiresome rehearsals just to oblige her. They were good-natured young fellows. Their trainer and stage-manager was young Upping, the jeweler who ordered Thea's music for her. Though barely thirty, he had followed half a dozen professions, and had once been a violinist in the orchestra of the Andrews Opera Company, then well known in little towns throughout Colorado and Nebraska.

By one amazing indiscretion Tillie very nearly lost her hold upon the Moonstone Drama Club. The club had decided to put on "The Drummer Boy of Shiloh,"* a very ambitious undertaking because of the many supers* needed and the scenic difficulties of the act which took place in Andersonville Prison. The members of the club consulted together in Tillie's absence as to who should play the part of the drummer boy. It must be taken by a very young person, and village boys of that age are self-conscious and are not apt at memorizing. The part was a long one, and clearly it must be given to a girl. Some members of the club suggested Thea Kronborg, others advocated Lily Fisher. Lily's partisans urged that she was much prettier than Thea, and had a much "sweeter disposition." Nobody denied these facts. But there was nothing in the least boyish about Lily, and she sang all songs and played all parts alike. Lily's simper was popular, but it seemed not quite the right thing for the heroic drummer boy.

Upping, the trainer, talked to one and another: "Lily's all right for girl parts," he insisted, "but you've got to get a girl with some ginger in her for this. Thea's got the voice, too. When she sings, 'Just Before the Battle, Mother,'* she'll bring down the house."

When all the members of the club had been privately consulted, they announced their decision to Tillie at the first regular meeting that was called to cast the parts. They expected Tillie to be overcome with joy, but, on the contrary, she seemed embarrassed. "I'm afraid Thea hasn't got time for that," she said jerkily. "She is always so busy with her music. Guess you'll have to get somebody else."

The club lifted its eyebrows. Several of Lily Fisher's friends coughed. Mr. Upping flushed. The stout woman who always played the injured wife called Tillie's attention to the fact that this would be a fine opportunity for her niece to show what she could do. Her tone was condescending.

Tillie threw up her head and laughed; there was something sharp and wild about Tillie's laugh—when it was not a giggle. "Oh, I guess Thea hasn't got time to do any showing off. Her time to show off ain't come yet. I expect she'll make us all sit up when it does. No use asking her to take the part. She'd turn her nose up at it. I guess they'd be glad to get her in the Denver Dramatics, if they could."

The company broke up into groups and expressed their amazement. Of course all Swedes were conceited, but they would never have believed that all the conceit of all the Swedes put together would reach such a pitch as this. They confided to each other that Tillie was "just a little off, on the subject of her niece," and agreed that it would be as well not to excite her further. Tillie got a cold reception at rehearsals for a long while afterward, and Thea had a crop of new enemies without even knowing it.

X

WUNSCH and old Fritz and Spanish Johnny celebrated Christmas together, so riotously that Wunsch was unable to give Thea her lesson the next day. In the middle of the vacation week Thea went to the Kohlers' through a soft, beautiful snowstorm. The air was a tender blue-gray, like the color on the doves that flew in and out of the white dove-house on the post in the Kohlers' garden. The sand hills looked dim and sleepy. The tamarisk hedge was full of snow, like a foam of blossoms drifted over it. When Thea opened the gate, old Mrs. Kohler was just coming in from the chicken yard, with five fresh eggs in her apron and a pair of old top-boots on her feet. She called Thea to come and look at a bantam egg, which she held up proudly. Her bantam hens were remiss in zeal, and she was always delighted when they accomplished anything. She took Thea into the sitting-room, very warm and smelling of food, and brought her a plateful of little Christmas cakes, made according to old and hallowed formulae, and put them before her while she warmed her feet. Then she went to the door of the kitchen stairs and called: "Herr Wunsch, Herr Wunsch!"

Wunsch came down wearing an old wadded jacket, with a velvet collar. The brown silk was so worn that the wadding stuck out almost everywhere. He avoided Thea's eyes when he came in, nodded without speaking, and pointed directly to the piano stool. He was not so insistent upon the scales as usual, and throughout the little sonata of Mozart's she was studying, he remained languid and absent-minded. His eyes looked very heavy, and he kept wiping them with one of the new silk handkerchiefs Mrs. Kohler had given him for Christmas. When the lesson was over he did not seem inclined to talk. Thea, loitering on the stool, reached for a tattered book she had taken off the music-rest when she sat down. It was a very old Leipsic* edition of the piano score of Gluck's "Orpheus."* She turned over the pages curiously.

"Is it nice?" she asked.

"It is the most beautiful opera ever made," Wunsch declared solemnly. "You know the story, eh? How, when she die, Orpheus went down below for his wife?"

"Oh, yes, I know. I didn't know there was an opera about it, though. Do people sing this now?"

"*Aber ja!** What else? You like to try? See." He drew her from the stool and sat down at the piano. Turning over the leaves to the third act, he handed the score to Thea. "Listen, I play it through and you get the *rhythmus*.* *Eins, zwei, drei, vier*." He played through Orpheus' lament, then pushed back his cuffs with awakening interest and nodded at Thea. "Now, *vom blatt, mit mir*."*

> *"Ach, ich habe sie verloren,*
> *All' mein Glück ist nun dahin."* *

Wunsch sang the aria with much feeling. It was evidently one that was very dear to him.

"*Noch einmal*,* alone, yourself." He played the introductory measures, then nodded at her vehemently, and she began:

> *"Ach, ich habe sie verloren."*

When she finished, Wunsch nodded again "*Schon*,"* he muttered as he finished the accompaniment softly. He dropped his hands on his knees and looked up at Thea. "That is very fine, eh? There is no such beautiful melody in the world. You can take the book for one week and learn something, to pass the time. It is good to know—always. *Euridice, Eu—ri—di—ce, weh dass ich auf Erden bin!*"* he sang softly, playing the melody with his right hand.

Thea, who was turning over the pages of the third act, stopped and scowled at a passage. The old German's blurred eyes watched her curiously.

"For what do you look so, *immer*?" puckering up his own face. "You see something a little difficult, may-be, and you make such a face like it was an enemy."

Thea laughed, disconcerted. "Well, difficult things are enemies, aren't they? When you have to get them?"

Wunsch lowered his head and threw it up as if he were butting something. "Not at all! By no means." He took the book from her and looked at it. "Yes, that is not so easy, there. This is an old book. They do not print it so now any more, I think. They leave it out, may-be. Only one woman could sing that good."*

Thea looked at him in perplexity.

Wunsch went on. "It is written for alto, you see. A woman sings the part, and there was only one to sing that good in there. You understand? Only one!" He glanced at her quickly and lifted his red forefinger upright before her eyes.

Thea looked at the finger as if she were hypnotized. "Only one?" she asked breathlessly; her hands, hanging at her sides, were opening and shutting rapidly.

Wunsch nodded and still held up that compelling finger. When he dropped his hands, there was a look of satisfaction in his face.

"Was she very great?"

Wunsch nodded.

"Was she beautiful?"

"*Aber gar nicht!* Not at all. She was ugly; big mouth, big teeth, no figure, nothing at all," indicating a luxuriant bosom by sweeping his hands over his chest. "A pole, a post! But for the voice—*ach!* She have something in there, behind the eyes," tapping his temples.

Thea followed all his gesticulations intently. "Was she German?"

"No, *Spanisch*." He looked down and frowned for a moment. "*Ach*, I tell you, she look like the Frau Tellamantez, some-thing. Long face, long chin, and ugly al-so."

"Did she die a long while ago?"

"Die? I think not. I never hear, anyhow. I guess she is alive somewhere in the world; Paris, may-be. But old, of course. I hear her when I was a youth. She is too old to sing now any more."

"Was she the greatest singer you ever heard?"

Wunsch nodded gravely. "Quite so. She was the most—" he hunted for an English word, lifted his hand over his head and snapped his fingers noiselessly in the air, enunciating fiercely, "*künst-ler-isch!*"* The word seemed to glitter in his uplifted hand, his voice was so full of emotion.

Wunsch rose from the stool and began to button his wadded jacket, preparing to return to his half-heated room in the loft. Thea regretfully put on her cloak and hood and set out for home.

When Wunsch looked for his score late that afternoon, he found that Thea had not forgotten to take it with her. He smiled his loose, sarcastic smile, and thoughtfully rubbed his stubbly chin with his red fingers. When Fritz came home in the early blue twilight the snow was flying faster, Mrs. Kohler was cooking *Hasenpfeffer** in the kitchen, and the professor was seated at the piano, playing the Gluck, which he knew by heart. Old Fritz took off his shoes quietly behind the stove and lay down on the lounge before his masterpiece, where the firelight was playing over the walls of Moscow. He listened, while the room grew darker and the windows duller. Wunsch always came back to the same thing:—

> *"Ach, ich habe sie verloren,*
>
> · · ·
>
> *Euridice, Euridice!"*

From time to time Fritz sighed softly. He, too, had lost a Euridice.

XI

ONE Saturday, late in June, Thea arrived early for her lesson. As she perched herself upon the piano stool,—a wobbly, old-fashioned thing that worked on a creaky screw,—she gave Wunsch a side glance, smiling. "You must not be cross to me to-day. This is my birthday."

"So?" he pointed to the keyboard.

After the lesson they went out to join Mrs. Kohler, who had asked Thea to come early, so that she could stay and smell the linden bloom. It was one of those still days of intense light, when every particle of mica in the soil flashed like a little mirror, and the glare from the plain below seemed more intense than the rays from above. The sand ridges ran glittering gold out to where the mirage licked them up, shining and steaming like a lake in the tropics. The sky looked like blue lava, forever incapable of clouds,—a turquoise bowl that was the lid of the desert. And yet within Mrs. Kohler's green patch the water dripped, the beds had all been hosed, and the air was fresh with rapidly evaporating moisture.

The two symmetrical linden trees were the proudest things in the garden. Their sweetness embalmed all the air. At every turn of the paths,—whether one went to see the hollyhocks or the bleeding heart, or to look at the purple morning-glories that ran over the bean-poles,—wherever one went, the sweetness of the lindens struck one afresh and one always came back to them. Under the round leaves, where the waxen yellow blossoms hung, bevies of wild bees were buzzing. The tamarisks were still pink, and the flower-beds were doing their best in honor of the linden festival. The white dove-house was shining with a fresh coat of paint, and the pigeons were crooning contentedly, flying down often to drink at the drip from the water tank. Mrs. Kohler, who was transplanting pansies, came up with her trowel and told Thea it was lucky to have your birthday when the lindens were in bloom, and she must go and look at the sweet peas. Wunsch accompanied her, and as they walked between the flower-beds he took Thea's hand.

"Es flüstern und sprechen die Blumen," —

he muttered. "You know that von Heine? *Im leuchtenden Sommermorgen?*" He looked down at Thea and softly pressed her hand.

"No, I don't know it. What does *flüstern* mean?"

"*Flüstern?*—to whisper. You must begin now to know such things. That is necessary. How many birthdays?"

"Thirteen. I'm in my 'teens now. But how can I know words like that? I only know what you say at my lessons. They don't teach German at school. How can I learn?"

"It is always possible to learn when one likes," said Wunsch. His words were peremptory, as usual, but his tone was mild, even confidential. "There is always a way. And if some day you are going to sing, it is necessary to know well the German language."

Thea stooped over to pick a leaf of rosemary. How did Wunsch know that, when the very roses on her wall-paper had never heard it? "But am I going to?" she asked, still stooping.

"That is for you to say," returned Wunsch coldly. "You would better marry some *Jacob** here and keep the house for him, maybe? That is as one desires."

Thea flashed up at him a clear, laughing look. "No I don't want to do that. You know," she brushed his coat-sleeve quickly with her yellow head. "Only how can I learn anything here? It's so far from Denver."

Wunsch's loose lower lip curled in amusement. Then, as if he suddenly remembered something, he spoke seriously. "Nothing is far and nothing is near, if one desires. The world is little, people are little, human life is little. There is only one big thing—desire. And before it, when it is big, all is little. It brought Columbus across the sea in a little boat, *und so weiter*."* Wunsch made a grimace, took his pupil's hand and drew her toward the grape arbor. "Hereafter I will more speak to you in German. Now, sit down and I will teach you for your birthday that little song. Ask me the words you do not know already. Now: *Im leuchtenden Sommermorgen*."

Thea memorized quickly because she had the power of listening intently. In a few moments she could repeat the eight lines for him. Wunsch nodded encouragingly and they went out of the arbor into the sunlight again. As they went up and down the gravel paths between the flower-beds, the white and yellow butterflies kept darting before them, and the pigeons were washing their pink feet at the drip and crooning in their husky bass. Over and over again Wunsch made her say the lines to him. "You see it is nothing. If you learn a great many of the *Lieder*,* you will know the German language already. *Weiter, nun*." He would incline his head gravely and listen.

> "*Im leuchtenden Sommermorgen*
> *Geh' ich im Garten herum;*
> *Es flüstern und sprechen die Blumen,*
> *Ich aber, ich wandte stumm.*
>
> "*Es flüstern und Sprechen die Blumen*
> *Und schau'n mitleidig mich an:*
> '*Sei unserer Schwester nicht böse,*
> *Du trauriger, blasser Mann!*'"*

(In the soft-shining summer morning
I wandered the garden within.

The flowers they whispered and murmured,
But I, I wandered dumb.

The flowers they whisper and murmur,
And me with compassion they scan:
"Oh, be not harsh to our sister,
Thou sorrowful, death-pale man!")

Wunsch had noticed before that when his pupil read anything in verse the character of her voice changed altogether; it was no longer the voice which spoke the speech of Moonstone. It was a soft, rich contralto, and she read quietly; the feeling was in the voice itself, not indicated by emphasis or change of pitch. She repeated the little verses musically, like a song, and the entreaty of the flowers was even softer than the rest, as the shy speech of flowers might be, and she ended with the voice suspended, almost with a rising inflection. It was a nature-voice, Wunsch told himself, breathed from the creature and apart from language, like the sound of the wind in the trees or the murmur of water.

"What is it the flowers mean when they ask him not to be harsh to their sister, eh?" he asked, looking down at her curiously and wrinkling his dull red forehead.

Thea glanced at him in surprise. "I suppose he thinks they are asking him not to be harsh to his sweetheart—or some girl they remind him of."

"And why *trauriger, blasser Mann?*"

They had come back to the grape arbor, and Thea picked out a sunny place on the bench, where a tortoise-shell cat was stretched at full length. She sat down, bending over the cat and teasing his whiskers. "Because he had been awake all night, thinking about her, wasn't it? Maybe that was why he was up so early."

Wunsch shrugged his shoulders. "If he think about her all night already, why do you say the flowers remind him?"

Thea looked up at him in perplexity. A flash of comprehension lit her face and she smiled eagerly. "Oh, I didn't mean 'remind' in that way! I didn't mean they brought her to his mind! I meant it was only when he came out in the morning, that she seemed to him like that,—like one of the flowers."

"And before he came out, how did she seem?"

This time it was Thea who shrugged her shoulders. The warm smile left her face. She lifted her eyebrows in annoyance and looked off at the sand hills.

Wunsch persisted. "Why you not answer me?"

"Because it would be silly. You are just trying to make me say things. It spoils things to ask questions."

Wunsch bowed mockingly; his smile was disagreeable. Suddenly his face grew grave, grew fierce, indeed. He pulled himself up from his clumsy stoop and folded his arms. "But it is necessary to know if you know somethings. Somethings cannot be taught. If you not know in the beginning, you not know in the end. For a singer there must be something in the inside from the beginning. I shall not be long in this place, may-be, and I like to know. Yes,"—he ground his heel in the gravel,—"yes, when you are barely six, you must know that already. That is the beginning of all things; *der Geist*, *die Phantasie*.* It must be in the baby, when it makes its first cry, like *der Rhythmus*, or it is not to be. You have some voice already, and if in the beginning, when you are with things-to-play, you know that what you will not tell me, then you can learn to sing, may-be."

Wunsch began to pace the arbor, rubbing his hands together. The dark flush of his face had spread up under the iron-gray bristles on his head. He was talking to himself, not to Thea. Insidious power of the linden bloom! "Oh, much you can learn! *Aber nicht die Americanischen Fräulein.** They have nothing inside them," striking his chest with both fists. "They are like the ones in the *Märchen*,* a grinning face and hollow in the insides. Something they can learn, oh, yes, may-be! But the secret—what make the rose to red, the sky to blue, the man to love—*in der Brust*, *in der Brust* it is, *und ohne dieses giebt es keine Kunst, giebt es keine Kunst!*"* He threw up his square hand and shook it, all the fingers apart and wagging. Purple and breathless he went out of the arbor and into the house, without saying good-bye. These outbursts frightened Wunsch. They were always harbingers of ill.

Thea got her music-book and stole quietly out of the garden.

She did not go home, but wandered off into the sand dunes, where the prickly pear was in blossom and the green lizards were racing each other in the glittering light. She was shaken by a passionate excitement. She did not altogether understand what Wunsch was talking about; and yet, in a way she knew. She knew, of course, that there was something about her that was different. But it was more like a friendly spirit than like anything that was a part of herself. She thought everything to it, and it answered her; happiness consisted of that backward and forward movement of herself. The something came and went, she never knew how. Sometimes she hunted for it and could not find it; again, she lifted her eyes from a book, or stepped out of doors, or wakened in the morning, and it was there,—under her cheek, it usually seemed to be, or over her breast,—a kind of warm sureness. And when it was there, everything was more interesting and beautiful, even people. When this companion was with her, she could get the most wonderful things out of Spanish Johnny, or Wunsch, or Dr. Archie.

On her thirteenth birthday she wandered for a long while about the sand ridges, picking up crystals and looking into the yellow prickly-pear blossoms with their thousand stamens. She looked at the sand hills until she wished she *were* a sand hill. And yet she knew that she was going to leave them all behind some day. They would be changing all day long, yellow and purple and lavender, and she would not be there. From that day on, she felt there was a secret between her and Wunsch. Together they had lifted a lid, pulled out a drawer, and looked at something. They hid it away and never spoke of what they had seen; but neither of them forgot it.

XII

ONE July night, when the moon was full, Dr. Archie was coming up from the depot, restless and discontented, wishing there were something to do. He carried his straw hat in his hand, and kept brushing his hair back from his forehead with a purposeless, unsatisfied gesture. After he passed Uncle Billy Beemer's cottonwood grove, the sidewalk ran out of the shadow into the white moonlight and crossed the sand gully on high posts, like a bridge. As the doctor approached this trestle, he saw a white figure, and recognized Thea Kronborg. He quickened his pace and she came to meet him.

"What are you doing out so late, my girl?" he asked as he took her hand.

"Oh, I don't know. What do people go to bed so early for? I'd like to run along before the houses and screech at them. Isn't it glorious out here?"

The young doctor gave a melancholy laugh and pressed her hand.

"Think of it," Thea snorted impatiently. "Nobody up but us and the rabbits! I've started up half a dozen of 'em. Look at that little one down there now,"—she stooped and pointed. In the gully below them there was, indeed, a little rabbit with a white spot of a tail, crouching down on the sand, quite motionless. It seemed to be lapping up the moonlight like cream. On the other side of the walk, down in the ditch, there was a patch of tall, rank sunflowers, their shaggy leaves white with dust. The moon stood over the cottonwood grove. There was no wind, and no sound but the wheezing of an engine down on the tracks.

"Well, we may as well watch the rabbits." Dr. Archie sat down on the sidewalk and let his feet hang over the edge. He pulled out a smooth linen handkerchief that smelled of German cologne water. "Well, how goes it? Working hard? You must know about all Wunsch can teach you by this time."

Thea shook her head. "Oh, no, I don't, Dr. Archie. He's hard to get at, but he's been a real musician in his time. Mother says she believes he's forgotten more than the music-teachers down in Denver ever knew."

"I'm afraid he won't be around here much longer," said Dr. Archie. "He's been making a tank of himself lately. He'll be pulling his freight one of these days. That's the way they do, you know. I'll be sorry on your account." He paused and ran his fresh handkerchief over his face. "What the deuce are we all here for anyway, Thea?" he said abruptly.

"On earth, you mean?" Thea asked in a low voice.

"Well, primarily, yes. But secondarily, why are we in Moonstone? It isn't as if we'd been born here. You were, but Wunsch wasn't, and I wasn't. I suppose I'm here because I married as soon as I got out of medical school and had to get a practice quick. If you hurry things, you always get left in the end. I don't learn anything here, and as for the people— In my own town in Michigan, now, there were people who liked me on my father's account, who had even known my grandfather. That meant something. But here it's all like the sand: blows north one day and south the next. We're all a lot of gamblers without much nerve, playing for small stakes. The railroad is the one real fact in this country. That has to be; the world has to be got back and forth. But the rest of us are here just because it's the end of a run and the engine has to have a drink. Some day I'll get up and find my hair turning gray, and I'll have nothing to show for it."

Thea slid closer to him and caught his arm. "No, no. I won't let you get gray. You've got to stay young for me. I'm getting young now, too."

Archie laughed. "Getting?"

"Yes. People aren't young when they're children. Look at Thor, now; he's just a little old man. But Gus has a sweetheart, and he's young!"

"Something in that!" Dr. Archie patted her head, and then felt the shape of her skull gently, with the tips of his fingers. "When you were little, Thea, I used always to be curious about the shape of your head. You seemed to have more inside it than most youngsters. I haven't examined it for a long time. Seems to be the usual shape, but uncommonly hard, some how. What are you going to do with yourself, anyway?"

"I don't know."

"Honest, now?" He lifted her chin and looked into her eyes.

Thea laughed and edged away from him.

"You've got something up your sleeve, haven't you? Anything

you like; only don't marry and settle down here without giving yourself a chance, will you?"

"Not much. See, there's another rabbit!"

"That's all right about the rabbits, but I don't want you to get tied up. Remember that."

Thea nodded. "Be nice to Wunsch, then. I don't know what I'd do if he went away."

"You've got older friends than Wunsch here, Thea."

"I know." Thea spoke seriously and looked up at the moon, propping her chin on her hand. "But Wunsch is the only one that can teach me what I want to know. I've got to learn to do something well, and that's the thing I can do best."

"Do you want to be a music-teacher?"

"Maybe, but I want to be a good one. I'd like to go to Germany to study, some day. Wunsch says that's the best place,—the only place you can really learn." Thea hesitated and then went on nervously, "I've got a book that says so, too. It's called 'My Musical Memories.' It made me want to go to Germany even before Wunsch said anything. Of course it's a secret. You're the first one I've told."

Dr. Archie smiled indulgently. "That's a long way off. Is that what you've got in your hard noddle?" He put his hand on her hair, but this time she shook him off.

"No, I don't think much about it. But you talk about going, and a body has to have something to go *to!*"

"That's so." Dr. Archie sighed. "You're lucky if you have. Poor Wunsch, now, he hasn't. What do such fellows come out here for? He's been asking me about my mining stock, and about mining towns. What would he do in a mining town? He wouldn't know a piece of ore if he saw one. He's got nothing to sell that a mining town wants to buy. Why don't those old fellows stay at home? We won't need them for another hundred years. An engine wiper can get a job, but a piano player! Such people can't make good."

"My grandfather Alstrom was a musician, and he made good."

Dr. Archie chuckled. "Oh, a Swede can make good anywhere, at anything! You've got that in your favor, miss. Come, you must be getting home."

Thea rose. "Yes, I used to be ashamed of being a Swede, but I'm not any more. Swedes are kind of common, but I think it's better to be *something*."

"It surely is! How tall you are getting. You come above my shoulder now."

"I'll keep on growing, don't you think? I particularly want to be tall. Yes, I guess I must go home. I wish there'd be a fire."

"A fire?"

"Yes, so the fire-bell would ring and the roundhouse whistle would blow, and everybody would come running out. Sometime I'm going to ring the fire-bell myself and stir them all up."

"You'd be arrested."

"Well, that would be better than going to bed."

"I'll have to lend you some more books."

Thea shook herself impatiently. "I can't read every night."

Dr. Archie gave one of his low, sympathetic chuckles as he opened the gate for her. "You're beginning to grow up, that's what's the matter with you. I'll have to keep an eye on you. Now you'll have to say good-night to the moon."

"No, I won't. I sleep on the floor now, right in the moonlight. My window comes down to the floor, and I can look at the sky all night."

She shot round the house to the kitchen door, and Dr. Archie watched her disappear with a sigh. He thought of the hard, mean, frizzy little woman who kept his house for him; once the belle of a Michigan town, now dry and withered up at thirty. "If I had a daughter like Thea to watch," he reflected, "I wouldn't mind anything. I wonder if all of my life's going to be a mistake just because I made a big one then? Hardly seems fair."

Howard Archie was "respected" rather than popular in Moonstone. Everyone recognized that he was a good physician, and a progressive Western town likes to be able to point to a handsome, well-set-up, well-dressed man among its citizens. But a great many people thought Archie "distant," and they were right. He had the uneasy manner of a man who is not among his own kind, and who has not seen enough of the world to feel that all people are in some sense his own kind. He knew that every one was curious about his wife, that she played a sort of character part in Moonstone, and that people made fun of her, not very delicately. Her own friends—most of them women who were distasteful to Archie—liked to ask her to contribute to church charities, just to see how mean she could be. The little, lop-sided cake at the church supper, the cheapest pincushion, the skimpiest apron at the bazaar, were always Mrs. Archie's contribution.

All this hurt the doctor's pride. But if there was one thing he had learned, it was that there was no changing Belle's nature. He had married a mean woman; and he must accept the consequences. Even in Colorado he would have had no pretext for divorce, and, to do him justice, he had never thought of such a thing. The tenets of the Presbyterian Church in which he had grown up, though he had long ceased to believe in them, still influenced his conduct and his conception of propriety. To him there was something vulgar about divorce. A divorced man was a disgraced man; at least, he had exhibited his hurt, and made it a matter for common gossip. Respectability was so necessary to Archie that he was willing to pay a high price for it. As long as he could keep up a decent exterior, he could manage to get on; and if he could have concealed his wife's littleness from all his friends, he would scarcely have complained. He was more afraid of pity than he was of any unhappiness. Had there been another woman for whom he cared greatly, he might have had plenty of courage; but he was not likely to meet such a woman in Moonstone.

There was a puzzling timidity in Archie's make-up. The thing that held his shoulders stiff, that made him resort to a mirthless little laugh when he was talking to dull people, that made him sometimes stumble over rugs and carpets, had its counterpart in his mind. He had not the courage to be an honest thinker. He could comfort himself by evasions and compromises. He consoled himself for his own marriage by telling himself that other people's were not much better. In his work he saw pretty deeply into marital relations in Moonstone, and he could honestly say that there were not many of his friends whom he envied. Their wives seemed to suit them well enough, but they would never have suited him.

Although Dr. Archie could not bring himself to regard marriage merely as a social contract, but looked upon it as somehow made sacred by a church in which he did not believe,—as a physician he knew that a young man whose marriage is merely nominal must yet go on living his life. When he went to Denver or to Chicago, he drifted about in careless company where gayety and good-humor can be bought, not because he had any taste for such society, but because he honestly believed that anything was better than divorce. He often told himself that "hanging and wiving go by destiny." If wiving went badly with a man,—and it did oftener than not,—then he must do the best he could to keep up appearances and help the tradition of domestic happiness along. The Moonstone gossips, assembled in Mrs. Smiley's millinery and notion store, often discussed Dr. Archie's politeness to his wife, and his pleasant manner of speaking about her. "Nobody has ever got a thing out of him yet," they agreed. And it was certainly not because no one had ever tried.

When he was down in Denver, feeling a little jolly, Archie could forget how unhappy he was at home, and could even make himself believe that he missed his wife. He always bought her presents, and would have liked to send her flowers if she had not repeatedly told him never to send her anything but bulbs,— which did not appeal to him in his expansive moments. At the Denver Athletic Club banquets, or at dinner with his colleagues at the Brown Palace Hotel,* he sometimes spoke sentimentally about "little Mrs. Archie," and he always drank the toast "to our wives, God bless them!" with gusto.

The determining factor about Dr. Archie was that he was romantic. He had married Belle White because he was romantic—too romantic to know anything about women, except what he wished them to be, or to repulse a pretty girl who had set her cap for him. At medical school, though he was a rather wild boy in behavior, he had always disliked coarse jokes and vulgar stories. In his old Flint's Physiology* there was still a poem he had pasted there when he was a student; some verses by Dr. Oliver Wendell Holmes* about the ideals of the medical profession. After so much and such disillusioning experience with it, he still had a romantic feeling about the human body; a sense that finer things dwelt in it than could be explained by anatomy. He never jested about birth or death or marriage, and did not like to hear other doctors do it. He was a good nurse, and had a reverence for the bodies of women and children. When he was tending them, one saw him at his best. Then his constraint and self-consciousness fell away from him. He was easy, gentle, competent, master of himself and of other people. Then the idealist in him was not afraid of being discovered and ridiculed.

In his tastes, too, the doctor was romantic. Though he read Balzac all the year through, he still enjoyed the Waverley Novels* as much as when he had first come upon them, in thick leather-bound volumes, in his grandfather's library. He nearly always read Scott on Christmas and holidays, because it brought back the pleasures of his boyhood so vividly. He liked Scott's women. Constance de Beverley* and the minstrel girl in "The Fair Maid of Perth," not the Duchesse de Langeais,* were his heroines. But better than anything that ever got from the heart of a man into printer's ink, he loved the poetry of Robert Burns.* "Death and Dr. Hornbook" and "The Jolly Beggars," Burns's "Reply to his Tailor," he often read aloud to himself in his office, late at night, after a glass of hot toddy. He used to read "Tam o' Shanter" to Thea Kronborg, and he got her some of the songs, set to the old airs for which they were written. He loved to hear her sing them. Sometimes when she sang, "Oh, wert thou in the cauld blast," the doctor and even Mr. Kronborg joined in. Thea never minded if people could not sing; she directed them with her head and somehow carried them along. When her father got off the pitch she let her own voice out and covered him.

XIII

AT the beginning of June, when school closed, Thea had told Wunsch that she didn't know how much practicing she could get in this summer because Thor had his worst teeth still to cut.

"My God! all last summer he was doing that!" Wunsch exclaimed furiously.

"I know, but it takes them two years, and Thor is slow," Thea answered reprovingly.

The summer went well beyond her hopes, however. She told herself that it was the best summer of her life, so far. Nobody was sick at home, and her lessons were uninterrupted. Now that she had four pupils of her own and made a dollar a week, her practicing was regarded more seriously by the household. Her mother had always arranged things so that she could have the parlor four hours a day in summer. Thor proved a friendly ally. He behaved handsomely about his molars, and never objected to being pulled off into remote places in his cart. When Thea dragged him over the hill and made a camp under the shade of a bush or a bank, he would waddle about and play with his blocks, or bury his monkey in the sand and dig him up again. Sometimes he got into the cactus and set up a howl, but usually he let his sister read peacefully, while he coated his hands and face, first with an all-day sucker and then with gravel.

Life was pleasant and uneventful until the first of September, when Wunsch began to drink so hard that he was unable to appear when Thea went to take her mid-week lesson, and Mrs. Kohler had to send her home after a tearful apology. On Saturday morning she set out for the Kohlers' again, but on her way, when she was crossing the ravine, she noticed a woman sitting at the bottom of the gulch, under the railroad trestle She turned from her path and saw that it was Mrs. Tellamantez, and she seemed to be doing drawn-work. Then Thea noticed that there was something beside her, covered up with a purple and yellow Mexican blanket. She ran up the gulch and called to Mrs. Tellamantez. The Mexican woman held up a warning finger. Thea glanced at the blanket and recognized a square red hand which protruded. The middle finger twitched slightly.

"Is he hurt?" she gasped.

Mrs. Tellamantez shook her head. "No; very sick. He knows nothing," she said quietly, folding her hands over her drawn-work.

Thea learned that Wunsch had been out all night, that this morning Mrs. Kohler had gone to look for him and found him under the trestle covered with dirt and cinders. Probably he had been trying to get home and had lost his way. Mrs. Tellamantez was watching beside the unconscious man while Mrs. Kohler and Johnny went to get help.

"You better go home now, I think," said Mrs. Tellamantez, in closing her narration.

Thea hung her head and looked wistfully toward the blanket.

"Couldn't I just stay till they come?" she asked "I'd like to know if he's very bad."

"Bad enough," sighed Mrs. Tellamantez, taking up her work again.

Thea sat down under the narrow shade of one of the trestle posts and listened to the locusts rasping in the hot sand while she watched Mrs. Tellamantez evenly draw her threads. The blanket looked as if it were over a heap of bricks.

"I don't see him breathing any," she said anxiously.

"Yes, he breathes," said Mrs. Tellamantez, not lifting her eyes.

It seemed to Thea that they waited for hours. At last they heard voices, and a party of men came down the hill and up the gulch. Dr. Archie and Fritz Kohler came first; behind were Johnny and Ray, and several men from the roundhouse. Ray had the canvas litter that was kept at the depot for accidents on the road. Behind them trailed half a dozen boys who had been hanging round the depot.

When Ray saw Thea, he dropped his canvas roll and hurried forward. "Better run along home, Thee. This is ugly business." Ray was indignant that anybody who gave Thea music lessons should behave in such a manner.

Thea resented both his proprietary tone and his superior virtue. "I won't. I want to know how bad he is. I'm not a baby!" she exclaimed indignantly, stamping her foot into the sand.

Dr. Archie, who had been kneeling by the blanket, got up and came toward Thea, dusting his knees. He smiled and nodded confidentially. "He'll be all right when we get him home. But he wouldn't want you to see him like this, poor old chap! Understand? Now, skip!"

Thea ran down the gulch and looked back only once, to see them lifting the canvas litter with Wunsch upon it, still covered with the blanket.

The men carried Wunsch up the hill and down the road to the Kohlers'. Mrs. Kohler had gone home and made up a bed in the sitting-room, as she knew the litter could not be got round the turn in the narrow stairway. Wunsch was like a dead man. He lay unconscious all day. Ray Kennedy stayed with him till two o'clock in the afternoon, when he had to go out on his run. It was the first time he had ever been inside the Kohlers' house, and he was so much impressed by Napoleon that the piece-picture formed a new bond between him and Thea.

Dr. Archie went back at six o'clock, and found Mrs. Kohler and Spanish Johnny with Wunsch, who was in a high fever, muttering and groaning.

"There ought to be some one here to look after him to-night, Mrs. Kohler," he said. "I'm on a confinement case, and I can't be here, but there ought to be somebody. He may get violent."

Mrs. Kohler insisted that she could always do anything with Wunsch, but the doctor shook his head and Spanish Johnny grinned. He said he would stay. The doctor laughed at him. "Ten fellows like you couldn't hold him, Spanish, if he got obstreperous; an Irishman would have his hands full. Guess I'd better put the soft pedal on him." He pulled out his hypodermic.

Spanish Johnny stayed, however, and the Kohlers went to bed. At about two o'clock in the morning Wunsch rose from his ignominious cot. Johnny, who was dozing on the lounge, awoke to find the German standing in the middle of the room in his undershirt and drawers, his arms bare, his heavy body seeming twice its natural girth. His face was snarling and savage, and his eyes were crazy. He had risen to avenge himself, to wipe out his shame, to destroy his enemy. One look was enough for Johnny. Wunsch raised a chair threateningly, and Johnny, with the lightness of a *picador*,* darted under the missile and out of the open window. He shot across the gully to get help, meanwhile leaving the Kohlers to their fate.

Fritz, upstairs heard the chair crash upon the stove. Then he heard doors opening and shutting, and some one stumbling about in the shrubbery of the garden. He and Paulina sat up in bed and held a consultation. Fritz slipped from under the covers, and going cautiously over to the window, poked out his head. Then he rushed to the door and bolted it.

"*Mein Gott*,* Paulina," he gasped, "he has the axe, he will kill us!"

"The dresser," cried Mrs. Kohler; "push the dresser before the door. *Ach*, if you had your rabbit gun now!"

"It is in the barn," said Fritz sadly. "It would do no good; he would not be afraid of anything now. Stay you in the bed, Paulina." The dresser had lost its casters years ago, but he managed to drag it in front of the door. "He is in the garden. He makes nothing. He will get sick again, maybe."

Fritz went back to bed and his wife pulled the quilt over him and made him lie down. They heard stumbling in the garden again, then a smash of glass.

"*Ach, das Mistbeet!*"* gasped Paulina, hearing her hot-bed shivered. "The poor soul, Fritz, he will cut himself. *Ach!* what is that?" They both sat up in bed. "*Wieder!** *Ach*, What is he doing?"

The noise came steadily, a sound of chopping. Paulina tore off her night-cap. "*Die Bäume, die Bäume!** He is cutting our trees, Fritz!" Before her husband could prevent her, she had sprung from the bed and rushed to the window. "*Der Taubenschlag! Gerechter Himmel*,* he is chopping the dove-house down!"

Fritz reached her side before she had got her breath again, and poked his head out beside hers. There, in the faint starlight, they saw a bulky man, barefoot, half dressed, chopping away at the white post that formed the pedestal of the dove-house. The startled pigeons were croaking and flying about his head, even beating their wings in his face, so that he struck at them furiously with the axe. In a few seconds there was a crash, and Wunsch had actually felled the dove-house.

"Oh, if only it is not the trees next!" prayed Paulina. "The dove-house you can make new again, but not *die Bäume*."

They watched breathlessly. In the garden below Wunsch stood in the attitude of a woodman, contemplating the fallen cote. Suddenly he threw the axe over his shoulder and went out of the front gate toward the town.

"The poor soul, he will meet his death!" Mrs. Kohler wailed. She ran back to her feather bed and hid her face in the pillow.

Fritz kept watch at the window. "No, no, Paulina," he called presently; "I see lanterns coming. Johnny must have gone for somebody. Yes, four lanterns, coming along the gulch. They stop; they must have seen him already. Now they are under the hill and I cannot see them, but I think they have him. They will bring him back. I must dress and go down." He caught his trousers and began pulling them on by the window. "Yes, here they come, half a dozen men. And they have tied him with a rope, Paulina!"

"*Ach*, the poor man! To be led like a cow," groaned Mrs. Kohler. "Oh, it is good that he has no wife!" She was reproaching herself for nagging Fritz when he drank himself into foolish pleasantry or mild sulks, and felt that she had never before appreciated her blessings.

Wunsch was in bed for ten days, during which time he was gossiped about and even preached about in Moonstone. The Baptist preacher took a shot at the fallen man from his pulpit, Mrs. Livery Johnson nodding approvingly from her pew. The mothers of Wunsch's pupils sent him notes informing him that their daughters would discontinue their music-lessons. The old maid who had rented him her piano sent the town dray for her contaminated instrument, and ever afterward declared that Wunsch had ruined its tone and scarred its glossy finish. The Kohlers were unremitting in their kindness to their friend. Mrs. Kohler made him soups and broths without stint, and Fritz repaired the dove-house and mounted it on a new post, lest it might be a sad reminder.

As soon as Wunsch was strong enough to sit about in his slippers and wadded jacket, he told Fritz to bring him some stout thread from the shop. When Fritz asked what he was going to sew, he produced the tattered score of "Orpheus" and said he would like to fix it up for a little present. Fritz carried it over to the shop and stitched it into pasteboards, covered with dark suiting-cloth. Over the stitches he glued a strip of thin red leather which he got from his friend, the harness-maker. After Paulina had cleaned the pages with fresh bread, Wunsch was amazed to see what a fine book he had. It opened stiffly, but that was no matter.

Sitting in the arbor one morning, under the ripe grapes and the brown, curling leaves, with a pen and ink on the bench beside him and the Gluck score on his knee, Wunsch pondered for a long while. Several times he dipped the pen in the ink, and then put it back again in the cigar box in which Mrs. Kohler kept her writing utensils. His thoughts wandered over a wide territory; over many countries and many years. There was no order or logical sequence in his ideas. Pictures came and went without reason. Faces, mountains, rivers, autumn days in other vineyards far away. He thought of a *Fuszreise** he had made through the Hartz Mountains in his student days; of the innkeeper's pretty daughter who had lighted his pipe for him in the garden one summer evening, of the woods above Wiesbaden, haymakers on an island in the river. The roundhouse whistle woke him from his reveries. Ah, yes, he was in Moonstone, Colorado. He frowned for a moment and looked at the book on his knee. He had thought of a great many appropriate things to write in it, but suddenly he rejected all of them, opened the book, and at the top of the much-engraved title-page he wrote rapidly in purple ink:—

*Einst, O Wunder!—**
A. Wunsch.

Moonstone, Colo.
    September 30, 18—

Nobody in Moonstone ever found what Wunsch's first name was. That "A" may have stood for Adam, or August, or even Amadeus; he got very angry if any one asked him. He remained A. Wunsch to the end of his chapter there. When he presented this score to Thea, he told her that in ten years she would either know what the inscription meant, or she would not have the least idea, in which case it would not matter.

When Wunsch began to pack his trunk, both the Kohlers were very unhappy. He said he was coming back some day, but that for the present, since he had lost all his pupils, it would be better for him to try some "new town." Mrs. Kohler darned and mended all his clothes, and gave him two new shirts she had made for Fritz. Fritz made him a new pair of trousers and would have made him an overcoat but for the fact that overcoats were so easy to pawn.

Wunsch would not go across the ravine to the town until he went to take the morning train for Denver. He said that after he got to Denver he would "look around." He left Moonstone one bright October morning, without telling anyone good-bye. He bought his ticket and went directly into the smoking-car. When the train was beginning to pull out, he heard his name called frantically, and looking out of the window he saw Thea Kronborg standing on the siding, bareheaded and panting. Some boys had brought word to school that they saw Wunsch's trunk going over to the station, and Thea had run away from school. She was at the end of the station platform, her hair in two braids, her blue gingham dress wet to the knees because she had run across lots through the weeds. It had rained during the night, and the tall sunflowers behind her were fresh and shining.

"Good-bye, Herr Wunsch, good-bye!" she called, waving to him.

He thrust his head out at the car window and called back, "*Leben sie wohl, leben sie wohl, mein Kind!*"* He watched her until the train swept around the curve beyond the roundhouse, and then sank back into his seat, muttering, "She had been running. Ah, she will run a long way; they cannot stop her!"

What was it about the child that one believed in? Was it her dogged industry, so unusual in this free-and-easy country? Was it her imagination? More likely it was because she had both imagination and a stubborn will, curiously balancing and inter-penetrating each other. There was something unconscious and unawakened about her, that tempted curiosity. She had a kind of seriousness that he had not met with in a pupil before. She hated difficult things, and yet she could never pass one by. They seemed to challenge her; she had no peace until she mastered them. She had the power to make a great effort, to lift a weight heavier than herself. Wunsch hoped he would always remember her as she stood by the track, looking up at him; her broad eager face, so fair in color, with its high cheek-bones, yellow eyebrows and greenish-hazel eyes. It was a face full of light and energy, of the unquestioning hopefulness of first youth. Yes, she was like a flower full of sun, but not the soft German flowers of his child-hood. He had it now, the comparison he had absently reached for before: she was like the yellow prickly-pear blossoms that open there in the desert; thornier and sturdier than the maiden flowers he remembered; not so sweet, but wonderful.

That night Mrs. Kohler brushed away many a tear as she got supper and set the table for two. When they sat down, Fritz was more silent than usual. People who have lived long together need a third at table: they know each other's thoughts so well that they have nothing left to say. Mrs. Kohler stirred and stirred her coffee and clattered the spoon, but she had no heart for her supper. She felt, for the first time in years, that she was tired of her own cooking. She looked across the glass lamp at her husband and asked him if the butcher liked his new overcoat, and whether he had got the shoulders right in a ready-made suit he was patching over for Ray Kennedy. After supper Fritz offered to wipe the dishes for her, but she told him to go about his business, and not to act as if she were sick or getting helpless.

When her work in the kitchen was all done, she went out to cover the oleanders against frost, and to take a last look at her chickens. As she came back from the hen-house she stopped by one of the linden trees and stood resting her hand on the trunk. He would never come back, the poor man; she knew that. He would drift on from new town to new town, from catastrophe to catastrophe. He would hardly find a good home for himself again. He would die at last in some rough place, and be buried in the desert or on the wild prairie, far enough from any linden tree!

Fritz, smoking his pipe on the kitchen doorstep, watched his Paulina and guessed her thoughts. He, too, was sorry to lose his friend. But Fritz was getting old; he had lived a long while and had learned to lose without struggle.

XIV

"MOTHER," said Peter Kronborg to his wife one morning about two weeks after Wunsch's departure, "how would you like to drive out to Copper Hole with me to-day?"

Mrs. Kronborg said she thought she would enjoy the drive. She put on her gray cashmere dress and gold watch and chain, as befitted a minister's wife, and while her husband was dressing she packed a black oilcloth satchel with such clothing as she and Thor would need overnight.

Copper Hole was a settlement fifteen miles northwest of Moonstone where Mr. Kronborg preached every Friday evening. There was a big spring there and a creek and a few irrigating ditches. It was a community of discouraged agriculturists who had disastrously experimented with dry farming. Mr. Kronborg always drove out one day and back the next, spending the night with one of his parishioners. Often, when the weather was fine, his wife accompanied him. To-day they set out from home after the midday meal, leaving Tillie in charge of the house. Mrs. Kronborg's maternal feeling was always garnered up in the baby, whoever the baby happened to be. If she had the baby with her, the others could look out for themselves. Thor, of course, was not, accurately speaking, a baby any longer. In the matter of nourishment he was quite independent of his mother, though this independence had not been won without a struggle. Thor was conservative in all things, and the whole family had anguished with him when he was being weaned. Being the youngest, he was still the baby for Mrs. Kronborg, though he was nearly four years old and sat up boldly on her lap this afternoon, holding on to the ends of the lines and shouting "'mup, 'mup, horsey." His father watched him affectionately and hummed hymn tunes in the jovial way that was sometimes such a trial to Thea.

Mrs. Kronborg was enjoying the sunshine and the brilliant sky and all the faintly marked features of the dazzling, monotonous landscape. She had a rather unusual capacity for getting the flavor of places and of people. Although she was so enmeshed in family cares most of the time, she could emerge serene when she was away from them. For a mother of seven, she had a singularly unprejudiced point of view. She was, moreover, a fatalist, and as she did not attempt to direct things beyond her control, she found a good deal of time to enjoy the ways of man and nature.

When they were well upon their road, out where the first lean pasture lands began and the sand grass made a faint showing between the sagebushes, Mr. Kronborg dropped his tune and turned to his wife. "Mother, I've been thinking about something."

"I guessed you had. What is it?" She shifted Thor to her left knee, where he would be more out of the way.

"Well, it's about Thea. Mr. Follansbee came to my study at the church the other day and said they would like to have their two girls take lessons of Thea. Then I sounded Miss Meyers" (Miss Meyers was the organist in Mr. Kronborg's church) "and she said there was a good deal of talk about whether Thea wouldn't take over Wunsch's pupils. She said if Thea stopped school she wouldn't wonder if she could get pretty much all Wunsch's class. People think Thea knows about all Wunsch could teach."

Mrs. Kronborg looked thoughtful. "Do you think we ought to take her out of school so young?"

"She is young, but next year would be her last year anyway. She's far along for her age. And she can't learn much under the principal we've got now, can she?"

"No, I'm afraid she can't," his wife admitted. "She frets a good deal and says that man always has to look in the back of the book for the answers. She hates all that diagramming they have to do, and I think myself it's a waste of time."

Mr. Kronborg settled himself back into the seat and slowed the mare to a walk. "You see, it occurs to me that we might raise

Thea's prices, so it would be worth her while. Seventy-five cents for hour lessons, fifty cents for half-hour lessons. If she got, say two thirds of Wunsch's class, that would bring her in upwards of ten dollars a week. Better pay than teaching a country school, and there would be more work in vacation than in winter. Steady work twelve months in the year; that's an advantage. And she'd be living at home, with no expenses."

"There'd be talk if you raised her prices," said Mrs. Kronborg dubiously.

"At first there would. But Thea is so much the best musician in town that they'd all come into line after a while. A good many people in Moonstone have been making money lately, and have bought new pianos. There were ten new pianos shipped in here from Denver in the last year. People ain't going to let them stand idle; too much money invested. I believe Thea can have as many scholars as she can handle, if we set her up a little."

"How set her up, do you mean?" Mrs. Kronborg felt a certain reluctance about accepting this plan, though she had not yet had time to think out her reasons.

"Well, I've been thinking for some time we could make good use of another room. We couldn't give up the parlor to her all the time. If we built another room on the ell and put the piano in there, she could give lessons all day long and it wouldn't bother us. We could build a clothes-press in it, and put in a bed-lounge and a dresser and let Anna have it for her sleeping-room. She needs a place of her own, now that she's beginning to be dressy."

"Seem's like Thea ought to have the choice of the room herself," said Mrs. Kronborg.

"But, my dear, she don't want it. Won't have it. I sounded her coming home from church on Sunday; asked her if she would like to sleep in a new room, if we built on. She fired up like a little wild-cat and said she'd made her own room all herself, and she didn't think anybody ought to take it away from her."

"She don't mean to be impertinent, father. She's made decided that way, like my father." Mrs. Kronborg spoke warmly. "I never have any trouble with the child. I remember my father's ways and go at her carefully. Thea's all right."

Mr. Kronborg laughed indulgently and pinched Thor's full cheek. "Oh, I didn't mean anything against your girl, mother! She's all right, but she's a little wild-cat, just the same. I think Ray Kennedy's planning to spoil a born old maid."

"Huh! She'll get something a good sight better than Ray Kennedy, you see! Thea's an awful smart girl. I've seen a good many girls take music lessons in my time, but I ain't seen one that took to it so. Wunsch said so, too. She's got the making of something in her."

"I don't deny that, and the sooner she gets at it in a business-like way, the better. She's the kind that takes responsibility, and it'll be good for her."

Mrs. Kronborg was thoughtful. "In some ways it will, maybe. But there's a good deal of strain about teaching youngsters, and she's always worked so hard with the scholars she has. I've often listened to her pounding it into 'em. I don't want to work her too hard. She's so serious that she's never had what you might call any real childhood. Seems like she ought to have the next few years sort of free and easy. She'll be tied down with responsibilities soon enough."

Mr. Kronborg patted his wife's arm. "Don't you believe it, mother. Thea is not the marrying kind. I've watched 'em. Anna will marry before long and make a good wife, but I don't see Thea bringing up a family. She's got a good deal of her mother in her, but she hasn't got all. She's too peppery and too fond of having her own way. Then she's always got to be ahead in everything. That kind make good church-workers and missionaries and school teachers, but they don't make good wives. They fret all their energy away, like colts, and get cut on the wire."

Mrs. Kronborg laughed. "Give me the graham crackers I put in your pocket for Thor. He's hungry. You're a funny man, Peter. A body wouldn't think, to hear you, you was talking about your own daughters. I guess you see through 'em. Still, even if Thea ain't apt to have children of her own, I don't know as that's a good reason why she should wear herself out on other people's."

"That's just the point, mother. A girl with all that energy has got to do something, same as a boy, to keep her out of mischief. If you don't want her to marry Ray, let her do something to make herself independent."

"Well, I'm not against it. It might be the best thing for her. I wish I felt sure she wouldn't worry. She takes things hard. She nearly cried herself sick about Wunsch's going away. She's the smartest child of 'em all, Peter, by a long ways."

Peter Kronborg smiled. "There you go, Anna. That's you all over again. Now, I have no favorites; they all have their good points. But you," with a twinkle, "always did go in for brains."

Mrs. Kronborg chuckled as she wiped the cracker crumbs from Thor's chin and fists. "Well, you're mighty conceited, Peter! But I don't know as I ever regretted it. I prefer having a family of my own to fussing with other folks' children, that's the truth."

Before the Kronborgs reached Copper Hole, Thea's destiny was pretty well mapped out for her. Mr. Kronborg was always delighted to have an excuse for enlarging the house.

Mrs. Kronborg was quite right in her conjecture that there would be unfriendly comment in Moonstone when Thea raised her prices for music-lessons. People said she was getting too conceited for anything. Mrs. Livery Johnson put on a new bonnet and paid up all her back calls to have the pleasure of announcing in each parlor she entered that her daughters, at least, would "never pay professional prices to Thea Kronborg."

Thea raised no objection to quitting school. She was now in the "high room," as it was called, in next to the highest class, and was studying geometry and beginning Caesar. She no longer recited her lessons to the teacher she liked, but to the Principal, a man who belonged, like Mrs. Livery Johnson, to the camp of Thea's natural enemies. He taught school because he was too lazy to work among grown-up people, and he made an easy job of it. He got out of real work by inventing useless activities for his pupils, such as the "tree-diagramming system."* Thea had spent hours making trees out of "Thanatopsis," Hamlet's soliloquy, Cato on "Immortality."* She agonized under this waste of time, and was only too glad to accept her father's offer of liberty.

So Thea left school the first of November. By the first of January she had eight one-hour pupils and ten half-hour pupils, and there would be more in the summer. She spent her earnings generously. She bought a new Brussels carpet for the parlor, and a rifle for Gunner and Axel, and an imitation tiger-skin coat and cap for Thor. She enjoyed being able to add to the family possessions, and thought Thor looked quite as handsome in his spots as the rich children she had seen in Denver. Thor was most complacent in his conspicuous apparel. He could walk anywhere by this time—though he always preferred to sit, or to be pulled in his cart. He was a blissfully lazy child, and had a number of long, dull plays, such as making nests for his china duck and waiting for her to lay him an egg. Thea thought him very intelligent, and she was proud that he was so big and burly. She found him restful, loved to hear him call her "sitter," and really liked his companionship, especially when she was tired. On Saturday, for instance, when she taught from nine in the morning until five in the afternoon, she liked to get off in a corner with Thor after supper, away from all the bathing and dressing and joking and talking that went on in the house, and ask him about his duck, or hear him tell one of his rambling stories.

XV

By the time Thea's fifteenth birthday came round, she was established as a music teacher in Moonstone. The new room had been added to the house early in the spring, and Thea had been giving her lessons there since the middle of May. She liked the personal independence which was accorded her as a wage-earner. The family questioned her comings and goings very little. She could go buggy-riding with Ray Kennedy, for instance, without taking Gunner or Axel. She could go to Spanish Johnny's and sing part songs with the Mexicans, and nobody objected.

Thea was still under the first excitement of teaching, and was terribly in earnest about it. If a pupil did not get on well, she fumed and fretted. She counted until she was hoarse. She listened to scales in her sleep. Wunsch had taught only one pupil seriously, but Thea taught twenty. The duller they were, the more furiously she poked and prodded them. With the little girls she was nearly always patient, but with pupils older than herself, she sometimes lost her temper. One of her mistakes was to let herself in for a calling-down from Mrs. Livery Johnson. That lady appeared at the Kronborgs' one morning and announced that she would allow no girl to stamp her foot at her daughter Grace. She added that Thea's bad manners with the older girls were being talked about all over town, and that if her temper did not speedily improve she would lose all her advanced pupils. Thea was frightened. She felt she could never bear the disgrace, if such a thing happened. Besides, what would her father say, after he had gone to the expense of building an addition to the house? Mrs. Johnson demanded an apology to Grace. Thea said she was willing to make it. Mrs. Johnson said that hereafter, since she had taken lessons of the best piano teacher in Grinnell, Iowa, she herself would decide what pieces Grace should study. Thea readily consented to that, and Mrs. Johnson rustled away to tell a neighbor woman that Thea Kronborg could be meek enough when you went at her right.

Thea was telling Ray about this unpleasant encounter as they were driving out to the sand hills the next Sunday.

"She was stuffing you, all right, Thee," Ray reassured her. "There's no general dissatisfaction among your scholars. She just wanted to get in a knock. I talked to the piano tuner the last time he was here, and he said all the people he tuned for expressed themselves very favorably about your teaching. I wish you didn't take so much pains with them, myself."

"But I have to, Ray. They're all so dumb. They've got no ambition," Thea exclaimed irritably. "Jenny Smiley is the only one who isn't stupid. She can read pretty well, and she has such good hands. But she don't care a rap about it. She has no pride."

Ray's face was full of complacent satisfaction as he glanced sidewise at Thea, but she was looking off intently into the mirage, at one of those mammoth cattle that are nearly always reflected there. "Do you find it easier to teach in your new room?" he asked.

"Yes; I'm not interrupted so much. Of course, if I ever happen to want to practice at night, that's always the night Anna chooses to go to bed early."

"It's a darned shame, Thee, you didn't cop that room for yourself. I'm sore at the *padre** about that. He ought to give you that room. You could fix it up so pretty."

"I didn't want it, honest I didn't. Father would have let me have it. I like my own room better. Somehow I can think better in a little room. Besides, up there I am away from everybody, and I can read as late as I please and nobody nags me."

"A growing girl needs lots of sleep," Ray providently remarked.

Thea moved restlessly on the buggy cushions "They need other things more," she muttered. "Oh I forgot. I brought something to show you. Look here, it came on my birthday. Wasn't it nice of him to remember?" She took from her pocket a postcard, bent in the middle and folded, and handed it to Ray. On it was a white dove, perched on a wreath of very blue forget-me-nots, and "Birthday Greetings" in gold letters. Under this was written, "From A. Wunsch."

Ray turned the card over, examined the postmark, and then began to laugh.

"Concord, Kansas. He has my sympathy!"

"Why, is that a poor town?"

"It's the jumping-off place, no town at all. Some houses dumped down in the middle of a cornfield. You get lost in the corn. Not even a saloon to keep things going; sell whiskey without a license at the butcher shop, beer on ice with the liver and beefsteak. I wouldn't stay there over Sunday for a ten-dollar bill."

"Oh, dear! What do you suppose he's doing there? Maybe he just stopped off there a few days to tune pianos," Thea suggested hopefully.

Ray gave her back the card. "He's headed in the wrong direction. What does he want to get back into a grass country for? Now, there are lots of good live towns down on the Santa Fé, and everybody down there is musical. He could always get a job playing in saloons if he was dead-broke. I've figured out that I've got no years of my life to waste in a Methodist country where they raise pork."

"We must stop on our way back and show this card to Mrs. Kohler. She misses him so."

"By the way, Thee, I hear the old woman goes to church every Sunday to hear you sing. Fritz tells me he has to wait till two o'clock for his Sunday dinner these days. The church people ought to give you credit for that, when they go for you."

Thea shook her head and spoke in a tone of resignation. "They'll always go for me, just as they did for Wunsch. It wasn't because he drank they went for him; not really. It was something else."

"You want to salt your money down, Thee, and go to Chicago and take some lessons. Then you come back, and wear a long feather and high heels and put on a few airs, and that'll fix 'em. That's what they like."

"I'll never have money enough to go to Chicago. Mother meant to lend me some, I think, but now they've got hard times back in Nebraska, and her farm don't bring her in anything. Takes all the tenant can raise to pay the taxes. Don't let's talk about that. You promised to tell me about the play you went to see in Denver."

Any one would have liked to hear Ray's simple and clear account of the performance he had seen at the Tabor Grand Opera House—Maggie Mitchell in *Little Barefoot**—and any one would have liked to watch his kind face. Ray looked his best out of doors, when his thick red hands were covered by gloves, and the dull red of his sunburned face somehow seemed right in the light and wind. He looked better, too, with his hat on; his hair was thin and dry, with no particular color or character, "regular Willy-boy hair," as he himself described it. His eyes were pale beside the reddish bronze of his skin. They had the faded look often seen in the eyes of men who have lived much in the sun and wind and who have been accustomed to train their vision upon distant objects.

Ray realized that Thea's life was dull and exacting, and that she missed Wunsch. He knew she worked hard, that she put up with a great many little annoyances, and that her duties as a teacher separated her more than ever from the boys and girls of her own age. He did everything he could to provide recreation for her. He brought her candy and magazines and pineapples—of which she was very fond—from Denver, and kept his eyes and ears open for anything that might interest her. He was, of course, living for Thea. He had thought it all out carefully and had made up his mind just when he would speak to her. When she was seventeen, then he would tell her his plan and ask her to marry him. He would be willing to wait two, or even three years, until she was twenty, if she thought best. By that time he would surely have got in on something: copper, oil, gold, silver, sheep,—something.

Meanwhile, it was pleasure enough to feel that she depended on him more and more, that she leaned upon his steady kindness. He never broke faith with himself about her; he never hinted to her of his hopes for the future, never suggested that she might be more intimately confidential with him, or talked to her of the thing he thought about so constantly. He had the chivalry which is perhaps the proudest possession of his race. He had never embarrassed her by so much as a glance. Sometimes, when they drove out to the sand hills, he let his left arm lie along the back of the buggy seat, but it never came any nearer to Thea than that, never touched her. He often turned to her a face full of pride, and frank admiration, but his glance was never so intimate or so penetrating as Dr. Archie's. His blue eyes were clear and shallow, friendly, uninquiring. He rested Thea because he was so different; because, though he often told her interesting things, he never set lively fancies going in her head; because he never misunderstood her, and because he never, by any chance, for a single instant, understood her! Yes, with Ray she was safe; by him she would never be discovered!

XVI

THE pleasantest experience Thea had that summer was a trip that she and her mother made to Denver in Ray Kennedy's caboose. Mrs. Kronborg had been looking forward to this excursion for a long while, but as Ray never knew at what hour his freight would leave Moonstone, it was difficult to arrange. The call-boy was as likely to summon him to start on his run at twelve o'clock midnight as at twelve o'clock noon. The first week in June started out with all the scheduled trains running on time, and a light freight business. Tuesday evening Ray, after consulting with the dispatcher, stopped at the Kronborgs' front gate to tell Mrs. Kronborg—who was helping Tillie water the flowers—that if she and Thea could be at the depot at eight o'clock the next morning, he thought he could promise them a pleasant ride and get them into Denver before nine o'clock in the evening. Mrs. Kronborg told him cheerfully, across the fence, that she would "take him up on it," and Ray hurried back to the yards to scrub out his car.

The one complaint Ray's brakemen had to make of him was that he was too fussy about his caboose. His former brakeman had asked to be transferred because, he said, "Kennedy was as fussy about his car as an old maid about her bird-cage." Joe Giddy, who was braking with Ray now, called him "the bride," because he kept the caboose and bunks so clean.

It was properly the brakeman's business to keep the car clean, but when Ray got back to the depot, Giddy was nowhere to be found. Muttering that all his brakemen seemed to consider him "easy," Ray went down to his car alone. He built a fire in the stove and put water on to heat while he got into his overalls and jumper. Then he set to work with a scrubbing-brush and plenty of soap and "cleaner." He scrubbed the floor and seats, blacked the stove, put clean sheets on the bunks, and then began to demolish Giddy's picture gallery. Ray found that his brakemen were likely to have what he termed "a taste for the nude in art," and Giddy was no exception. Ray took down half a dozen girls in tights and ballet skirts,—premiums for cigarette coupons,—and some racy calendars advertising saloons and sporting clubs, which had cost Giddy both time and trouble; he even removed Giddy's particular pet, a naked girl lying on a couch with her knee carelessly poised in the air. Underneath the picture was printed the title, "The Odalisque."* Giddy was under the happy delusion that this title meant something wicked,—there was a wicked look about the consonants,—but Ray, of course, had looked it up, and Giddy was indebted to the dictionary for the privilege of keeping his lady. If "odalisque" had been what Ray called an objectionable word, he would have thrown the picture out in the first place. Ray even took down a picture of Mrs. Langtry in evening dress, because it was entitled the "Jersey Lily," and because there was a small head of Edward VII, then Prince of Wales,* in one corner. Albert Edward's conduct was a popular subject of discussion among railroad men in those days, and as Ray pulled the tacks out of this lithograph he felt more indignant with the English than ever. He deposited all these pictures under the mattress of Giddy's bunk, and stood admiring his clean car in the lamplight; the walls now exhibited only a wheatfield, advertising agricultural implements, a map of Colorado, and some pictures of race-horses and hunting-dogs. At this moment Giddy, freshly shaved and shampooed, his shirt shining with the highest polish known to Chinese laundrymen, his straw hat tipped over his right eye, thrust his head in at the door.

"What in hell—" he brought out furiously. His good-humored, sunburned face seemed fairly to swell with amazement and anger.

"That's all right, Giddy," Ray called in a conciliatory tone. "Nothing injured. I'll put 'em all up again as I found 'em. Going to take some ladies down in the car to-morrow."

Giddy scowled. He did not dispute the propriety of Ray's measures, if there were to be ladies on board, but he felt injured. "I suppose you'll expect me to behave like a Y.M.C.A.* secretary," he growled. "I can't do my work and serve tea at the same time."

"No need to have a tea-party," said Ray with determined cheerfulness. "Mrs. Kronborg will bring the lunch, and it will be a darned good one."

Giddy lounged against the car, holding his cigar between two thick fingers. "Then I guess she'll get it," he observed knowingly. "I don't think your musical friend is much on the grub-box. Has to keep her hands white to tickle the ivories." Giddy had nothing against Thea, but he felt cantankerous and wanted to get a rise out of Kennedy.

"Every man to his own job," Ray replied agreeably, pulling his white shirt on over his head.

Giddy emitted smoke disdainfully. "I suppose so. The man that gets her will have to wear an apron and bake the pancakes. Well, some men like to mess about the kitchen." He paused, but Ray was intent on getting into his clothes as quickly as possible. Giddy thought he could go a little further. "Of course, I don't dispute your right to haul women in this car if you want to; but personally, so far as I'm concerned, I'd a good deal rather drink a can of tomatoes and do without the women *and* their lunch. I was never much enslaved to hard-boiled eggs, anyhow."

"You'll eat 'em to-morrow, all the same." Ray's tone had a steely glitter as he jumped out of the car, and Giddy stood aside to let him pass. He knew that Kennedy's next reply would be delivered by hand. He had once seen Ray beat up a nasty fellow for insulting a Mexican woman who helped about the grub-car in the work train, and his fists had worked like two steel hammers. Giddy wasn't looking for trouble.

At eight o'clock the next morning Ray greeted his ladies and helped them into the car. Giddy had put on a clean shirt and yellow pig-skin gloves and was whistling his best. He considered Kennedy a fluke as a ladies' man, and if there was to be a party, the honors had to be done by some one who wasn't a blacksmith at small-talk. Giddy had, as Ray sarcastically admitted, "a local reputation as a jollier," and he was fluent in gallant speeches of a not too-veiled nature. He insisted that Thea should take his seat in the cupola, opposite Ray's, where she could look out over the country. Thea told him, as she clambered up, that she cared a good deal more about riding in that seat than about going to Denver. Ray was never so companionable and easy as when he sat chatting in the lookout of his little house on wheels. Good stories came to him, and interesting recollections. Thea had a great respect for the reports he had to write out, and for the telegrams that were handed to him at stations; for all the knowledge and experience it must take to run a freight train.

Giddy, down in the car, in the pauses of his work, made himself agreeable to Mrs. Kronborg.

"It's a great rest to be where my family can't get at me, Mr. Giddy," she told him. "I thought you and Ray might have some housework here for me to look after, but I couldn't improve any on this car."

"Oh, we like to keep her neat," returned Giddy glibly, winking up at Ray's expressive back. "If you want to see a clean ice-box, look at this one. Yes, Kennedy always carries fresh cream to eat on his oatmeal. I'm not particular. The tin cow's good enough for me."

"Most of you boys smoke so much that all victuals taste alike to you," said Mrs. Kronborg. "I've got no religious scruples against smoking, but I couldn't take as much interest cooking for a man that used tobacco. I guess it's all right for bachelors who have to eat round."

Mrs. Kronborg took off her hat and veil and made herself comfortable. She seldom had an opportunity to be idle, and she enjoyed it. She could sit for hours and watch the sage-hens fly up and the jack-rabbits dart away from the track, without being bored. She wore a tan bombazine dress, made very plainly, and carried a roomy, worn, mother-of-the-family handbag.

Ray Kennedy always insisted that Mrs. Kronborg was "a fine-looking lady," but this was not the common opinion in Moonstone. Ray had lived long enough among the Mexicans to dislike fussiness, to feel that there was something more attractive in ease of manner than in absent-minded concern about hairpins and dabs of lace. He had learned to think that the way a woman stood, moved, sat in her chair, looked at you, was more important than the absence of wrinkles from her skirt. Ray had, indeed, such unusual perceptions in some directions, that one could not help wondering what he would have been if he had ever, as he said, had "half a chance."

He was right: Mrs. Kronborg was a fine-looking woman. She was short and square, but her head was a real head, not a mere jerky termination of the body. It had some individuality apart from hats and hairpins. Her hair, Moonstone women admitted, would have been very pretty "on anybody else." Frizzy bangs were worn then, but Mrs. Kronborg always dressed her hair in the same way, parted in the middle, brushed smoothly back from her low, white forehead, pinned loosely on the back of her head in two thick braids. It was growing gray about the temples, but after the manner of yellow hair it seemed only to have grown paler there, and had taken on a color like that of English primroses. Her eyes were clear and untroubled; her face smooth and calm, and, as Ray said, "strong."

Thea and Ray, up in the sunny cupola, were laughing and talking. Ray got great pleasure out of seeing her face there in the little box where he so often imagined it. They were crossing a plateau where great red sandstone boulders lay about, most of them much wider at the top than at the base, so that they looked like great toadstools.

"The sand has been blowing against them for a good many hundred years," Ray explained, directing Thea's eyes with his gloved hand. "You see the sand blows low, being so heavy, and cuts them out underneath. Wind and sand are pretty high-class architects. That's the principle of most of the Cliff-Dweller remains down at Canyon de Chelly.* The sandstorms had dug out big depressions in the face of a cliff, and the Indians built their houses back in that depression."

"You told me that before, Ray, and of course you know. But the geography says their houses were cut out of the face of the living rock, and I like that better."

Ray sniffed. "What nonsense does get printed! It's enough to give a man disrespect for learning. How could them Indians cut houses out of the living rock, when they knew nothing about the art of forging metals?" Ray leaned back in his chair, swung his foot, and looked thoughtful and happy. He was in one of his favorite fields of speculation, and nothing gave him more pleasure than talking these things over with Thea Kronborg. "I'll tell you, Thee, if those old fellows had learned to work metals once, your ancient Egyptians and Assyrians wouldn't have beat them very much. Whatever they did do, they did well. Their masonry's standing there to-day, the corners as true as the Denver Capitol.

They were clever at most everything but metals; and that one failure kept them from getting across. It was the quicksand that swallowed 'em up, as a race. I guess civilization proper began when men mastered metals."

Ray was not vain about his bookish phrases. He did not use them to show off, but because they seemed to him more adequate than colloquial speech. He felt strongly about these things, and groped for words, as he said, "to express himself." He had the lamentable American belief that "expression" is obligatory. He still carried in his trunk, among the unrelated possessions of a railroad man, a notebook on the title-page of which was written "Impressions on First Viewing the Grand Canyon, Ray H. Kennedy." The pages of that book were like a battlefield; the laboring author had fallen back from metaphor after metaphor, abandoned position after position. He would have admitted that the art of forging metals was nothing to this treacherous business of recording impressions, in which the material you were so full of vanished mysteriously under your striving hand. "Escaping steam!" he had said to himself, the last time he tried to read that notebook.

Thea didn't mind Ray's travel-lecture expressions. She dodged them, unconsciously, as she did her father's professional palaver. The light in Ray's pale-blue eyes and the feeling in his voice more than made up for the stiffness of his language.

"Were the Cliff-Dwellers really clever with their hands, Ray, or do you always have to make allowance and say, 'That was pretty good for an Indian'?" she asked

Ray went down into the car to give some instructions to Giddy. "Well," he said when he returned, "about the aborigines: once or twice I've been with some fellows who were cracking burial mounds. Always felt a little ashamed of it, but we did pull out some remarkable things. We got some pottery out whole; seemed pretty fine to me. I guess their women were their artists. We found lots of old shoes and sandals made out of yucca fiber, neat and strong; and feather blankets, too."

"Feather blankets? You never told me about them."

"Didn't I? The old fellows—or the squaws—wove a close

netting of yucca fiber, and then tied little bunches of down feathers, overlapping, just the way feathers grow on a bird. Some of them were feathered on both sides. You can't get anything warmer than that, now, can you?—or prettier. What I like about those old aborigines is, that they got all their ideas from nature."

Thea laughed. "That means you're going to say something about girls' wearing corsets. But some of your Indians flattened their babies' heads, and that's worse than wearing corsets."

"Give me an Indian girl's figure for beauty," Ray insisted. "And a girl with a voice like yours ought to have plenty of lung-action. But you know my sentiments on that subject. I was going to tell you about the handsomest thing we ever looted out of those burial mounds. It was on a woman, too, I regret to say. She was preserved as perfect as any mummy that ever came out of the pyramids. She had a big string of turquoises around her neck, and she was wrapped in a fox-fur cloak, lined with little yellow feathers that must have come off wild canaries. Can you beat that, now? The fellow that claimed it sold it to a Boston man for a hundred and fifty dollars."

Thea looked at him admiringly. "Oh, Ray, and didn't you get anything off her, to remember her by, even? She must have been a princess."

Ray took a wallet from the pocket of the coat that was hanging beside him, and drew from it a little lump wrapped in worn tissue paper. In a moment a stone, soft and blue as a robin's egg, lay in the hard palm of his hand. It was a turquoise, rubbed smooth in the Indian finish, which is so much more beautiful than the incongruous high polish the white man gives that tender stone. "I got this from her necklace. See the hole where the string went through? You know how the Indians drill them? Work the drill with their teeth. You like it, don't you? They're just right for you. Blue and yellow are the Swedish colors." Ray looked intently at her head, bent over his hand, and then gave his whole attention to the track.

"I'll tell you, Thee," he began after a pause, "I'm going to form a camping party one of these days and persuade your *padre* to take you and your mother down to that country, and we'll live in the rock houses—they're as comfortable as can be—and start the cook fires up in 'em once again. I'll go into the burial mounds and get you more keepsakes than any girl ever had before." Ray had planned such an expedition for his wedding journey, and it made his heart thump to see how Thea's eyes kindled when he talked about it. "I've learned more down there about what makes history," he went on, "than in all the books I've ever read. When you sit in the sun and let your heels hang out of a doorway that drops a thousand feet, ideas come to you. You begin to feel what the human race has been up against from the beginning. There's something mighty elevating about those old habitations. You feel like it's up to you to do your best, on account of those fellows having it so hard. You feel like you owed them something."

At Wassiwappa, Ray got instructions to sidetrack until Thirty-six went by. After reading the message, he turned to his guests. "I'm afraid this will hold us up about two hours, Mrs. Kronborg, and we won't get into Denver till near midnight."

"That won't trouble me," said Mrs. Kronborg contentedly. "They know me at the Y.W.C.A., and they'll let me in any time of night. I came to see the country, not to make time. I've always wanted to get out at this white place and look around, and now I'll have a chance. What makes it so white?"

"Some kind of chalky rock." Ray sprang to the ground and gave Mrs. Kronborg his hand. "You can get soil of any color in Colorado; match most any ribbon."

While Ray was getting his train on to a side track, Mrs Kronborg strolled off to examine the post-office and station house; these, with the water tank, made up the town. The station agent "batched"* and raised chickens. He ran out to meet Mrs. Kronborg; clutched at her feverishly, and began telling her at once how lonely he was and what bad luck he was having with his poultry. She went to his chicken yard with him, and prescribed for gapes.

Wassiwappa seemed a dreary place enough to people who looked for verdure, a brilliant place to people who liked color. Beside the station house there was a blue-grass plot, protected by a red plank fence, and six fly-bitten box-elder trees, not much larger than bushes, were kept alive by frequent hosings from the water plug. Over the windows some dusty morning-glory vines were trained on strings. All the country about was broken up into low chalky hills, which were so intensely white, and spotted so evenly with sage, that they looked like white leopards crouching. White dust powdered everything, and the light was so intense that the station agent usually wore blue glasses. Behind the station there was a water course, which roared in flood time, and a basin in the soft white rock where a pool of alkali water flashed in the sun like a mirror. The agent looked almost as sick as his chickens, and Mrs. Kronborg at once invited him to lunch with her party. He had, he confessed, a distaste for his own cooking, and lived mainly on soda crackers and canned beef. He laughed apologetically when Mrs. Kronborg said she guessed she'd look about for a shady place to eat lunch.

She walked up the track to the water tank, and there, in the narrow shadows cast by the uprights on which the tank stood, she found two tramps. They sat up and stared at her, heavy with sleep. When she asked them where they were going, they told her "to the coast." They rested by day and traveled by night; walked the ties unless they could steal a ride, they said; adding that "these Western roads were getting strict." Their faces were blistered, their eyes blood-shot, and their shoes looked fit only for the trash pile.

"I suppose you're hungry?" Mrs. Kronborg asked. "I suppose you both drink?" she went on thoughtfully, not censoriously.

The huskier of the two hoboes, a bushy, bearded fellow, rolled his eyes and said, "I wonder?" But the other, who was old and spare, with a sharp nose and watery eyes, sighed. "Some has one affliction, some another," he said.

Mrs. Kronborg reflected. "Well," she said at last, "you can't get liquor here, anyway. I am going to ask you to vacate, because I want to have a little picnic under this tank for the freight crew that brought me along. I wish I had lunch enough to provide you, but I ain't. The station agent says he gets his provisions over there at the post-office store, and if you are hungry you can get some canned stuff there." She opened her handbag and gave each of the tramps a half-dollar.

The old man wiped his eyes with his forefinger. "Thank 'ee, ma'am. A can of tomatters will taste pretty good to me. I wasn't always walkin' ties; I had a good job in Cleveland before—"

The hairy tramp turned on him fiercely. "Aw, shut up on that, grandpaw! Ain't you got no gratitude? What do you want to hand the lady that fur?"

The old man hung his head and turned away. As he went off, his comrade looked after him and said to Mrs. Kronborg: "It's true, what he says. He had a job in the car shops; but he had bad luck." They both limped away toward the store, and Mrs. Kronborg sighed. She was not afraid of tramps. She always talked to them, and never turned one away. She hated to think how many of them there were, crawling along the tracks over that vast country.

Her reflections were cut short by Ray and Giddy and Thea, who came bringing the lunch box and water bottles. Although there was not shadow enough to accommodate all the party at once, the air under the tank was distinctly cooler than the surrounding air, and the drip made a pleasant sound in that breathless noon. The station agent ate as if he had never been fed before, apologizing every time he took another piece of fried chicken. Giddy was unabashed before the devilled eggs of which he had spoken so scornfully last night. After lunch the men lit their pipes and lay back against the uprights that supported the tank.

"This is the sunny side of railroading, all right," Giddy drawled luxuriously.

"You fellows grumble too much," said Mrs. Kronborg as she corked the pickle jar. "Your job has its drawbacks, but it don't tie you down. Of course there's the risk; but I believe a man's watched over, and he can't be hurt on the railroad or anywhere else if it's intended he shouldn't be."

Giddy laughed. "Then the trains must be operated by fellows the Lord has it in for, Mrs. Kronborg. They figure it out that a railroad man's only due to last eleven years; then it's his turn to be smashed."

"That's a dark Providence, I don't deny," Mrs. Kronborn admitted. "But there's lots of things in life that's hard to understand."

"I guess!" murmured Giddy, looking off at the spotted white hills.

Ray smoked in silence, watching Thea and her mother clear away the lunch. He was thinking that Mrs. Kronborg had in her face the same serious look that Thea had; only hers was calm and satisfied, and Thea's was intense and questioning. But in both it was a large kind of look, that was not all the time being broken up and convulsed by trivial things. They both carried their heads like Indian women, with a kind of noble unconsciousness. He got so tired of women who were always nodding and jerking; apologizing, deprecating, coaxing, insinuating with their heads.

When Ray's party set off again that afternoon the sun beat fiercely into the cupola, and Thea curled up in one of the seats at the back of the car and had a nap.

As the short twilight came on, Giddy took a turn in the cupola, and Ray came down and sat with Thea on the rear platform of the caboose and watched the darkness come in soft waves over the plain. They were now about thirty miles from Denver, and the mountains looked very near. The great toothed wall behind which the sun had gone down now separated into four distinct ranges, one behind the other. They were a very pale blue, a color scarcely stronger than wood smoke, and the sunset had left bright streaks in the snow-filled gorges. In the clear, yellow-streaked sky the stars were coming out, flickering like newly lighted lamps, growing steadier and more golden as the sky darkened and the land beneath them fell into complete shadow. It was a cool, restful darkness that was not black or forbidding, but somehow open and free; the night of high plains where there is no moistness or mistiness in the atmosphere.

Ray lit his pipe. "I never get tired of them old stars, Thee. I miss 'em up in Washington and Oregon where it's misty. Like 'em best down in Mother Mexico, where they have everything their own way. I'm not for any country where the stars are dim." Ray paused and drew on his pipe. "I don't know as I ever really noticed 'em much till that first year I herded sheep up in Wyoming. That was the year the blizzard caught me."

"And you lost all your sheep, didn't you, Ray?" Thea spoke sympathetically. "Was the man who owned them nice about it?"

"Yes, he was a good loser. But I didn't get over it for a long while. Sheep are so damned resigned. Sometimes, to this day, when I'm dog-tired, I try to save them sheep all night long. It comes kind of hard on a boy when he first finds out how little he is, and how big everything else is."

Thea moved restlessly toward him and dropped her chin on her hand, looking at a low star that seemed to rest just on the rim of the earth. "I don't see how you stood it. I don't believe I could. I don't see how people can stand it to get knocked out, anyhow!" She spoke with such fierceness that Ray glanced at her in surprise. She was sitting on the floor of the car, crouching like a little animal about to spring.

"No occasion for you to see," he said warmly. "There'll always be plenty of other people to take the knocks for you."

"That's nonsense, Ray." Thea spoke impatiently and leaned lower still, frowning at the red star. "Everybody's up against it for himself, succeeds or fails—himself."

"In one way, yes," Ray admitted, knocking the sparks from his pipe out into the soft darkness that seemed to flow like a river beside the car. "But when you look at it another way, there are a lot of halfway people in this world who help the winners win, and the failers fail. If a man stumbles, there's plenty of people to push him down. But if he's like 'the youth who bore,'* those same people are foreordained to help him along. They may hate to, worse than blazes, and they may do a lot of cussin' about it, but they have to help the winners and they can't dodge it. It's a natural law, like what keeps the big clock up there going, little wheels and big, and no mix-up." Ray's hand and his pipe were suddenly outlined against the sky. "Ever occur to you, Thee, that they have to be on time close enough to *make time*? The Dispatcher up there must have a long head." Pleased with his similitude, Ray went back to the lookout. Going into Denver, he had to keep a sharp watch.

Giddy came down, cheerful at the prospect of getting into port, and singing a new topical ditty had come up from the Santa Fé by way of La Junta. Nobody knows who makes these songs; they seem to follow events automatically. Mrs. Kronborg made Giddy sing the whole twelve verses of this one, and laughed until she wiped her eyes. The story was that of Katie Casey, head dining-room girl at Winslow, Arizona, who was unjustly discharged by the Harvey House manager. Her suitor, the yard-master, took the switchmen out on a strike until she was re-instated. Freight trains from the east and the west piled up at Winslow until the yards looked like a log-jam. The division superintendent, who was in California, had to wire instructions for Katie Casey's restoration before he could get his trains running. Giddy's song told all this with much detail, both tender and technical, and after each of the dozen verses came the refrain:—

"Oh, who would think that Katie Casey owned the Santa Fé?
But it really looks that way,
The dispatcher's turnin' gray,
All the crews is off their pay;
She can hold the freight from Albuquerq' to Needles any day;
The division superintendent, he come home from Monterey,
Just to see if things was pleasin' Katie Ca—a—a—sey."

Thea laughed with her mother and applauded Giddy. Everything was so kindly and comfortable; Giddy and Ray, and their hospitable little house, and the easy-going country, and the stars. She curled up on the seat again with that warm, sleepy feeling of the friendliness of the world—which nobody keeps very long, and which she was to lose early and irrevocably.

XVII

THE summer flew by. Thea was glad when Ray Kennedy had a Sunday in town and could take her driving. Out among the sand hills she could forget the "new room" which was the scene of wearing and fruitless labor. Dr. Archie was away from home a good deal that year. He had put all his money into mines above Colorado Springs, and he hoped for great returns from them.

In the fall of that year, Mr. Kronborg decided that Thea ought to show more interest in church work. He put it to her frankly, one night at supper, before the whole family. "How can I insist on the other girls in the congregation being active in the work, when one of my own daughters manifests so little interest?"

"But I sing every Sunday morning, and I have to give up one night a week to choir practice," Thea declared rebelliously, pushing back her plate with an angry determination to eat nothing more.

"One night a week is not enough for the pastor's daughter," her father replied. "You won't do anything in the sewing society, and you won't take part in the Christian Endeavor or the Band of Hope. Very well, you must make it up in other ways. I want some one to play the organ and lead the singing at prayer-meeting this winter. Deacon Potter told me some time ago that he thought there would be more interest in our prayer-meetings if we had the organ. Miss Meyers don't feel that she can play on Wednesday nights. And there ought to be somebody to start the hymns. Mrs. Potter is getting old, and she always starts them too high. It won't take much of your time, and it will keep people from talking."

This argument conquered Thea, though she left the table sullenly. The fear of the tongue, that terror of little towns, is usually felt more keenly by the minister's family than by other households. Whenever the Kronborgs wanted to do anything, even to buy a new carpet, they had to take counsel together as to whether people would talk. Mrs. Kronborg had her own conviction that people talked when they felt like it, and said what they chose, no matter how the minister's family conducted themselves. But she did not impart these dangerous ideas to her children. Thea was still under the belief that public opinion could be placated; that if you clucked often enough, the hens would mistake you for one of themselves.

Mrs. Kronborg did not have any particular zest for prayer-meetings, and she stayed at home whenever she had a valid excuse. Thor was too old to furnish such an excuse now, so every Wednesday night, unless one of the children was sick, she trudged off with Thea, behind Mr. Kronborg. At first Thea was terribly bored. But she got used to prayer-meeting, got even to feel a mournful interest in it.

The exercises were always pretty much the same. After the first hymn her father read a passage from the Bible, usually a Psalm. Then there was another hymn, and then her father commented upon the passage he had read and, as he said, "applied the Word to our necessities." After a third hymn, the meeting was declared open, and the old men and women took turns at praying and talking. Mrs. Kronborg never spoke in meeting. She told people firmly that she had been brought up to keep silent and let the men talk, but she gave respectful attention to the others, sitting with her hands folded in her lap.

The prayer-meeting audience was always small. The young and energetic members of the congregation came only once or twice a year, "to keep people from talking." The usual Wednesday night gathering was made up of old women, with perhaps six or eight old men, and a few sickly girls who had not much interest in life; two of them, indeed, were already preparing to die. Thea accepted the mournfulness of the prayer-meetings as a kind of spiritual discipline, like funerals. She always read late after she went home and felt a stronger wish than usual to live and to be happy.

The meetings were conducted in the Sunday-School room, where there were wooden chairs instead of pews; an old map of Palestine hung on the wall, and the bracket lamps gave out only a dim light. The old women sat motionless as Indians in their shawls and bonnets; some of them wore long black mourning veils. The old men drooped in their chairs. Every back, every face, every head said "resignation." Often there were long silences, when you could hear nothing but the crackling of the soft coal in the stove and the muffled cough of one of the sick girls.

There was one nice old lady,—tall, erect, self-respecting, with a delicate white face and a soft voice. She never whined, and what she said was always cheerful, though she spoke so nervously that Thea knew she dreaded getting up, and that she made a real

sacrifice to, as she said, "testify to the goodness of her Saviour."
She was the mother of the girl who coughed, and Thea used to
wonder how she explained things to herself. There was, indeed,
only one woman who talked because she was, as Mr. Kronborg
said, "tonguey." The others were somehow impressive. They told
about the sweet thoughts that came to them while they were at
their work; how, amid their household tasks, they were suddenly
lifted by the sense of a divine Presence. Sometimes they told of
their first conversion, of how in their youth that higher Power
had made itself known to them. Old Mr. Carsen, the carpenter,
who gave his services as janitor to the church, used often to tell
how, when he was a young man and a scoffer, bent on the destruction of both body and soul, his Saviour had come to him in the
Michigan woods and had stood, it seemed to him, beside the tree
he was felling; and how he dropped his axe and knelt in prayer "to
Him who died for us upon the tree." Thea always wanted to ask
him more about it; about his mysterious wickedness, and about
the vision.

Sometimes the old people would ask for prayers for their
absent children. Sometimes they asked their brothers and sisters
in Christ to pray that they might be stronger against temptations.
One of the sick girls used to ask them to pray that she might have
more faith in the times of depression that came to her, "when all
the way before seemed dark." She repeated that husky phrase so
often, that Thea always remembered it.

One old woman, who never missed a Wednesday night, and
who nearly always took part in the meeting, came all the way up
from the depot settlement. She always wore a black crocheted
"fascinator"* over her thin white hair, and she made long, tremu-
lous prayers, full of railroad terminology. She had six sons in the
service of different railroads, and she always prayed "for the boys
on the road, who know not at what moment they may be cut off.
When, in Thy divine wisdom, their hour is upon them, may they,
O our Heavenly Father, see only white lights along the road to
Eternity." She used to speak, too, of "the engines that race with
death"; and though she looked so old and little when she was on
her knees, and her voice was so shaky, her prayers had a thrill of

speed and danger in them; they made one think of the deep black canyons, the slender trestles, the pounding trains. Thea liked to look at her sunken eyes that seemed full of wisdom, at her black thread gloves, much too long in the fingers and so meekly folded one over the other. Her face was brown, and worn away as rocks are worn by water. There are many ways of describing that color of age, but in reality it is not like parchment, or like any of the things it is said to be like. That brownness and that texture of skin are found only in the faces of old human creatures, who have worked hard and who have always been poor.

One bitterly cold night in December the prayer-meeting seemed to Thea longer than usual. The prayers and the talks went on and on. It was as if the old people were afraid to go out into the cold, or were stupefied by the hot air of the room. She had left a book at home that she was impatient to get back to. At last the Doxology* was sung, but the old people lingered about the stove to greet each other, and Thea took her mother's arm and hurried out to the frozen sidewalk, before her father could get away. The wind was whistling up the street and whipping the naked cottonwood trees against the telegraph poles and the sides of the houses. Thin snow clouds were flying overhead, so that the sky looked gray, with a dull phosphorescence. The icy streets and the shingle roofs of the houses were gray, too. All along the street, shutters banged or windows rattled, or gates wobbled, held by their latch but shaking on loose hinges. There was not a cat or a dog in Moonstone that night that was not given a warm shelter; the cats under the kitchen stove, the dogs in barns or coal-sheds. When Thea and her mother reached home, their mufflers were covered with ice, where their breath had frozen. They hurried into the house and made a dash for the parlor and the hard-coal burner, behind which Gunner was sitting on a stool, reading his Jules Verne* book. The door stood open into the dining-room, which was heated from the parlor. Mr. Kronborg always had a lunch when he came home from prayer-meeting, and his pumpkin pie and milk were set out on the dining-table. Mrs. Kronborg said she thought she felt hungry, too, and asked Thea if she didn't want something to eat.

"No, I'm not hungry, mother. I guess I'll go upstairs."

"I expect you've got some book up there," said Mrs. Kronborg, bringing out another pie. "You'd better bring it down here and read. Nobody'll disturb you, and it's terrible cold up in that loft."

Thea was always assured that no one would disturb her if she read downstairs, but the boys talked when they came in, and her father fairly delivered discourses after he had been renewed by half a pie and a pitcher of milk.

"I don't mind the cold. I'll take a hot brick up for my feet. I put one in the stove before I left, if one of the boys hasn't stolen it. Good-night, mother." Thea got her brick and lantern, and dashed upstairs through the windy loft. She undressed at top speed and got into bed with her brick. She put a pair of white knitted gloves on her hands, and pinned over her head a piece of soft flannel that had been one of Thor's long petticoats when he was a baby. Thus equipped, she was ready for business. She took from her table a thick paper-backed volume, one of the "line" of paper novels the druggist kept to sell to traveling men. She had bought it, only yesterday, because the first sentence interested her very much, and because she saw, as she glanced over the pages, the magical names of two Russian cities. The book was a poor translation of "Anna Karenina."* Thea opened it at a mark, and fixed her eyes intently upon the small print. The hymns, the sick girl, the resigned black figures were forgotten. It was the night of the ball in Moscow.

Thea would have been astonished if she could have known how, years afterward, when she had need of them, those old faces were to come back to her, long after they were hidden away under the earth; that they would seem to her then as full of meaning, as mysteriously marked by Destiny, as the people who danced the mazurka under the elegant Korsunsky.*

XVIII

MR. KRONBORG was too fond of his ease and too sensible to worry his children much about religion. He was more sincere than many preachers, but when he spoke to his family about matters of conduct it was usually with a regard for keeping up appearances. The church and church work were discussed in the family like the routine of any other business. Sunday was the hard day of the week with them, just as Saturday was the busy day with the merchants on Main Street. Revivals were seasons of extra work and pressure, just as threshing-time was on the farms. Visiting elders had to be lodged and cooked for, the folding-bed in the parlor was let down, and Mrs. Kronborg had to work in the kitchen all day long and attend the night meetings.

During one of these revivals Thea's sister Anna professed religion with, as Mrs. Kronborg said, "a good deal of fluster." While Anna was going up to the mourners' bench nightly and asking for the prayers of the congregation, she disseminated general gloom throughout the household, and after she joined the church she took on an air of "set-apartness" that was extremely trying to her brothers and her sister, though they realized that Anna's sanctimoniousness was perhaps a good thing for their father. A preacher ought to have one child who did more than merely acquiesce in religious observances, and Thea and the boys were glad enough that it was Anna and not one of themselves who assumed this obligation.

"Anna, she's American," Mrs. Kronborg used to say. The Scandinavian mould of countenance, more or less marked in each of the other children, was scarcely discernible in her, and she looked enough like other Moonstone girls to be thought pretty. Anna's nature was conventional, like her face. Her position as the minister's eldest daughter was important to her, and she tried to live up to it. She read sentimental religious story-books and emulated the spiritual struggles and magnanimous behavior of their persecuted heroines. Everything had to be interpreted for Anna. Her opinions about the smallest and most commonplace things were gleaned from the Denver papers, the church weeklies, from sermons and Sunday-School addresses. Scarcely anything was attractive to her in its natural state—indeed, scarcely anything was decent until it was clothed by the opinion of some authority. Her ideas about habit, character, duty, love, marriage, were grouped under heads, like a book of popular quotations, and were totally unrelated to the emergencies of human living. She discussed all these subjects with other Methodist girls of her age. They would spend hours, for instance, in deciding what they would or would not tolerate in a suitor or a husband, and the frailties of masculine nature were too often a subject of discussion among them. In her behavior Anna was a harmless girl, mild except where her prejudices were concerned, neat and industrious, with no graver fault than priggishness; but her mind had really shocking habits of classification. The wickedness of Denver and of Chicago, and even of Moonstone, occupied her thoughts too much. She had none of the delicacy that goes with a nature of warm impulses, but the kind of fishy curiosity which justifies itself by an expression of horror.

Thea, and all Thea's ways and friends, seemed indecorous to Anna. She not only felt a grave social discrimination against the Mexicans; she could not forget that Spanish Johnny was a drunkard and that "nobody knew what he did when he ran away from home." Thea pretended, of course, that she liked the Mexicans because they were fond of music; but every one knew that music was nothing very real, and that it did not matter in a girl's relations with people. What was real, then, and what did matter? Poor Anna!

Anna approved of Ray Kennedy as a young man of steady habits and blameless life, but she regretted that he was an atheist, and that he was not a passenger conductor with brass buttons on his coat. On the whole, she wondered what such an exemplary young man found to like in Thea. Dr. Archie she treated respectfully because of his position in Moonstone, but she *knew* he had kissed the Mexican barytone's pretty daughter, and she had a whole *dossier** of evidence about his behavior in his hours of relaxation in Denver. He was "fast," and it was because he was "fast" that Thea liked him. Thea always liked that kind of people. Dr. Archie's whole manner with Thea, Anna often told her mother, was too free. He was always putting his hand on Thea's head, or holding her hand while he laughed and looked down at her. The kindlier manifestation of human nature (about which Anna sang and talked, in the interests of which she went to conventions and wore white ribbons) were never realities to her after all. She did not believe in them. It was only in attitudes of protest or reproof, clinging to the cross, that human beings could be even temporarily decent.

Preacher Kronborg's secret convictions were very much like Anna's. He believed that his wife was absolutely good, but there was not a man or woman in his congregation whom he trusted all the way.

Mrs. Kronborg, on the other hand, was likely to find something to admire in almost any human conduct that was positive and energetic. She could always be taken in by the stories of tramps and runaway boys. She went to the circus and admired the bareback riders, who were "likely good enough women in their way." She admired Dr. Archie's fine physique and well-cut clothes as much as Thea did, and said she "felt it was a privilege to be handled by such a gentleman when she was sick."

Soon after Anna became a church member she began to remonstrate with Thea about practicing—playing "secular music"—on Sunday. One Sunday the dispute in the parlor grew warm and was carried to Mrs. Kronborg in the kitchen. She listened judicially and told Anna to read the chapter about how Naaman the leper was permitted to bow down in the house of Rimmon.* Thea went back to the piano, and Anna lingered to say that, since she was in the right, her mother should have supported her.

"No," said Mrs. Kronborg, rather indifferently, "I can't see it that way, Anna. I never forced you to practice, and I don't see as I should keep Thea from it. I like to hear her, and I guess your father does. You and Thea will likely follow different lines, and I don't see as I'm called upon to bring you up alike."

Anna looked meek and abused. "Of course all the church

people must hear her. Ours is the only noisy house on this street. You hear what she's playing now, don't you?"

Mrs. Kronborg rose from browning her coffee. "Yes; it's the Blue Danube waltzes. I'm familiar with 'em. If any of the church people come at you, you just send 'em to me. I ain't afraid to speak out on occasion, and I wouldn't mind one bit telling the Ladies' Aid a few things about standard composers." Mrs. Kronborg smiled, and added thoughtfully, "No, I wouldn't mind that one bit."

Anna went about with a reserved and distant air for a week, and Mrs. Kronborg suspected that she held a larger place than usual in her daughter's prayers; but that was another thing she didn't mind.

Although revivals were merely a part of the year's work, like examination week at school, and although Anna's piety impressed her very little, a time came when Thea was perplexed about religion. A scourge of typhoid broke out in Moonstone and several of Thea's schoolmates died of it. She went to their funerals, saw them put into the ground, and wondered a good deal about them. But a certain grim incident, which caused the epidemic, troubled her even more than the death of her friends.

Early in July, soon after Thea's fifteenth birthday, a particularly disgusting sort of tramp came into Moonstone in an empty box car. Thea was sitting in the hammock in the front yard when he first crawled up to the town from the depot, carrying a bundle wrapped in dirty ticking under one arm, and under the other a wooden box with rusty screening nailed over one end. He had a thin, hungry face covered with black hair. It was just before supper-time when he came along, and the street smelled of fried potatoes and fried onions and coffee. Thea saw him sniffing the air greedily and walking slower and slower. He looked over the fence. She hoped he would not stop at their gate, for her mother never turned any one away, and this was the dirtiest and most utterly wretched-looking tramp she had ever seen. There was a terrible odor about him, too. She caught it even at that distance, and put her handkerchief to her nose. A moment later she was sorry, for she knew that he had noticed it. He looked away and shuffled a little faster.

A few days later Thea heard that the tramp had camped in an empty shack over on the east edge of town, beside the ravine, and was trying to give a miserable sort of show there. He told the boys who went to see what he was doing, that he had traveled with a circus. His bundle contained a filthy clown's suit, and his box held half a dozen rattlesnakes.

Saturday night, when Thea went to the butcher shop to get the chickens for Sunday, she heard the whine of an accordion and saw a crowd before one of the saloons. There she found the tramp, his bony body grotesquely attired in the clown's suit, his face shaved and painted white,—the sweat trickling through the paint and washing it away,—and his eyes wild and feverish. Pulling the accordion in and out seemed to be almost too great an effort for him, and he panted to the tune of "Marching through Georgia." After a considerable crowd had gathered, the tramp exhibited his box of snakes, announced that he would now pass the hat, and that when the onlookers had contributed the sum of one dollar, he would eat "one of these living reptiles." The crowd began to cough and murmur, and the saloon keeper rushed off for the marshal, who arrested the wretch for giving a show without a license and hurried him away to the calaboose.

The calaboose stood in a sunflower patch,—an old hut with a barred window and a padlock on the door. The tramp was utterly filthy and there was no way to give him a bath. The law made no provision to grub-stake vagrants, so after the constable had detained the tramp for twenty-four hours, he released him and told him to "get out of town, and get quick." The fellow's rattlesnakes had been killed by the saloon keeper. He hid in a box car in the freight yard, probably hoping to get a ride to the next station, but he was found and put out. After that he was seen no more. He had disappeared and left no trace except an ugly, stupid word, chalked on the black paint of the seventy-five-foot standpipe which was the reservoir for the Moonstone water-supply; the same word, in another tongue, that the French soldier shouted at Waterloo to the English officer who bade the Old Guard surrender;* a comment on life which the defeated, along the hard roads of the world, sometimes bawl at the victorious.

A week after the tramp excitement had passed over, the city water began to smell and to taste. The Kronborgs had a well in their back yard and did not use city water, but they heard the complaints of their neighbors. At first people said that the town well was full of rotting cottonwood roots, but the engineer at the pumping-station convinced the mayor that the water left the well untainted. Mayors reason slowly, but, the well being eliminated, the official mind had to travel toward the standpipe— there was no other track for it to go in. The standpipe amply rewarded investigation. The tramp had got even with Moonstone. He had climbed the standpipe by the handholds and let himself down into seventy-five feet of cold water, with his shoes and hat and roll of ticking. The city council had a mild panic and passed a new ordinance about tramps. But the fever had already broken out, and several adults and half a dozen children died of it.

Thea had always found everything that happened in Moonstone exciting, disasters particularly so. It was gratifying to read sensational Moonstone items in the Denver paper. But she wished she had not chanced to see the tramp as he came into town that evening, sniffing the supper-laden air. His face remained unpleasantly clear in her memory, and her mind struggled with the problem of his behavior as if it were a hard page in arithmetic. Even when she was practicing, the drama of the tramp kept going on in the back of her head, and she was constantly trying to make herself realize what pitch of hatred or despair could drive a man to do such a hideous thing. She kept seeing him in his bedraggled clown suit, the white paint on his roughly shaven face, playing his accordion before the saloon. She had noticed his lean body, his high, bald forehead that sloped back like a curved metal lid. How could people fall so far out of fortune? She tried to talk to Ray Kennedy about her perplexity, but Ray would not discuss things of that sort with her. It was in his sentimental conception of women that they should be deeply religious, though men were at liberty to doubt and finally to deny. A picture called "The

Soul Awakened,"* popular in Moonstone parlors, pretty well
interpreted Ray's idea of woman's spiritual nature.

One evening when she was haunted by the figure of the tramp,
Thea went up to Dr. Archie's office. She found him sewing up
two bad gashes in the face of a little boy who had been kicked by a
mule. After the boy had been bandaged and sent away with his
father, Thea helped the doctor wash and put away the surgical
instruments. Then she dropped into her accustomed seat beside
his desk and began to talk about the tramp. Her eyes were hard
and green with excitement, the doctor noticed.

"It seems to me, Dr. Archie, that the whole town's to blame.
I'm to blame, myself. I know he saw me hold my nose when he
went by. Father's to blame. If he believes the Bible, he ought to
have gone to the calaboose and cleaned that man up and taken
care of him. That's what I can't understand; do people believe the
Bible, or don't they? If the next life is all that matters, and we're
put here to get ready for it, then why do we try to make money, or
learn things or have a good time? There's not one person in
Moonstone that really lives the way the New Testament says.
Does it matter, or don't it?"

Dr. Archie swung round in his chair and looked at her, honestly and leniently. "Well, Thea, it seems to me like this. Every
people has had its religion. All religions are good, and all are
pretty much alike. But I don't see how we could live up to them in
the sense you mean. I've thought about it a good deal, and I can't
help feeling that while we are in this world we have to live for the
best things of this world, and those things are material and positive. Now, most religions are passive, and they tell us chiefly what
we should not do." The doctor moved restlessly, and his eyes
hunted for something along the opposite wall: "See here, my girl,
take out the years of early childhood and the time we spend in
sleep and dull old age, and we only have about twenty able, waking
years. That's not long enough to get acquainted with half the fine
things that have been done in the world, much less to do anything
ourselves. I think we ought to keep the Commandments and help
other people all we can; but the main thing is to live those twenty
splendid years; to do all we can and enjoy all we can."

Dr. Archie met his little friend's searching gaze, the look of acute inquiry which always touched him.

"But poor fellows like that tramp—" she hesitated and wrinkled her forehead.

The doctor leaned foward and put his hand protectingly over hers, which lay clenched on the green felt desk-top. "Ugly accidents happen, Thea; always have and always will. But the failures are swept back into the pile and forgotten. They don't leave any lasting scar in the world, and they don't affect the future. The things that last are the good things. The people who forge ahead and do something, they really count." He saw tears on her cheeks, and he remembered that he had never seen her cry before, not even when she crushed her finger when she was little. He rose and walked to the window, came back and sat down on the edge of his chair.

"Forget the tramp, Thea. This is a great big world, and I want you to get about and see it all. You're going to Chicago some day, and do something with that fine voice of yours. You're going to be a number one musician and make us proud of you. Take Mary Anderson,* now; even the tramps are proud of her. There isn't a tramp along the 'Q' system who hasn't heard of her. We all like people who do things, even if we only see their faces on a cigar-box lid."

They had a long talk. Thea felt that Dr. Archie had never let himself out to her so much before. It was the most grown-up conversation she had ever had with him. She left his office happy, flattered and stimulated. She ran for a long while about the white, moonlit streets, looking up at the stars and the bluish night, at the quiet houses sunk in black shade, the glittering sand hills. She loved the familiar trees, and the people in those little houses, and she loved the unknown world beyond Denver. She felt as if she were being pulled in two, between the desire to go away forever and the desire to stay forever. She had only twenty years—no time to lose.

Many a night that summer she left Dr. Archie's office with a desire to run and run about those quiet streets until she wore out her shoes, or wore out the streets themselves; when her chest ached and it seemed as if her heart were spreading all over the

desert. When she went home, it was not to go to sleep. She used
to drag her mattress beside her low window and lie awake for a
long while, vibrating with excitement, as a machine vibrates from
speed. Life rushed in upon her through that window—or so it
seemed. In reality, of course, life rushes from within, not from
without. There is no work of art so big or so beautiful that it was
not once all contained in some youthful body, like this one which
lay on the floor in the moonlight, pulsing with ardor and anticipation. It was on such nights that Thea Kronborg learned the thing
that old Dumas* meant when he told the Romanticists* that to
make a drama he needed but one passion and four walls.

XIX

It is well for its peace of mind that the traveling public takes
railroads so much for granted. The only men who are incurably
nervous about railway travel are the railroad operatives. A railroad man never forgets that the next run may be his turn.

On a single-track road, like that upon which Ray Kennedy
worked, the freight trains make their way as best they can
between passenger trains. Even when there is such a thing as a
freight time-schedule, it is merely a form. Along the one track
dozens of fast and slow trains dash in both directions, kept from
collision only by the brains in the dispatcher's office. If one passenger train is late, the whole schedule must be revised in an
instant; the trains following must be warned, and those moving
toward the belated train must be assigned new meeting-places.

Between the shifts and modifications of the passenger schedule, the freight trains play a game of their own. They have no right
to the track at any given time, but are supposed to be on it when it
is free, and to make the best time they can between passenger
trains. A freight train, on a single-track road, gets anywhere at all
only by stealing bases.

Ray Kennedy had stuck to the freight service, although he had
had opportunities to go into passenger service at higher pay. He
always regarded railroading as a temporary makeshift, until he

"got into something," and he disliked the passenger service. No brass buttons for him, he said; too much like a livery. While he was railroading he would wear a jumper, thank you!

The wreck that "caught" Ray was a very commonplace one; nothing thrilling about it, and it got only six lines in the Denver papers. It happened about daybreak one morning, only thirty-two miles from home.

At four o'clock in the morning Ray's train had stopped to take water at Saxony, having just rounded the long curve which lies south of that station. It was Joe Giddy's business to walk back along the curve about three hundred yards and put out torpedoes to warn any train which might be coming up from behind—a freight crew is not notified of trains following, and the brakeman is supposed to protect his train. Ray was so fussy about the punctilious observance of orders that almost any brakeman would take a chance once in a while, from natural perversity.

When the train stopped for water that morning, Ray was at the desk in his caboose, making out his report. Giddy took his torpedoes, swung off the rear platform, and glanced back at the curve. He decided that he would not go back to flag this time. If anything was coming up behind, he could hear it in plenty of time. So he ran forward to look after a hot journal that had been bothering him. In a general way, Giddy's reasoning was sound. If a freight train, or even a passenger train, had been coming up behind them, he could have heard it in time. But as it happened, a light engine, which made no noise at all, was coming,—ordered out to help with the freight that was piling up at the other end of the division. This engine got no warning, came round the curve, struck the caboose, went straight through it, and crashed into the heavy lumber car ahead.

The Kronborgs were just sitting down to breakfast, when the night telegraph operator dashed into the yard at a run, and hammered on the front door. Gunner answered the knock, and the telegraph operator told him he wanted to see his father a minute, quick. Mr. Kronborg appeared at the door, napkin in hand. The operator was pale and panting.

"Fourteen was wrecked down at Saxony this morning," he shouted, "and Kennedy's all broke up. We're sending an engine down with the doctor, and the operator at Saxony says Kennedy wants you to come along with us and bring your girl." He stopped for breath.

Mr. Kronborg took off his glasses and began rubbing them with his napkin.

"Bring—I don't understand," he muttered. "How did this happen?"

"No time for that, sir. Getting the engine out now. Your girl, Thea. You'll surely do that for the poor chap. Everybody knows he thinks the world of her." Seeing that Mr. Kronborg showed no indication of having made up his mind, the operator turned to Gunner. "Call your sister, kid. I'm going to ask the girl herself," he blurted out

"Yes, yes, certainly. Daughter," Mr. Kronborg called. He had somewhat recovered himself and reached to the hall hatrack for his hat.

Just as Thea came out on the front porch before the operator had had time to explain to her, Dr. Archie's ponies came up to the gate at a brisk trot. Archie jumped out the moment his driver stopped the team and came up to the bewildered girl without so much as saying good morning to any one. He took her hand with the sympathetic reassuring graveness which had helped her at more than one hard time in her life. "Get your hat, my girl. Kennedy's hurt down the road, and he wants you to run down with me. They'll have a car for us. Get into my buggy, Mr. Kronborg. I'll drive you down, and Larry can come for the team."

The driver jumped out of the buggy and Mr. Kronborg and the doctor got in. Thea, still bewildered, sat on her father's knee. Dr. Archie gave his ponies a smart cut with the whip.

When they reached the depot, the engine, with one car attached, was standing on the main track. The engineer had got his steam up, and was leaning out of the cab impatiently. In a moment they were off. The run to Saxony took forty minutes. Thea sat still in her seat while Dr. Archie and her father talked about the wreck. She took no part in the conversation and asked no questions, but occasionally she looked at Dr. Archie with a frightened, inquiring glance, which he answered by an encouraging nod. Neither he nor her father said anything about how badly Ray was hurt. When the engine stopped near Saxony, the main track was already cleared. As they got out of the car, Dr. Archie pointed to a pile of ties.

"Thea, you'd better sit down here and watch the wreck crew while your father and I go up and look Kennedy over. I'll come back for you when I get him fixed up."

The two men went off up the sand gulch, and Thea sat down and looked at the pile of splintered wood and twisted iron that had lately been Ray's caboose. She was frightened and absentminded. She felt that she ought to be thinking about Ray, but her mind kept racing off to all sorts of trivial and irrelevant things. She wondered whether Grace Johnson would be furious when she came to take her music lesson and found nobody there to give it to her; whether she had forgotten to close the piano last night and whether Thor would get into the new room and mess the keys all up with his sticky fingers; whether Tillie would go upstairs and make her bed for her. Her mind worked fast, but she could fix it upon nothing. The grasshoppers, the lizards, distracted her attention and seemed more real to her than poor Ray.

On their way to the sand bank where Ray had been carried, Dr. Archie and Mr. Kronborg met the Saxony doctor. He shook hands with them.

"Nothing you can do, doctor. I couldn't count the fractures. His back's broken, too. He wouldn't be alive now if he weren't so confoundedly strong, poor chap. No use bothering him. I've given him morphia, one and a half, in eighths."

Dr. Archie hurried on. Ray was lying on a flat canvas litter, under the shelter of a shelving bank, lightly shaded by a slender cottonwood tree. When the doctor and the preacher approached, he looked at them intently.

"Didn't—" he closed his eyes to hide his bitter disappointment.

Dr. Archie knew what was the matter. "Thea's back there, Ray. I'll bring her as soon as I've had a look at you."

Ray looked up. "You might clean me up a trifle, doc. Won't need you for anything else, thank you all the same."

However little there was left of him, that little was certainly Ray Kennedy. His personality was as positive as ever, and the blood and dirt on his face seemed merely accidental, to have nothing to do with the man himself. Dr. Archie told Mr. Kronborg to bring a pail of water, and he began to sponge Ray's face and neck. Mr. Kronborg stood by, nervously rubbing his hands together and trying to think of something to say. Serious situations always embarrassed him and made him formal, even when he felt real sympathy.

"In times like this, Ray," he brought out at last, crumpling up his handkerchief in his long fingers—"in times like this, we don't want to forget the Friend that sticketh closer than a brother."

Ray looked up at him; a lonely, disconsolate smile played over his mouth and his square cheeks. "Never mind about all that, *padre*," he said quietly. "Christ and me fell out long ago."

There was a moment of silence. Then Ray took pity on Mr. Kronborg's embarrassment. "You go back for the little girl, *padre*. I want a word with the doc in private."

Ray talked to Dr. Archie for a few moments, then stopped suddenly, with a broad smile. Over the doctor's shoulder he saw Thea coming up the gulch, in her pink chambray dress, carrying her sun-hat by the strings. Such a yellow head! He often told himself that he "was perfectly foolish about her hair." The sight of her, coming, went through him softly, like the morphia. "There she is," he whispered. "Get the old preacher out of the way, doc. I want to have a little talk with her."

Dr. Archie looked up. Thea was hurrying and yet hanging back. She was more frightened than he had thought she would be. She had gone with him to see very sick people and had always been steady and calm. As she came up, she looked at the ground, and he could see that she had been crying.

Ray Kennedy made an unsuccessful effort to put out his hand. "Hello, little kid, nothing to be afraid of. Darned if I don't believe they've gone and scared you! Nothing to cry about. I'm the same old goods, only a little dented. Sit down on my coat there, and keep me company. I've got to lay still a bit."

Dr. Archie and Mr. Kronborg disappeared. Thea cast a timid glance after them, but she sat down resolutely and took Ray's hand.

"You ain't scared now, are you?" he asked affectionately. "You were a regular brick to come, Thee. Did you get any breakfast?"

"No, Ray, I'm not scared. Only I'm dreadful sorry you're hurt, and I can't help crying."

His broad, earnest face, languid from the opium and smiling with such simple happiness, reassured her. She drew nearer to him and lifted his hand to her knee. He looked at her with his clear, shallow blue eyes. How he loved everything about that face and head! How many nights in his cupola, looking up the track, he had seen that face in the darkness; through the sleet and snow, or in the soft blue air when the moonlight slept on the desert.

"You needn't bother to talk, Thee. The doctor's medicine makes me sort of dopey. But it's nice to have company. Kind of cozy, don't you think? Pull my coat under you more. It's a darned shame I can't wait on you."

"No, no, Ray. I'm all right. Yes, I like it here. And I guess you ought not to talk much, ought you? If you can sleep, I'll stay right here, and be awful quiet. I feel just as much at home with you as ever, now."

That simple, humble, faithful something in Ray's eyes went straight to Thea's heart. She did feel comfortable with him, and happy to give him so much happiness. It was the first time she had ever been conscious of that power to bestow intense happiness by simply being near any one. She always remembered this day as the beginning of that knowledge. She bent over him and put her lips softly to his cheek.

Ray's eyes filled with light. "Oh, do that again, kid!" he said impulsively. Thea kissed him on the forehead, blushing faintly. Ray held her hand fast and closed his eyes with a deep sigh of happiness. The morphia and the sense of her nearness filled him with content. The gold mine, the oil well, the copper ledge—all pipe dreams, he mused, and this was a dream, too. He might have known it before. It had always been like that; the things he admired had always been away out of his reach: a college education, a gentleman's manner, an Englishman's accent—things over his head. And Thea was farther out of his reach than all the rest put together. He had been a fool to imagine it, but he was glad he had been a fool. She had given him one grand dream. Every mile of his run, from Moonstone to Denver, was painted with the colors of that hope. Every cactus knew about it. But now that it was not to be, he knew the truth. Thea was never meant for any rough fellow like him—hadn't he really known that all along, he asked himself? She wasn't meant for common men. She was like wedding cake, a thing to dream on. He raised his eyelids a little. She was stroking his hand and looking off into the distance. He felt in her face that look of unconscious power that Wunsch had seen there. Yes, she was bound for the big terminals of the world; no way stations for her. His lids drooped. In the dark he could see her as she would be after a while; in a box at the Tabor Grand in Denver, with diamonds on her neck and a tiara in her yellow hair, with all the people looking at her through their opera-glasses, and a United States Senator, maybe, talking to her. "Then you'll remember me!" He opened his eyes, and they were full of tears.

Thea leaned closer. "What did you say, Ray? I couldn't hear."

"Then you'll remember me," he whispered.

The spark in his eye, which is one's very self, caught the spark in hers that was herself, and for a moment they looked into each other's natures. Thea realized how good and how great-hearted he was, and he realized about her many things. When that elusive spark of personality retreated in each of them, Thea still saw in his wet eyes her own face, very small, but much prettier than the cracked glass at home had ever shown it. It was the first time she had seen her face in that kindest mirror a woman can ever find.

Ray had felt things in that moment when he seemed to be looking into the very soul of Thea Kronborg. Yes, the gold mine, the oil well, the copper ledge, they'd all got away from him, as things will; but he'd backed a winner once in his life! With all his might he gave his faith to the broad little hand he held. He wished he could leave her the rugged strength of his body to help her through with it all. He would have liked to tell her a little about his old dream,—there seemed long years between him and it already,—but to tell her now would somehow be unfair; wouldn't be quite the straightest thing in the world. Probably she knew, anyway. He looked up quickly. "You know, don't you, Thee, that I think you are just the finest thing I've struck in this world?"

The tears ran down Thea's cheeks. "You're too good to me, Ray. You're a lot too good to me," she faltered.

"Why, kid," he murmured, "everybody in this world's going to be good to you!"

Dr. Archie came to the gulch and stood over his patient. "How's it going?"

"Can't you give me another punch with your pacifier, doc? The little girl had better run along now." Ray released Thea's hand. "See you later, Thee."

She got up and moved away aimlessly, carrying her hat by the strings. Ray looked after her with the exaltation born of bodily pain and said between his teeth, "Always look after that girl, doc. She's a queen!"

Thea and her father went back to Moonstone on the one-o'clock passenger. Dr. Archie stayed with Ray Kennedy until he died, late in the afternoon.

XX

On Monday morning, the day after Ray Kennedy's funeral, Dr. Archie called at Mr. Kronborg's study, a little room behind the church. Mr. Kronborg did not write out his sermons, but spoke from notes jotted upon small pieces of cardboard in a kind of shorthand of his own. As sermons go, they were not worse than most. His conventional rhetoric pleased the majority of his congregation, and Mr. Kronborg was generally regarded as a model preacher. He did not smoke, he never touched spirits. His indulgence in the pleasures of the table was an endearing bond between him and the women of his congregation. He ate enormously, with a zest which seemed incongruous with his spare frame.

This morning the doctor found him opening his mail and reading a pile of advertising circulars with deep attention.

"Good morning, Mr. Kronborg," said Dr. Archie, sitting down. "I came to see you on business. Poor Kennedy asked me to look after his affairs for him. Like most railroad men he spent his wages, except for a few investments in mines which don't look to me very promising. But his life was insured for six hundred dollars in Thea's favor."

Mr. Kronborg wound his feet about the standard of his desk-chair. "I assure you, doctor, this is a complete surprise to me.

"Well, it's not very surprising to me," Dr. Archie went on. "He talked to me about it the day he was hurt. He said he wanted the money to be used in a particular way, and in no other." Dr. Archie paused meaningly.

Mr. Kronborg fidgeted. "I am sure Thea would observe his wishes in every respect."

"No doubt; but he wanted me to see that you agreed to his plan. It seems that for some time Thea has wanted to go away to study music. It was Kennedy's wish that she should take this money and go to Chicago this winter. He felt that it would be an advantage to her in a business way: that even if she came back here to teach, it would give her more authority and make her position here more comfortable."

Mr. Kronborg looked a little startled. "She is very young," he hesitated; "she is barely seventeen. Chicago is a long way from home. We would have to consider. I think, Dr. Archie, we had better consult Mrs. Kronborg."

"I think I can bring Mrs. Kronborg around, if I have your consent. I've always found her pretty level-headed. I have several old classmates practicing in Chicago. One is a throat specialist. He has a good deal to do with singers. He probably knows the best piano teachers and could recommend a boarding-house where music students stay. I think Thea needs to get among a lot of young people who are clever like herself. Here she has no companions but old fellows like me. It's not a natural life for a young girl. She'll either get warped, or wither up before her time. If it will make you and Mrs. Kronborg feel any easier, I'll be glad to take Thea to Chicago and see that she gets started right. This throat man I speak of is a big fellow in his line, and if I can get him interested, he may be able to put her in the way of a good many things. At any rate, he'll know the right teachers. Of course, six hundred dollars won't take her very far, but even half the winter there would be a great advantage. I think Kennedy sized the situation up exactly."

"Perhaps; I don't doubt it. You are very kind, Dr. Archie." Mr. Kronborg was ornamenting his desk-blotter with hieroglyphics. "I should think Denver might be better. There we could watch over her. She is very young."

Dr. Archie rose. "Kennedy didn't mention Denver. He said Chicago, repeatedly. Under the circumstances it seems to me we ought to try to carry out his wishes exactly, if Thea is willing."

"Certainly, certainly. Thea is conscientious. She would not waste her opportunities." Mr. Kronborg paused. "If Thea were your own daughter, doctor, would you consent to such a plan, at her present age?"

"I most certainly should. In fact, if she were my daughter, I'd have sent her away before this. She's a most unusual child, and she's only wasting herself here. At her age she ought to be learning, not teaching. She'll never learn so quickly and easily as she will right now."

"Well, doctor, you had better talk it over with Mrs. Kronborg. I make it a point to defer to her wishes in such matters. She understands all her children perfectly. I may say that she has all a mother's insight, and more."

Dr. Archie smiled. "Yes, and then some; I feel quite confident about Mrs. Kronborg. We usually agree. Good-morning."

Dr. Archie stepped out into the hot sunshine and walked rapidly toward his office, with a determined look on his face. He found his waiting-room full of patients, and it was one o'clock before he had dismissed the last one. Then he shut his door and took a drink before going over to the hotel for his lunch. He smiled as he locked his cupboard. "I feel almost as gay as if I were going to get away for a winter myself," he thought.

*

Afterward Thea could never remember much about that summer, or how she lived through her impatience. She was to set off with Dr. Archie on the fifteenth of October, and she gave lessons until the first of September. Then she began to get her clothes ready, and spent whole afternoons in the village dressmaker's stuffy, littered little sewing-room. Thea and her mother made a trip to Denver to buy the materials for her dresses. Ready-made clothes for girls were not to be had in those days. Miss Spencer, the dressmaker, declared that she could do handsomely by Thea if they would only let her carry out her own ideas. But Mrs. Kronborg and Thea felt that Miss Spencer's most daring productions might seem out of place in Chicago, so they restrained her with a firm hand. Tillie, who always helped Mrs. Kronborg with the family sewing, was for letting Miss Spencer challenge Chicago on Thea's person. Since Ray Kennedy's death, Thea had become more than ever one of Tillie's heroines. Tillie swore each of her friends to secrecy, and, coming home from church or leaning over the fence, told them the most touching stories about Ray's devotion, and how Thea would "never get over it."

Tillie's confidences stimulated the general discussion of Thea's venture. This discussion went on, upon front porches and in back yards, pretty much all summer. Some people approved of Thea's going to Chicago, but most people did not. There were others who changed their minds about it every day.

Tillie said she wanted Thea to have a ball dress "above all things." She bought a fashion book especially devoted to evening clothes and looked hungrily over the colored plates, picking out costumes that would be becoming to "a blonde." She wanted Thea to have all the gay clothes she herself had always longed for; clothes she often told herself she needed "to recite in."

"Tillie," Thea used to cry impatiently, "can't you see that if Miss Spencer tried to make one of those things, she'd make me look like a circus girl? Anyhow, I don't know anybody in Chicago. I won't be going to parties."

Tillie always replied with a knowing toss of her head, "You see! You'll be in society before you know it. There ain't many girls as accomplished as you."

On the morning of the fifteenth of October the Kronborg family, all of them but Gus, who couldn't leave the store, started for the station an hour before train time. Charley had taken Thea's trunk and telescope to the depot in his delivery wagon early that morning. Thea wore her new blue serge traveling-dress, chosen for its serviceable qualities. She had done her hair up carefully, and had put a pale-blue ribbon around her throat, under a little lace collar that Mrs. Kohler had crocheted for her. As they went out of the gate, Mrs. Kronborg looked her over thoughtfully. Yes, that blue ribbon went very well with the dress, and with Thea's eyes. Thea had a rather unusual touch about such things, she reflected comfortably. Tillie always said that Thea was "so indifferent to dress," but her mother noticed that she usually put her clothes on well. She felt the more at ease about letting Thea go away from home, because she had good sense about her clothes and never tried to dress up too much. Her coloring was so individual, she was so unusually fair, that in the wrong clothes she might easily have been "conspicuous."

It was a fine morning, and the family set out from the house in good spirits. Thea was quiet and calm. She had forgotten nothing, and she clung tightly to her handbag, which held her trunk-key and all of her money that was not in an envelope pinned to her chemise. Thea walked behind the others, holding Thor by the hand, and this time she did not feel that the procession was too long. Thor was uncommunicative that morning, and would only talk about how he would rather get a sand bur in his toe every day than wear shoes and stockings. As they passed the cottonwood grove where Thea often used to bring him in his cart, she asked him who would take him for nice long walks after sister went away.

"Oh, I can walk in our yard," he replied unappreciatively. "I guess I can make a pond for my duck."

Thea leaned down and looked into his face. "But you won't forget about sister, will you?" Thor shook his head. "And won't you be glad when sister comes back and can take you over to Mrs. Kohler's to see the pigeons?"

"Yes, I'll be glad. But I'm going to have a pigeon my own self."

"But you haven't got any little house for one. Maybe Axel would make you a little house."

"Oh, her can live in the barn, her can," Thor drawled indifferently.

Thea laughed and squeezed his hand. She always liked his sturdy matter-of-factness. Boys ought to be like that, she thought.

When they reached the depot, Mr. Kronborg paced the platform somewhat ceremoniously with his daughter. Any member of his flock would have gathered that he was giving her good counsel about meeting the temptations of the world. He did, indeed, begin to admonish her not to forget that talents come from our Heavenly Father and are to be used for his glory; but he cut his remarks short and looked at his watch. He believed that Thea was a religious girl, but when she looked at him with that intent, that passionately inquiring gaze which used to move even Wunsch, Mr. Kronborg suddenly felt his eloquence fail. Thea was like her mother, he reflected; you couldn't put much sentiment across with her. As a usual thing, he liked girls to be a little more responsive. He liked them to blush at his compliments; as Mrs. Kronborg candidly said, "Father could be very soft with the girls." But this morning he was thinking that hard-headedness was a reassuring quality in a daughter who was going to Chicago alone.

Mr. Kronborg believed that big cities were places where people went to lose their identity and to be wicked. He himself, when he was a student at the Seminary—he coughed and opened his watch again. He knew, of course, that a great deal of business went on in Chicago, that there was an active Board of Trade, and that hogs and cattle were slaughtered there. But when, as a young man, he had stopped over in Chicago, he had not interested himself in the commercial activities of the city. He remembered it as a place full of cheap shows and dance halls and boys from the country who were behaving disgustingly.

Dr. Archie drove up to the station about ten minutes before the train was due. His man tied the ponies and stood holding the doctor's alligator-skin bag—very elegant, Thea thought it. Mrs. Kronborg did not burden the doctor with warnings and cautions. She said again that she hoped he could get Thea a comfortable place to stay, where they had good beds, and she hoped the land-lady would be a woman who'd had children of her own. "I don't go much on old maids looking after girls," she remarked as she took a pin out of her own hat and thrust it into Thea's blue turban. "You'll be sure to lose your hatpins on the train, Thea. It's better to have an extra one in case." She tucked in a little curl that had escaped from Thea's careful twist. "Don't forget to brush your dress often, and pin it up to the curtains of your berth to-night, so it won't wrinkle. If you get it wet, have a tailor press it before it draws."

She turned Thea about by the shoulders and looked her over a last time. Yes, she looked very well. She wasn't pretty, exactly,—her face was too broad and her nose was too big. But she had that lovely skin, and she looked fresh and sweet. She had always been a sweet-smelling child. Her mother had always liked to kiss her, when she happened to think of it.

The train whistled in, and Mr. Kronborg carried the canvas "telescope" into the car. Thea kissed them all good-bye. Tillie cried, but she was the only one who did. They all shouted things up at the closed window of the Pullman car, from which Thea looked down at them as from a frame, her face glowing with excitement, her turban a little tilted in spite of three hatpins. She had already taken off her new gloves to save them. Mrs. Kronborg reflected that she would never see just that same picture again, and as Thea's car slid off along the rails, she wiped a tear from her eye. "She won't come back a little girl," Mrs. Kronborg said to her husband as they turned to go home. "Anyhow, she's been a sweet one."

While the Kronborg family were trooping slowly homeward, Thea was sitting in the Pullman, her telescope in the seat beside her, her handbag tightly gripped in her fingers. Dr. Archie had gone into the smoker. He thought she might be a little tearful, and that it would be kinder to leave her alone for a while. Her eyes did fill once, when she saw the last of the sand hills and realized that she was going to leave them behind for a long while. They always made her think of Ray, too. She had had such good times with him out there.

But, of course, it was herself and her own adventure that mattered to her. If youth did not matter so much to itself, it would never have the heart to go on. Thea was surprised that she did not feel a deeper sense of loss at leaving her old life behind her. It seemed, on the contrary, as she looked out at the yellow desert speeding by, that she had left very little. Everything that was essential seemed to be right there in the car with her. She lacked nothing. She even felt more compact and confident than usual. She was all there, and something else was there, too,—in her heart, was it, or under her cheek? Anyhow, it was about her somewhere, that warm sureness, that sturdy little companion with whom she shared a secret.

When Dr. Archie came in from the smoker, she was sitting still, looking intently out of the window and smiling, her lips a little parted, her hair in a blaze of sunshine. The doctor thought she was the prettiest thing he had ever seen, and very funny, with her telescope and big handbag. She made him feel jolly, and a little mournful, too. He knew that the splendid things of life are few, after all, and so very easy to miss.

PART II

THE SONG OF THE LARK

PART II

I

THEA and Dr. Archie had been gone from Moonstone four days. On the afternoon of the nineteenth of October they were in a street-car, riding through the depressing, unkept wastes of North Chicago, on their way to call upon the Reverend Lars Larsen, a friend to whom Mr. Kronborg had written. Thea was still staying at the rooms of the Young Women's Christian Association, and was miserable and homesick there. The housekeeper watched her in a way that made her uncomfortable. Things had not gone very well, so far. The noise and confusion of a big city tired and disheartened her. She had not had her trunk sent to the Christian Association rooms because she did not want to double cartage charges, and now she was running up a bill for storage on it. The contents of her gray telescope were becoming untidy, and it seemed impossible to keep one's face and hands clean in Chicago. She felt as if she were still on the train, traveling without enough clothes to keep clean. She wanted another nightgown, and it did not occur to her that she could buy one. There were other clothes in her trunk that she needed very much, and she seemed no nearer a place to stay than when she arrived in the rain, on that first disillusioning morning.

Dr. Archie had gone at once to his friend Hartley Evans, the throat specialist, and had asked him to tell him of a good piano teacher and direct him to a good boarding-house. Dr. Evans said he could easily tell him who was the best piano teacher in Chicago, but that most students' boarding-houses were "abominable places, where girls got poor food for body and mind." He gave Dr. Archie several addresses, however, and the doctor went to look the places over. He left Thea in her room, for she seemed tired and was not at all like herself. His inspection of boarding-houses was not encouraging. The only place that seemed to him at all desirable was full, and the mistress of the house could not give Thea a room in which she could have a piano. She said Thea might use the piano in her parlor; but when Dr. Archie went to look at the parlor he found a girl talking to a young man on one of the corner sofas. Learning that the boarders received all their callers there, he gave up that house, too, as hopeless.

So when they set out to make the acquaintance of Mr. Larsen on the afternoon he had appointed, the question of a lodging was still undecided. The Swedish Reform Church was in a sloughy, weedy district, near a group of factories. The church itself was a very neat little building. The parsonage, next door, looked clean and comfortable, and there was a well-kept yard about it, with a picket fence. Thea saw several little children playing under a swing, and wondered why ministers always had so many. When they rang at the parsonage door, a capable-looking Swedish servant girl answered the bell and told them that Mr. Larsen's study was in the church, and that he was waiting for them there.

Mr. Larsen received them very cordially. The furniture in his study was so new and the pictures were so heavily framed, that Thea thought it looked more like the waiting-room of the fashionable Denver dentist to whom Dr. Archie had taken her that summer, than like a preacher's study. There were even flowers in a glass vase on the desk. Mr. Larsen was a small, plump man, with a short, yellow beard, very white teeth, and a little turned-up nose on which he wore gold-rimmed eye-glasses. He looked about thirty-five, but he was growing bald, and his thin, hair was parted above his left ear and brought up over the bare spot on the top of his head. He looked cheerful and agreeable. He wore a blue coat and no cuffs.

After Dr. Archie and Thea sat down on a slippery leather couch, the minister asked for an outline of Thea's plans. Dr. Archie explained that she meant to study piano with Andor Harsanyi; that they had already seen him, that Thea had played for him and he said he would be glad to teach her.

Mr. Larsen lifted his pale eyebrows and rubbed his plump

white hands together. "But he is a concert pianist already. He will be very expensive."

"That's why Miss Kronborg wants to get a church position if possible. She has not money enough to see her through the winter. There's no use her coming all the way from Colorado and studying with a second-rate teacher. My friends here tell me Harsanyi is the best."

"Oh, very likely! I have heard him play with Thomas. You Western people do things on a big scale. There are half a dozen teachers that I should think— However, you know what you want." Mr. Larsen showed his contempt for such extravagant standards by a shrug. He felt that Dr. Archie was trying to impress him. He had succeeded, indeed, in bringing out the doctor's stiffest manner. Mr. Larsen went on to explain that he managed the music in his church himself, and drilled his choir, though the tenor was the official choirmaster. Unfortunately there were no vacancies in his choir just now. He had his four voices, very good ones. He looked away from Dr. Archie and glanced at Thea. She looked troubled, even a little frightened when he said this, and drew in her lower lip. She, certainly, was not pretentious, if her protector was. He continued to study her. She was sitting on the lounge, her knees far apart, her gloved hands lying stiffly in her lap, like a country girl. Her turban, which seemed a little too big for her, had got tilted in the wind,— it was always windy in that part of Chicago,—and she looked tired. She wore no veil, and her hair, too, was the worse for the wind and dust. When he said he had all the voices he required, he noticed that her gloved hands shut tightly. Mr. Larsen reflected that she was not, after all, responsible for the lofty manner of her father's physician; that she was not even responsible for her father, whom he remembered as a tiresome fellow. As he watched her tired, worried face, he felt sorry for her.

"All the same, I would like to try your voice," he said, turning pointedly away from her companion. "I am interested in voices. Can you sing to the violin?"

"I guess so," Thea replied dully. "I don't know. I never tried."

Mr. Larsen took his violin out of the case and began to tighten the keys. "We might go into the lecture-room and see how it goes. I can't tell much about a voice by the organ. The violin is really the proper instrument to try a voice." He opened a door at the back of his study, pushed Thea gently through it, and looking over his shoulder to Dr. Archie said, "Excuse us, sir. We will be back soon."

Dr. Archie chuckled. All preachers were alike, officious and on their dignity; liked to deal with women and girls, but not with men. He took up a thin volume from the minister's desk. To his amusement it proved to be a book of "Devotional and Kindred Poems; by Mrs. Aurelia S. Larsen." He looked them over, thinking that the world changed very little. He could remember when the wife of his father's minister had published a volume of verses, which all the church members had to buy and all the children were encouraged to read. His grandfather had made a face at the book and said, "Puir body!" Both ladies seemed to have chosen the same subjects, too: Jephthah's Daughter, Rizpah, David's Lament for Absalom, etc.* The doctor found the book very amusing.

The Reverend Lars Larsen was a reactionary Swede. His father came to Iowa in the sixties, married a Swedish girl who was ambitious, like himself, and they moved to Kansas and took up land under the Homestead Act.* After that, they bought land and leased it from the Government, acquired land in every possible way. They worked like horses, both of them; indeed, they would never have used any horse-flesh they owned as they used themselves. They reared a large family and worked their sons and daughters as mercilessly as they worked themselves; all of them but Lars. Lars was the fourth son, and he was born lazy. He seemed to bear the mark of overstrain on the part of his parents. Even in his cradle he was an example of physical inertia; anything to lie still. When he was a growing boy his mother had to drag him out of bed every morning, and he had to be driven to his chores. At school he had a model "attendance record," because he found getting his lessons easier than farm work. He was the only one of the family who went through the high school, and by the time he graduated he had already made up his mind to study for the ministry, because it seemed to him the least laborious of all callings. In so far as he could see, it was the only business in which there was practically no competition, in which a man was not all the time pitted against other men who were willing to work themselves to death. His father stubbornly opposed Lars's plan, but after keeping the boy at home for a year and finding how useless he was on the farm, he sent him to a theological seminary—as much to conceal his laziness from the neighbors as because he did not know what else to do with him.

Larsen, like Peter Kronborg, got on well in the ministry, because he got on well with the women. His English was no worse than that of most young preachers of American parentage, and he made the most of his skill with the violin. He was supposed to exert a very desirable influence over young people and to stimulate their interest in church work. He married an American girl, and when his father died he got his share of the property—which was very considerable. He invested his money carefully and was that rare thing, a preacher of independent means. His white, well-kept hands were his result,—the evidence that he had worked out his life successfully in the way that pleased him. His Kansas brothers hated the sight of his hands.

Larsen liked all the softer things of life,—in so far as he knew about them. He slept late in the morning, was fussy about his food, and read a great many novels, preferring sentimental ones. He did not smoke, but he ate a great deal of candy "for his throat," and always kept a box of chocolate drops in the upper right-hand drawer of his desk. He always bought season tickets for the symphony concerts, and he played his violin for women's culture clubs. He did not wear cuffs, except on Sunday, because he believed that a free wrist facilitated his violin practice. When he drilled his choir he always held his hand with the little and index fingers curved higher than the other two, like a noted German conductor he had seen. On the whole, the Reverend Larsen was not an insincere man; he merely spent his life resting and playing, to make up for the time his forebears had wasted grubbing in the earth. He was simple-hearted and kind; he enjoyed his candy and his children and his sacred cantatas. He could work energetically at almost any form of play.

Dr. Archie was deep in "The Lament of Mary Magdalen,"* when Mr. Larsen and Thea came back to the study. From the minister's expression he judged that Thea had succeeded in interesting him.

Mr. Larsen seemed to have forgotten his hostility toward him, and addressed him frankly as soon as he entered. He stood holding his violin, and as Thea sat down he pointed to her with his bow:—

"I have just been telling Miss Kronborg that though I cannot promise her anything permanent, I might give her something for the next few months. My soprano is a young married woman and is temporarily indisposed. She would be glad to be excused from her duties for a while. I like Miss Kronborg's singing very much, and I think she would benefit by the instruction in my choir. Singing here might very well lead to something else. We pay our soprano only eight dollars a Sunday, but she always gets ten dollars for singing at funerals. Miss Kronborg has a sympathetic voice, and I think there could be a good deal of demand for her at funerals. Several American churches apply to me for a soloist on such occasions, and I could help her to pick up quite a little money that way."

This sounded lugubrious to Dr. Archie, who had a physician's dislike of funerals, but he tried to accept the suggestion cordially.

"Miss Kronborg tells me she is having some trouble getting located," Mr. Larsen went on with animation, still holding his violin. "I would advise her to keep away from boarding-houses altogether. Among my parishioners there are two German women, a mother and daughter. The daughter is a Swede by marriage, and clings to the Swedish Church. They live near here, and they rent some of their rooms. They have now a large room vacant, and have asked me to recommend some one. They have never taken boarders, but Mrs. Lorch, the mother, is a good cook,—at least, I am always glad to take supper with her,—and I think I could persuade her to let this young woman partake of the family table. The daughter, Mrs. Andersen, is musical, too, and sings in the Mozart Society. I think they might like to have a music student in the house. You speak German, I suppose?" he turned to Thea.

"Oh, no; a few words. I don't know the grammar," she murmured.

Dr. Archie noticed that her eyes looked alive again, not frozen as they had looked all morning. "If this fellow can help her, it's not for me to be stand-offish," he said to himself.

"Do you think you would like to stay in such a quiet place, with old-fashioned people?" Mr. Larsen asked. "I shouldn't think you could find a better place to work, if that's what you want."

"I think mother would like to have me with people like that," Thea replied. "And I'd be glad to settle down most anywhere. I'm losing time."

"Very well, there's no time like the present. Let us go to see Mrs. Lorch and Mrs. Andersen."

The minister put his violin in its case and caught up a black-and-white checked traveling-cap that he wore when he rode his high Columbia wheel. The three left the church together.

II

So Thea did not go to a boarding-house after all. When Dr. Archie left Chicago she was comfortably settled with Mrs. Lorch, and her happy reunion with her trunk somewhat consoled her for his departure.

Mrs. Lorch and her daughter lived half a mile from the Swedish Reform Church, in an old square frame house with a porch supported by frail pillars, set in a damp yard full of big lilac bushes. The house, which had been left over from country times, needed paint badly, and looked gloomy and despondent among its smart Queen Anne neighbors. There was a big back yard with two rows of apple trees and a grape arbor, and a warped walk, two planks wide which led to the coal bins at the back of the lot. Thea's room was on the second floor, overlooking this back yard, and she understood that in the winter she must carry up her own coal and kindling from the bin. There was no furnace in the house, no running water except in the kitchen and that was why the room rent was small. All the rooms were heated by stoves, and the lodgers pumped the water they needed from the cistern under the porch, or from the well at the entrance of the grape arbor. Old Mrs Lorch could never bring herself to have costly improvements made in her house; indeed she had very little money. She preferred to keep the house just as her husband built it, and she thought her way of living good enough for plain people.

Thea's room was large enough to admit a rented upright piano without crowding. It was, the widowed daughter said, "a double room that had always before been occupied by two gentlemen"; the piano now took the place of a second occupant. There was a ingrain carpet on the floor, green ivy leaves on a red ground, and clumsy, old-fashioned walnut furniture. The bed was very wide, and the mattress thin and hard. Over the fat pillows were "shams" embroidered in Turkey red, each with a flowering scroll—one with "Gute Nacht," the other with "Guten Morgen."* The dresser was so big that Thea wondered how it had ever been got into the house and up the narrow stairs. Besides an old horsehair armchair, there were two low plush "spring-rockers," against the massive pedestals of which one was always stumbling in the dark. Thea sat in the dark a good deal those first weeks, and sometimes a painful bump against one of those brutally immovable pedestals roused her temper and pulled her out of a heavy hour. The wall-paper was brownish yellow, with blue flowers. When it was put on, the carpet, certainly, had not been consulted. There was only one picture on the wall when Thea moved in: a large colored print of a brightly lighted church in a snow-storm, on Christmas Eve, with greens hanging about the stone doorway and arched windows. There was something warm and home-like about this picture, and Thea grew fond of it. One day, on her way into town to take her lesson, she stopped at a bookstore and bought a photograph of the Naples bust of Julius Caesar.* This she had framed, and hung it on the big bare wall behind her stove. It was a curious choice, but she was at the age when people do inexplicable things. She had been interested in Caesar's "Commentaries"* when she left school to begin teaching, and she loved to read about great generals; but these facts would scarcely explain her wanting that grim bald head to share her daily existence. It seemed a strange freak, when she bought so few things, and when she had, as Mrs. Andersen said to Mrs. Lorch, "no pictures of the composers at all."

Both the widows were kind to her, but Thea liked the mother better. Old Mrs. Lorch was fat and jolly, with a red face, always shining as if she had just come from the stove, bright little eyes, and hair of several colors. Her own hair was one cast of iron-gray, her switch another and her false front still another. Her clothes always smelled of savory cooking, except when she was dressed for church or *Kaffeeklatsch*,* and then she smelled of bay rum or of the lemon-verbena sprig which she tucked inside her puffy black kid glove. Her cooking justified all that Mr. Larsen had said of it, and Thea had never been so well nourished before.

The daughter, Mrs. Andersen,—Irene, her mother called her,—was a different sort of woman altogether. She was perhaps forty years old, angular, big-boned, with large, thin features, light-blue eyes and dry yellow hair, the bang tightly frizzed. She was pale, anaemic, and sentimental. She had married the youngest son of a rich, arrogant Swedish family who were lumber merchants in St. Paul. There she dwelt during her married life. Oscar Andersen was a strong, full-blooded fellow who had counted on a long life and had been rather careless about his business affairs. He was killed by the explosion of a steam boiler in the mills, and his brothers managed to prove that he had very little stock in the big business. They had strongly disapproved of his marriage and they agreed among themselves that they were entirely justified in defrauding his widow, who, they said, "would only marry again and give some fellow a good thing of it." Mrs. Andersen would not go to law with the family that had always snubbed and wounded her—she felt the humiliation of being thrust out more than she felt her impoverishment; so she went back to Chicago to live with her widowed mother on an income of five hundred a year. This experience had given her sentimental nature an incurable hurt. Something withered away in her. Her head had a downward droop; her step was soft and apologetic, even in her mother's house, and her smile had the sickly, uncertain flicker that so often comes from a secret humiliation. She was affable and yet shrinking, like one who has come down in the world, who has known better clothes, better carpets, better people, brighter hopes. Her husband was buried in the Andersen lot in St. Paul, with a locked iron fence around it. She had to go to his eldest brother for the key when she went to say good-bye to his grave. She clung to the Swedish Church because it had been her husband's church.

As her mother had no room for her household belongings, Mrs. Andersen had brought home with her only her bedroom set, which now furnished her own room at Mrs. Lorch's. There she spent most of her time, doing fancy-work or writing letters to sympathizing German friends in St. Paul, surrounded by keepsakes and photographs of the burly Oscar Andersen. Thea, when she was admitted to this room, and shown these photographs, found herself wondering, like the Andersen family, why such a lusty, gay-looking fellow ever thought he wanted this pallid, long-cheeked woman, whose manner was always that of withdrawing, and who must have been rather thin-blooded even as a girl.

Mrs. Andersen was certainly a depressing person. It sometimes annoyed Thea very much to hear her insinuating knock on the door, her flurried explanation of why she had come, as she backed toward the stairs. Mrs. Andersen admired Thea greatly. She thought it a distinction to be even a "temporary soprano"— Thea called herself so quite seriously—in the Swedish Church. She also thought it distinguished to be a pupil of Harsanyi's. She considered Thea very handsome, very Swedish, very talented. She fluttered about the upper floor when Thea was practicing. In short, she tried to make a heroine of her, just as Tillie Kronborg had always done, and Thea was conscious of something of the sort. When she was working and heard Mrs. Andersen tip-toeing past her door, she used to shrug her shoulders and wonder whether she was always to have a Tillie diving furtively about her in some disguise or other.

At the dressmaker's Mrs. Andersen recalled Tillie even more painfully. After her first Sunday in Mr. Larsen's choir, Thea saw that she must have a proper dress for morning service. Her Moonstone party dress might do to wear in the evening, but she must have one frock that could stand the light of day. She, of course, knew nothing about Chicago dressmakers, so she let Mrs. Andersen take her to a German woman whom she recommended warmly. The German dressmaker was excitable and dramatic. Concert dresses, she said, were her specialty. In her fitting-room there were photographs of singers in the dresses she had made them for this or that *Sängerfest*.* She and Mrs. Andersen together achieved a costume which would have warmed Tillie Kronborg's heart. It was clearly intended for a woman of forty, with violent tastes. There seemed to be a piece of every known fabric in it somewhere. When it came home, and was spread out on her huge bed, Thea looked it over and told herself candidly that it was "a horror." However, her money was gone, and there was nothing to do but make the best of the dress. She never wore it except, as she said, "to sing in," as if it were an unbecoming uniform. When Mrs. Lorch and Irene told her that she "looked like a little bird-of-Paradise in it," Thea shut her teeth and repeated to herself words she had learned from Joe Giddy and Spanish Johnny.

In these two good women Thea found faithful friends, and in their house she found the quiet and peace which helped her to support the great experiences of that winter.

III

ANDOR HARSANYI had never had a pupil in the least like Thea Kronborg. He had never had one more intelligent, and he had never had one so ignorant. When Thea sat down to take her first lesson from him, she had never heard a work by Beethoven or a composition by Chopin. She knew their names vaguely. Wunsch had been a musician once, long before he wandered into

Moonstone, but when Thea awoke his interest there was not much left of him. From him Thea had learned something about the works of Gluck and Bach, and he used to play her some of the compositions of Schumann. In his trunk he had a mutilated score of the F sharp minor sonata, which he had heard Clara Schumann play at a festival in Leipsic. Though his powers of execution were at such a low ebb, he used to play at this sonata for his pupil and managed to give her some idea of its beauty. When Wunsch was a young man, it was still daring to like Schumann; enthusiasm for his work was considered an expression of youthful waywardness. Perhaps that was why Wunsch remembered him best. Thea studied some of the *Kinderszenen** with him, as well as some little sonatas by Mozart and Clementi. But for the most part Wunsch stuck to Czerny and Hummel.

Harsanyi found in Thea a pupil with sure, strong hands, one who read rapidly and intelligently, who had, he felt, a richly gifted nature. But she had been given no direction, and her ardor was unawakened. She had never heard a symphony orchestra. The literature of the piano was an undiscovered world to her. He wondered how she had been able to work so hard when she knew so little of what she was working toward. She had been taught according to the old Stuttgart method; stiff back, stiff elbows, a very formal position of the hands. The best thing about her pre-paration was that she had developed an unusual power of work. He noticed at once her way of charging at difficulties. She ran to meet them as if they were foes she had long been seeking, seized them as if they were destined for her and she for them. Whatever she did well, she took for granted. Her eagerness aroused all the young Hungarian's chivalry. Instinctively one went to the rescue of a creature who had so much to overcome and who struggled so hard. He used to tell his wife that Miss Kronborg's hour took more out of him than half a dozen other lessons. He usually kept her long over time; he changed her lessons about so that he could do so, and often gave her time at the end of the day, when he could talk to her afterward and play for her a little from what he happened to be studying. It was always interesting to play for her. Sometimes she was so silent that he wondered, when she left him, whether she had got anything out of it. But a week later, two weeks later, she would give back his idea again in a way that set him vibrating.

All this was very well for Harsanyi; an interesting variation in the routine of teaching. But for Thea Kronborg, that winter was almost beyond enduring. She always remembered it as the happiest and wildest and saddest of her life. Things came too fast for her; she had not had enough preparation. There were times when she came home from her lesson and lay upon her bed hating Wunsch and her family, hating a world that had let her grow up so ignorant; when she wished that she could die then and there, and be born over again to begin anew. She said something of this kind once to her teacher, in the midst of a bitter struggle. Harsanyi turned the light of his wonderful eye upon her—poor fellow, he had but one, though that was set in such a handsome head—and said slowly: "Every artist makes himself born. It is very much harder than the other time, and longer. Your mother did not bring anything into the world to play piano. That you must bring into the world yourself."

This comforted Thea temporarily, for it seemed to give her a chance. But a great deal of the time she was comfortless. Her letters to Dr. Archie were brief and businesslike. She was not apt to chatter much, even in the stimulating company of people she liked, and to chatter on paper was simply impossible for her. If she tried to write him anything definite about her work, she immediately scratched it out as being only partially true, or not true at all. Nothing that she could say about her studies seemed unqualifiedly true, once she put it down on paper.

Late one afternoon, when she was thoroughly tired and wanted to struggle on into the dusk, Harsanyi, tired too, threw up his hands and laughed at her. "Not to-day, Miss Kronborg. That sonata will keep; it won't run away. Even if you and I should not waken up to-morrow, it will be there."

Thea turned to him fiercely. "No, it isn't here unless I have it—not for me," she cried passionately. "Only what I hold in my two hands is there for me!"

Harsanyi made no reply. He took a deep breath and sat down

again. "The second movement now, quietly, with the shoulders relaxed."

There were hours, too, of great exaltation; when she was at her best and became a part of what she was doing and ceased to exist in any other sense. There were other times when she was so shattered by ideas that she could do nothing worth while; when they trampled over her like an army and she felt as if she were bleeding to death under them. She sometimes came home from a late lesson so exhausted that she could eat no supper. If she tried to eat, she was ill afterward. She used to throw herself upon the bed and lie there in the dark, not thinking, not feeling, but evaporating. That same night, perhaps, she would waken up rested and calm, and as she went over her work in her mind, the passages seemed to become something of themselves, to take a sort of pattern in the darkness. She had never learned to work away from the piano until she came to Harsanyi, and it helped her more than anything had ever helped her before.

She almost never worked now with the sunny, happy contentment that had filled the hours when she worked with Wunsch—"like a fat horse turning a sorgum mill," she said bitterly to herself. Then, by sticking to it, she could always do what she set out to do. Now, everything that she really wanted was impossible; a *cantabile** like Harsanyi's, for instance, instead of her own cloudy tone. No use telling her she might have it in ten years. She wanted it now. She wondered how she had ever found other things interesting: books, "Anna Karenina"—all that seemed so unreal and on the outside of things. She was not born a musician, she decided; there was no other way of explaining it.

Sometimes she got so nervous at the piano that she left it, and snatching up her hat and cape went out and walked, hurrying through the streets like Christian fleeing from the City of Destruction.* And while she walked she cried. There was scarcely a street in the neighborhood that she had not cried up and down before that winter was over. The thing that used to lie under her cheek, that sat so warmly over her heart when she glided away from the sand hills that autumn morning, was far from her. She had come to Chicago to be with it, and it had deserted her, leaving in its place a painful longing, an unresigned despair.

Harsanyi knew that his interesting pupil—"the savage blonde," one of his male students called her—was sometimes very unhappy. He saw in her discontent a curious definition of character. He would have said that a girl with so much musical feeling, so intelligent, with good training of eye and hand, would, when thus suddenly introduced to the great literature of the piano, have found boundless happiness. But he soon learned that she was not able to forget her own poverty in the richness of the world he opened to her. Often when he played to her, her face was the picture of restless misery. She would sit crouching forward, her elbows on her knees, her brows drawn together and her gray-green eyes smaller than ever, reduced to mere pin-points of cold, piercing light. Sometimes, while she listened, she would swallow hard, two or three times, and look nervously from left to right, drawing her shoulders together. "Exactly," he thought, "as if she were being watched, or as if she were naked and heard some one coming."

On the other hand, when she came several times to see Mrs. Harsanyi and the two babies, she was like a little girl, jolly and gay and eager to play with the children, who loved her. The little daughter, Tanya, liked to touch Miss Kronborg's yellow hair and pat it, saying, "Dolly, dolly," because it was of a color much oftener seen on dolls than on people. But if Harsanyi opened the piano and sat down to play, Miss Kronborg gradually drew away from the children, retreated to a corner and became sullen or troubled. Mrs. Harsanyi noticed this, also, and thought it very strange behavior.

Another thing that puzzled Harsanyi was Thea's apparent lack of curiosity. Several times he offered to give her tickets to concerts, but she said she was too tired or that it "knocked her out to be up late." Harsanyi did not know that she was singing in a choir, and had often to sing at funerals, neither did he realize how much her work with him stirred her and exhausted her. Once, just as she was leaving his studio, he called her back and told her he

could give her some tickets that had been sent him for Emma
Juch that evening. Thea fingered the black wool on the edge of
her plush cape and replied, "Oh, thank you, Mr. Harsanyi, but I
have to wash my hair to-night."

Mrs. Harsanyi liked Miss Kronborg thoroughly. She saw in her
the making of a pupil who would reflect credit upon Harsanyi.
She felt that the girl could be made to look strikingly handsome,
and that she had the kind of personality which takes hold of
audiences. Moreover, Miss Kronborg was not in the least sentimental about her husband. Sometimes from the show pupils one
had to endure a good deal. "I like that girl," she used to say, when
Harsanyi told her of one of Thea's *gaucheries.** "She doesn't sigh
every time the wind blows. With her one swallow doesn't make a
summer."

Thea told them very little about herself. She was not naturally
communicative, and she found it hard to feel confidence in new
people. She did not know why, but she could not talk to Harsanyi
as she could to Dr. Archie, or to Johnny and Mrs. Tellamantez.
With Mr. Larsen she felt more at home, and when she was walking she sometimes stopped at his study to eat candy with him or
to hear the plot of the novel he happened to be reading.

One evening toward the middle of December Thea was to dine
with the Harsanyis. She arrived early, to have time to play with
the children before they went to bed. Mrs. Harsanyi took her into
her own room and helped her take off her country "fascinator"
and her clumsy plush cape. Thea had bought this cape at a big
department store and had paid $16.50 for it. As she had never
paid more than ten dollars for a coat before, that seemed to her a
large price. It was very heavy and not very warm, ornamented
with a showy pattern in black disks, and trimmed around the
collar and the edges with some kind of black wool that "crocked"
badly in snow or rain. It was lined with a cotton stuff called
"farmer's satin." Mrs. Harsanyi was one woman in a thousand.
As she lifted this cape from Thea's shoulders and laid it on her
white bed, she wished that her husband did not have to charge
pupils like this one for their lessons. Thea wore her Moonstone
party dress, white organdie, made with a "V" neck and elbow

sleeves, and a blue sash. She looked very pretty in it, and around her throat she had a string of pink coral and tiny white shells that Ray once brought her from Los Angeles. Mrs. Harsanyi noticed that she wore high heavy shoes which needed blacking. The choir in Mr. Larsen's church stood behind a railing, so Thea did not pay much attention to her shoes.

"You have nothing to do to your hair," Mrs. Harsanyi said kindly, as Thea turned to the mirror. "However it happens to lie, it's always pretty. I admire it as much as Tanya does."

Thea glanced awkwardly away from her and looked stern, but Mrs. Harsanyi knew that she was pleased. They went into the living-room, behind the studio, where the two children were playing on the big rug before the coal grate. Andor, the boy, was six, a sturdy, handsome child, and the little girl was four. She came tripping to meet Thea, looking like a little doll in her white net dress—her mother made all her clothes. Thea picked her up and hugged her. Mrs. Harsanyi excused herself and went to the dining-room. She kept only one maid and did a good deal of the housework herself, besides cooking her husband's favorite dishes for him. She was still under thirty, a slender, graceful woman, gracious, intelligent, and capable. She adapted herself to circumstances with a well-bred ease which solved many of her husband's difficulties, and kept him, as he said, from feeling cheap and down at the heel. No musician ever had a better wife. Unfortunately her beauty was of a very frail and impressionable kind, and she was beginning to lose it. Her face was too thin now, and there were often dark circles under her eyes.

Left alone with the children, Thea sat down on Tanya's little chair—she would rather have sat on the floor, but was afraid of rumpling her dress—and helped them play "cars" with Andor's iron railway set. She showed him new ways to lay his tracks and how to make switches, set up his Noah's ark village for stations and packed the animals in the open coal cars to send them to the stockyards. They worked out their shipment so realistically that when Andor put the two little reindeer into the stock car, Tanya snatched them out and began to cry, saying she wasn't going to have all their animals killed.

Harsanyi came in, jaded and tired, and asked Thea to go on with her game, as he was not equal to talking much before dinner. He sat down and made pretense of glancing at the evening paper, but he soon dropped it. After the railroad began to grow tiresome, Thea went with the children to the lounge in the corner, and played for them the game with which she used to amuse Thor for hours together behind the parlor stove at home, making shadow pictures against the wall with her hands. Her fingers were very supple, and she could make a duck and a cow and a sheep and a fox and a rabbit and even an elephant. Harsanyi, from his low chair, watched them, smiling. The boy was on his knees, jumping up and down with the excitement of guessing the beasts, and Tanya sat with her feet tucked under her and clapped her frail little hands. Thea's profile, in the lamplight, teased his fancy. Where had he seen a head like it before?

When dinner was announced, little Andor took Thea's hand and walked to the dining-room with her. The children always had dinner with their parents and behaved very nicely at table. "Mamma," said Andor seriously as he climbed into his chair and tucked his napkin into the collar of his blouse, "Miss Kronborg's hands are every kind of animal there is."

His father laughed. "I wish somebody would say that about my hands, Andor."

When Thea dined at the Harsanyis before, she noticed that there was an intense suspense from the moment they took their places at the table until the master of the house had tasted the soup. He had a theory that if the soup went well, the dinner would go well; but if the soup was poor, all was lost. To-night he tasted his soup and smiled, and Mrs. Harsanyi sat more easily in her chair and turned her attention to Thea. Thea loved their dinner table, because it was lighted by candles in silver candlesticks, and she had never seen a table so lighted anywhere else. There were always flowers, too. To-night there was a little orange tree, with oranges on it, that one of Harsanyi's pupils had sent him at Thanksgiving time. After Harsanyi had finished his soup and a glass of red Hungarian wine, he lost his fagged look and became cordial and witty. He persuaded Thea to drink a little wine to-night. The first time she dined with them, when he urged her to taste the glass of sherry beside her plate, she astonished them by telling them that she "never drank."

Harsanyi was then a man of thirty-two. He was to have a very brilliant career, but he did not know it then. Theodore Thomas* was perhaps the only man in Chicago who felt that Harsanyi might have a great future. Harsanyi belonged to the softer Slavic type, and was more like a Pole than a Hungarian. He was tall, slender, active, with sloping, graceful shoulders and long arms. His head was very fine, strongly and delicately modelled, and, as Thea put it, "so independent." A lock of his thick brown hair usually hung over his forehead. His eye was wonderful; full of light and fire when he was interested, soft and thoughtful when he was tired or melancholy. The meaning and power of two very fine eyes must all have gone into this one—the right one, fortunately, the one next his audience when he played. He believed that the glass eye which gave one side of his face such a dull, blind look, had ruined his career, or rather had made a career impossible for him. Harsanyi lost his eye when he was twelve years old, in a Pennsylvania mining town where explosives happened to be kept too near the frame shanties in which the company packed newly arrived Hungarian families.

His father was a musician and a good one, but he had cruelly over-worked the boy; keeping him at the piano for six hours a day and making him play in cafés and dance halls for half the night. Andor ran away and crossed the ocean with an uncle, who smuggled him through the port as one of his own many children. The explosion in which Andor was hurt killed a score of people, and he was thought lucky to get off with an eye. He still had a clipping from a Pittsburg paper, giving a list of the dead and injured. He appeared as "Harsanyi, Andor, left eye and slight injuries about the head." That was his first American "notice"; and he kept it. He held no grudge against the coal company; he understood that the accident was merely one of the things that are bound to happen in the general scramble of American life, where every one comes to grab and takes his chance.

While they were eating dessert, Thea asked Harsanyi if she could change her Tuesday lesson from afternoon to morning. "I have to be at a choir rehearsal in the afternoon, to get ready for the Christmas music, and I expect it will last until late."

Harsanyi put down his fork and looked up. "A choir rehearsal? You sing in a church?"

"Yes. A little Swedish church, over on the North side."

"Why did you not tell us?"

"Oh, I'm only a temporary. The regular soprano is not well."

"How long have you been singing there?"

"Ever since I came. I had to get a position of some kind," Thea explained, flushing, "and the preacher took me on. He runs the choir himself. He knew my father, and I guess he took me to oblige."

Harsanyi tapped the tablecloth with the ends of his fingers. "But why did you never tell us? Why are you so reticent with us?"

Thea looked shyly at him from under her brows. "Well, it's certainly not very interesting. It's only a little church. I only do it for business reasons."

"What do you mean? Don't you like to sing? Don't you sing well?".

"I like it well enough, but, of course, I don't know anything about singing. I guess that's why I never said anything about it. Anybody that's got a voice can sing in a little church like that."

Harsanyi laughed softly—a little scornfully, Thea thought. "So you have a voice, have you?"

Thea hesitated, looked intently at the candles and then at Harsanyi. "Yes," she said firmly; "I have got some, anyway."

"Good girl," said Mrs. Harsanyi, nodding and smiling at Thea. "You must let us hear you sing after dinner."

This remark seemingly closed the subject, and when the coffee was brought they began to talk of other things. Harsanyi asked Thea how she happened to know so much about the way in which freight trains are operated, and she tried to give him some idea of how the people in little desert towns live by the railway and order their lives by the coming and going of the trains. When they left the dining-room the children were sent to bed and Mrs. Harsanyi took Thea into the studio. She and her husband usually sat there in the evening.

Although their apartment seemed so elegant to Thea, it was small and cramped. The studio was the only spacious room. The Harsanyis were poor, and it was due to Mrs. Harsanyi's good management that their lives, even in hard times, moved along with dignity and order. She had long ago found out that bills or debts of any kind frightened her husband and crippled his working power. He said they were like bars on the windows, and shut out the future; they meant that just so many hundred dollars' worth of his life was debilitated and exhausted before he got to it. So Mrs. Harsanyi saw to it that they never owed anything. Harsanyi was not extravagant, though he was sometimes careless about money. Quiet and order and his wife's good taste were the things that meant most to him. After these, good food, good cigars, a little good wine. He wore his clothes until they were shabby, until his wife had to ask the tailor to come to the house and measure him for new ones. His neckties she usually made herself, and when she was in shops she always kept her eye open for silks in very dull or pale shades, grays and olives, warm blacks and browns.

When they went into the studio Mrs. Harsanyi took up her embroidery and Thea sat down beside her on a low stool, her hands clasped about her knees. While his wife and his pupil talked, Harsanyi sank into a *chaise longue** in which he sometimes snatched a few moments' rest between his lessons, and smoked. He sat well out of the circle of the lamplight, his feet to the fire. His feet were slender and well shaped, always elegantly shod. Much of the grace of his movements was due to the fact that his feet were almost as sure and flexible as his hands. He listened to the conversation with amusement. He admired his wife's tact and kindness with crude young people; she taught them so much without seeming to be instructing. When the clock struck nine, Thea said she must be going home.

Harsanyi rose and flung away his cigarette. "Not yet. We have just begun the evening. Now you are going to sing for us. I have been waiting for you to recover from dinner. Come, what shall it be?" he crossed to the piano.

Thea laughed and shook her head, locking her elbows still tighter about her knees. "Thank you, Mr. Harsanyi, but if you really make me sing, I'll accompany myself. You couldn't stand it to play the sort of things I have to sing."

As Harsanyi still pointed to the chair at the piano, she left her stool and went to it, while he returned to his *chaise longue*. Thea looked at the keyboard uneasily for a moment, then she began "Come, ye Disconsolate," the hymn Wunsch had always liked to hear her sing. Mrs. Harsanyi glanced questioningly at her husband, but he was looking intently at the toes of his boots, shading his forehead with his long white hand. When Thea finished the hymn she did not turn around, but immediately began "The Ninety and Nine."* Mrs. Harsanyi kept trying to catch her husband's eye; but his chin only sank lower on his collar.

> "There were ninety and nine that safely lay
>   In the shelter of the fold,
> But one was out on the hills away,
>   Far off from the gates of gold."

Harsanyi looked at her, then back at the fire.

> "Rejoice, for the Shepherd has found his sheep."

Thea turned on the chair and grinned. "That's about enough, isn't it? That song got me my job. The preacher said it was sympathetic," she minced the word, remembering Mr. Larsen's manner.

Harsanyi drew himself up in his chair, resting his elbows on the low arms. "Yes? That is better suited to your voice. Your upper tones are good, above G. I must teach you some songs. Don't you know anything—pleasant?"

Thea shook her head ruefully. "I'm afraid I don't. Let me see— Perhaps," she turned to the piano and put her hands on the keys. "I used to sing this for Mr. Wunsch a long while ago. It's for contralto, but I'll try it." She frowned at the keyboard a moment, played the few introductory measures, and began

> *"Ach, ich habe sie verloren,"*

She had not sung it for a long time; and it came back like an old friendship. When she finished, Harsanyi sprang from his chair and dropped lightly upon his toes, a kind of *entre-chat** that he sometimes executed when he formed a sudden resolution, or when he was about to follow a pure intuition, against reason. His wife said that when he gave that spring he was shot from the bow of his ancestors, and now when he left his chair in that manner she knew he was intensely interested. He went quickly to the piano.

"Sing that again. There is nothing the matter with your low voice, my girl. I will play for you. Let your voice out." Without looking at her he began the accompaniment. Thea drew back her shoulders, relaxed them instinctively, and sang.

When she finished the aria, Harsanyi beckoned her nearer. "Sing *ah—ah* for me, as I indicate." He kept his right hand on the keyboard and put his left to her throat, placing the tips of his delicate fingers over her larynx. "Again,—until your breath is gone.—Trill between the two tones, always; good! Again; excellent!—Now up,—stay there. E and F. Not so good, is it? F is always a hard one.—Now, try the half-tone.—That's right, nothing difficult about it.—Now, pianissimo,* *ah—ah*. Now, swell it, *ah—ah*.—Again, follow my hand.—Now, carry it down.—Anybody ever tell you anything about your breathing?"

"Mr. Larsen says I have an unusually long breath," Thea replied with spirit.

Harsanyi smiled. "So you have, so you have. That was what I meant. Now, once more; carry it up and then down, *ah—ah*." He put his hand back to her throat and sat with his head bent, his one eye closed. He loved to hear a big voice throb in a relaxed, natural throat, and he was thinking that no one had ever felt this voice vibrate before. It was like a wild bird that had flown into his studio on Middleton Street from goodness knew how far! No one knew that it had come, or even that it existed; least of all the strange, crude girl in whose throat it beat its passionate wings. What a simple thing it was, he reflected; why had he never guessed it before? Everything about her indicated it,—the big mouth, the wide jaw and chin, the strong white teeth, the deep

laugh. The machine was so simple and strong, seemed to be so
easily operated. She sang from the bottom of herself. Her breath
came from down where her laugh came from, the deep laugh
which Mrs. Harsanyi had once called "the laugh of the people."
A relaxed throat, a voice that lay on the breath, that had never
been forced off the breath; it rose and fell in the air-column like
the little balls which are put to shine in the jet of a fountain. The
voice did not thin as it went up; the upper tones were as full and
rich as the lower, produced in the same way and as unconsciously,
only with deeper breath.

At last Harsanyi threw back his head and rose. "You must be
tired, Miss Kronborg."

When she replied, she startled him; he had forgotten how hard
and full of burs her speaking voice was. "No," she said, "singing
never tires me."

Harsanyi pushed back his hair with a nervous hand. "I don't
know much about the voice, but I shall take liberties and teach
you some good songs. I think you have a very interesting voice."

"I'm glad if you like it. Good-night, Mr. Harsanyi." Thea went
with Mrs. Harsanyi to get her wraps.

When Mrs. Harsanyi came back to her husband, she found him
walking restlessly up and down the room.

"Don't you think her voice wonderful, dear?" she asked.

"I scarcely know what to think. All I really know about that girl
is that she tires me to death. We must not have her often. If I did
not have my living to make, then—" he dropped into a chair and
closed his eyes. "How tired I am. What a voice!"

IV

AFTER that evening Thea's work with Harsanyi changed somewhat. He insisted that she should study some songs with him, and
after almost every lesson he gave up half an hour of his own time
to practicing them with her. He did not pretend to know much
about voice production, but so far, he thought, she had acquired
no really injurious habits. A healthy and powerful organ had

found its own method, which was not a bad one. He wished to find out a good deal before he recommended a vocal teacher. He never told Thea what he thought about her voice, and made her general ignorance of anything worth singing his pretext for the trouble he took. That was in the beginning. After the first few lessons his own pleasure and hers were pretext enough. The singing came at the end of the lesson hour, and they both treated it as a form of relaxation.

Harsanyi did not say much even to his wife about his discovery. He brooded upon it in a curious way. He found that these unscientific singing lessons stimulated him in his own study. After Miss Kronborg left him he often lay down in his studio for an hour before dinner, with his head full of musical ideas, with an effervescence in his brain which he had sometimes lost for weeks together under the grind of teaching. He had never got so much back for himself from any pupil as he did from Miss Kronborg. From the first she had stimulated him; something in her personality invariably affected him. Now that he was feeling his way toward her voice, he found her more interesting than ever before. She lifted the tedium of the winter for him, gave him curious fancies and reveries. Musically, she was sympathetic to him. Why all this was true, he never asked himself. He had learned that one must take where and when one can the mysterious mental irritant that rouses one's imagination; that it is not to be had by order. She often wearied him, but she never bored him. Under her crudeness and brusque hardness, he felt there was a nature quite different, of which he never got so much as a hint except when she was at the piano, or when she sang. It was toward this hidden creature that he was trying, for his own pleasure, to find his way. In short, Harsanyi looked forward to his hour with Thea for the same reason that poor Wunsch had sometimes dreaded his; because she stirred him more than anything she did could adequately explain.

One afternoon Harsanyi, after the lesson, was standing by the window putting some collodion on a cracked finger, and Thea was at the piano trying over "Die Lorelei"* which he had given her last week to practise. It was scarcely a song which a singing master would have given her, but he had his own reasons. How she sang it mattered only to him and to her. He was playing his own game now, without interference; he suspected that he could not do so always.

When she finished the song, she looked back over her shoulder at him and spoke thoughtfully. "That wasn't right, at the end, was it?"

"No, that should be an open, flowing tone, something like this,"—he waved his fingers rapidly in the air. "You get the idea?"

"No, I don't. Seems a queer ending, after the rest."

Harsanyi corked his little bottle and dropped it into the pocket of his velvet coat. "Why so? Shipwrecks come and go, *Märchen* come and go, but the river keeps right on. There you have your open, flowing tone."

Thea looked intently at the music. "I see," she said dully. "Oh, I see!" she repeated quickly and turned to him a glowing countenance. "It is the river.—Oh, yes, I get it now!" She looked at him but long enough to catch his glance, then turned to the piano again. Harsanyi was never quite sure where the light came from when her face suddenly flashed out at him in that way. Her eyes were too small to account for it, though they glittered like green ice in the sun. At such moments her hair was yellower, her skin whiter, her cheeks pinker, as if a lamp had suddenly been turned up inside of her. She went at the song again:

> "*Ich weiss nicht, was soll es bedeuten,
> Das ich so traurig bin.*"*

A kind of happiness vibrated in her voice. Harsanyi noticed how much and how unhesitatingly she changed her delivery of the whole song, the first part as well as the last. He had often noticed that she could not think a thing out in passages. Until she saw it as a whole, she wandered like a blind man surrounded by torments. After she once had her "revelation," after she got the idea that to her—not always to him—explained everything, then she went forward rapidly. But she was not always easy to help. She was some times impervious to suggestion; she would stare at him as if she were deaf and ignore everything he told her to do.

Then, all at once, something would happen in her brain and she would begin to do all that he had been for weeks telling her to do, without realizing that he had ever told her.

To-night Thea forgot Harsanyi and his finger. She finished the song only to begin it with fresh enthusiasm.

> "*Und das hat mit ihrem singen*
> *Die Lorelei gethan.*"*

She sat there singing it until the darkening room was so flooded with it that Harsanyi threw open a window.

"You really must stop it, Miss Kronborg. I shan't be able to get it out of my head to-night."

Thea laughed tolerantly as she began to gather up her music. "Why, I thought you had gone, Mr. Harsanyi. I like that song."

That evening at dinner Harsanyi sat looking intently into a glass of heavy yellow wine; boring into it, indeed, with his one eye, when his face suddenly broke into a smile.

"What is it, Andor?" his wife asked.

He smiled again, this time at her, and took up the nut-crackers and a Brazil nut. "Do you know," he said in a tone so intimate and confidential that he might have been speaking to himself,—"do you know, I like to see Miss Kronborg get hold of an idea. In spite of being so talented, she's not quick. But when she does get an idea, it fills her up to the eyes. She had my room so reeking of a song this afternoon that I couldn't stay there."

Mrs. Harsanyi looked up quickly, "'Die Lorelei,' you mean? One couldn't think of anything else anywhere in the house. I thought she was possessed. But don't you think her voice is wonderful sometimes?"

Harsanyi tasted his wine slowly. "My dear, I've told you before that I don't know what I think about Miss Kronborg, except that I'm glad there are not two of her. I sometimes wonder whether she is not glad. Fresh as she is at it all, I've occasionally fancied that, if she knew how, she would like to—diminish." He moved his left hand out into the air as if he were suggesting a *diminuendo**
to an orchestra.

V

BY the first of February Thea had been in Chicago almost four months, and she did not know much more about the city than if she had never quitted Moonstone. She was, as Harsanyi said, incurious. Her work took most of her time, and she found that she had to sleep a good deal. It had never before been so hard to get up in the morning. She had the bother of caring for her room, and she had to build her fire and bring up her coal. Her routine was frequently interrupted by a message from Mr. Larsen summoning her to sing at a funeral. Every funeral took half a day, and the time had to be made up. When Mrs. Harsanyi asked her if it did not depress her to sing at funerals, she replied that she "had been brought up to go to funerals and didn't mind."

Thea never went into shops unless she had to, and she felt no interest in them. Indeed, she shunned them, as places where one was sure to be parted from one's money in some way. She was nervous about counting her change, and she could not accustom herself to having her purchases sent to her address. She felt much safer with her bundles under her arm.

During this first winter Thea got no city consciousness. Chicago was simply a wilderness through which one had to find one's way. She felt no interest in the general briskness and zest of the crowds. The crash and scramble of that big, rich, appetent Western city she did not take in at all, except to notice that the noise of the drays and street-cars tired her. The brilliant window displays, the splendid furs and stuffs, the gorgeous flower-shops, the gay candy-shops, she scarcely noticed. At Christmas-time she did feel some curiosity about the toy-stores, and she wished she held Thor's little mittened fist in her hand as she stood before the windows. The jewelers' windows, too, had a strong attraction for her—she had always liked bright stones. When she went into the city she used to brave the biting lake winds and stand gazing in at the displays of diamonds and pearls and emeralds; the tiaras and necklaces and ear-rings, on white velvet. These seemed very well worth while to her, things worth coveting.

Mrs. Lorch and Mrs. Andersen often told each other it was strange that Miss. Kronborg had so little initiative about "visiting points of interest." When Thea came to live with them she had expressed a wish to see two places: Montgomery Ward and Company's big mail-order store, and the packing-houses, to which all the hogs and cattle that went through Moonstone were bound. One of Mrs. Lorch's lodgers worked in a packing-house, and Mrs. Andersen brought Thea word that she had spoken to Mr. Eckman and he would gladly take her to Packingtown. Eckman was a toughish young Swede, and he thought it would be something of a lark to take a pretty girl through the slaughter-houses. But he was disappointed. Thea neither grew faint nor clung to the arm he kept offering her. She asked innumerable questions and was impatient because he knew so little of what was going on outside of his own department. When they got off the street-car and walked back to Mrs. Lorch's house in the dusk, Eckman put her hand in his overcoat pocket—she had no muff—and kept squeezing it ardently until she said, "Don't do that; my ring cuts me." That night he told his roommate that he "could have kissed her as easy as rolling off a log, but she wasn't worth the trouble." As for Thea, she had enjoyed the afternoon very much, and wrote her father a brief but clear account of what she had seen.

One night at supper Mrs. Andersen was talking about the exhibit of students' work she had seen at the Art Institute* that afternoon. Several of her friends had sketches in the exhibit. Thea, who always felt that she was behindhand in courtesy to Mrs. Andersen, thought that here was an opportunity to show interest without committing herself to anything. "Where is that, the Institute?" she asked absently.

Mrs. Andersen clasped her napkin in both hands. "The Art Institute? Our beautiful Art Institute on Michigan Avenue? Do you mean to say you have never visited it?"

"Oh, is it the place with the big lions out in front? I remember; I saw it when I went to Montgomery Ward's. Yes, I thought the lions were beautiful."

"But the pictures! Didn't you visit the galleries?"

"No. The sign outside said it was a pay-day. I've always meant to go back, but I haven't happened to be down that way since."

Mrs. Lorch and Mrs. Andersen looked at each other. The old mother spoke, fixing her shining little eyes upon Thea across the table. "Ah, but Miss Kronborg, there are old masters! Oh, many of them, such as you could not see anywhere out of Europe."

"And Corots," breathed Mrs. Andersen, tilting her head feelingly. "Such examples of the Barbizon school!"* This was meaningless to Thea, who did not read the art columns of the Sunday *Inter-Ocean** as Mrs. Andersen did.

"Oh, I'm going there some day," she reassured them. "I like to look at oil paintings."

One bleak day in February, when the wind was blowing clouds of dirt like a Moonstone sandstorm, dirt that filled your eyes and ears and mouth, Thea fought her way across the unprotected space in front of the Art Institute and into the doors of the building. She did not come out again until the closing hour. In the street-car, on the long cold ride home, while she sat staring at the waistcoat buttons of a fat strap-hanger, she had a serious reckoning with herself. She seldom thought about her way of life, about what she ought or ought not to do; usually there was but one obvious and important thing to be done. But that afternoon she remonstrated with herself severely. She told herself that she was missing a great deal; that she ought to be more willing to take advice and to go to see things. She was sorry that she had let months pass without going to the Art Institute. After this she would go once a week.

The Institute proved, indeed, a place of retreat, as the sand hills or the Kohlers' garden used to be; a place where she could forget Mrs. Andersen's tiresome overtures of friendship, the stout contralto in the choir whom she so unreasonably hated, and even, for a little while, the torment of her work. That building was a place in which she could relax and play, and she could hardly ever play now. On the whole, she spent more time with the casts than with the pictures. They were at once more simple and more perplexing; and some way they seemed more important, harder to overlook. It never occurred to her to buy a catalogue, so she called most of the casts by names she made up for them. Some of them she knew; the Dying Gladiator she had read about in "Childe Harold"* almost as long ago as she could remember; he was strongly associated with Dr. Archie and childish illnesses. The Venus di Milo* puzzled her; she could not see why people thought her so beautiful. She told herself over and over that she did not think the Apollo Belvedere* "at all handsome." Better than anything else she liked a great equestrian statue of an evil, cruel-looking general with an unpronounceable name.* She used to walk round and round this terrible man and his terrible horse, frowning at him, brooding upon him, as if she had to make some momentous decision about him.

The casts, when she lingered long among them, always made her gloomy. It was with a lightening of the heart, a feeling of throwing off the old miseries and old sorrows of the world, that she ran up the wide staircase to the pictures. There she liked best the ones that told stories. There was a painting by Gérôme called "The Pasha's Grief"* which always made her wish for Gunner and Axel. The Pasha was seated on a rug, beside a green candle almost as big as a telegraph pole, and before him was stretched his dead tiger, a splendid beast, and there were pink roses scattered about him. She loved, too, a picture of some boys bringing in a newborn calf on a litter, the cow walking beside it and licking it. The Corot which hung next to this painting she did not like or dislike; she never saw it.

But in that same room there was a picture—oh, that was the thing she ran upstairs so fast to see! That was her picture. She imagined that nobody cared for it but herself, and that it waited for her. That was a picture indeed. She liked even the name of it, "The Song of the Lark." The flat country, the early morning light, the wet fields, the look in the girl's heavy face—well, they were all hers, anyhow, whatever was there. She told herself that that picture was "right." Just what she meant by this it would take a clever person to explain. But to her the word covered the almost boundless satisfaction she felt when she looked at the picture.

*

Before Thea had any idea how fast the weeks were flying, before Mr. Larsen's "permanent" soprano had returned to her duties, spring came; windy, dusty, strident, shrill; a season almost more violent in Chicago than the winter from which it releases one, or the heat to which it eventually delivers one. One sunny morning the apple trees in Mrs. Lorch's back yard burst into bloom, and for the first time in months Thea dressed without building a fire. The morning shone like a holiday, and for her it was to be a holiday. There was in the air that sudden, treacherous softness which makes the Poles who work in the packing-houses get drunk. At such times beauty is necessary and in Packingtown there is no place to get it except at the saloons, where one can buy for a few hours the illusion of comfort, hope, love,—whatever one most longs for.

Harsanyi had given Thea a ticket for the symphony concert that afternoon, and when she looked out at the white apple trees her doubts as to whether she ought to go vanished at once. She would make her work light that morning, she told herself. She would go to the concert full of energy. When she set off, after dinner, Mrs. Lorch, who knew Chicago weather, prevailed upon her to take her cape. The old lady said that such sudden mildness, so early in April, presaged a sharp return of winter, and she was anxious about her apple trees.

The concert began at two-thirty, and Thea was in her seat in the Auditorium at ten minutes after two—a fine seat in the first row of the balcony, on the side, where she could see the house as well as the orchestra. She had been to so few concerts that the great house, the crowd of people, and the lights, all had a stimulating effect. She was surprised to see so many men in the audience, and wondered how they could leave their business in the afternoon. During the first number Thea was so much interested in the orchestra itself, in the men, the instruments, the volume of sound, that she paid little attention to what they were playing. Her excitement impaired her power of listening. She kept saying to herself, "Now I must stop this foolishness and listen; I may never hear this again"; but her mind was like a glass that is hard to focus. She was not ready to listen until the second number,

Dvorak's Symphony in E minor, called on the programme, "From the New World."* The first theme had scarcely been given out when her mind became clear; instant composure fell upon her, and with it came the power of concentration. This was music she could understand, music from the New World indeed! Strange how, as the first movement went on, it brought back to her that high tableland above Laramie; the grass-grown wagon trails, the far-away peaks of the snowy range, the wind and the eagles, that old man and the first telegraph message.

When the first movement ended, Thea's hands and feet were cold as ice. She was too much excited to know anything except that she wanted something desperately, and when the English horns gave out the theme of the Largo,* she knew that what she wanted was exactly that. Here were the sand hills, the grass-hoppers and locusts, all the things that wakened and chirped in the early morning; the reaching and reaching of high plains, the immeasurable yearning of all flat lands. There was home in it, too; first memories, first mornings long ago; the amazement of a new soul in a new world; a soul new and yet old that had dreamed something despairing, something glorious, in the dark before it was born; a soul obsessed by what it did not know, under the cloud of a past it could not recall.

If Thea had had much experience in concert-going, and had known her own capacity, she would have left the hall when the symphony was over. But she sat still, scarcely knowing where she was, because her mind had been far away and had not yet come back to her. She was startled when the orchestra began to play again—the entry of the gods into Walhalla. She heard it as people hear things in their sleep. She knew scarcely anything about the Wagner operas. She had a vague idea that "Rhinegold"* was about the strife between gods and men; she had read something about it in Mr. Haweis's book long ago. Too tired to follow the orchestra with much understanding, she crouched down in her seat and closed her eyes. The cold, stately measures of the Walhalla music rang out, far away; the rainbow bridge* throbbed out into the air, under it the wailing of the Rhine daughters and the singing of the Rhine. But Thea was sunk in twilight; it was all going on in another world. So it happened that with a dull, almost listless ear she heard for the first time that troubled music, ever-darkening, ever-brightening, which was to flow through so many years of her life.

When Thea emerged from the concert hall, Mrs. Lorch's predictions had been fulfilled. A furious gale was beating over the city from Lake Michigan. The streets were full of cold, hurrying, angry people, running for street-cars and barking at each other. The sun was setting in a clear windy sky, that flamed with red as if there were a great fire somewhere on the edge of the city. For almost the first time Thea was conscious of the city itself, of the congestion of life all about her, of the brutality and power of those streams that flowed in the streets, threatening to drive one under. People jostled her, ran into her, poked her aside with their elbows, uttering angry exclamations. She got on the wrong car and was roughly ejected by the conductor at a windy corner, in front of a saloon. She stood there dazed and shivering. The cars passed, screaming as they rounded curves, but either they were full to the doors, or were bound for places where she did not want to go. Her hands were so cold that she took off her tight kid gloves. The street lights began to gleam in the dusk. A young man came out of the saloon and stood eyeing her questioningly while he lit a cigarette. "Looking for a friend to-night?" he asked. Thea drew up the collar of her cape and walked on a few paces. The young man shrugged his shoulders and drifted away.

Thea came back to the corner and stood there irresolutely. An old man approached her. He, too, seemed to be waiting for a car. He wore an overcoat with a black fur collar, his gray mustache was waxed into little points, and his eyes were watery. He kept thrusting his face up near hers. Her hat blew off and he ran after it—a stiff, pitiful skip he had—and brought it back to her. Then, while she was pinning her hat on, her cape blew up, and he held it down for her, looking at her intently. His face worked as if he were going to cry or were frightened. He leaned over and whispered something to her. It struck her as curious that he was really quite timid, like an old beggar. "Oh, let me *alone!*" she cried miserably between her teeth. He vanished, disappeared like the

Devil in a play. But in the mean time something had got away from her; she could not remember how the violins came in after the horns, just there. When her cape blew up, perhaps—Why did these men torment her? A cloud of dust blew in her face and blinded her. There was some power abroad in the world bent upon taking away from her that feeling with which she had come out of the concert hall. Everything seemed to sweep down on her to tear it out from under her cape. If one had that, the world became one's enemy; people, buildings, wagons, cars, rushed at one to crush it under, to make one let go of it. Thea glared round her at the crowds, the ugly, sprawling streets, the long lines of lights, and she was not crying now. Her eyes were brighter than even Harsanyi had ever seen them. All these things and people were no longer remote and negligible; they had to be met, they were lined up against her, they were there to take something from her. Very well; they should never have it. They might trample her to death, but they should never have it. As long as she lived that ecstasy was going to be hers. She would live for it, work for it, die for it; but she was going to have it, time after time, height after height. She could hear the crash of the orchestra again, and she rose on the brasses. She would have it, what the trumpets were singing! She would have it, have it,—it! Under the old cape she pressed her hands upon her heaving bosom, that was a little girl's no longer.

VI

ONE afternoon in April, Theodore Thomas, the conductor of the Chicago Symphony Orchestra, had turned out his desk light and was about to leave his office in the Auditorium Building, when Harsanyi appeared in the doorway. The conductor welcomed him with a hearty hand-grip and threw off the overcoat he had just put on. He pushed Harsanyi into a chair and sat down at his burdened desk, pointing to the piles of papers and railway folders upon it.

"Another tour, clear to the coast. This traveling is the part of my work that grinds me, Andor. You know what it means: bad food, dirt, noise, exhaustion for the men and for me. I'm not so young as I once was. It's time I quit the highway. This is the last tour, I swear!"

"Then I'm sorry for the 'highway.' I remember when I first heard you in Pittsburg, long ago. It was a life-line you threw me. It's about one of the people along your highway that I've come to see you. Whom do you consider the best teacher for voice in Chicago?"

Mr. Thomas frowned and pulled his heavy mustache. "Let me see; I suppose on the whole Madison Bowers is the best. He's intelligent, and he had good training. I don't like him."

Harsanyi nodded. "I thought there was no one else. I don't like him, either, so I hesitated. But I suppose he must do, for the present."

"Have you found anything promising? One of your own students?"

"Yes, sir. A young Swedish girl from somewhere in Colorado. She is very talented, and she seems to me to have a remarkable voice."

"High voice?"

"I think it will be; though her low voice has a beautiful quality, very individual. She has had no instruction in voice at all, and I shrink from handing her over to anybody; her own instinct about it has been so good. It is one of those voices that manages itself easily, without thinning as it goes up; good breathing and perfect relaxation. But she must have a teacher, of course. There is a break in the middle voice, so that the voice does not all work together; an unevenness."

Thomas looked up. "So? Curious; that cleft often happens with the Swedes. Some of their best singers have had it. It always reminds me of the space you so often see between their front teeth. Is she strong physically?"

Harsanyi's eye flashed. He lifted his hand before him and clenched it. "Like a horse, like a tree! Every time I give her a lesson, I lose a pound. She goes after what she wants."

"Intelligent, you say? Musically intelligent?"

"Yes; but no cultivation whatever. She came to me like a fine young savage, a book with nothing written in it. That is why I feel the responsibility of directing her." Harsanyi paused and crushed his soft gray hat over his knee. "She would interest you, Mr. Thomas," he added slowly. "She has a quality—very individual."

"Yes; the Scandinavians are apt to have that, too. She can't go to Germany, I suppose?"

"Not now, at any rate. She is poor."

Thomas frowned again. "I don't think Bowers a really first-rate man. He's too petty to be really first-rate; in his nature, I mean. But I dare say he's the best you can do if you can't give her time enough yourself."

Harsanyi waved his hand. "Oh, the time is nothing—she may have all she wants. But I cannot teach her to sing."

"Might not come amiss if you made a musician of her, however," said Mr. Thomas dryly.

"I have done my best. But I can only play with a voice, and this is not a voice to be played with. I think she will be a musician, whatever happens. She is not quick, but she is solid, real; not like these others. My wife says that with that girl one swallow does not make a summer."

Mr. Thomas laughed. "Tell Mrs. Harsanyi that her remark conveys something to me. Don't let yourself get too much interested. Voices are so often disappointing; especially women's voices. So much chance about it, so many factors."

"Perhaps that is why they interest one. All the intelligence and talent in the world can't make a singer. The voice is a wild thing. It can't be bred in captivity. It is a sport, like the silver fox. It happens."

Mr. Thomas smiled into Harsanyi's gleaming eye. "Why haven't you brought her to sing for me?"

"I've been tempted to, but I knew you were driven to death, with this tour confronting you."

"Oh, I can always find time to listen to a girl who has a voice, if she means business. I'm sorry I'm leaving so soon. I could advise you better if I had heard her. I can sometimes give a singer suggestions. I've worked so much with them."

"You're the only conductor I know who is not snobbish about singers." Harsanyi spoke warmly.

"Dear me, why should I be? They've learned from me, and I've learned from them." As they rose, Thomas took the younger man affectionately by the arm. "Tell me about that wife of yours. Is she well, and as lovely as ever? And such fine children! Come to see me oftener, when I get back. I miss it when you don't."

The two men left the Auditorium Building together. Harsanyi walked home. Even a short talk with Thomas always stimulated him. As he walked he was recalling an evening they once spent together in Cincinnati.

Harsanyi was the soloist at one of Thomas's concerts there, and after the performance the conductor had taken him off to a *Rathskeller** where there was excellent German cooking, and where the proprietor saw to it that Thomas had the best wines procurable. Thomas had been working with the great chorus of the Festival Association and was speaking of it with enthusiasm when Harsanyi asked him how it was that he was able to feel such an interest in choral directing and in voices generally. Thomas seldom spoke of his youth or his early struggles, but that night he turned back the pages and told Harsanyi a long story.

He said he had spent the summer of his fifteenth year wandering about alone in the South, giving violin concerts in little towns. He traveled on horseback. When he came into a town, he went about all day tacking up posters announcing his concert in the evening. Before the concert, he stood at the door taking in the admission money until his audience had arrived, and then he went on the platform and played. It was a lazy, hand-to-mouth existence, and Thomas said he must have got to like that easy way of living and the relaxing Southern atmosphere. At any rate, when he got back to New York in the fall, he was rather torpid; perhaps he had been growing too fast. From this adolescent drowsiness the lad was awakened by two voices, by two women who sang in New York in 1851,—Jenny Lind and Henrietta Sontag.* They were the first great artists he had ever heard, and he never forgot his debt to them.

As he said, "It was not voice and execution alone. There was a greatness about them. They were great women, great artists. They opened a new world to me." Night after night he went to hear them, striving to reproduce the quality of their tone upon his violin. From that time his idea about strings was completely changed, and on his violin he tried always for the singing, vibrating tone, instead of the loud and somewhat harsh tone then prevalent among even the best German violinists. In later years he often advised violinists to study singing, and singers to study violin. He told Harsanyi that he got his first conception of tone quality from Jenny Lind.

"But, of course," he added, "the great thing I got from Lind and Sontag was the indefinite, not the definite, thing. For an impressionable boy, their inspiration was incalculable. They gave me my first feeling for the Italian style—but I could never say how much they gave me. At that age, such influences are actually creative. I always think of my artistic consciousness as beginning then."

All his life Thomas did his best to repay what he felt he owed to the singer's art. No man could get such singing from choruses, and no man worked harder to raise the standard of singing in schools and churches and choral societies.

VII

ALL through the lesson Thea had felt that Harsanyi was restless and abstracted. Before the hour was over, he pushed back his chair and said resolutely, "I am not in the mood, Miss Kronborg. I have something on my mind, and I must talk to you. When do you intend to go home?"

Thea turned to him in surprise. "The first of June, about. Mr. Larsen will not need me after that, and I have not much money ahead. I shall work hard this summer, though."

"And to-day is the first of May; May-day." Harsanyi leaned forward, his elbows on his knees, his hands locked between them. "Yes, I must talk to you about something. I have asked Madison Bowers to let me bring you to him on Thursday, at your usual lesson-time. He is the best vocal teacher in Chicago, and it is time you began to work seriously with your voice."

Thea's brow wrinkled. "You mean take lessons of Bowers?"

Harsanyi nodded, without lifting his head.

"But I can't, Mr. Harsanyi. I haven't got the time, and, besides—" she blushed and drew her shoulders up stiffly— "besides, I can't afford to pay two teachers." Thea felt that she had blurted this out in the worst possible way, and she turned back to the keyboard to hide her chagrin.

"I know that. I don't mean that you shall pay two teachers. After you go to Bowers you will not need me. I need scarcely tell you that I shan't be happy at losing you."

Thea turned to him, hurt and angry. "But I don't want to go to Bowers. I don't want to leave you. What's the matter? Don't I work hard enough? I'm sure you teach people that don't try half as hard."

Harsanyi rose to his feet. "Don't misunderstand me, Miss Kronborg. You interest me more than any pupil I have. I have been thinking for months about what you ought to do, since that night when you first sang for me." He walked over to the window, turned, and came toward her again. "I believe that your voice is worth all that you can put into it. I have not come to this decision rashly. I have studied you, and I have become more and more convinced, against my own desires. I cannot make a singer of you, so it was my business to find a man who could. I have even consulted Theodore Thomas about it."

"But suppose I don't want to be a singer? I want to study with you. What's the matter? Do you really think I've no talent? Can't I be a pianist?"

Harsanyi paced up and down the long rug in front of her. "My girl, you are very talented. You could be a pianist, a good one. But the early training of a pianist, such a pianist as you would want to be, must be something tremendous. He must have had no other life than music. At your age he must be the master of his instrument. Nothing can ever take the place of that first training. You know very well that your technique is good, but it is not remarkable. It will never overtake your intelligence. You have a fine power of work, but you are not by nature a student. You are not by nature, I think, a pianist. You would never find yourself. In the effort to do so, I'm afraid your playing would become warped, eccentric." He threw back his head and looked at his pupil intently with that one eye which sometimes seemed to see deeper than any two eyes, as if its singleness gave it privileges. "Oh, I have watched you very carefully, Miss Kronborg. Because you had had so little and had yet done so much for yourself, I had a great wish to help you. I believe that the strongest need of your nature is to find yourself, to emerge *as* yourself. Until I heard you sing I wondered how you were to do this, but it has grown clearer to me every day."

Thea looked away toward the window with hard, narrow eyes. "You mean I can be a singer because I haven't brains enough to be a pianist."

"You have brains enough and talent enough. But to do what you will want to do, it takes more than these—it takes vocation. Now, I think you have vocation, but for the voice, not for the piano. If you knew,"—he stopped and sighed,—"if you knew how fortunate I sometimes think you. With the voice the way is so much shorter, the rewards are more easily won. In your voice I think Nature herself did for you what it would take you many years to do at the piano. Perhaps you were not born in the wrong place after all. Let us talk frankly now. We have never done so before, and I have respected your reticence. What you want more than anything else in the world is to be an artist; is that true?"

She turned her face away from him and looked down at the keyboard. Her answer came in a thickened voice. "Yes, I suppose so."

"When did you first feel that you wanted to be an artist?"

"I don't know. There was always—something."

"Did you never think that you were going to sing?"

"Yes."

"How long ago was that?"

"Always, until I came to you. It was you who made me want to play piano." Her voice trembled. "Before, I tried to think I did, but I was pretending."

Harsanyi reached out and caught the hand that was hanging at her side. He pressed it as if to give her something. "Can't you see, my dear girl, that was only because I happened to be the first artist you have ever known? If I had been a trombone player, it would have been the same; you would have wanted to play trombone. But all the while you have been working with such goodwill, something has been struggling against me. See, here we were, you and I and this instrument,"—he tapped the piano,— "three good friends, working so hard. But all the while there was something fighting us: your gift, and the woman you were meant to be. When you find your way to that gift and to that woman, you will be at peace. In the beginning it was an artist that you wanted to be; well, you may be an artist, always."

Thea drew a long breath. Her hands fell in her lap. "So I'm just where I began. No teacher, nothing done. No money."

Harsanyi turned away. "Feel no apprehension about the money, Miss Kronborg. Come back in the fall and we shall manage that. I shall even go to Mr. Thomas if necessary. This year will not be lost. If you but knew what an advantage this winter's study, all your study of the piano, will give you over most singers. Perhaps things have come out better for you than if we had planned them knowingly."

"You mean they have *if* I can sing."

Thea spoke with a heavy irony, so heavy, indeed, that it was coarse. It grated upon Harsanyi because he felt that it was not sincere, an awkward affectation.

He wheeled toward her. "Miss Kronborg, answer me this. *You know that you can sing*, do you not? You have always known it. While we worked here together you sometimes said to yourself, 'I have something you know nothing about; I could surprise you.' Is that also true?"

Thea nodded and hung her head.

"Why were you not frank with me? Did I not deserve it?"

She shuddered. Her bent shoulders trembled. "I don't know," she muttered. "I didn't mean to be like that. I couldn't. I can't. It's different."

"You mean it is very personal?" he asked kindly.

She nodded. "Not at church or funerals, or with people like Mr. Larsen. But with you it was—personal. I'm not like you and Mrs. Harsanyi. I come of rough people. I'm rough. But I'm independent, too. It was—all I had. There is no use my talking, Mr. Harsanyi. I can't tell you."

"You needn't tell me. I know. Every artist knows." Harsanyi stood looking at his pupil's back, bent as if she were pushing something, at her lowered head. "You can sing for those people because with them you do not commit yourself. But the reality, one cannot uncover *that* until one is sure. One can fail one's self, but one must not live to see that fail; better never reveal it. Let me help you to make yourself sure of it. That I can do better than Bowers."

Thea lifted her face and threw out her hands.

Harsanyi shook his head and smiled. "Oh, promise nothing! You will have much to do. There will not be voice only, but French, German, Italian. You will have work enough. But sometimes you will need to be understood; what you never show to any one will need companionship. And then you must come to me." He peered into her face with that searching, intimate glance. "You know what I mean, the thing in you that has no business with what is little, that will have to do only with beauty and power."

Thea threw out her hands fiercely, as if to push him away. She made a sound in her throat, but it was not articulate. Harsanyi took one of her hands and kissed it lightly upon the back. His salute was one of greeting, not of farewell, and it was for some one he had never seen.

When Mrs. Harsanyi came in at six o'clock, she found her husband sitting listlessly by the window. "Tired?" she asked.

"A little. I've just got through a difficulty. I've sent Miss Kronborg away; turned her over to Bowers, for voice."

"Sent Miss Kronborg away? Andor, what is the matter with you?"

"It's nothing rash. I've known for a long while I ought to do it. She is made for a singer, not a pianist."

Mrs. Harsanyi sat down on the piano chair. She spoke a little bitterly: "How can you be sure of that? She was, at least, the best you had. I thought you meant to have her play at your students' recital next fall. I am sure she would have made an impression. I could have dressed her so that she would have been very striking. She had so much individuality."

Harsanyi bent forward, looking at the floor. "Yes, I know. I shall miss her, of course."

Mrs. Harsanyi looked at her husband's fine head against the gray window. She had never felt deeper tenderness for him than she did at that moment. Her heart ached for him. "You will never get on, Andor," she said mournfully.

Harsanyi sat motionless. "No, I shall never get on," he repeated quietly. Suddenly he sprang up with that light movement she knew so well, and stood in the window, with folded arms. "But some day I shall be able to look her in the face and laugh because I did what I could for her. I believe in her. She will do nothing common. She is uncommon, in a common, common world. That is what I get out of it. It means more to me than if she played at my concert and brought me a dozen pupils. All this drudgery will kill me if once in a while I cannot hope something, for somebody! If I cannot sometimes see a bird fly and wave my hand to it."

His tone was angry and injured. Mrs. Harsanyi understood that this was one of the times when his wife was a part of the drudgery, of the "common, common world." He had let something he cared for go, and he felt bitterly about whatever was left. The mood would pass, and he would be sorry. She knew him. It wounded her, of course, but that hurt was not new. It was as old as her love for him. She went out and left him alone.

VIII

ONE warm damp June night the Denver Express was speeding westward across the earthy-smelling plains of Iowa. The lights in the day-coach were turned low and the ventilators were open, admitting showers of soot and dust upon the occupants of the narrow green plush chairs which were tilted at various angles of discomfort. In each of these chairs some uncomfortable human being lay drawn up, or stretched out, or writhing from one position to another. There were tired men in rumpled shirts, their necks bare and their suspenders down; old women with their heads tied up in black handkerchiefs; bedraggled young women who went to sleep while they were nursing their babies and forgot to button up their dresses; dirty boys who added to the general discomfort by taking off their boots. The brakeman, when he came through at midnight, sniffed the heavy air disdainfully and looked up at the ventilators. As he glanced down the double rows of contorted figures, he saw one pair of eyes that were wide open and bright, a yellow head that was not overcome by the stupefying heat and smell in the car. "There's a girl for you," he thought as he stopped by Thea's chair.

"Like to have the window up a little?" he asked.

Thea smiled up at him, not misunderstanding his friendliness. "The girl behind me is sick; she can't stand a draft. What time is it, please?"

He took out his open-faced watch and held it before her eyes with a knowing look. "In a hurry?" he asked. "I'll leave the end door open and air you out. Catch a wink; the time'll go faster."

Thea nodded good-night to him and settled her head back on her pillow, looking up at the oil lamps. She was going back to Moonstone for her summer vacation, and she was sitting up all night in a day-coach because that seemed such an easy way to save money. At her age discomfort was a small matter, when one made five dollars a day by it. She had confidently expected to sleep after the car got quiet, but in the two chairs behind her were a sick girl and her mother, and the girl had been coughing steadily since ten o'clock. They had come from somewhere in Pennsylvania, and this was their second night on the road. The mother said they were going to Colorado "for her daughter's lungs." The daughter was a little older than Thea, perhaps nineteen, with patient dark eyes and curly brown hair. She was pretty in spite of being so sooty and travel-stained. She had put on an ugly figured satine kimono over her loosened clothes. Thea, when she boarded the train in Chicago, happened to stop and plant her heavy telescope on this seat. She had not intended to remain there, but the sick girl had looked up at her with an eager smile and said, "Do sit there, miss. I'd so much rather not have a gentleman in front of me."

After the girl began to cough there were no empty seats left, and if there had been Thea could scarcely have changed without hurting her feelings. The mother turned on her side and went to sleep; she was used to the cough. But the girl lay wide awake, her eyes fixed on the roof of the car, as Thea's were. The two girls must have seen very different things there.

Thea fell to going over her winter in Chicago. It was only under unusual or uncomfortable conditions like these that she could keep her mind fixed upon herself or her own affairs for any length of time. The rapid motion and the vibration of the wheels under her seemed to give her thoughts rapidity and clearness. She had taken twenty very expensive lessons from Madison Bowers, but she did not yet know what he thought of her or of her ability. He was different from any man with whom she had ever had to do. With her other teachers she had felt a personal relation; but with him she did not. Bowers was a cold, bitter, avaricious man, but he knew a great deal about voices. He worked with a voice as if he were in a laboratory, conducting a series of experiments. He was conscientious and industrious, even capable of a certain cold fury when he was working with an interesting voice, but Harsanyi declared that he had the soul of a shrimp, and could no more make an artist than a throat specialist could. Thea realized that he had taught her a great deal in twenty lessons.

Although she cared so much less for Bowers than for Harsanyi, Thea was, on the whole, happier since she had been studying with him than she had been before. She had always told herself that she studied piano to fit herself to be a music teacher. But she never asked herself why she was studying voice. Her voice, more than any other part of her, had to do with that confidence, that sense of wholeness and inner well-being that she had felt at moments ever since she could remember.

Of this feeling Thea had never spoken to any human being

until that day when she told Harsanyi that "there had always been—something." Hitherto she had felt but one obligation toward it—secrecy; to protect it even from herself. She had always believed that by doing all that was required of her by her family, her teachers, her pupils, she kept that part of herself from being caught up in the meshes of common things. She took it for granted that some day, when she was older, she would know a great deal more about it. It was as if she had an appointment to meet the rest of herself sometime, somewhere. It was moving to meet her and she was moving to meet it. That meeting awaited her, just as surely as, for the poor girl in the seat behind her, there awaited a hole in the earth, already dug.

For Thea, so much had begun with a hole in the earth. Yes, she reflected, this new part of her life had all begun that morning when she sat on the clay bank beside Ray Kennedy, under the flickering shade of the cottonwood tree. She remembered the way Ray had looked at her that morning. Why had he cared so much? And Wunsch, and Dr. Archie, and Spanish Johnny, why had they? It was something that had to do with her that made them care, but it was not she. It was something they believed in, but it was not she. Perhaps each of them concealed another person in himself, just as she did. Why was it that they seemed to feel and to hunt for a second person in her and not in each other? Thea frowned up at the dull lamp in the roof of the car. What if one's second self could somehow speak to all these second selves? What if one could bring them out, as whiskey did Spanish Johnny's? How deep they lay, these second persons, and how little one knew about them, except to guard them fiercely. It was to music, more than to anything else, that these hidden things in people responded. Her mother—even her mother had something of that sort which replied to music.

Thea found herself listening for the coughing behind her and not hearing it. She turned cautiously and looked back over the head-rest of her chair. The poor girl had fallen asleep. Thea looked at her intently. Why was she so afraid of men? Why did she shrink into herself and avert her face whenever a man passed her chair? Thea thought she knew; of course, she knew. How horrible to waste away like that, in the time when one ought to be growing fuller and stronger and rounder every day. Suppose there were such a dark hole open for her, between to-night and that place where she was to meet herself? Her eyes narrowed. She put her hand on her breast and felt how warm it was; and within it there was a full, powerful pulsation. She smiled—though she was ashamed of it—with the natural contempt of strength for weakness, with the sense of physical security which makes the savage merciless. Nobody could die while they felt like that inside. The springs there were wound so tight that it would be a long while before there was any slack in them. The life in there was rooted deep. She was going to have a few things before she died. She realized that there were a great many trains dashing east and west on the face of the continent that night, and that they all carried young people who meant to have things. But the difference was that *she was going to get them!* That was all. Let people try to stop her! She glowered at the rows of feckless bodies that lay sprawled in the chairs. Let them try it once! Along with the yearning that came from some deep part of her, that was selfless and exalted, Thea had a hard kind of cockiness, a determination to get ahead. Well, there are passages in life when that fierce, stubborn self-assertion will stand its ground after the nobler feeling is overwhelmed and beaten under.

Having told herself once more that she meant to grab a few things, Thea went to sleep.

She was wakened in the morning by the sunlight, which beat fiercely through the glass of the car window upon her face. She made herself as clean as she could, and while the people all about her were getting cold food out of their lunch-baskets she escaped into the dining-car. Her thrift did not go to the point of enabling her to carry a lunch-basket. At that early hour there were few people in the dining-car. The linen was white and fresh, the darkies were trim and smiling, and the sunlight gleamed pleasantly upon the silver and the glass water-bottles. On each table there was a slender vase with a single pink rose in it. When Thea sat down she looked into her rose and though it the most beautiful thing in the world; it was wide open, recklessly offering its yellow heart, and there were drops of water on the petals. All the future was in that rose, all that one would like to be. The flower put her in an absolutely regal mood. She had a whole pot of coffee, and scrambled eggs with chopped ham, utterly disregarding the astonishing price they cost. She had faith enough in what she could do, she told herself, to have eggs if she wanted them. At the table opposite her sat a man and his wife and little boy—Thea classified them as being "from the East." They spoke in that quick, sure staccato, which Thea, like Ray Kennedy, pretended to scorn and secretly admired. People who could use words in that confident way, and who spoke them elegantly, had a great advantage in life, she reflected. There were so many words which she could not pronounce in speech as she had to do in singing. Language was like clothes; it could be a help to one, or it could give one away. But the most important thing was that one should not pretend to be what one was not.

When she paid her check she consulted the waiter. "Waiter, do, you suppose I could buy one of those roses? I'm out of the day-coach, and there is a sick girl in there. I'd like to take her a cup of coffee and one of those flowers."

The waiter liked nothing better than advising travelers less sophisticated than himself. He told Thea there were a few roses left in the icebox and he would get one. He took the flower and the coffee into the day-coach. Thea pointed out the girl, but she did not accompany him. She hated thanks and never received them gracefully. She stood outside on the platform to get some fresh air into her lungs. The train was crossing the Platte River now, and the sunlight was so intense that it seemed to quiver in little flames on the glittering sandbars, the scrub willows, and the curling, fretted shallows.

Thea felt that she was coming back to her own land. She had often heard Mrs. Kronborg say that she "believed in immigration," and so did Thea believe in it. This earth seemed to her young and fresh and kindly, a place where refugees from old, sad countries were given another chance. The mere absence of rocks gave the soil a kind of amiability and generosity, and the absence of natural boundaries gave the spirit a wider range. Wire fences might mark the end of a man's pasture, but they could not shut in his thoughts as mountains and forests can. It was over flat lands like this, stretching out to drink the sun, that the larks sang—and one's heart sang there, too. Thea was glad that this was her country, even if one did not learn to speak elegantly there. It was, somehow, an honest country, and there was a new song in that blue air which had never been sung in the world before. It was hard to tell about it, for it had nothing to do with words; it was like the light of the desert at noon, or the smell of the sagebrush after rain; intangible but powerful. She had the sense of going back to a friendly soil, whose friendship was somehow going to strengthen her; a naive, generous country that gave one its joyous force, its large-hearted, childlike power to love, just as it gave one its coarse, brilliant flowers.

As she drew in that glorious air Thea's mind went back to Ray Kennedy. He, too, had that feeling of empire; as if all the South-west really belonged to him because he had knocked about over it so much, and knew it, as he said, "like the blisters on his own hands." That feeling, she reflected, was the real element of companionship between her and Ray. Now that she was going back to Colorado, she realized this as she had not done before.

IX

THEA reached Moonstone in the late afternoon, and all the Kronborgs were there to meet her except her two older brothers. Gus and Charley were young men now, and they had declared at noon that it would "look silly if the whole bunch went down to the train." "There's no use making a fuss over Thea just because she's been to Chicago," Charley warned his mother. "She's inclined to think pretty well of herself, anyhow, and if you go treating her like company, there'll be no living in the house with her." Mrs. Kronborg simply leveled her eyes at Charley, and he faded away, muttering. She had, as Mr. Kronborg always said with an inclination of his head, good control over her children. Anna, too, wished to absent herself from the party, but in the end her curiosity got the better of her. So when Thea stepped down from the porter's stool, a very creditable Kronborg representation was grouped on the platform to greet her. After they had all kissed her (Gunner and Axel shyly), Mr. Kronborg hurried his flock into the hotel omnibus, in which they were to be driven ceremoniously home, with the neighbors looking out of their windows to see them go by.

All the family talked to her at once, except Thor,—impressive in new trousers,—who was gravely silent and who refused to sit on Thea's lap. One of the first things Anna told her was that Maggie Evans, the girl who used to cough in prayer meeting, died yesterday, and had made a request that Thea sing at her funeral.

Thea's smile froze. "I'm not going to sing at all this summer, except my exercises. Bowers says I taxed my voice last winter, singing at funerals so much. If I begin the first day after I get home, there'll be no end to it. You can tell them I caught cold on the train, or something."

Thea saw Anna glance at their mother. Thea remembered having seen that look on Anna's face often before, but she had never thought anything about it because she was used to it. Now she realized that the look was distinctly spiteful, even vindictive. She suddenly realized that Anna had always disliked her.

Mrs. Kronborg seemed to notice nothing, and changed the trend of the conversation, telling Thea that Dr. Archie and Mr. Upping, the jeweler, were both coming in to see her that evening, and that she had asked Spanish Johnny to come, because he had behaved well all winter and ought to be encouraged.

The next morning Thea wakened early in her own room up under the eaves and lay watching the sunlight shine on the roses of her wall-paper. She wondered whether she would ever like a plastered room as well as this one lined with scantlings. It was snug and tight, like the cabin of a little boat. Her bed faced the window and stood against the wall, under the slant of the ceiling. When she went away she could just touch the ceiling with the tips of her fingers; now she could touch it with the palm of her hand. It was so little that it was like a sunny cave, with roses running all over the roof. Through the low window, as she lay there, she could watch people going by on the farther side of the street; men, going downtown to open their stores. Thor was over there, rattling his express wagon along the sidewalk. Tillie had put a bunch of French pinks in a tumbler of water on her dresser, and they gave out a pleasant perfume. The blue jays were fighting and screeching in the cottonwood tree outside her window, as they always did, and she could hear the old Baptist deacon across the street calling his chickens, as she had heard him do every summer morning since she could remember. It was pleasant to waken up in that bed, in that room, and to feel the brightness of the morning, while light quivered about the low, papered ceiling in golden spots, refracted by the broken mirror and the glass of water that held the pinks. "*Im leuchtenden Sommermorgen*"; those lines, and the face of her old teacher, came back to Thea, floated to her out of sleep, perhaps. She had been dreaming something pleasant, but she could not remember what. She would go to call upon Mrs. Kohler to-day, and see the pigeons washing their pink feet in the drip under the water tank, and flying about their house that was sure to have a fresh coat of white paint on it for summer. On the way home she would stop to see Mrs. Tellamantez. On Sunday she would coax Gunner to take her out to the sand hills. She had missed them in Chicago; had been homesick for their brilliant morning gold and for their soft colors at evening. The Lake, somehow, had never taken their place.

While she lay planning, relaxed in warm drowsiness, she heard a knock at her door. She supposed it was Tillie, who sometimes fluttered in on her before she was out of bed to offer some service which the family would have ridiculed. But instead, Mrs. Kronborg herself came in, carrying a tray with Thea's breakfast set out on one of the best white napkins. Thea sat up with some embarrassment and pulled her nightgown together across her chest. Mrs. Kronborg was always busy downstairs in the morning, and Thea could not remember when her mother had come to her room before.

"I thought you'd be tired, after traveling, and might like to take it easy for once." Mrs. Kronborg put the tray on the edge of the bed. "I took some thick cream for you before the boys got at it. They raised a howl." She chuckled and sat down in the big wooden rocking chair. Her visit made Thea feel grown-up, and, somehow, important.

Mrs. Kronborg asked her about Bowers and the Harsanyis. She felt a great change in Thea, in her face and in her manner. Mr. Kronborg had noticed it, too, and had spoken of it to his wife with great satisfaction while they were undressing last night. Mrs. Kronborg sat looking at her daughter, who lay on her side, supporting herself on her elbow and lazily drinking her coffee from the tray before her. Her short-sleeved nightgown had come open at the throat again, and Mrs. Kronborg noticed how white her arms and shoulders were, as if they had been dipped in new milk. Her chest was fuller than when she went away, her breasts rounder and firmer, and though she was so white where she was uncovered, they looked rosy through the thin muslin. Her body had the elasticity that comes of being highly charged with the desire to live. Her hair, hanging in two loose braids, one by either cheek, was just enough disordered to catch the light in all its curly ends.

Thea always woke with a pink flush on her cheeks, and this morning her mother thought she had never seen her eyes so wide-open and bright; like clear green springs in the wood, when the early sunlight sparkles in them. She would make a very handsome woman, Mrs. Kronborg said to herself, if she would only get rid of that fierce look she had sometimes. Mrs. Kronborg took great pleasure in good looks, wherever she found them. She still remembered that, as a baby, Thea had been the "best-formed" of any of her children.

"I'll have to get you a longer bed," she remarked, as she put the tray on the table. "You're getting too long for that one."

Thea looked up at her mother and laughed, dropping back on her pillow with a magnificent stretch of her whole body. Mrs. Kronborg sat down again.

"I don't like to press you, Thea, but I think you'd better sing at that funeral to-morrow. I'm afraid you'll always be sorry if you don't. Sometimes a little thing like that, that seems nothing at the time, comes back on one afterward and troubles one a good deal. I don't mean the church shall run you to death this summer, like they used to. I've spoken my mind to your father about that, and he's very reasonable. But Maggie talked a good deal about you to people this winter; always asked what word we'd had, and said how she missed your singing and all. I guess you ought to do that much for her."

"All right, mother, if you think so." Thea lay looking at her mother with intensely bright eyes.

"That's right, daughter." Mrs. Kronborg rose and went over to get the tray, stopping to put her hand on Thea's chest. "You're filling out nice," she said, feeling about. "No, I wouldn't bother about the buttons. Leave 'em stay off. This is a good time to harden your chest."

Thea lay still and heard her mother's firm step receding along the bare floor of the trunk loft. There was no sham about her mother, she reflected. Her mother knew a great many things of which she never talked, and all the church people were forever chattering about things of which they knew nothing. She liked her mother.

Now for Mexican Town and the Kohlers! She meant to run in on the old woman without warning, and hug her.

X

SPANISH JOHNNY had no shop of his own, but he kept a table and an order-book in one corner of the drug store where paints and wall-paper were sold, and he was sometimes to be found there for an hour or so about noon. Thea had gone into the drug store to have a friendly chat with the proprietor, who used to lend her books from his shelves. She found Johnny there, trimming rolls of wall-paper for the parlor of Banker Smith's new house. She sat down on the top of his table and watched him.

"Johnny," she said suddenly, "I want you to write down the words of that Mexican serenade you used to sing; you know, 'Rosa de Noche.'* It's an unusual song. I'm going to study it. I know enough Spanish for that."

Johnny looked up from his roller with his bright, affable

smile, "*Si*, but it is low for you, I think; *voz contralto*. It is low for me."

"Nonsense. I can do more with my low voice than I used to. I'll show you. Sit down and write it out for me, please." Thea beckoned him with the short yellow pencil tied to his order-book.

Johnny ran his fingers through his curly, black hair. "If you wish. I do not know if that *serenata** all right for young ladies. Down there it is more for married ladies. They sing it for husbands—or somebody else, may-bee." Johnny's eyes twinkled and he apologized gracefully with his shoulders. He sat down at the table, and while Thea looked over his arm, began to write the song down in a long, slanting script, with highly ornamental capitals. Presently he looked up. "This-a song not exactly Mexican," he said thoughtfully. "It come from farther down; Brazil, Venezuela, may-bee. I learn it from some fellow down there, and he learn it from another fellow. It is-a most like Mexican, but not quite." Thea did not release him, but pointed to the paper. There were three verses of the song in all, and when Johnny had written them down, he sat looking at them meditatively, his head on one side. "I don' think for a high voice, *señorita*," he objected with polite persistence. "How you accompany with piano?"

"Oh, that will be easy enough."

"For you, may-bee!" Johnny smiled and drummed on the table with the tips of his agile brown fingers. "You know something? Listen, I tell you." He rose and sat down on the table beside her, putting his foot on the chair. He loved to talk at the hour of noon. "When you was a little girl, no bigger than that, you come to my house one day 'bout noon, like this, and I was in the door, playing guitar. You was barehead, barefoot; you run away from home. You stand there and make a frown at me an' listen. By 'n by you say for me to sing. I sing some lil' ting, and then I say for you to sing with me. You don' know no words, of course, but you take the air and you sing it just-a beauti-ful! I never see a child do that, outside Mexico. You was, oh, I do' know—seven year, may-bee. By 'n by the preacher come look for you and begin for scold. I say, 'Don' scold, Meester Kronborg. She come for hear guitar. She gotta some music in her, that child. Where she get?' Then he tell me 'bout your gran'papa play oboe in the old country. I never forgetta that time." Johnny chuckled softly.

Thea nodded. "I remember that day, too. I liked your music better than the church music. When are you going to have a dance over there, Johnny?"

Johnny tilted his head. "Well, Saturday night the Spanish boys have a lil' party, some *danza*. You know Miguel Ramas? He have some young cousins, two boys, very nice-a, come from Torreon.* They going to Salt Lake for some job-a, and stay off with him two-three days, and he mus' have a party. You like to come?"

That was how Thea came to go to the Mexican ball. Mexican Town had been increased by half a dozen new families during the last few years, and the Mexicans had put up an adobe dance-hall, that looked exactly like one of their own dwellings, except that it was a little longer, and was so unpretentious that nobody in Moonstone knew of its existence. The "Spanish boys" are reticent about their own affairs. Ray Kennedy used to know about all their little doings, but since his death there was no one whom the Mexicans considered *simpatico*.*

On Saturday evening after supper Thea told her mother that she was going over to Mrs. Tellamantez's to watch the Mexicans dance for a while, and that Johnny would bring her home.

Mrs. Kronborg smiled. She noticed that Thea had put on a white dress and had done her hair up with unusual care, and that she carried her best blue scarf. "Maybe you'll take a turn yourself, eh? I wouldn't mind watching them Mexicans. They're lovely dancers."

Thea made a feeble suggestion that her mother might go with her, but Mrs. Kronborg was too wise for that. She knew that Thea would have a better time if she went alone, and she watched her daughter go out of the gate and down the sidewalk that led to the depot.

Thea walked slowly. It was a soft, rosy evening. The sand hills were lavender. The sun had gone down a glowing copper disk, and the fleecy clouds in the east were a burning rose-color, flecked with gold. Thea passed the cottonwood grove and then the depot, where she left the sidewalk and took the sandy path toward Mexican Town. She could hear the scraping of violins being tuned, the tinkle of mandolins, and the growl of a double bass. Where had they got a double bass? She did not know there was one in Moonstone. She found later that it was the property of one of Ramas's young cousins, who was taking it to Utah with him to cheer him at his "job-a."

The Mexicans never wait until it is dark to begin to dance, and Thea had no difficulty in finding the new hall because every other house in the town was deserted. Even the babies had gone to the ball; a neighbor was always willing to hold the baby while the mother danced. Mrs. Tellamantez came out to meet Thea and led her in. Johnny bowed to her from the platform at the end of the room, where he was playing the mandolin along with two fiddles and the bass. The hall was a long low room, with whitewashed walls, a fairly tight plank floor, wooden benches along the sides, and a few bracket lamps screwed to the frame timbers. There must have been fifty people there, counting the children. The Mexican dances were very much family affairs. The fathers always danced again and again with their little daughters, as well as with their wives. One of the girls came up to greet Thea, her dark cheeks glowing with pleasure and cordiality, and introduced her brother, with whom she had just been dancing. "You better take him every time he asks you," she whispered. "He's the best dancer here, except Johnny."

Thea soon decided that the poorest dancer was herself. Even Mrs. Tellamantez, who always held her shoulders so stiffly, danced better than she did. The musicians did not remain long at their post. When one of them felt like dancing, he called some other boy to take his instrument, put on his coat, and went down on the floor. Johnny, who wore a blousy white silk shirt, did not even put on his coat.

The dances the railroad men gave in Firemen's Hall were the only dances Thea had ever been allowed to go to, and they were very different from this. The boys played rough jokes and thought it smart to be clumsy and to run into each other on the floor. For the square dances there was always the bawling voice of the caller, who was also the county auctioneer.

This Mexican dance was soft and quiet. There was no calling, the conversation was very low, the rhythm of the music was smooth and engaging, the men were graceful and courteous. Some of them Thea had never before seen out of their working clothes, smeared with grease from the round-house or clay from the brickyard. Sometimes, when the music happened to be a popular Mexican waltz song, the dancers sang it softly as they moved. There were three little girls under twelve, in their first communion dresses, and one of them had an orange marigold in her black hair, just over her ear. They danced with the men and with each other. There was an atmosphere of ease and friendly pleasure in the low, dimly lit room, and Thea could not help wondering whether the Mexicans had no jealousies or neighborly grudges as the people in Moonstone had. There was no constraint of any kind there to-night, but a kind of natural harmony about their movements, their greetings, their low conversation, their smiles.

Ramas brought up his two young cousins, Silvo and Felipe, and presented them. They were handsome, smiling youths, of eighteen and twenty, with pale-gold skins, smooth cheeks, aquiline features, and wavy black hair, like Johnny's. They were dressed alike, in black velvet jackets and soft silk shirts, with opal shirt-buttons and flowing black ties looped through gold rings. They had charming manners, and low, guitar-like voices. They knew almost no English, but a Mexican boy can pay a great many compliments with a very limited vocabulary. The Ramas boys thought Thea dazzlingly beautiful. They had never seen a Scandinavian girl before, and her hair and fair skin bewitched them. "*Bianco y oro, semejante la Pascua!*" (White and gold, like Easter!) they exclaimed to each other. Silvo, the younger, declared that he could never go on to Utah; that he and his double bass had reached their ultimate destination. The elder was more crafty; he asked Miguel Ramas whether there would be "plenty more girls like that *a* Salt Lake, may-bee?"

Silvo, overhearing, gave his brother a contemptuous glance.

"Plenty more *a Paraíso** may-bee!" he retorted. When they were not dancing with her, their eyes followed her, over the coiffures of their other partners. That was not difficult; one blonde head moving among so many dark ones.

Thea had not meant to dance much, but the Ramas boys danced so well and were so handsome and adoring that she yielded to their entreaties. When she sat out a dance with them, they talked to her about their family at home, and told her how their mother had once punned upon their name. *Rama*, in Spanish, meant a branch, they explained. Once when they were little lads their mother took them along when she went to help the women decorate the church for Easter. Some one asked her whether she had brought any flowers, and she replied that she had brought her "ramas." This was evidently a cherished family story.

When it was nearly midnight, Johnny announced that every one was going to his house to have "some lil' ice-cream and some lil' *musica*." He began to put out the lights and Mrs. Tellamantez led the way across the square to her *casa*.* The Ramas brothers escorted Thea, and as they stepped out of the door, Silvo exclaimed, "*Hace frio!*"* and threw his velvet coat about her shoulders.

Most of the company followed Mrs. Tellamantez, and they sat about on the gravel in her little yard while she and Johnny and Mrs. Miguel Ramas served the ice-cream. Thea sat on Felipe's coat, since Silvo's was already about her shoulders. The youths lay down on the shining gravel beside her, one on her right and one on her left. Johnny already called them "*los acolitos*," the altar-boys. The talk all about them was low, and indolent. One of the girls was playing on Johnny's guitar, another was picking lightly at a mandolin. The moonlight was so bright that one could see every glance and smile, and the flash of their teeth. The moonflowers over Mrs. Tellamantez's door were wide open and of an unearthly white. The moon itself looked like a great pale flower in the sky.

After all the ice-cream was gone, Johnny approached Thea, his guitar under his arm, and the elder Ramas boy politely gave up his place. Johnny sat down, took a long breath, struck a fierce chord, and then hushed it with his other hand. "Now we have some lil' *serenata*, eh? You wan' a try?"

When Thea began to sing, instant silence fell upon the company. She felt all those dark eyes fix themselves upon her intently. She could see them shine. The faces came out of the shadow like the white flowers over the door. Felipe leaned his head upon his hand. Silvo dropped on his back and lay looking at the moon, under the impression that he was still looking at Thea. When she finished the first verse, Thea whispered to Johnny, "Again, I can do it better than that."

She had sung for churches and funerals and teachers, but she had never before sung for a really musical people, and this was the first time she had ever felt the response that such a people can give. They turned themselves and all they had over to her. For the moment they cared about nothing in the world but what she was doing. Their faces confronted her, open, eager, unprotected. She felt as if all these warm-blooded people débouched into her. Mrs. Tellamantez's fateful resignation, Johnny's madness, the adoration of the boy who lay still in the sand; in an instant these things seemed to be within her instead of without, as if they had come from her in the first place.

When she finished, her listeners broke into excited murmur. The men began hunting feverishly for cigarettes. Famos Serraños, the barytone bricklayer, touched Johnny's arm, gave him a questioning look, then heaved a deep sigh. Johnny dropped on his elbow, wiping his face and neck and hands with his handkerchief. "*Señorita*," he panted, "if you sing like that once in the City of Mexico they just-a go crazy. In the City of Mexico they ain't-a sit like stumps when they hear that, not-a much! When they like, they just-a give you the town."

Thea laughed. She, too, was excited. "Think so, Johnny? Come, sing something with me. *El Parreño*;* I haven't sung that for a long time."

Johnny laughed and hugged his guitar. "You not-a forget him?" He began teasing his strings. "Come!" He threw back his head, "*Anoche-e-e—*"

*"Anoche me confesse
Con un padre carmelite,
Y me dio penitencia
Que besaras tu boquita."*

(Last night I made confession
With a Carmelite father,
And he gave me absolution
For the kisses you imprinted.)

Johnny had almost every fault that a tenor can have. His voice was thin, unsteady, husky in the middle tones. But it was distinctly a voice, and sometimes he managed get something very sweet out of it. Certainly it made him happy to sing. Thea kept glancing down at him as he lay there on his elbow. His eyes seemed twice as large as usual and had lights in them like those the moonlight makes on black, running water. Thea remembered the old stories about his "spells." She had never seen him when his madness was on him, but she felt something to-night at her elbow that gave her an idea of what it might be like. For the first time she fully understood the cryptic explanation that Mrs. Tellamantez had made to Dr. Archie, long ago. There were the same shells along the walk; she believed she could pick out the very one. There was the same moon up yonder, and panting at her elbow was the same Johnny—fooled by the same old things!

When they had finished, Famos, the barytone, murmured something to Johnny; who replied, "Sure we can sing 'Trovatore.'* We have no alto, but all the girls can sing alto and make some noise."

The women laughed. Mexican women of the poorer class do not sing like the men. Perhaps they are too indolent. In the evening, when the men are singing their throats dry on the doorstep, or around the camp-fire beside the work-train, the women usually sit and comb their hair.

While Johnny was gesticulating and telling everybody what to sing and how to sing it, Thea put out her foot and touched the corpse of Silvo with the toe of her slipper. "Aren't you going to sing, Silvo?" she asked teasingly.

The boy turned on his side and raised himself on his elbow for a moment. "Not this night, *señorita*," he pleaded softly, "not this night!" He dropped back again, and lay with his cheek on his right arm, the hand lying passive on the sand above his head.

"How does he flatten himself into the ground like that?" Thea asked herself. "I wish I knew. It's very effective, somehow."

Across the gulch the Kohlers' little house slept among its trees, a dark spot on the white face of the desert. The windows of their upstairs bedroom were open, and Paulina had listened to the dance music for a long while before she drowsed off. She was a light sleeper, and when she woke again, after midnight, Johnny's concert was at its height. She lay still until she could bear it no longer. Then she wakened Fritz and they went over to the window and leaned out. They could hear clearly there.

"*Die Thea*," whispered Mrs. Kohler; "it must be. *Ach, wunderschön!*"*

Fritz was not so wide awake as his wife. He grunted and scratched on the floor with his bare foot. They were listening to a Mexican part-song; the tenor, then the soprano, then both together; the barytone joins them, rages, is extinguished; the tenor expires in sobs, and the soprano finishes alone. When the soprano's last note died away, Fritz nodded to his wife. "*Ja*," he said; "*schön*."

There was silence for a few moments. Then the guitar sounded fiercely, and several male voices began the sextette from "Lucia."* Johnny's reedy tenor they knew well, and the bricklayer's big, opaque barytone; the others might be anybody over there—just Mexican voices. Then at the appointed, at the acute, moment, the soprano voice, like a fountain jet, shot up into the light. "*Horch! Horch!*"* the old people whispered, both at once. How it leaped from among those dusky male voices! How it played in and about and around and over them, like a goldfish darting among creek minnows, like a yellow butterfly soaring above a swarm of dark ones. "Ah," said Mrs. Kohler softly, "the dear man; if he could hear her now!"

XI

Mrs. Kronborg had said that Thea was not to be disturbed on Sunday morning, and she slept until noon. When she came downstairs the family were just sitting down to dinner, Mr. Kronborg at one end of the long table, Mrs. Kronborg at the other. Anna, stiff and ceremonious, in her summer silk, sat at her father's right, and the boys were strung along on either side of the table. There was a place left for Thea between her mother and Thor. During the silence which preceded the blessing, Thea felt something uncomfortable in the air. Anna and her older brothers had lowered their eyes when she came in. Mrs. Kronborg nodded cheerfully, and after the blessing, as she began to pour the coffee, turned to her.

"I expect you had a good time at that dance, Thea. I hope you got your sleep out."

"High society, that," remarked Charley, giving the mashed potatoes a vicious swat. Anna's mouth and eyebrows became half-moons.

Thea looked across the table at the uncompromising countenances of her older brothers. "Why, what's the matter with the Mexicans?" she asked, flushing. "They don't trouble anybody, and they are kind to their families and have good manners."

"Nice clean people; got some style about them. Do you really like that kind, Thea, or do you just pretend to? That's what I'd like to know." Gus looked at her with pained inquiry. But he at least looked at her.

"They're just as clean as white people, and they have a perfect right to their own ways. Of course I like 'em. I don't pretend things."

"Everybody according to their own taste," remarked Charley bitterly. "Quit crumbing your bread up, Thor. Ain't you learned how to eat yet?"

"Children, children!" said Mr. Kronborg nervously, looking up from the chicken he was dismembering. He glanced at his wife, whom he expected to maintain harmony in the family.

"That's all right, Charley. Drop it there," said Mrs. Kronborg. "No use spoiling your Sunday dinner with race prejudices. The Mexicans suit me and Thea very well. They are a useful people. Now you can just talk about something else."

Conversation, however, did not flourish at that dinner. Everybody ate as fast as possible. Charley and Gus said they had engagements and left the table as soon as they finished their apple pie. Anna sat primly and ate with great elegance. When she spoke at all she spoke to her father, about church matters, and always in a commiserating tone, as if he had met with some misfortune. Mr. Kronborg, quite innocent of her intentions, replied kindly and absent-mindedly. After the dessert he went to take his usual Sunday afternoon nap, and Mrs. Kronborg carried some dinner to a sick neighbor. Thea and Anna began to clear the table.

"I should think you would show more consideration for father's position, Thea," Anna began as soon as she and her sister were alone.

Thea gave her a sidelong glance. "Why, what have I done to father?"

"Everybody at Sunday-School was talking about you going over there and singing with the Mexicans all night, when you won't sing for the church. Somebody heard you, and told it all over town. Of course, we all get the blame for it."

"Anything disgraceful about singing?" Thea asked with a provoking yawn.

"I must say you choose your company! You always had that streak in you, Thea. We all hoped that going away would improve you. Of course, it reflects on father when you are scarcely polite to the nice people here and make up to the rowdies."

"Oh, it's my singing with the Mexicans you object to?" Thea put down a tray full of dishes. "Well, I like to sing over there, and I don't like to over here. I'll sing for them any time they ask me to. They know something about what I'm doing. They're a talented people."

"Talented!" Anna made the word sound like escaping steam. "I suppose you think it's smart to come home and throw that at your family!"

Thea picked up the tray. By this time she was as white as the Sunday tablecloth. "Well," she replied in a cold, even tone, "I'll have to throw it at them sooner or later. It's just a question of when, and it might as well be now as any time." She carried the tray blindly into the kitchen.

Tillie, who was always listening and looking out for her, took the dishes from her with a furtive, frightened glance at her stony face. Thea went slowly up the back stairs to her loft. Her legs seemed as heavy as lead as she climbed the stairs, and she felt as if everything inside her had solidified and grown hard.

After shutting her door and locking it, she sat down on the edge of her bed. This place had always been her refuge, but there was a hostility in the house now which this door could not shut out. This would be her last summer in that room. Its services were over; its time was done. She rose and put her hand on the low ceiling. Two tears ran down her cheeks, as if they came from ice that melted slowly. She was not ready to leave her little shell. She was being pulled out too soon. She would never be able to think anywhere else as well as here. She would never sleep so well or have such dreams in any other bed; even last night, such sweet, breathless dreams— Thea hid her face in the pillow. Wherever she went she would like to take that little bed with her. When she went away from it for good, she would leave something that she could never recover; memories of pleasant excitement, of happy adventures in her mind; of warm sleep on howling winter nights, and joyous awakenings on summer mornings. There were certain dreams that might refuse to come to her at all except in a little morning cave, facing the sun—where they came to her so powerfully, where they beat a triumph in her!

The room was hot as an oven. The sun was beating fiercely on the shingles behind the board ceiling. She undressed, and before she threw herself upon her bed in her chemise, she frowned at herself for a long while in her looking-glass. Yes, she and It must fight it out together. The thing that looked at her out of her own eyes was the only friend she could count on. Oh, she would make these people sorry enough! There would come a time when they would want to make it up with her. But, never again!

She had no little vanities, only one big one, and she would never forgive.

Her mother was all right, but her mother was a part of the family, and she was not. In the nature of things, her mother had to be on both sides. Thea felt that she had been betrayed. A truce had been broken behind her back. She had never had much individual affection for any of her brothers except Thor, but she had never been disloyal, never felt scorn or held grudges. As a little girl she had always been good friends with Gunner and Axel, whenever she had time to play. Even before she got her own room, when they were all sleeping and dressing together, like little cubs, and breakfasting in the kitchen, she had led an absorbing personal life of her own. But she had a cub loyalty to the other cubs. She thought them nice boys and tried to make them get their lessons. She once fought a bully who "picked on" Axel at school. She never made fun of Anna's crimpings and curlings and beauty-rites.

Thea had always taken it for granted that her sister and brothers recognized that she had special abilities, and that they were proud of it. She had done them the honor, she told herself bitterly, to believe that though they had no particular endowments, *they were of her kind*, and not of the Moonstone kind. Now they had all grown up and become persons. They faced each other as individuals, and she saw that Anna and Gus and Charley were among the people whom she had always recognized as her natural enemies. Their ambitions and sacred proprieties were meaningless to her. She had neglected to congratulate Charley upon having been promoted from the grocery department of Commings's store to the drygoods department. Her mother had reproved her for this omission. And how was she to know, Thea asked herself, that Anna expected to be teased because Bert Rice now came and sat in the hammock with her every night? No, it was all clear enough. Nothing that she would ever do in the world would seem important to them, and nothing they would ever do would seem important to her.

Thea lay thinking intently all through the stifling afternoon. Tillie whispered something outside her door once, but she did not answer. She lay on her bed until the second church bell rang, and she saw the family go trooping up the sidewalk on the opposite side of the street, Anna and her father in the lead. Anna seemed to have taken on a very story-book attitude toward her father; patronizing and condescending, it seemed to Thea. The older boys were not in the family band. They now took their girls to church. Tillie had stayed at home to get supper. Thea got up, washed her hot face and arms, and put on the white organdie dress she had worn last night; it was getting too small for her, and she might as well wear it out. After she was dressed she unlocked her door and went cautiously downstairs. She felt as if chilling hostilities might be awaiting her in the trunk loft, on the stairway, almost anywhere. In the dining-room she found Tillie, sitting by the open window, reading the dramatic news in a Denver Sunday paper. Tillie kept a scrapbook in which she pasted clippings about actors and actresses.

"Come look at this picture of Pauline Hall* in tights, Thea," she called. "Ain't she cute? It's too bad you didn't go to the theater more when you was in Chicago; such a good chance! Didn't you even get to see Clara Morris or Modjeska?"*

"No; I didn't have time. Besides, it costs money, Tillie," Thea replied wearily, glancing at the paper Tillie held out to her.

Tillie looked up at her niece. "Don't you go and be upset about any of Anna's notions. She's one of these narrow kind. Your father and mother don't pay any attention to what she says. Anna's fussy; she is with me, but I don't mind her."

"Oh, I don't mind her. That's all right, Tillie. I guess I'll take a walk."

Thea knew that Tillie hoped she would stay and talk to her for a while, and she would have liked to please her. But in a house as small as that one, everything was too intimate and mixed up together. The family was the family, an integral thing. One couldn't discuss Anna there. She felt differently toward the house and everything in it, as if the battered old furniture that seemed so kindly, and the old carpets on which she had played, had been nourishing a secret grudge against her and were not to be trusted any more.

She went aimlessly out of the front gate, not knowing what to do with herself. Mexican Town, somehow, was spoiled for her just then, and she felt that she would hide if she saw Silvo or Felipe coming toward her. She walked down through the empty main street. All the stores were closed, their blinds down. On the steps of the bank some idle boys were sitting, telling disgusting stories because there was nothing else to do. Several of them had gone to school with Thea, but when she nodded to them they hung their heads and did not speak. Thea's body was often curiously expressive of what was going on in her mind, and to-night there was something in her walk and carriage that made these boys feel that she was "stuck up." If she had stopped and talked to them, they would have thawed out on the instant and would have been friendly and grateful. But Thea was hurt afresh, and walked on, holding her chin higher than ever. As she passed the Duke Block, she saw a light in Dr. Archie's office, and she went up the stairs and opened the door into his study. She found him with a pile of papers and account-books before him. He pointed her to her old chair at the end of his desk and leaned back in his own, looking at her with satisfaction. How handsome she was growing!

"I'm still chasing the elusive metal, Thea,"—he pointed to the papers before him,—"I'm up to my neck in mines, and I'm going to be a rich man some day."

"I hope you will; awfully rich. That's the only thing that counts." She looked restlessly about the consulting-room. "To do any of the things one wants to do, one has to have lots and lots of money."

Dr. Archie was direct. "What's the matter? Do you need some?"

Thea shrugged. "Oh, I can get along, in a little way." She looked intently out of the window at the arc street-lamp that was just beginning to sputter. "But it's silly to live at all for little things," she added quietly. "Living's too much trouble unless one can get something big out of it."

Dr. Archie rested his elbows on the arms of his chair, dropped his chin on his clasped hands and looked at her. "Living is no trouble for little people, believe me!" he exclaimed. "What do you want to get out of it?"

"Oh—so many things!" Thea shivered.

"But what? Money? You mentioned that. Well, you can make money, if you care about that more than anything else." He nodded prophetically above his interlacing fingers.

"But I don't. That's only one thing. Anyhow, I couldn't if I did." She pulled her dress lower at the neck as if she were suffocating. "I only want impossible things," she said roughly. "The others don't interest me."

Dr. Archie watched her contemplatively, as if she were a beaker full of chemicals working. A few years ago, when she used to sit there, the light from under his green lampshade used to fall full upon her broad face and yellow pig-tails. Now her face was in the shadow and the line of light fell below her bare throat, directly across her bosom. The shrunken white organdie rose and fell as if she were struggling to be free and to break out of it altogether. He felt that her heart must be laboring heavily in there, but he was afraid to touch her; he was, indeed. He had never seen her like this before. Her hair, piled high on her head, gave her a commanding look, and her eyes, that used to be so inquisitive, were stormy.

"Thea," he said slowly, "I won't say that you can have everything you want—that means having nothing, in reality. But if you decide what it is you want most, *you can get it*." His eye caught hers for a moment. "Not everybody can, but you can. Only, if you want a big thing, you've got to have nerve enough to cut out all that's easy, everything that's to be had cheap." Dr. Archie paused. He picked up a paper-cutter and, feeling the edge of it softly with his fingers, he added slowly, as if to himself:—

> "He either fears his fate too much,
> Or his deserts are small,
> Who dares not put it to the touch
> To win . . . or lose it all."*

Thea's lips parted; she looked at him from under a frown, searching his face. "Do you mean to break loose, too, and—do something?" she asked in a low voice.

"I mean to get rich, if you call that doing anything. I've found what I can do without. You make such bargains in your mind, first."

Thea sprang up and took the paper-cutter he had put down, twisting it in her hands. "A long while first, sometimes," she said with a short laugh. "But suppose one can never get out what they've got in them? Suppose they make a mess of it in the end; then what?" She threw the paper-cutter on the desk and took a step toward the doctor, until her dress touched him. She stood looking down at him. "Oh, it's easy to fail!" She was breathing through her mouth and her throat was throbbing with excitement.

As he looked up at her, Dr. Archie's hands tightened on the arms of his chair. He had thought he knew Thea Kronborg pretty well, but he did not know the girl who was standing there. She was beautiful, as his little Swede had never been, but she frightened him. Her pale cheeks, her parted lips, her flashing eyes, seemed suddenly to mean one thing—he did not know what. A light seemed to break upon her from far away—or perhaps from far within. She seemed to grow taller, like a scarf drawn out long; looked as if she were pursued and fleeing, and—yes, she looked tormented. "It's easy to fail," he heard her say again, "and if I fail, you'd better forget about me, for I'll be one of the worst women that ever lived. I'll be an awful woman!"

In the shadowy light above the lampshade he caught her glance again and held it for a moment. Wild as her eyes were, that yellow gleam at the back of them was as hard as a diamond drill-point. He rose with a nervous laugh and dropped his hand lightly on her shoulder. "No, you won't. You'll be a splendid one!"

She shook him off before he could say anything more, and went out of his door with a kind of bound. She left so quickly and so lightly that he could not even hear her footstep in the hallway outside. Archie dropped back into his chair and sat motionless for a long while.

So it went; one loved a quaint little girl, cheerful, industrious, always on the run and hustling through her tasks; and suddenly one lost her. He had thought he knew that child like the glove on his hand. But about this tall girl who threw up her head and glittered like that all over, he knew nothing. She was goaded by desires, ambitions, revulsions that were dark to him. One thing he knew: the old highroad of life, worn safe and easy, hugging the sunny slopes, would scarcely hold her again.

After that night Thea could have asked pretty much anything of him. He could have refused her nothing. Years ago a crafty little bunch of hair and smiles had shown him what she wanted, and he had promptly married her. Tonight a very different sort of girl—driven wild by doubts and youth, by poverty and riches—had let him see the fierceness of her nature. She went out still distraught, not knowing or caring what she had shown him. But to Archie knowledge of that sort was obligation. Oh, he was the same old Howard Archie!

That Sunday in July was the turning-point; Thea's peace of mind did not come back. She found it hard even to practice at home. There was something in the air there that froze her throat. In the morning, she walked as far as she could walk. In the hot afternoons she lay on her bed in her nightgown, planning fiercely. She haunted the post-office. She must have worn a path in the sidewalk that led to the post-office, that summer. She was there the moment the mail-sacks came up from the depot, morning and evening, and while the letters were being sorted and distributed she paced up and down outside, under the cottonwood trees, listening to the thump, thump, thump of Mr. Thompson's stamp. She hung upon any sort of word from Chicago; a card from Bowers, a letter from Mrs. Harsanyi, from Mr. Larsen, from her landlady,—anything to reassure her that Chicago was still there. She began to feel the same restlessness that had tortured her the last spring when she was teaching in Moonstone. Suppose she never got away again, after all? Suppose one broke a leg and had to lie in bed at home for weeks, or had pneumonia and died there. The desert was so big and thirsty; if one's foot slipped, it could drink one up like a drop of water.

This time, when Thea left Moonstone to go back to Chicago, she went alone. As the train pulled out, she looked back at her mother and father and Thor. They were calm and cheerful; they did not know, they did not understand. Something pulled in her—and broke. She cried all the way to Denver, and that night, in her berth, she kept sobbing and waking herself. But when the sun rose in the morning, she was far away. It was all behind her, and she knew that she would never cry like that again. People live through such pain only once; pain comes again, but it finds a tougher surface. Thea remembered how she had gone away the first time, with what confidence in everything, and what pitiful ignorance. Such a silly! She felt resentful toward that stupid, good-natured child. How much older she was now, and how much harder! She was going away to fight, and she was going away forever.

PART III

STUPID FACES

PART III

STUPID FACES

I

So many grinning, stupid faces! Thea was sitting by the window in Bowers's studio, waiting for him to come back from lunch. On her knee was the latest number of an illustrated musical journal in which musicians great and little stridently advertised their wares. Every afternoon she played accompaniments for people who looked and smiled like these. She was getting tired of the human countenance.

Thea had been in Chicago for two months. She had a small church position which partly paid her living expenses, and she paid for her singing lessons by playing Bowers's accompaniments every afternoon from two until six. She had been compelled to leave her old friends Mrs. Lorch and Mrs. Andersen, because the long ride from North Chicago to Bowers's studio on Michigan Avenue took too much time—an hour in the morning, and at night, when the cars were crowded, an hour and a half. For the first month she had clung to her old room, but the bad air in the cars, at the end of a long day's work, fatigued her greatly and was bad for her voice. Since she left Mrs. Lorch, she had been staying at a students' club to which she was introduced by Miss Adler, Bowers's morning accompanist, an intelligent Jewish girl from Evanston.

Thea took her lesson from Bowers every day from eleven-thirty until twelve. Then she went out to lunch with an Italian grammar under her arm, and came back to the studio to begin her work at two. In the afternoon Bowers coached professionals and taught his advanced pupils. It was his theory that Thea ought to be able to learn a great deal by keeping her ears open while she played for him.

The concert-going public of Chicago still remembers the long, sallow, discontented face of Madison Bowers. He seldom missed an evening concert, and was usually to be seen lounging somewhere at the back of the concert hall, reading a newspaper or review, and conspicuously ignoring the efforts of the performers. At the end of a number he looked up from his paper long enough to sweep the applauding audience with a contemptuous eye. His face was intelligent, with a narrow lower jaw, a thin nose, faded gray eyes, and a close-cut brown mustache. His hair was iron-gray, thin and dead-looking. He went to concerts chiefly to satisfy himself as to how badly things were done and how gullible the public was. He hated the whole race of artists; the work they did, the wages they got, and the way they spent their money. His father, old Hiram Bowers, was still alive and at work, a genial old choirmaster in Boston, full of enthusiasm at seventy. But Madison was of the colder stuff of his grandfathers, a long line of New Hampshire farmers; hard workers, close traders, with good minds, mean natures, and flinty eyes. As a boy Madison had a fine barytone voice, and his father made great sacrifices for him, sending him to Germany at an early age and keeping him abroad at his studies for years. Madison worked under the best teachers, and afterward sang in England in oratorio. His cold nature and academic methods were against him. His audiences were always aware of the contempt he felt for them. A dozen poorer singers succeeded, but Bowers did not.

Bowers had all the qualities which go to make a good teacher—except generosity and warmth. His intelligence was of a high order, his taste never at fault. He seldom worked with a voice without improving it, and in teaching the delivery of oratorio he was without a rival. Singers came from far and near to study Bach and Handel with him. Even the fashionable sopranos and contraltos of Chicago, St. Paul, and St. Louis (they were usually ladies with very rich husbands, and Bowers called them the "pampered jades of Asia") humbly endured his sardonic humor for the sake of what he could do for them. He was not at all above helping a very lame singer across, if her husband's check-book warranted it. He had a whole bag of tricks for stupid people, "life-preservers," he called them. "Cheap repairs for a cheap 'un," he used to say, but the husbands never found the repairs very cheap. Those were the days when lumbermen's daughters and brewers' wives contended in song; studied in Germany and then floated from *Sängerfest* to *Sängerfest*. Choral societies flourished in all the rich lake cities and river cities. The soloists came to Chicago to coach with Bowers, and he often took long journeys to hear and instruct a chorus. He was intensely avaricious, and from these semi-professionals he reaped a golden harvest. They fed his pockets and they fed his ever-hungry contempt, his scorn of himself and his accomplices. The more money he made, the more parsimonious he became. His wife was so shabby that she never went anywhere with him, which suited him exactly. Because his clients were luxurious and extravagant, he took a revengeful pleasure in having his shoes half-soled a second time, and in getting the last wear out of a broken collar. He had first been interested in Thea Kronborg because of her bluntness, her country roughness, and her manifest carefulness about money. The mention of Harsanyi's name always made him pull a wry face. For the first time Thea had a friend who, in his own cool and guarded way, liked her for whatever was least admirable in her.

Thea was still looking at the musical paper, her grammar unopened on the window-sill, when Bowers sauntered in a little before two o'clock. He was smoking a cheap cigarette and wore the same soft felt hat he had worn all last winter. He never carried a cane or wore gloves.

Thea followed him from the reception-room into the studio. "I may cut my lesson out to-morrow, Mr. Bowers. I have to hunt a new boarding-place."

Bowers looked up languidly from his desk where he had begun to go over a pile of letters. "What's the matter with the Studio Club? Been fighting with them again?"

"The Club's all right for people who like to live that way. I don't."

Bowers lifted his eyebrows. "Why so tempery?" he asked as he drew a check from an envelope postmarked "Minneapolis."

"I can't work with a lot of girls around. They're too familiar. I never could get along with girls of my own age. It's all too chummy. Gets on my nerves. I didn't come here to play kinder-garten games." Thea began energetically to arrange the scattered music on the piano.

Bowers grimaced good-humoredly at her over the three checks he was pinning together. He liked to play at a rough game of banter with her. He flattered himself that he had made her harsher than she was when she first came to him; that he had got off a little of the sugar-coating Harsanyi always put on his pupils.

"The art of making yourself agreeable never comes amiss, Miss Kronborg. I should say you rather need a little practice along that line. When you come to marketing your wares in the world, a little smoothness goes farther than a great deal of talent some-times. If you happen to be cursed with a real talent, then you've got to be very smooth indeed, or you'll never get your money back." Bowers snapped the elastic band around his bank-book.

Thea gave him a sharp, recognizing glance. "Well, that's the money I'll have to go without," she replied.

"Just what do you mean?"

"I mean the money people have to grin for. I used to know a railroad man who said there was money in every profession that you couldn't take. He'd tried a good many jobs," Thea added musingly; "perhaps he was too particular about the kind he could take, for he never picked up much. He was proud, but I liked him for that."

Bowers rose and closed his desk. "Mrs. Priest is late again. By the way, Miss Kronborg, remember not to frown when you are playing for Mrs. Priest. You did not remember yesterday."

"You mean when she hits a tone with her breath like that? Why do you let her? You wouldn't let me."

"I certainly would not. But that is a mannerism of Mrs. Priest's. The public like it, and they pay a great deal of money for the pleasure of hearing her do it. There she is. Remember!"

Bowers opened the door of the reception-room and a tall, imposing woman rustled in, bringing with her a glow of anima-tion which pervaded the room as if half a dozen persons, all talking gayly, had come in instead of one. She was large, hand-some, expansive, uncontrolled; one felt this the moment she

crossed the threshold. She shone with care and cleanliness,
mature vigor, unchallenged authority, gracious good-humor, and
absolute confidence in her person, her powers, her position, and
her way of life; a glowing, overwhelming self-satisfaction, only to
be found where human society is young and strong and without
yesterdays. Her face had a kind of heavy, thoughtless beauty, like a
pink peony just at the point of beginning to fade. Her brown hair
was waved in front and done up behind in a great twist, held by a
tortoiseshell comb with gold filigree. She wore a beautiful little
green hat with three long green feathers sticking straight up in
front, a little cape made of velvet and fur with a yellow satin rose
on it. Her gloves, her shoes, her veil, somehow made themselves
felt. She gave the impression of wearing a cargo of splendid
merchandise.

Mrs. Priest nodded graciously to Thea, coquettishly to Bowers,
and asked him to untie her veil for her. She threw her splendid
wrap on a chair, the yellow lining out. Thea was already at the
piano. Mrs. Priest stood behind her.

"'Rejoice Greatly'* first, please. And please don't hurry it in
there," she put her arm over Thea's shoulder, and indicated the
passage by a sweep of her white glove. She threw out her chest,
clasped her hands over her abdomen, lifted her chin, worked the
muscles of her cheeks back and forth for a moment, and then
began with conviction, "Re–jo–oice! Re–jo–oice!"

Bowers paced the room with his catlike tread. When he
checked Mrs. Priest's vehemence at all, he handled her roughly;
poked and hammered her massive person with cold satisfaction,
almost as if he were taking out a grudge on this splendid creation.
Such treatment the imposing lady did not at all resent. She tried
harder and harder, her eyes growing all the while more lustrous
and her lips redder. Thea played on as she was told, ignoring the
singer's struggles.

When she first heard Mrs. Priest sing in church, Thea admired
her. Since she had found out how dull the good-natured soprano
really was, she felt a deep contempt for her. She felt that Mrs.
Priest ought to be reproved and even punished for her shortcom-
ings; that she ought to be exposed,—at least to herself,—and not

be permitted to live and shine in happy ignorance of what a poor thing it was she brought across so radiantly. Thea's cold looks of reproof were lost upon Mrs. Priest; although the lady did murmur one day when she took Bowers home in her carriage, "How handsome your afternoon girl would be if she did not have that unfortunate squint; it gives her that vacant Swede look, like an animal." That amused Bowers. He liked to watch the germination and growth of antipathies.

One of the first disappointments Thea had to face when she returned to Chicago that fall, was the news that the Harsanyis were not coming back. They had spent the summer in a camp in the Adirondacks and were moving to New York. An old teacher and friend of Harsanyi's, one of the best-known piano teachers in New York, was about to retire because of failing health and had arranged to turn his pupils over to Harsanyi. Andor was to give two recitals in New York in November, to devote himself to his new students until spring, and then to go on a short concert tour. The Harsanyis had taken a furnished apartment in New York, as they would not attempt to settle a place of their own until Andor's recitals were over. The first of December, however, Thea received a note from Mrs. Harsanyi, asking her to call at the old studio, where she was packing their goods for shipment.

The morning after this invitation reached her, Thea climbed the stairs and knocked at the familiar door. Mrs. Harsanyi herself opened it, and embraced her visitor warmly. Taking Thea into the studio, which was littered with excelsior and packing-cases, she stood holding her hand and looking at her in the strong light from the big window before she allowed her to sit down. Her quick eye saw many changes. The girl was taller, her figure had become definite, her carriage positive. She had got used to living in the body of a young woman, and she no longer tried to ignore it and behave as if she were a little girl. With that increased independence of body there had come a change in her face; an indifference, something hard and skeptical. Her clothes, too, were different, like the attire of a shopgirl who tries to follow the fashions; a purple suit, a piece of cheap fur, a three-cornered purple hat with a pompon sticking up in front. The queer country clothes she used to wear suited her much better, Mrs. Harsanyi thought. But such trifles, after all, were accidental and remediable. She put her hand on the girl's strong shoulder.

"How much the summer has done for you! Yes, you are a young lady at last. Andor will be so glad to hear about you."

Thea looked about at the disorder of the familiar room. The pictures were piled in a corner, the piano and the *chaise longue* were gone. "I suppose I ought to be glad you have gone away," she said, "but I'm not. It's a fine thing for Mr. Harsanyi, I suppose."

Mrs. Harsanyi gave her a quick glance that said more than words. "If you knew how long I have wanted to get him away from here, Miss Kronborg! He is never tired, never discouraged, now."

Thea sighed. "I'm glad for that, then." Her eyes traveled over the faint discolorations on the walls where the pictures had hung. "I may run away myself. I don't know whether I can stand it here without you."

"We hope that you can come to New York to study before very long. We have thought of that. And you must tell me how you are getting on with Bowers. Andor will want to know all about it."

"I guess I get on more or less. But I don't like my work very well. It never seems serious as my work with Mr. Harsanyi did. I play Bowers's accompaniments in the afternoons, you know. I thought I would learn a good deal from the people who work with him, but I don't think I get much."

Mrs. Harsanyi looked at her inquiringly. Thea took out a carefully folded handkerchief from the bosom of her dress and began to draw the corners apart. "Singing doesn't seem to be a very brainy profession, Mrs. Harsanyi," she said slowly. "The people I see now are not a bit like the ones I used to meet here. Mr. Harsanyi's pupils, even the dumb ones, had more—well, more of everything, it seems to me. The people I have to play accompaniments for are discouraging. The professionals, like Katharine Priest and Miles Murdstone, are worst of all. If I have to play 'The Messiah' much longer for Mrs. Priest, I'll go out of my mind!" Thea brought her foot down sharply on the bare floor.

Mrs. Harsanyi looked down at the foot in perplexity. "You mustn't wear such high heels, my dear. They will spoil your walk and make you mince along. Can't you at least learn to avoid what you dislike in these singers? I was never able to care for Mrs. Priest's singing."

Thea was sitting with her chin lowered. Without moving her head she looked up at Mrs. Harsanyi and smiled; a smile much too cold and desperate to be seen on a young face, Mrs. Harsanyi felt. "Mrs. Harsanyi, it seems to me that what I learn is just *to dislike*. I dislike so much and so hard that it tires me out. I've got no heart for anything." She threw up her head suddenly and sat in defiance, her hand clenched on the arm of the chair. "Mr. Harsanyi couldn't stand these people an hour, I know he couldn't. He'd put them right out of the window there, frizzes and feathers and all. Now, take that new soprano they're all making such a fuss about, Jessie Darcey. She's going on tour with a symphony orchestra and she's working up her repertory with Bowers. She's singing some Schumann songs Mr. Harsanyi used to go over with me. Well, I don't know what he *would* do if he heard her."

"But if your own work goes well, and you know these people are wrong, why do you let them discourage you?"

Thea shook her head. "That's just what I don't understand myself. Only, after I've heard them all afternoon, I come out frozen up. Somehow it takes the shine off of everything. People want Jessie Darcey and the kind of thing she does; so what's the use?"

Mrs. Harsanyi smiled. "That stile you must simply vault over. You must not begin to fret about the successes of cheap people. After all, what have they to do with you?"

"Well, if I had somebody like Mr. Harsanyi, perhaps I wouldn't fret about them. He was the teacher for me. Please tell him so."

Thea rose and Mrs. Harsanyi took her hand again. "I am sorry you have to go through this time of discouragement. I wish Andor could talk to you, he would understand it so well. But I feel like urging you to keep clear of Mrs. Priest and Jessie Darcey and all their works."

Thea laughed discordantly. "No use urging me. I don't get on with them *at all*. My spine gets like a steel rail when they come near me. I liked them at first, you know. Their clothes and their manners were so fine, and Mrs. Priest *is* handsome. But now I keep wanting to tell them how stupid they are. Seems like they ought to be informed, don't you think so?" There was a flash of the shrewd grin that Mrs. Harsanyi remembered. Thea pressed her hand. "I must go now. I had to give my lesson hour this morning to a Duluth woman who has come on to coach, and I must go, and play 'On Mighty Pens'* for her. Please tell Mr. Harsanyi that I think oratorio is a great chance for bluffers."

Mrs. Harsanyi detained her. "But he will want to know much more than that about you. You are free at seven? Come back this evening, then, and we will go to dinner somewhere, to some cheerful place. I think you need a party."

Thea brightened. "Oh, I do! I'll love to come; that will be like old times. You see," she lingered a moment, softening, "I wouldn't mind if there were only *one* of them I could really admire."

"How about Bowers?" Mrs. Harsanyi asked as they were approaching the stairway.

"Well, there's nothing he loves like a good fakir,* and nothing he hates like a good artist. I always remember something Mr. Harsanyi said about him. He said Bowers was the cold muffin that had been left on the plate."

Mrs. Harsanyi stopped short at the head of the stairs and said decidedly: "I think Andor made a mistake. I can't believe that is the right atmosphere for you. It would hurt you more than most people. It's all wrong."

"Something's wrong," Thea called back as she clattered down the stairs in her high heels.

II

DURING that winter Thea lived in so many places that sometimes at night when she left Bowers's studio and emerged into the street she had to stop and think for a moment to remember where she was living now and what was the best way to get there.

When she moved into a new place her eyes challenged the beds, the carpets, the food, the mistress of the house. The boarding-houses were wretchedly conducted and Thea's complaints some-times took an insulting form. She quarreled with one landlady after another and moved on. When she moved into a new room, she was almost sure to hate it on sight and to begin planning to hunt another place before she unpacked her trunk. She was moody and contemptuous toward her fellow boarders, except to-ward the young men, whom she treated with a careless familiarity which they usually misunderstood. They liked her, however, and when she left the house after a storm, they helped her to move her things and came to see her after she got settled in a new place. But she moved so often that they soon ceased to follow her. They could see no reason for keeping up with a girl who, under her jocularity, was cold, self-centered, and unimpressionable. They soon felt that she did not admire them.

Thea used to waken up in the night and wonder why she was so unhappy. She would have been amazed if she had known how much the people whom she met in Bowers's studio had to do with her low spirits. She had never been conscious of those instinctive standards which are called ideals, and she did not know that she was suffering for them. She often found herself sneering when she was on a street-car, or when she was brushing out her hair before her mirror, as some inane remark or too familiar mannerism flitted across her mind.

She felt no creature kindness, no tolerant good-will for Mrs. Priest or Jessie Darcey. After one of Jessie Darcey's concerts the glowing press notices, and the admiring comments that floated about Bowers's studio, caused Thea bitter unhappiness. It was not the torment of personal jealousy. She had never thought of herself as even a possible rival of Miss Darcey. She was a poor music student, and Jessie Darcey was a popular and petted pro-fessional. Mrs. Priest, whatever one held against her, had a fine, big, showy voice and an impressive presence. She read indiffer-ently, was inaccurate, and was always putting other people wrong, but she at least had the material out of which singers can be made. But people seemed to like Jessie Darcey exactly because she could not sing; because, as they put it, she was "so natural and unprofessional." Her singing was pronounced "artless," her voice "birdlike." Miss Darcey was thin and awkward in person, with a sharp, sallow face. Thea noticed that her plainness was accounted to her credit, and that people spoke of it affectionately. Miss Darcey was singing everywhere just then; one could not help hearing about her. She was backed by some of the packing-house people and by the Chicago Northwestern Railroad. Only one critic raised his voice against her. Thea went to several of Jessie Darcey's concerts. It was the first time she had had an opportunity to observe the whims of the public which singers live by interesting. She saw that people liked in Miss Darcey every quality a singer ought not to have, and especially the nervous complacency that stamped her as a commonplace young woman. They seemed to have a warmer feeling for Jessie than for Mrs. Priest, an affectionate and cherishing regard. Chicago was not so very different from Moonstone, after all, and Jessie Darcey was only Lily Fisher under another name.

Thea particularly hated to accompany for Miss Darcey because she sang off pitch and didn't mind it in the least. It was excruciating to sit there day after day and hear her; there was something shameless and indecent about not singing true.

One morning Miss Darcey came by appointment to go over the programme for her Peoria concert. She was such a frail-looking girl that Thea ought to have felt sorry for her. True, she had an arch, sprightly little manner, and a flash of salmon-pink on either brown cheek. But a narrow upper jaw gave her face a pinched look, and her eyelids were heavy and relaxed. By the morning light, the purplish brown circles under her eyes were pathetic enough, and foretold no long or brilliant future. A singer with a poor digestion and low vitality; she needed no seer to cast her horoscope. If Thea had ever taken the pains to study her, she would have seen that, under all her smiles and archness, poor Miss Darcey was really frightened to death. She could not understand her success any more than Thea could; she kept catching

her breath and lifting her eyebrows and trying to believe that it
was true. Her loquacity was not natural, she forced herself to it,
and when she confided to you how many defects she could overcome by her unusual command of head resonance, she was not so
much trying to persuade you as to persuade herself.

When she took a note that was high for her, Miss Darcey
always put her right hand out into the air, as if she were indicating
height, or giving an exact measurement. Some early teacher had
told her that she could "place" a tone more surely by the help of
such a gesture, and she firmly believed that it was of great assistance to her. (Even when she was singing in public, she kept her
right hand down with difficulty, nervously clasping her white kid
fingers together when she took a high note. Thea could always see
her elbows stiffen.) She unvaryingly executed this gesture with a
smile of gracious confidence, as if she were actually putting her
finger on the tone: "There it is, friends!"

This morning, in Gounod's "Ave Maria," as Miss Darcey
approached her B natural,— .

> *Dans——nos a–lár———mes!**

out went the hand, with the sure airy gesture, though it was little
above A she got with her voice, whatever she touched with her
finger. Often Bowers let such things pass—with the right
people—but this morning he snapped his jaws together and
muttered, "God!" Miss Darcey tried again, with the same gesture
as of putting the crowning touch, tilting her head and smiling
radiantly at Bowers, as if to say, "It is for you I do all this!"

> *Dans——nos a—lár———mes!"*

This time she made B flat, and went on in the happy belief that
she had done well enough, when she suddenly found that her
accompanist was not going on with her, and this put her out
completely.

She turned to Thea, whose hands had fallen in her lap. "Oh
why did you stop just there! It *is* too trying! Now we'd better go
back to that other *crescendo** and try it from there."

"I beg your pardon," Thea muttered. "I thought you wanted

to get that B natural." She began again, as Miss Darcey indicated.

After the singer was gone, Bowers walked up to Thea and asked languidly, "Why do you hate Jessie so? Her little variations from pitch are between her and her public; they don't hurt you. Has she ever done anything to you except be very agreeable?"

"Yes, she has done things to me," Thea retorted hotly.

Bowers looked interested. "What, for example?"

"I can't explain, but I've got it in for her."

Bowers laughed. "No doubt about that. I'll have to suggest that you conceal it a little more effectually. That is—necessary, Miss Kronborg," he added, looking back over the shoulder of the overcoat he was putting on.

He went out to lunch and Thea thought the subject closed. But late in the afternoon, when he was taking his dyspepsia tablet and a glass of water between lessons, he looked up and said in a voice ironically coaxing:—

"Miss Kronborg, I wish you would tell me why you hate Jessie."

Taken by surprise Thea put down the score she was reading and answered before she knew what she was saying, "I hate her for the sake of what I used to think a singer might be."

Bowers balanced the tablet on the end of his long forefinger and whistled softly. "And how did you form your conception of what a singer ought to be?" he asked.

"I don't know." Thea flushed and spoke under her breath; "but I suppose I got most of it from Harsanyi."

Bowers made no comment upon this reply, but opened the door for the next pupil, who was waiting in the reception-room.

It was dark when Thea left the studio that night. She knew she had offended Bowers. Somehow she had hurt herself, too. She felt unequal to the boarding-house table, the sneaking divinity student who sat next her and had tried to kiss her on the stairs last night. She went over to the waterside of Michigan Avenue and walked along beside the lake. It was a clear, frosty winter night. The great empty space over the water was restful and spoke of freedom. If she had any money at all, she would go away. The stars glittered over the wide black water. She looked up at them wearily and shook her head. She believed that what she felt was despair, but it was only one of the forms of hope. She felt, indeed, as if she were bidding the stars good-bye; but she was renewing a promise. Though their challenge is universal and eternal, the stars get no answer but that,—the brief light flashed back to them from the eyes of the young who unaccountably aspire.

The rich, noisy, city, fat with food and drink, is a spent thing; its chief concern is its digestion and its little game of hide-and-seek with the undertaker. Money and office and success are the consolations of impotence. Fortune turns kind to such solid people and lets them suck their bone in peace. She flecks her whip upon flesh that is more alive, upon that stream of hungry boys and girls who tramp the streets of every city, recognizable by their pride and discontent, who are the Future, and who possess the treasure of creative power.

III

WHILE her living arrangements were so casual and fortuitous, Bowers's studio was the one fixed thing in Thea's life. She went out from it to uncertainties, and hastened to it from nebulous confusion. She was more influenced by Bowers than she knew. Unconsciously she began to take on something of his dry contempt, and share his grudge without understanding exactly what it was about. His cynicism seemed to her honest, and the amiability of his pupils artificial. She admired his drastic treatment of his dull pupils. The stupid deserved all they got, and more. Bowers knew that she thought him a very clever man.

One afternoon when Bowers came in from lunch Thea handed him a card on which he read the name, "Mr Philip Frederick Ottenburg."

"He said he would be in again to-morrow and that he wanted some time. Who is he? I like him better than the others."

Bowers nodded. "So do I. He's not a singer. He's a beer prince:

son of the big brewer in St. Louis. He's been in Germany with his mother. I didn't know he was back."

"Does he take lessons?"

"Now and again. He sings rather well. He's at the head of the Chicago branch of the Ottenburg business, but he can't stick to work and is always running away. He has great ideas in beer, people tell me. He's what they call an imaginative business man; goes over to Bayreuth* and seems to do nothing but give parties and spend money, and brings back more good notions for the brewery than the fellows who sit tight dig out in five years. I was born too long ago to be much taken in by these chesty boys with flowered vests, but I like Fred, all the same."

"So do I," said Thea positively.

Bowers made a sound between a cough and a laugh. "Oh, he's a lady-killer, all right! The girls in here are always making eyes at him. You won't be the first." He threw some sheets of music on the piano. "Better look that over; accompaniment's a little tricky. It's for that new woman from Detroit. And Mrs. Priest will be in this afternoon."

Thea sighed. "'I Know that my Redeemer Liveth'?"*

"The same. She starts on her concert tour next week, and we'll have a rest. Until then, I suppose we'll have to be going over her programme."

The next day Thea hurried through her luncheon at a German bakery and got back to the studio at ten minutes past one. She felt sure that the young brewer would come early, before it was time for Bowers to arrive. He had not said he would, but yesterday, when he opened the door to go, he had glanced about the room and at her, and something in his eye had conveyed that suggestion.

Sure enough, at twenty minutes past one the door of the reception-room opened, and a tall, robust young man with a cane and an English hat and ulster looked in expectantly. "Ah—ha!" he exclaimed, "I thought if I came early I might have good luck. And how are you to-day, Miss Kronborg?"

Thea was sitting in the window chair. At her left elbow there was a table, and upon this table the young man sat down, holding his hat and cane in his hand, loosening his long coat so that it fell back from his shoulders. He was a gleaming, florid young fellow. His hair, thick and yellow, was cut very short, and he wore a closely trimmed beard, long enough on the chin to curl a little. Even his eyebrows were thick and yellow, like fleece. He had lively blue eyes—Thea looked up at them with great interest as he sat chatting and swinging his foot rhythmically. He was easily famil- iar, and frankly so. Wherever people met young Ottenburg, in his office, on shipboard, in a foreign hotel or railway compartment, they always felt (and usually liked) that artless presumption which seemed to say, "In this case we may waive formalities. We really haven't time. This is to-day, but it will soon be to-morrow, and then we may be very different people, and in some other country." He had a way of floating people out of dull or awkward situations, out of their own torpor or constraint or discourage- ment. It was a marked personal talent, of almost incalculable value in the representative of a great business founded on social amenities. Thea had liked him yesterday for the way in which he had picked her up out of herself and her German grammar for a few exciting moments.

"By the way, will you tell me your first name, please? Thea? Oh, then you *are* a Swede, sure enough! I thought so. Let me call you Miss Thea, after the German fashion. You won't mind? Of course not!" He usually made his assumption of a special under- standing seem a tribute to the other person and not to himself.

"How long have you been with Bowers here? Do you like the old grouch? So do I. I've come to tell him about a new soprano I heard at Bayreuth. He'll pretend not to care, but he does. Do you warble with him? Have you anything of a voice? Honest? You look it, you know. What are you going in for, something big? Opera?"

Thea blushed crimson. "Oh, I'm not going in for anything. I'm trying to learn to sing at funerals."

Ottenburg leaned forward. His eyes twinkled. "I'll engage you to sing at mine. You can't fool me, Miss Thea. May I hear you take your lesson this afternoon?"

"No, you may not. I took it this morning."

He picked up a roll of music that lay behind him on the table. "Is this yours? Let me see what you are doing." He snapped back the clasp and began turning over the songs. "All very fine, but tame. What's he got you at this Mozart stuff for? I shouldn't think it would suit your voice. Oh, I can make a pretty good guess at what will suit you! This from 'Gioconda'* is more in your line. What's this Grieg?* It looks interesting. *Tak for Ditt Råd.* What does that mean?"

" 'Thanks for your Advice.' Don't you know it?"

"No; not at all. Let's try it." He rose, pushed open the door into the music-room, and motioned Thea to enter before him. She hung back.

"I couldn't give you much of an idea of it. It's a big song."

Ottenburg took her gently by the elbow and pushed her into the other room. He sat down carelessly at the piano and looked over the music for a moment. "I think I can get you through it. But how stupid not to have the German words. Can you really sing the Norwegian? What an infernal language to sing. Translate the text for me." He handed her the music.

Thea looked at it, then at him, and shook her head. "I can't. The truth is I don't know either English or Swedish very well, and Norwegian's still worse," she said confidentially. She not infrequently refused to do what she was asked to do, but it was not like her to explain her refusal, even when she had a good reason.

"I understand. We immigrants never speak any language well. But you know what it means, don't you?"

"Of course I do!"

"Then don't frown at me like that, but tell me."

Thea continued to frown, but she also smiled. She was confused, but not embarrassed. She was not afraid of Ottenburg. He was not one of those people who made her spine like a steel rail. On the contrary, he made one venturesome.

"Well, it goes something like this: *Thanks for your advice! But I prefer to steer my boat into the din of roaring breakers. Even if the journey is my last, I may find what I have never found before. Onward must I go, for I yearn for the wild sea. I long to fight my way through the angry waves, and to see how far, and how long I can make them carry me.*"

Ottenburg took the music and began: "Wait a moment. Is that too fast? How do you take it? That right?" He pulled up his cuffs and began the accompaniment again. He had become entirely serious, and he played with fine enthusiasm and with understanding.

Fred's talent was worth almost as much to old Otto Ottenburg as the steady industry of his older sons. When Fred sang the Prize Song* at an interstate meet of the *Turnverein*, ten thousand *Turners** went forth pledged to Ottenburg beer.

As Thea finished the song Fred turned back to the first page, without looking up from the music. "Now, once more," he called. They began again, and did not hear Bowers when he came in and stood in the doorway. He stood still, blinking like an owl at their two heads shining in the sun. He could not see their faces, but there was something about his girl's back that he had not noticed before: a very slight and yet very free motion, from the toes up. Her whole back seemed plastic, seemed to be moulding itself to the galloping rhythm of the song. Bowers perceived such things sometimes—unwillingly. He had known to-day that there was something afoot. The river of sound which had its source in his pupil had caught him two flights down. He had stopped and listened with a kind of sneering admiration. From the door he watched her with a half-incredulous, half-malicious smile.

When he had struck the keys for the last time, Ottenburg dropped his hands on his knees and looked up with a quick breath. "I got you through. What a stunning song! Did I play it right?"

Thea studied his excited face. There was a good deal of meaning in it, and there was a good deal in her own as she answered him. "You suited me," she said ungrudgingly.

After Ottenburg was gone, Thea noticed that Bowers was more agreeable than usual. She had heard the young brewer ask Bowers to dine with him at his club that evening, and she saw that he looked forward to the dinner with pleasure. He dropped a remark to the effect that Fred knew as much about food and wines as any man in Chicago. He said this boastfully.

"If he's such a grand business man, how does he have time to run around listening to singing-lessons?" Thea asked suspiciously.

As she went home to her boarding-house through the February slush, she wished she were going to dine with them. At nine o'clock she looked up from her grammar to wonder what Bowers and Ottenburg were having to eat. At that moment they were talking of her.

IV

THEA noticed that Bowers took rather more pains with her now that Fred Ottenburg often dropped in at eleven-thirty to hear her lesson. After the lesson the young man took Bowers off to lunch with him, and Bowers liked good food when another man paid for it. He encouraged Fred's visits, and Thea soon saw that Fred knew exactly why.

One morning, after her lesson, Ottenburg turned to Bowers. "If you'll lend me Miss Thea, I think I have an engagement for her. Mrs. Henry Nathanmeyer is going to give three musical evenings in April, first three Saturdays, and she has consulted me about soloists. For the first evening she has a young violinist, and she would be charmed to have Miss Kronborg. She will pay fifty dollars. Not much, but Miss Thea would meet some people there who might be useful. What do you say?"

Bowers passed the question on to Thea. "I guess you could use the fifty, couldn't you, Miss Kronborg? You can easily work up some songs."

Thea was perplexed. "I need the money awfully," she said frankly; "but I haven't got the right clothes for that sort of thing. I suppose I'd better try to get some."

Ottenburg spoke up quickly, "Oh, you'd make nothing out of it if you went to buying evening clothes. I've thought of that. Mrs. Nathanmeyer has a troop of daughters, a perfect seraglio, all ages and sizes. She'll be glad to fit you out, if you aren't sensitive about wearing kosher clothes. Let me take you to see her, and you'll find

that she'll arrange that easily enough. I told her she must produce
something nice, blue or yellow, and properly cut. I brought half a
dozen Worth gowns* through the customs for her two weeks ago,
and she's not ungrateful. When can we go to see her?"

"I haven't any time free, except at night," Thea replied in some
confusion.

"To-morrow evening, then? I shall call for you at eight. Bring
all your songs along; she will want us to give her a little rehearsal,
perhaps. I'll play your accompaniments, if you've no objection.
That will save money for you and Mrs. Nathanmeyer. She needs
it." Ottenburg chuckled as he took down the number of Thea's
boarding-house.

The Nathanmeyers were so rich and great that even Thea had
heard of them, and this seemed a very remarkable opportunity.
Ottenburg had brought it about by merely lifting a finger, appar-
ently. He was a beer prince sure enough, as Bowers had said.

The next evening at a quarter to eight Thea was dressed and
waiting in the boarding-house parlor. She was nervous and
fidgety and found it difficult to sit still on the hard, convex upholstery of the chairs. She tried them one after another, moving
about the dimly lighted, musty room, where the gas always leaked
gently and sang in the burners. There was no one in the parlor
but the medical student, who was playing one of Sousa's marches
so vigorously that the china ornaments on the top of the piano
rattled. In a few moments some of the pension-office girls would
come in and begin to two-step. Thea wished that Ottenburg
would come and let her escape. She glanced at herself in the long,
somber mirror. She was wearing her pale-blue broadcloth church
dress, which was not unbecoming but was certainly too heavy to
wear to anybody's house in the evening. Her slippers were run
over at the heel and she had not had time to have them mended,
and her white gloves were not so clean as they should be. However, she knew that she would forget these annoying things as
soon as Ottenburg came.

Mary, the Hungarian chambermaid, came to the door, stood
between the plush portières, beckoned to Thea, and made an
inarticulate sound in her throat. Thea jumped up and ran into the

hall, where Ottenburg stood smiling, his caped cloak open, his silk hat in his white-kid hand. The Hungarian girl stood like a monument on her flat heels, staring at the pink carnation in Ottenburg's coat. Her broad, pockmarked face wore the only expression of which it was capable, a kind of animal wonder. As the young man followed Thea out, he glanced back over his shoulder through the crack of the door; the Hun clapped her hands over her stomach, opened her mouth, and made another raucous sound in her throat.

"Isn't she awful?" Thea exclaimed. "I think she's half-witted. Can you understand her?"

Ottenburg laughed as he helped her into the carriage. "Oh, yes; I can understand her!" He settled himself on the front seat opposite Thea. "Now, I want to tell you about the people we are going to see. We may have a musical public in this country some day, but as yet there are only the Germans and the Jews. All the other people go to hear Jessie Darcey sing, 'O, Promise Me!' The Nathanmeyers are the finest kind of Jews. If you do anything for Mrs. Henry Nathanmeyer, you must put yourself into her hands. Whatever she says about music, about clothes, about life, will be correct. And you may feel at ease with her. She expects nothing of people; she has lived in Chicago twenty years. If you were to behave like the Magyar who was so interested in my buttonhole, she would not be surprised. If you were to sing like Jessie Darcey, she would not be surprised; but she would manage not to hear you again."

"Would she? Well, that's the kind of people I want to find." Thea felt herself growing bolder.

"You will be all right with her so long as you do not try to be anything that you are not. Her standards have nothing to do with Chicago. Her perceptions—or her grandmother's, which is the same thing—were keen when all this was an Indian village. So merely be yourself, and you will like her. She will like you because the Jews always sense talent, and," he added ironically, "they admire certain qualities of feeling that are found only in the white-skinned races."

Thea looked into the young man's face as the light of a street lamp flashed into the carriage. His somewhat academic manner amused her.

"What makes you take such an interest in singers?" she asked curiously. "You seem to have a perfect passion for hearing music-lessons. I wish I could trade jobs with you!"

"I'm not interested in singers." His tone was offended. "I am interested in talent. There are only two interesting things in the world, anyhow; and talent is one of them."

"What's the other?" The question came meekly from the figure opposite him. Another arc-light flashed in at the window.

Fred saw her face and broke into a laugh. "Why, you're guying me, you little wretch! You won't let me behave properly." He dropped his gloved hand lightly on her knee, took it away and let it hang between his own. "Do you know," he said confidentially, "I believe I'm more in earnest about all this than you are."

"About all what?"

"All you've got in your throat there."

"Oh! I'm in earnest all right; only I never was much good at talking. Jessie Darcey is the smooth talker. 'You notice the effect I get there—' If she only got 'em, she'd be a wonder, you know!"

Mr. and Mrs. Nathanmeyer were alone in their great library. Their three unmarried daughters had departed in successive carriages, one to a dinner, one to a Nietzsche club,* one to a ball given for the girls employed in the big department stores. When Ottenburg and Thea entered, Henry Nathanmeyer and his wife were sitting at a table at the farther end of the long room, with a reading-lamp and a tray of cigarettes and cordial-glasses between them. The overhead lights were too soft to bring out the colors of the big rugs, and none of the picture lights were on. One could merely see that there were pictures there. Fred whispered that they were Rousseaus* and Corots, very fine ones which the old banker had bought long ago for next to nothing. In the hall Ottenburg had stopped Thea before a painting of a woman eating grapes out of a paper bag, and had told her gravely that there was the most beautiful Manet in the world.* He made her take off her hat and gloves in the hall, and looked her over a little before he took her in. But once they were in the library he seemed perfectly satisfied with her and led her down the long room to their hostess.

Mrs. Nathanmeyer was a heavy, powerful old Jewess, with a great pompadour of white hair, a swarthy complexion, an eagle nose, and sharp, glittering eyes. She wore a black velvet dress with a long train, and a diamond necklace and earrings. She took Thea to the other side of the table and presented her to Mr. Nathanmeyer, who apologized for not rising, pointing to a slippered foot on a cushion; he said that he suffered from gout. He had a very soft voice and spoke with an accent which would have been heavy if it had not been so caressing. He kept Thea standing beside him for some time. He noticed that she stood easily, looked straight down into his face, and was not embarrassed. Even when Mrs. Nathanmeyer told Ottenburg to bring a chair for Thea, the old man did not release her hand, and she did not sit down. He admired her just as she was, as she happened to be standing, and she felt it. He was much handsomer than his wife, Thea thought. His forehead was high, his hair soft and white, his skin pink, a little puffy under his clear blue eyes. She noticed how warm and delicate his hands were, pleasant to touch and beautiful to look at. Ottenburg had told her that Mr. Nathanmeyer had a very fine collection of medals and cameos, and his fingers looked as if they had never touched anything but delicately cut surfaces.

He asked Thea where Moonstone was; how many inhabitants it had; what her father's business was; from what part of Sweden her grandfather came; and whether she spoke Swedish as a child. He was interested to hear that her mother's mother was still living, and that her grandfather had played the oboe. Thea felt at home standing there beside him; she felt that he was very wise, and that he some way took one's life up and looked it over kindly, as if it were a story. She was sorry when they left him to go into the music-room.

As they reached the door of the music-room, Mrs. Nathanmeyer turned a switch that threw on many lights. The room was even larger than the library, all glittering surfaces, with two Steinway pianos.

Mrs. Nathanmeyer rang for her own maid. "Selma will take you upstairs, Miss Kronborg, and you will find some dresses on the bed. Try several of them, and take the one you like best. Selma will help you. She has a great deal of taste. When you are dressed, come down and let us go over some of your songs with Mr. Ottenburg."

After Thea went away with the maid, Ottenburg came up to Mrs. Nathanmeyer and stood beside her, resting his hand on the high back of her chair.

"Well, *gnädige Frau,** do you like her?"

"I think so. I liked her when she talked to father. She will always get on better with men."

Ottenburg leaned over her chair. "Prophetess! Do you see what I meant?"

"About her beauty? She has great possibilities, but you can never tell about those Northern women. They look so strong, but they are easily battered. The face falls so early under those wide cheek-bones. A single idea—hate or greed, or even love—can tear them to shreds. She is nineteen? Well, in ten years she may have quite a regal beauty, or she may have a heavy, discontented face, all dug out in channels. That will depend upon the kind of ideas she lives with."

"Or the kind of people?" Ottenburg suggested.

The old Jewess folded her arms over her massive chest, drew back her shoulders, and looked up at the young man. "With that hard glint in her eye? The people won't matter much, I fancy. They will come and go. She is very much interested in herself— as she should be."

Ottenburg frowned. "Wait until you hear her sing. Her eyes are different then. That gleam that comes in them is curious, isn't it? As you say, it's impersonal."

The object of this discussion came in, smiling. She had chosen neither the blue nor the yellow gown, but a pale rose-color, with silver butterflies. Mrs. Nathanmeyer lifted her lorgnette and studied her as she approached. She caught the characteristic things at once: the free, strong walk, the calm carriage of the head, the milky whiteness of the girl's arms and shoulders.

"Yes, that color is good for you," she said approvingly. "The yellow one probably killed your hair? Yes; this does very well indeed, so we need think no more about it."

Thea glanced questioningly at Ottenburg. He smiled and bowed, seemed perfectly satisfied. He asked her to stand in the elbow of the piano, in front of him, instead of behind him as she had been taught to do.

"Yes," said the hostess with feeling. "That other position is barbarous."

Thea sang an aria from "Gioconda," some songs by Schumann which she had studied with Harsanyi, and the "*Tak for Dit Råd*," which Ottenburg liked.

"That you must do again," he declared when they finished this song. "You did it much better the other day. You accented it more, like a dance or a galop. How did you do it?"

Thea laughed, glancing sidewise at Mrs. Nathanmeyer. "You want it rough-house, do you? Bowers likes me to sing it more seriously, but it always makes me think about a story my grandmother used to tell."

Fred pointed to the chair behind her. "Won't you rest a moment and tell us about it? I thought you had some notion about it when you first sang it for me."

Thea sat down. "In Norway my grandmother knew a girl who was awfully in love with a young fellow. She went into service on a big dairy farm to make enough money for her outfit. They were married at Christmastime, and everybody was glad, because they'd been sighing around about each other for so long. That very summer, the day before St. John's Day,* her husband caught her carrying on with another farm-hand. The next night all the farm people had a bonfire and a big dance up on the mountain, and everybody was dancing and singing. I guess they were all a little drunk, for they got to seeing how near they could make the girls dance to the edge of the cliff. Ole—he was the girl's husband—seemed the jolliest and the drunkest of anybody. He danced his wife nearer and nearer the edge of the rock, and his wife began to scream so that the others stopped dancing and the music stopped; but Ole went right on singing, and he danced her over the edge of the cliff and they fell hundreds of feet and were all smashed to pieces."

Ottenburg turned back to the piano. "That's the idea! Now, come Miss Thea. Let it go!"

Thea took her place. She laughed and drew herself up out of her corsets, threw her shoulders high and let them drop again. She had never sung in a low dress before, and she found it comfortable. Ottenburg jerked his head and they began the song. The accompaniment sounded more than ever like the thumping and scraping of heavy feet.

When they stopped, they heard a sympathetic tapping at the end of the room. Old Mr. Nathanmeyer had come to the door and was sitting back in the shadow, just inside the library, applauding with his cane. Thea threw him a bright smile. He continued to sit there, his slippered foot on a low chair, his cane between his fingers, and she glanced at him from time to time. The doorway made a frame for him, and he looked like a man in a picture, with the long, shadowy room behind him.

Mrs. Nathanmeyer summoned the maid again. "Selma will pack that gown in a box for you, and you can take it home in Mr. Ottenburg's carriage."

Thea turned to follow the maid, but hesitated. "Shall I wear gloves?" she asked, turning again to Mrs. Nathanmeyer.

"No, I think not. Your arms are good, and you will feel freer without. You will need light slippers, pink—or white, if you have them, will do quite as well."

Thea went upstairs with the maid and Mrs. Nathanmeyer rose, took Ottenburg's arm, and walked toward her husband. "That's the first real voice I have heard in Chicago," she said decidedly. "I don't count that stupid Priest woman. What do you say, father?"

Mr. Nathanmeyer shook his white head and smiled softly, as if he were thinking about something very agreeable. "*Svensk sommar*," he murmured. "She is like a Swedish summer. I spent nearly a year there when I was a young man," he explained to Ottenburg.

When Ottenburg got Thea and her big box into the carriage, it occurred to him that she must be hungry, after singing so much.

When he asked her, she admitted that she was very hungry, indeed.

He took out his watch. "Would you mind stopping somewhere with me? It's only eleven."

"Mind? Of course, I wouldn't mind. I wasn't brought up like that. I can take care of myself."

Ottenburg laughed. "And I can take care of myself, so we can do lots of jolly things together." He opened the carriage door and spoke to the driver. "I'm stuck on the way you sing that Grieg song," he declared.

When Thea got into bed that night she told herself that this was the happiest evening she had had in Chicago. She had enjoyed the Nathanmeyers and their grand house, her new dress, and Ottenburg, her first real carriage ride, and the good supper when she was so hungry. And Ottenburg *was* jolly! He made you want to come back at him. You weren't always being caught up and mystified. When you started in with him, you went; you cut the breeze, as Ray used to say. He had some go in him.

Philip Frederick Ottenburg was the third son of the great brewer. His mother was Katarina Fürst, the daughter and heiress of a brewing business older and richer than Otto Ottenburg's. As a young woman she had been a conspicuous figure in German-American society in New York, and not untouched by scandal. She was a handsome, headstrong girl, a rebellious and violent force in a provincial society. She was brutally sentimental and heavily romantic. Her free speech, her Continental ideas, and her proclivity for championing new causes, even when she did not know much about them, made her an object of suspicion. She was always going abroad to seek out intellectual affinities, and was one of the group of young women who followed Wagner about in his old age, keeping at a respectful distance, but receiving now and then a gracious acknowledgment that he appreciated their homage. When the composer died, Katarina, then a matron with a family, took to her bed and saw no one for a week.

After having been engaged to an American actor, a Welsh socialist agitator, and a German army officer, Fräulein Fürst at last placed herself and her great brewery interests into the trustworthy hands of Otto Ottenburg, who had been her suitor ever since he was a clerk, learning his business in her father's office.

Her first two sons were exactly like their father. Even as children they were industrious, earnest little tradesmen. As Frau Ottenburg said, "she had to wait for her Fred, but she got him at last," the first man who had altogether pleased her. Frederick entered Harvard when he was eighteen. When his mother went to Boston to visit him, she not only got him everything he wished for, but she made handsome and often embarrassing presents to all his friends. She gave dinners and supper parties for the Glee Club, made the crew break training, and was a generally disturbing influence. In his third year Fred left the university because of a serious escapade which had somewhat hampered his life ever since. He went at once into his father's business, where, in his own way, he had made himself very useful.

Fred Ottenburg was now twenty-eight, and people could only say of him that he had been less hurt by his mother's indulgence than most boys would have been. He had never wanted anything that he could not have it, and he might have had a great many things that he had never wanted. He was extravagant, but not prodigal. He turned most of the money his mother gave him into the business, and lived on his generous salary.

Fred had never been bored for a whole day in his life. When he was in Chicago or St. Louis, he went to ball games, prize-fights, and horse-races. When he was in Germany, he went to concerts and to the opera. He belonged to a long list of sporting-clubs and hunting-clubs, and was a good boxer. He had so many natural interests that he had no affectations. At Harvard he kept away from the aesthetic circle that had already discovered Francis Thompson.* He liked no poetry but German poetry. Physical energy was the thing he was full to the brim of, and music was one of its natural forms of expression. He had a healthy love of sport and art, of eating and drinking. When he was in Germany, he scarcely knew where the soup ended and the symphony began.

V

MARCH began badly for Thea. She had a cold during the first week, and after she got through her church duties on Sunday she had to go to bed with tonsilitis. She was still in the boarding-house at which young Ottenburg had called when he took her to see Mrs. Nathanmeyer. She had stayed on there because her room, although it was inconvenient and very small, was at the corner of the house and got the sunlight.

Since she left Mrs. Lorch, this was the first place where she had got away from a north light. Her rooms had all been as damp and mouldy as they were dark, with deep foundations of dirt under the carpets, and dirty walls. In her present room there was no running water and no clothes closet, and she had to have the dresser moved out to make room for her piano. But there were two windows, one on the south and one on the west, a light wall-paper with morning-glory vines, and on the floor a clean matting. The landlady had tried to make the room look cheerful, because it was hard to let. It was so small that Thea could keep it clean herself, after the Hun had done her worst. She hung her dresses on the door under a sheet, used the washstand for a dresser, slept on a cot, and opened both the windows when she practiced. She felt less walled in than she had in the other houses.

Wednesday was her third day in bed. The medical student who lived in the house had been in to see her, had left some tablets and a foamy gargle, and told her that she could probably go back to work on Monday. The landlady stuck her head in once a day, but Thea did not encourage her visits. The Hungarian chambermaid brought her soup and toast. She made a sloppy pretense of put-ting the room in order, but she was such a dirty creature that Thea would not let her touch her cot; she got up every morning and turned the mattress and made the bed herself. The exertion made her feel miserably ill, but at least she could lie still contentedly for a long while afterward. She hated the poisoned feeling in her throat, and no matter how often she gargled she felt unclean and disgusting. Still, if she had to be ill, she was almost glad that she had a contagious illness. Otherwise she would have been at the mercy of the people in the house. She knew that they disliked her, yet now that she was ill, they took it upon themselves to tap at her door, send her messages, books, even a miserable flower or two. Thea knew that their sympathy was an expression of self-righteousness, and she hated them for it. The divinity student, who was always whispering soft things to her, sent "The Kreutzer Sonata."*

The medical student had been kind to her: he knew that she did not want to pay a doctor. His gargle had helped her, and he gave her things to make her sleep at night. But he had been a cheat, too. He had exceeded his rights. She had no soreness in her chest, and had told him so clearly. All this thumping of her back, and listening to her breathing, was done to satisfy personal curiosity. She had watched him with a contemptuous smile. She was too sick to care; if it amused him— She made him wash his hands before he touched her; he was never very clean. All the same, it wounded her and made her feel that the world was a pretty disgusting place. "The Kreutzer Sonata" did not make her feel any more cheerful. She threw it aside with hatred. She could not believe it was written by the same man who wrote the novel that had thrilled her.

Her cot was beside the south window, and on Wednesday afternoon she lay thinking about the Harsanyis, about old Mr. Nathanmeyer, and about how she was missing Fred Ottenburg's visits to the studio. That was much the worst thing about being sick. If she were going to the studio every day, she might be having pleasant encounters with Fred. He was always running away, Bowers said, and he might be planning to go away as soon as Mrs. Nathanmeyer's evenings were over. And here she was losing all this time!

After a while she heard the Hun's clumsy trot in the hall, and then a pound on the door. Mary came in, making her usual uncouth sounds, carrying a long box and a big basket. Thea sat up in bed and tore off the strings and paper. The basket was full of fruit, with a big Hawaiian pineapple in the middle, and in the box there were layers of pink roses with long, woody stems and dark-green leaves. They filled the room with a cool smell that made another air to breathe. Mary stood with her apron full of paper and cardboard. When she saw Thea take an envelope out from under the flowers, she uttered an exclamation, pointed to the roses, and then to the bosom of her own dress, on the left side. Thea laughed and nodded. She understood that Mary associated the color with Ottenburg's *boutonnière*. She pointed to the water pitcher,—she had nothing else big enough to hold the flowers,—and made Mary put it on the window sill beside her.

After Mary was gone Thea locked the door. When the landlady knocked, she pretended that she was asleep. She lay still all afternoon and with drowsy eyes watched the roses open. They were the first hothouse flowers she had ever had. The cool fragrance they released was soothing, and as the pink petals curled back, they were the only things between her and the gray sky. She lay on her side, putting the room and the boarding-house behind her. Fred knew where all the pleasant things in the world were, she reflected, and knew the road to them. He had keys to all the nice places in his pocket, and seemed to jingle them from time to time. And then, he was young; and her friends had always been old. Her mind went back over them. They had all been teachers; wonderfully kind, but still teachers. Ray Kennedy, she knew, had wanted to marry her, but he was the most protecting and teacher-like of them all. She moved impatiently in her cot and threw her braids away from her hot neck, over her pillow. "I don't want him for a teacher," she thought, frowning petulantly out of the window. "I've had such a string of them. I want him for a sweetheart."

VI

"THEA," said Fred Ottenburg one drizzly afternoon in April, while they sat waiting for their tea at a restaurant in the Pullman Building, overlooking the lake, "what are you going to do this summer?"

"I don't know. Work, I suppose."

"With Bowers, you mean? Even Bowers goes fishing for a month. Chicago's no place to work, in the summer. Haven't you made any plans?"

Thea shrugged her shoulders. "No use having any plans when you haven't any money. They are unbecoming."

"Aren't you going home?"

She shook her head. "No. It won't be comfortable there till I've got something to show for myself. I'm not getting on at all, you know. This year has been mostly wasted."

"You're stale; that's what's the matter with you. And just now you're dead tired. You'll talk more rationally after you've had some tea. Rest your throat until it comes." They were sitting by a window. As Ottenburg looked at her in the gray light, he remembered what Mrs. Nathanmeyer had said about the Swedish face "breaking early." Thea was as gray as the weather. Her skin looked sick. Her hair, too, though on a damp day it curled charmingly about her face, looked pale.

Fred beckoned the waiter and increased his order for food. Thea did not hear him. She was staring out of the window, down at the roof of the Art Institute and the green lions, dripping in the rain. The lake was all rolling mist, with a soft shimmer of robin's-egg blue in the gray. A lumber boat, with two very tall masts, was emerging gaunt and black out of the fog. When the tea came Thea ate hungrily, and Fred watched her. He thought her eyes became a little less bleak. The kettle sang cheerfully over the spirit lamp, and she seemed to concentrate her attention upon that pleasant sound. She kept looking toward it listlessly and indulgently, in a way that gave him a realization of her loneliness. Fred lit a cigarette and smoked thoughtfully. He and Thea were alone in the quiet, dusky room full of white tables. In those days Chicago people never stopped for tea. "Come," he said at last, "what would you do this summer, if you could do whatever you wished?"

"I'd go a long way from here! West, I think. Maybe I could get some of my spring back. All this cold, cloudy weather,"—she looked out at the lake and shivered,—"I don't know, it does things to me," she ended abruptly.

Fred nodded. "I know. You've been going down ever since you had tonsilitis. I've seen it. What you need is to sit in the sun and bake for three months. You've got the right idea. I remember once when we were having dinner somewhere you kept asking me about the Cliff-Dweller ruins. Do they still interest you?"

"Of course they do. I've always wanted to go down there—long before I ever got in for this."

"I don't think I told you, but my father owns a whole canyon full of Cliff-Dweller ruins. He has a big worthless ranch down in Arizona, near a Navajo reservation, and there's a canyon on the place they call Panther Canyon,* chock full of that sort of thing. I often go down there to hunt. Henry Biltmer and his wife live there and keep a tidy place. He's an old German who worked in the brewery until he lost his health. Now he runs a few cattle. Henry likes to do me a favor. I've done a few for him." Fred drowned his cigarette in his saucer and studied Thea's expression, which was wistful and intent, envious and admiring. He continued with satisfaction: "If you went down there and stayed with them for two or three months, they wouldn't let you pay anything. I might send Henry a new gun, but even I couldn't offer him money for putting up a friend of mine. I'll get you transportation. It would make a new girl of you. Let me write to Henry, and you pack your trunk. That's all that's necessary. No red tape about it. What do you say, Thea?"

She bit her lip, and sighed as if she were waking up.

Fred crumpled his napkin impatiently. "Well, isn't it easy enough?"

"That's the trouble; it's *too* easy. Doesn't sound probable. I'm not used to getting things for nothing."

Ottenburg laughed. "Oh, if that's all, I'll show you how to begin. You won't get this for nothing, quite. I'll ask you to let me stop off and see you on my way to California. Perhaps by that time you will be glad to see me. Better let me break the news to Bowers. I can manage him. He needs a little transportation himself now and then. You must get corduroy riding-things and leather leggings. There are a few snakes about. Why do you keep frowning?"

"Well, I don't exactly see why you take the trouble. What do you get out of it? You haven't liked me so well the last two or three weeks."

Fred dropped his third cigarette and looked at his watch. "If you don't see that, it's because you need a tonic. I'll show you what I'll get out of it. Now I'm going to get a cab and take you home. You are too tired to walk a step. You'd better get to bed as soon as you get there. Of course, I don't like you so well when you're half anaesthetized all the time. What have you been doing to yourself?"

Thea rose. "I don't know. Being bored eats the heart out of me, I guess." She walked meekly in front of him to the elevator. Fred noticed for the hundredth time how vehemently her body proclaimed her state of feeling. He remembered how remarkably brilliant and beautiful she had been when she sang at Mrs. Nathanmeyer's: flushed and gleaming, round and supple, something that couldn't be dimmed or downed. And now she seemed a moving figure of discouragement. The very waiters glanced at her apprehensively. It was not that she made a fuss, but her back was most extraordinarily vocal. One never needed to see her face to know what she was full of that day. Yet she was certainly not mercurial. Her flesh seemed to take a mood and to "set," like plaster. As he put her into the cab, Fred reflected once more that he "gave her up." He would attack her when his lance was brighter.

PART IV

THE ANCIENT PEOPLE

PART IV

THE ANCIENT PEOPLE

I

THE San Francisco Mountain lies in Northern Arizona, above Flagstaff, and its blue slopes and snowy summit entice the eye for a hundred miles across the desert. About its base lie the pine forests of the Navajos, where the great red-trunked trees live out their peaceful centuries in that sparkling air. The *piñons** and scrub begin only where the forest ends, where the country breaks into open, stony clearings and the surface of the earth cracks into deep canyons. The great pines stand at a considerable distance from each other. Each tree grows alone, murmurs alone, thinks alone. They do not intrude upon each other. The Navajos are not much in the habit of giving or of asking help. Their language is not a communicative one, and they never attempt an interchange of personality in speech. Over their forests there is the same inexorable reserve. Each tree has its exalted power to bear.

That was the first thing Thea Kronborg felt about the forest as she drove through it one May morning in Henry Biltmer's democrat wagon—and it was the first great forest she had ever seen. She had got off the train at Flagstaff that morning, rolled off into the high, chill air when all the pines on the mountain were fired by sunrise, so that she seemed to fall from sleep directly into the forest.

Old Biltmer followed a faint wagon trail which ran southeast and which, as they traveled, continually dipped lower, falling away from the high plateau on the slope of which Flagstaff sits. The white peak of the mountain, the snow gorges above the timber, now disappeared from time to time as the road dropped and dropped, and the forest closed behind the wagon. More than the mountain disappeared as the forest closed thus. Thea seemed to be taking very little through the wood with her. The

personality of which she was so tired seemed to let go of her.
The high, sparkling air drank it up like blotting-paper. It was
lost in the thrilling blue of the new sky and the song of the thin
wind in the *piñons*. The old, fretted lines which marked one
off, which defined her,—made her Thea Kronborg, Bowers's
accompanist, a soprano with a faulty middle voice,—were all
erased.

So far she had failed. Her two years in Chicago had not
resulted in anything. She had failed with Harsanyi, and she had
made no great progress with her voice. She had come to believe
that whatever Bowers had taught her was of secondary importance, and that in the essential things she had made no advance.
Her student life closed behind her, like the forest, and she doubted whether she could go back to it if she tried. Probably she
would teach in little country towns all her life. Failure was not so
tragic as she would have supposed; she was tired enough not to
care.

She was getting back to the earliest sources of gladness that she
could remember. She had loved the sun, and the brilliant solitudes of sand and sun, long before these other things had come
along to fasten themselves upon her and torment her. That night,
when she clambered into her big German feather bed, she felt
completely released from the enslaving desire to get on in the
world. Darkness had once again the sweet wonder that it had in
childhood.

II

THEA'S life at the Ottenburg ranch was simple and full of light,
like the days themselves. She awoke every morning when the first
fierce shafts of sunlight darted through the curtainless windows
of her room at the ranch house. After breakfast she took her
lunch-basket and went down to the canyon. Usually she did not
return until sunset.

Panther Canyon was like a thousand others—one of those
abrupt fissures with which the earth in the Southwest is riddled;

so abrupt that you might walk over the edge of any one of them on a dark night and never know what had happened to you. This canyon headed on the Ottenburg ranch, about a mile from the ranch house, and it was accessible only at its head. The canyon walls, for the first two hundred feet below the surface, were perpendicular cliffs, striped with even-running strata of rock. From there on to the bottom the sides were less abrupt, were shelving, and lightly fringed with *piñons* and dwarf cedars. The effect was that of a gentler canyon within a wilder one. The dead city lay at the point where the perpendicular outer wall ceased and the V-shaped inner gorge began. There a stratum of rock, softer than those above, had been hollowed out by the action of time until it was like a deep groove running along the sides of the canyon. In this hollow (like a great fold in the rock) the Ancient People had built their houses of yellowish stone and mortar. The over-hanging cliff above made a roof two hundred feet thick. The hard stratum below was an ever-lasting floor. The houses stood along in a row, like the buildings in a city block, or like a barracks.

In both walls of the canyon the same streak of soft rock had been washed out, and the long horizontal groove had been built up with houses. The dead city had thus two streets, one set in either cliff, facing each other across the ravine, with a river of blue air between them.

The canyon twisted and wound like a snake, and these two streets went on for four miles or more, interrupted by the abrupt turnings of the gorge, but beginning again within each turn. The canyon had a dozen of these false endings near its head. Beyond, the windings were larger and less perceptible, and it went on for a hundred miles, too narrow, precipitous, and terrible for man to follow it. The Cliff-Dwellers liked wide canyons, where the great cliffs caught the sun. Panther Canyon had been deserted for hundreds of years when the first Spanish missionaries came into Arizona, but the masonry of the houses was still wonderfully firm; had crumbled only where a landslide or a rolling boulder had torn it.

All the houses in the canyon were clean with the cleanness of sun-baked, wind-swept places, and they all smelled of the tough little cedars that twisted themselves into the very doorways. One of these rock-rooms Thea took for her own. Fred had told her how to make it comfortable. The day after she came old Henry brought over on one of the pack-ponies a roll of Navajo blankets that belonged to Fred, and Thea lined her cave with them. The room was not more than eight by ten feet, and she could touch the stone roof with her finger-tips. This was her old idea: a nest in a high cliff, full of sun. All morning long the sun beat upon her cliff, while the ruins on the opposite side of the canyon were in shadow. In the afternoon, when she had the shade of two hundred feet of rock wall, the ruins on the other side of the gulf stood out in the blazing sunlight. Before her door ran the narrow, winding path that had been the street of the Ancient People. The yucca and niggerhead cactus grew everywhere. From her doorstep she looked out on the ocher-colored slope that ran down several hundred feet to the stream, and this hot rock was sparsely grown with dwarf trees. Their colors were so pale that the shadows of the little trees on the rock stood out sharper than the trees themselves. When Thea first came, the chokecherry bushes were in blossom, and the scent of them was almost sickeningly sweet after a shower. At the very bottom of the canyon, along the stream, there was a thread of bright, flickering, golden-green,—cottonwood seedlings. They made a living, chattering screen behind which she took her bath every morning.

Thea went down to the stream by the Indian water trail. She had found a bathing-pool with a sand bottom, where the creek was damned by fallen trees. The climb back was long and steep, and when she reached her little house in the cliff she always felt fresh delight in its comfort and inaccessibility. By the time she got there, the woolly red-and-gray blankets were saturated with sunlight, and she sometimes fell asleep as soon as she stretched her body on their warm surfaces. She used to wonder at her own inactivity. She could lie there hour after hour in the sun and listen to the strident whir of the big locusts, and to the light, ironical laughter of the quaking asps. All her life she had been hurrying and sputtering, as if she had been born behind time and had been trying to catch up. Now, she reflected, as she drew herself out long upon the rugs, it was as if she were waiting for something to catch up with her. She had got to a place where she was out of the stream of meaningless activity and undirected effort.

Here she could lie for half a day undistracted, holding pleasant and incomplete conceptions in her mind—almost in her hands. They were scarcely clear enough to be called ideas. They had something to do with fragrance and color and sound, but almost nothing to do with words. She was singing very little now, but a song would go through her head all morning, as a spring keeps welling up, and it was like a pleasant sensation indefinitely prolonged. It was much more like a sensation than like an idea, or an act of remembering. Music had never come to her in that sensuous form before. It had always been a thing to be struggled with, had always brought anxiety and exaltation and chagrin—never content and indolence. Thea began to wonder whether people could not utterly lose the power to work, as they can lose their voice or their memory. She had always been a little drudge, hurrying from one task to another—as if it mattered! And now her power to think seemed converted into a power of sustained sensation. She could become a mere receptacle for heat, or become a color, like the bright lizards that darted about on the hot stones outside her door; or she could become a continuous repetition of sound, like the cicadas.

III

THE faculty of observation was never highly developed in Thea Kronborg. A great deal escaped her eye as she passed through the world. But the things which were for her, she saw; she experienced them physically and remembered them as if they had once been a part of herself. The roses she used to see in the florists' shops in Chicago were merely roses. But when she thought of the moonflowers that grew over Mrs. Tellamantez's door, it was as if she had been that vine and had opened up in white flowers every night. There were memories of light on the sand hills, of masses of prickly-pear blossoms she had found in the desert in early childhood, of the late afternoon sun pouring through the grape leaves and the mint bed in Mrs. Kohler's garden, which she would never lose. These recollections were a part of her mind and personality. In Chicago she had got almost nothing that went into her subconscious self and took root there. But here, in Panther Canyon, there were again things which seemed destined for her.

Panther Canyon was the home of innumerable swallows. They built nests in the wall far above the hollow groove in which Thea's own rock chamber lay. They seldom ventured above the rim of the canyon, to the flat, wind-swept tableland. Their world was the blue air-river between the canyon walls. In that blue gulf the arrow-shaped birds swam all day long, with only an occasional movement of the wings. The only sad thing about them was their timidity; the way in which they lived their lives between the echoing cliffs and never dared to rise out of the shadow of the canyon walls. As they swam past her door, Thea often felt how easy it would be to dream one's life out in some cleft in the world.

From the ancient dwelling there came always a dignified, unobtrusive sadness; now stronger, now fainter,—like the aromatic smell which the dwarf cedars gave out in the sun,—but always present, a part of the air one breathed. At night, when Thea dreamed about the canyon,—or in the early morning when she hurried toward it, anticipating it,—her conception of it was of yellow rocks baking in sunlight, the swallows, the cedar smell, and that peculiar sadness—a voice out of the past, not very loud, that went on saying a few simple things to the solitude eternally.

Standing up in her lodge, Thea could with her thumb nail dislodge flakes of carbon from the rock roof—the cooking-smoke of the Ancient People. They were that near! A timid, nest-building folk, like the swallows. How often Thea remembered Ray Kennedy's moralizing about the cliff cities. He used to say that he never felt the hardness of the human struggle or the sadness of history as he felt it among those ruins. He used to say, too, that it made one feel an obligation to do one's best. On the first day that Thea climbed the water trail she began to have intuitions about the women who had worn the path, and who had spent so great a part of their lives going up and down it. She found herself trying to walk as they must have walked, with a feeling in her feet and knees and loins which she had never known before,—which must have come up to her out of the accustomed dust of that rocky trail. She could feel the weight of an Indian baby hanging to her back as she climbed.

The empty houses, among which she wandered in the afternoon, the blanketed one in which she lay all morning, were haunted by certain fears and desires; feelings about warmth and cold and water and physical strength. It seemed to Thea that a certain understanding of those old people came up to her out of the rock shelf on which she lay; that certain feelings were transmitted to her, suggestions that were simple, insistent, and monotonous, like the beating of Indian drums. They were not expressible in words, but seemed rather to translate themselves into attitudes of body, into degrees of muscular tension or relaxation; the naked strength of youth, sharp as the sunshafts; the crouching timorousness of age, the sullenness of women who waited for their captors. At the first turning of the canyon there was a half-ruined tower of yellow masonry, a watch-tower upon which the young men used to entice eagles and snare them with nets. Sometimes for a whole morning Thea could see the coppery breast and shoulders of an Indian youth there against the sky; see him throw the net, and watch the struggle with the eagle.

Old Henry Biltmer, at the ranch, had been a great deal among the Pueblo Indians who are the descendants of the Cliff-Dwellers. After supper he used to sit and smoke his pipe by the kitchen stove and talk to Thea about them. He had never found any one before who was interested in his ruins. Every Sunday the old man prowled about in the canyon, and he had come to know a good deal more about it than he could account for. He had gathered up a whole chestful of Cliff-Dweller relics which he meant to take back to Germany with him some day. He taught Thea how to find things among the ruins: grinding-stones, and drills and needles made of turkey-bones. There were fragments of pottery everywhere. Old Henry explained to her that the Ancient People had developed masonry and pottery far beyond any other crafts.

After they had made houses for themselves, the next thing was to house the precious water. He explained to her how all their customs and ceremonies and their religion went back to water. The men provided the food, but water was the care of the women. The stupid women carried water for most of their lives; the cleverer ones made the vessels to hold it. Their pottery was their most direct appeal to water, the envelope and sheath of the precious element itself. The strongest Indian need was expressed in those graceful jars, fashioned slowly by hand, without the aid of a wheel.

When Thea took her bath at the bottom of the canyon, in the sunny pool behind the screen of cottonwoods, she sometimes felt as if the water must have sovereign qualities, from having been the object of so much service and desire. That stream was the only living thing left of the drama that had been played out in the canyon centuries ago. In the rapid, restless heart of it, flowing swifter than the rest, there was a continuity of life that reached back into the old time. The glittering thread of current had a kind of lightly worn, loosely knit personality, graceful and laughing. Thea's bath came to have a ceremonial gravity. The atmosphere of the canyon was ritualistic.

One morning, as she was standing upright in the pool, splashing water between her shoulder-blades with a big sponge, something flashed through her mind that made her draw herself up and stand still until the water had quite dried upon her flushed skin. The stream and the broken pottery: what was any art but an effort to make a sheath, a mould in which to imprison for a moment the shining, elusive element which is life itself,—life hurrying past us and running away, too strong to stop, too sweet to lose? The Indian women had held it in their jars. In the sculpture she had seen in the Art Institute, it had been caught in a flash of arrested motion. In singing, one made a vessel of one's throat and nostrils and held it on one's breath, caught the stream in a scale of natural intervals.

IV

THEA had a superstitious feeling about the potsherds, and liked better to leave them in the dwellings where she found them. If she took a few bits back to her own lodge and hid them under the blankets, she did it guiltily, as if she were being watched. She was a guest in these houses, and ought to behave as such. Nearly every afternoon she went to the chambers which contained the most interesting fragments of pottery, sat and looked at them for a while. Some of them were beautifully decorated. This care, expended upon vessels that could not hold food or water any better for the additional labor put upon them, made her heart go out to those ancient potters. They had not only expressed their desire, but they had expressed it as beautifully as they could. Food, fire, water, and something else—even here, in this crack in the world, so far back in the night of the past! Down here at the beginning that painful thing was already stirring; the seed of sorrow, and of so much delight.

There were jars done in a delicate overlay, like pine cones; and there were many patterns in a low relief, like basket-work. Some of the pottery was decorated in color, red and brown, black and white, in graceful geometrical patterns. One day, on a fragment of a shallow bowl, she found a crested serpent's head, painted in red on terra-cotta. Again she found half a bowl with a broad band of white cliff-houses painted on a black ground. They were scarcely conventionalized at all; there they were in the black border, just as they stood in the rock before her. It brought her centuries nearer to these people to find that they saw their houses exactly as she saw them.

Yes, Ray Kennedy was right. All these things made one feel that one ought to do one's best, and help to fulfill some desire of the dust that slept there. A dream had been dreamed there long ago, in the night of ages, and the wind had whispered some promise to the sadness of the savage. In their own way, those people had felt the beginnings of what was to come. These potsherds were like fetters that bound one to a long chain of human endeavor.

Not only did the world seem older and richer to Thea now, but she herself seemed older. She had never been alone for so long before, or thought so much. Nothing had ever engrossed her so deeply as the daily contemplation of that line of pale-yellow houses tucked into the wrinkle of the cliff. Moonstone and Chicago had become vague. Here everything was simple and definite, as things had been in childhood. Her mind was like a ragbag into which she had been frantically thrusting whatever she could grab. And here she must throw this lumber away. The things that were really hers separated themselves from the rest. Her ideas were simplified, became sharper and clearer. She felt united and strong.

When Thea had been at the Ottenburg ranch for two months, she got a letter from Fred announcing that he "might be along at almost any time now." The letter came at night, and the next morning she took it down into the canyon with her. She was delighted that he was coming soon. She had never felt so grateful to any one, and she wanted to tell him everything that had happened to her since she had been there—more than had happened in all her life before. Certainly she liked Fred better than any one else in the world. There was Harsanyi, of course—but Harsanyi was always tired. Just now, and here, she wanted some one who had never been tired, who could catch an idea and run with it.

She was ashamed to think what an apprehensive drudge she must always have seemed to Fred, and she wondered why he had concerned himself about her at all. Perhaps she would never be so happy or so good-looking again, and she would like Fred to see her, for once, at her best. She had not been singing much, but she knew that her voice was more interesting than it had ever been before. She had begun to understand that—with her, at least— voice was, first of all, vitality; a lightness in the body and driving power in the blood. If she had that, she could sing. When she felt so keenly alive, lying on that insensible shelf of stone, when her body bounded like a rubber ball away from its hardness, then she could sing. This, too, she could explain to Fred. He would know what she meant.

Another week passed. Thea did the same things as before, felt the same influences, went over the same ideas; but there was a livelier movement in her thoughts, and a freshening of sensation, like the brightness which came over the underbrush after a shower. A persistent affirmation—or denial—was going on in her, like the tapping of the woodpecker in the one tall pine tree across the chasm. Musical phrases drove each other rapidly through her mind, and the song of the cicada was now too long and too sharp. Everything seemed suddenly to take the form of a desire for action.

It was while she was in this abstracted state, waiting for the clock to strike, that Thea at last made up her mind what she was going to try to do in the world, and that she was going to Germany to study without further loss of time. Only by the merest chance had she ever got to Panther Canyon. There was certainly no kindly Providence that directed one's life; and one's parents did not in the least care what became of one, so long as one did not misbehave and endanger their comfort. One's life was at the mercy of blind chance. She had better take it in her own hands and lose everything than meekly draw the plough under the rod of parental guidance. She had seen it when she was at home last summer,—the hostility of comfortable, self-satisfied people toward any serious effort. Even to her father it seemed indecorous. Whenever she spoke seriously, he looked apologetic. Yet she had clung fast to whatever was left of Moonstone in her mind. No more of that! The Cliff-Dwellers had lengthened her past. She had older and higher obligations.

V.

ONE Sunday afternoon late in July old Henry Biltmer was rheumatically descending into the head of the canyon. The Sunday before had been one of those cloudy days—fortunately rare—when the life goes out of that country and it becomes a gray ghost, an empty, shivering uncertainty. Henry had spent the day in the barn; his canyon was a reality only when it was flooded with the light of its great lamp, when the yellow rocks cast purple shadows, and the resin was fairly cooking in the corkscrew cedars. The yuccas were in blossom now. Out of each clump of sharp bayonet leaves rose a tall stalk hung with greenish-white bells with thick, fleshy petals. The niggerhead cactus was thrusting its crimson blooms up out of every crevice in the rocks.

Henry had come out on the pretext of hunting a spade and pick-axe that young Ottenburg had borrowed, but he was keeping his eyes open. He was really very curious about the new occupants of the canyon, and what they found to do there all day long. He let his eye travel along the gulf for a mile or so to the first turning, where the fissure zigzagged out and then receded behind a stone promontory on which stood the yellowish, crumbling ruin of the old watch-tower.

From the base of this tower, which now threw its shadow forward, bits of rock kept flying out into the open gulf—skating upon the air until they lost their momentum, then falling like chips until they rang upon the ledges at the bottom of the gorge or splashed into the stream. Biltmer shaded his eyes with his hand. There on the promontory, against the cream-colored cliff, were two figures nimbly moving in the light, both slender and agile, entirely absorbed in their game. They looked like two boys. Both were hatless and both wore white shirts.

Henry forgot his pick-axe and followed the trail before the cliff-houses toward the tower. Behind the tower, as he well knew, were heaps of stones, large and small, piled against the face of the cliff. He had always believed that the Indian watchmen piled them there for ammunition. Thea and Fred had come upon these missiles and were throwing them for distance. As Biltmer approached he could hear them laughing, and he caught Thea's voice, high and excited, with a ring of vexation in it. Fred was teaching her to throw a heavy stone like a discus. When it was Fred's turn, he sent a triangular-shaped stone out into the air with considerable skill. Thea watched it enviously, standing in a half-defiant posture, her sleeves rolled above her elbows and her face flushed with heat and excitement. After Fred's third missile had rung upon the rocks below, she snatched up a stone and stepped impatiently out on the ledge in front of him. He caught her by the elbows and pulled her back.

"Not so close, you silly! You'll spin yourself off in a minute."

"You went that close. There's your heel-mark," she retorted.

"Well, I know how. That makes a difference." He drew a mark in the dust with his toe. "There, that's right. Don't step over that. Pivot yourself on your spine, and make a half turn. When you've swung your length, let it go."

Thea settled the flat piece of rock between her wrist and fingers, faced the cliff wall, stretched her arm in position, whirled round on her left foot to the full stretch of her body, and let the missile spin out over the gulf. She hung expectantly in the air, forgetting to draw back her arm, her eyes following the stone as if it carried her fortunes with it. Her comrade watched her; there weren't many girls who could show a line like that from the toe to the thigh, from the shoulder to the tip of the outstretched hand. The stone spent itself and began to fall. Thea drew back and struck her knee furiously with her palm.

"There it goes again! Not nearly so far as yours. What *is* the matter with me? Give me another." She faced the cliff and whirled again. The stone spun out, not quite so far as before.

Ottenburg laughed. "Why do you keep on working *after* you've thrown it? You can't help it along then."

Without replying, Thea stooped and selected another stone, took a deep breath and made another turn. Fred watched the disk, exclaiming, "Good girl! You got past the pine that time. That's a good throw."

She took out her handkerchief and wiped her glowing face and throat, pausing to feel her right shoulder with her left hand.

"Ah—ha, you've made yourself sore, haven't you? What did I tell you? You go at things too hard. I'll tell you what I'm going to do, Thea," Fred dusted his hands and began tucking in the blouse of his shirt, "I'm going to make some single-sticks and teach you to fence. You'd be all right there. You're light and quick and you've got lots of drive in you. I'd like to have you come at me with foils; you'd look so fierce," he chuckled.

She turned away from him and stubbornly sent out another

stone, hanging in the air after its flight. Her fury amused Fred, who took all games lightly and played them well. She was breathing hard, and little beads of moisture had gathered on her upper lip. He slipped his arm about her. "If you will look as pretty as that—" he bent his head and kissed her. Thea was startled, gave him an angry push, drove at him with her free hand in a manner quite hostile. Fred was on his mettle in an instant. He pinned both her arms down and kissed her resolutely.

When he released her, she turned away and spoke over her shoulder. "That was mean of you, but I suppose I deserved what I got."

"I should say you did deserve it," Fred panted, "turning savage on me like that! I should say you did deserve it!"

He saw her shoulders harden. "Well, I just said I deserved it, didn't I? What more do you want?"

"I want you to tell me why you flew at me like that! You weren't playing; you looked as if you'd like to murder me."

She brushed back her hair impatiently. "I didn't mean anything, really. You interrupted me when I was watching the stone. I can't jump from one thing to another. I pushed you without thinking."

Fred thought her back expressed contrition. He went up to her, stood behind her with his chin above her shoulder, and said something in her ear. Thea laughed and turned toward him. They left the stone-pile carelessly, as if they had never been interested in it, rounded the yellow tower, and disappeared into the second turn of the canyon where the dead city, interrupted by the jutting promontory, began again.

Old Biltmer had been somewhat embarrassed by the turn the game had taken. He had not heard their conversation, but the pantomime against the rocks was clear enough. When the two young people disappeared, their host retreated rapidly toward the head of the canyon.

"I guess that young lady can take care of herself," he chuckled. "Young Fred, though, he has quite a way with them."

VI

DAY was breaking over Panther Canyon. The gulf was cold and full of heavy, purplish twilight. The wood smoke which drifted from one of the cliff-houses hung in a blue scarf across the chasm, until the draft caught it and whirled it away. Thea was crouching in the doorway of her rock house, while Ottenburg looked after the crackling fire in the next cave. He was waiting for it to burn down to coals before he put the coffee on to boil.

They had left the ranch house that morning a little after three o'clock, having packed their camp equipment the day before, and had crossed the open pasture land with their lantern while the stars were still bright. During the descent into the canyon by lantern-light, they were chilled through their coats and sweaters. The lantern crept slowly along the rock trail, where the heavy air seemed to offer resistance. The voice of the stream at the bottom of the gorge was hollow and threatening, much louder and deeper than it ever was by day—another voice altogether. The sullenness of the place seemed to say that the world could get on very well without people, red or white; that under the human world there was a geological world, conducting its silent, immense operations which were indifferent to man. Thea had often seen the desert sunrise,—a light-hearted affair, where the sun springs out of bed and the world is golden in an instant. But this canyon seemed to waken like an old man, with rheum and stiffness of the joints, with heaviness, and a dull, malignant mind. She crouched against the wall while the stars faded, and thought what courage the early races must have had to endure so much for the little they got out of life.

At last a kind of hopefulness broke in the air. In a moment the pine trees up on the edge of the rim were flashing with coppery fire. The thin red clouds which hung above their pointed tops began to boil and move rapidly, weaving in and out like smoke. The swallows darted out of their rock houses as at a signal, and flew upward, toward the rim. Little brown birds began to chirp in the bushes along the watercourse down at the bottom of the

ravine, where everything was still dusky and pale. At first the
golden light seemed to hang like a wave upon the rim of the
canyon; the trees and bushes up there, which one scarcely noticed
at noon stood out magnified by the slanting rays. Long, thin
streaks of light began to reach quiveringly down into the canyon.
The red sun rose rapidly above the tops of the blazing pines, and
its glow burst into the gulf, about the very doorstep on which
Thea sat. It bored into the wet, dark underbrush. The dripping
cherry bushes, the pale aspens, and the frosty *piñons* were glittering and trembling, swimming in the liquid gold. All the pale,
dusty little herbs of the bean family, never seen by any one but a
botanist, became for a moment individual and important, their
silky leaves quite beautiful with dew and light. The arch of sky
overhead, heavy as lead a little while before, lifted, became more
and more transparent, and one could look up into depths of
pearly blue.

The savor of coffee and bacon mingled with the smell of wet
cedars drying, and Fred called to Thea that he was ready for her.
They sat down in the doorway of his kitchen, with the warmth of
the live coals behind them and the sunlight on their faces, and
began their breakfast. Mrs. Biltmer's thick coffee cups and the
cream bottle between them, the coffee-pot and frying-pan con-
veniently keeping hot among the embers.

"I thought you were going back on the whole proposition,
Thea, when you were crawling along with that lantern. I couldn't
get a word out of you."

"I know. I was cold and hungry, and I didn't believe there was
going to be any morning, anyway. Didn't you feel queer, at all?"

Fred squinted above his smoking cup. "Well, I am never strong
for getting up before the sun. The world looks unfurnished.
When I first lit the fire and had a square look at you, I thought I'd
got the wrong girl. Pale, grim—you were a sight!"

Thea leaned back into the shadow of the rock room and
warmed her hands over the coals. "It was dismal enough. How
warm these walls are, all the way round; and your breakfast is so
good. I'm all right now, Fred."

"Yes, you're all right now." Fred lit a cigarette and looked at her critically as her head emerged into the sun again. "You get up every morning just a little bit handsomer than you were the day before. I'd love you just as much if you were not turning into one of the loveliest women I've ever seen; but you are, and that's a fact to be reckoned with." He watched her across the thin line of smoke he blew from his lips. "What are you going to do with all that beauty and all that talent, Miss Kronborg?"

She turned away to the fire again. "I don't know what you're talking about," she muttered with an awkwardness which did not conceal her pleasure.

Ottenburg laughed softly. "Oh, yes, you do! Nobody better! You're a close one, but you give yourself away sometimes, like everybody else. Do you know, I've decided that you never do a single thing without an ulterior motive." He threw away his cigarette, took out his tobacco-pouch and began to fill his pipe. "You ride and fence and walk and climb, but I know that all the while you're getting somewhere in your mind. All these things are instruments; and I, too, am an instrument." He looked up in time to intercept a quick, startled glance from Thea. "Oh, I don't mind," he chuckled; "not a bit. Every woman, every interesting woman, has ulterior motives, many of 'em less creditable than yours. It's your constancy that amuses me. You must have been doing it ever since you were two feet high."

Thea looked slowly up at her companion's good-humored face. His eyes, sometimes too restless and sympathetic in town, had grown steadier and clearer in the open air. His short curly beard and yellow hair had reddened in the sun and wind. The pleasant vigor of his person was always delightful to her, something to signal to and laugh with in a world of negative people. With Fred she was never becalmed. There was always life in the air, always something coming and going, a rhythm of feeling and action, stronger than the natural accord of youth. As she looked at him, leaning against the sunny wall, she felt a desire to be frank with him. She was not willfully holding anything back. But, on the other hand, she could not force things that held themselves back. "Yes, it was like that when I was little," she said at last. "I had to be close, as you call it, or go under. But I didn't know I had been like that since you came. I've had nothing to be close about. I haven't thought about anything but having a good time with you. I've just drifted."

Fred blew a trail of smoke out into the breeze and looked knowing. "Yes, you drift like a rifle ball, my dear. It's your—your direction that I like best of all. Most fellows wouldn't, you know. I'm unusual."

They both laughed, but Thea frowned questioningly. "Why wouldn't most fellows? Other fellows have liked me."

"Yes, serious fellows. You told me yourself they were all old, or solemn. But jolly fellows want to be the whole target. They would say you were all brain and muscle; that you have no feeling."

She glanced at him sidewise. "Oh, they would, would they?"

"Of course they would," Fred continued blandly. "Jolly fellows have no imagination. They want to be the animating force. When they are not around, they want a girl to be—extinct," he waved his hand. "Old fellows like Mr. Nathanmeyer understand your kind; but among the young ones, you are rather lucky to have found me. Even I wasn't always so wise. I've had my time of thinking it would not bore me to be the Apollo of a homey flat, and I've paid out a trifle to learn better. All those things get very tedious unless they are hooked up with an idea of some sort. It's because we *don't* come out here only to look at each other and drink coffee that it's so pleasant to—look at each other." Fred drew on his pipe for a while, studying Thea's abstraction. She was staring up at the far wall of the canyon with a troubled expression that drew her eyes narrow and her mouth hard. Her hands lay in her lap, one over the other, the fingers interlacing. "Suppose," Fred came out at length,—"suppose I were to offer you what most of the young men I know would offer a girl they'd been sitting up nights about: a comfortable flat in Chicago, a summer camp up in the woods, musical evenings, and a family to bring up. Would it look attractive to you?"

Thea sat up straight and stared at him in alarm, glared into his eyes. "Perfectly hideous!" she exclaimed.

Fred dropped back against the old stonework and laughed deep in his chest. "Well, don't be frightened. I won't offer them.

You're not a nest-building bird. You know I always liked your song, 'Me for the jolt of the breakers!' I understand."

She rose impatiently and walked to the edge of the cliff. "It's not that so much. It's waking up every morning with the feeling that your life is your own, and your strength is your own, and your talent is your own; that you're all there, and there's no sag in you." She stood for a moment as if she were tortured by uncertainty, then turned suddenly back to him. "Don't talk about these things any more now," she entreated. "It isn't that I want to keep anything from you. The trouble is that I've got nothing to keep—except (you know as well as I) that feeling. I told you about it in Chicago once. But it always makes me unhappy to talk about it. It will spoil the day. Will you go for a climb with me?" She held out her hands with a smile so eager that it made Ottenburg feel how much she needed to get away from herself.

He sprang up and caught the hands she put out so cordially, and stood swinging them back and forth. "I won't tease you. A word's enough to me. But I love it, all the same. Understand?" He pressed her hands and dropped them. "Now, where are you going to drag me?"

"I want you to drag me. Over there, to the other houses. They are more interesting than these." She pointed across the gorge to the row of white houses in the other cliff. "The trail is broken away, but I got up there once. It's possible. You have to go to the bottom of the canyon, cross the creek, and then go up hand-over-hand."

Ottenburg, lounging against the sunny wall, his hands in the pockets of his jacket, looked across at the distant dwellings. "It's an awful climb," he sighed, "when I could be perfectly happy here with my pipe. However—" He took up his stick and hat and followed Thea down the water trail. "Do you climb this path every day? You surely earn your bath. I went down and had a look at your pool the other afternoon. Neat place, with all those little cottonwoods. Must be very becoming."

"Think so?" Thea said over her shoulder, as she swung round a turn.

"Yes, and so do you, evidently. I'm becoming expert at reading your meaning in your back. I'm behind you so much on these single-foot trails. You don't wear stays, do you?"

"Not here."

"I wouldn't, anywhere, if I were you. They will make you less elastic. The side muscles get flabby. If you go in for opera, there's a fortune in a flexible body. Most of the German singers are clumsy, even when they're well set up."

Thea switched a *piñon* branch back at him. "Oh, I'll never get fat! That I can promise you."

Fred smiled, looking after her. "Keep that promise, no matter how many others you break," he drawled.

The upward climb, after they had crossed the stream, was at first a breathless scramble through underbrush. When they reached the big boulders, Ottenburg went first because he had the longer leg-reach, and gave Thea a hand when the step was quite beyond her, swinging her up until she could get a foothold. At last they reached a little platform among the rocks, with only a hundred feet of jagged, sloping wall between them and the cliff-houses.

Ottenburg lay down under a pine tree and declared that he was going to have a pipe before he went any farther. "It's a good thing to know when to stop, Thea," he said meaningly.

"I'm not going to stop now until I get there," Thea insisted. "I'll go on alone."

Fred settled his shoulder against the tree-trunk. "Go on if you like, but I'm here to enjoy myself. If you meet a rattler on the way, have it out with him."

She hesitated, fanning herself with her felt hat. "I never have met one."

"There's reasoning for you," Fred murmured languidly.

Thea turned away resolutely and began to go up the wall, using an irregular cleft in the rock for a path. The cliff, which looked almost perpendicular from the bottom, was really made up of ledges and boulders, and behind these she soon disappeared. For a long while Fred smoked with half-closed eyes, smiling to himself now and again. Occasionally he lifted an eyebrow as he heard the rattle of small stones among the rocks above. "In a temper," he concluded; "do her good." Then he subsided into warm drowsiness and listened to the locusts in the yuccas, and the tap-tap of the old woodpecker that was never weary of assaulting the big pine.

Fred had finished his pipe and was wondering whether he wanted another, when he heard a call from the cliff far above him. Looking up, he saw Thea standing on the edge of a projecting crag. She waved to him and threw her arm over her head, as if she were snapping her fingers in the air.

As he saw her there between the sky and the gulf, with that great wash of air and the morning light about her, Fred recalled the brilliant figure at Mrs. Nathanmeyer's. Thea was one of those people who emerge, unexpectedly, larger than we are accustomed to see them. Even at this distance one got the impression of muscular energy and audacity,—a kind of brilliancy of motion,— of a personality that carried across big spaces and expanded among big things. Lying still, with his hands under his head, Ottenburg rhetorically addressed the figure in the air. "You are the sort that used to run wild in Germany, dressed in their hair and a piece of skin. Soldiers caught 'em in nets. Old Nathanmeyer," he mused, "would like a peep at her now. Knowing old fellow. Always buying those Zorn etchings* of peasant girls bathing. No sag in them either. Must be the cold climate." He sat up. "She'll begin to pitch rocks on me if I don't move." In response to another impatient gesture from the crag, he rose and began swinging slowly up the trail.

It was the afternoon of that long day. Thea was lying on a blanket in the door of her rock house. She and Ottenburg had come back from their climb and had lunch, and he had gone off for a nap in one of the cliff-houses farther down the path. He was sleeping peacefully, his coat under his head and his face turned toward the wall.

Thea, too, was drowsy, and lay looking through half-closed eyes up at the blazing blue arch over the rim of the canyon. She was thinking of nothing at all. Her mind, like her body, was full of warmth, lassitude, physical content. Suddenly an eagle, tawny and of great size, sailed over the cleft in which she lay, across the arch of sky. He dropped for a moment into the gulf between the walls, then wheeled, and mounted until his plumage was so steeped in light that he looked like a golden bird. He swept on, following the course of the canyon a little way and then disappearing beyond the rim. Thea sprang to her feet as if she had been thrown up from the rock by volcanic action. She stood rigid on the edge of the stone shelf, straining her eyes after that strong, tawny flight. O eagle of eagles! Endeavor, achievement, desire, glorious striving of human art! From a cleft in the heart of the world she saluted it. . . . It had come all the way; when men lived in caves, it was there. A vanished race; but along the trails, in the stream, under the spreading cactus, there still glittered in the sun the bits of their frail clay vessels, fragments of their desire.

VII

FROM the day of Fred's arrival, he and Thea were unceasingly active. They took long rides into the Navajo pine forests, bought turquoises and silver bracelets from the wandering Indian herdsmen, and rode twenty miles to Flagstaff upon the slightest pretext. Thea had never felt this pleasant excitement about any man before, and she found herself trying very hard to please young Ottenburg. She was never tired, never dull. There was a zest about waking up in the morning and dressing, about walking, riding, even about sleep.

One morning when Thea came out from her room at seven o'clock, she found Henry and Fred on the porch looking up at the sky. The day was already hot and there was no breeze. The sun was shining, but heavy brown clouds were hanging in the west, like the smoke of a forest fire. She and Fred had meant to ride to Flagstaff that morning, but Biltmer advised against it, foretelling a storm. After breakfast they lingered about the house waiting for the weather to make up its mind. Fred brought his guitar, and as they had the dining-room to themselves, he made Thea go over some songs with him. They got interested and kept it up until

Mrs. Biltmer came to set the table for dinner. Ottenburg knew some of the Mexican things Spanish Johnny used to sing. Thea had never before happened to tell him about Spanish Johnny, and he seemed more interested in Johnny than in Dr. Archie or Wunsch.

After dinner they were too restless to endure the ranch house any longer, and ran away to the canyon to practice with single-sticks. Fred carried a slicker and a sweater, and he made Thea wear one of the rubber hats that hung in Biltmer's gun-room. As they crossed the pasture land the clumsy slicker kept catching in the lacings of his leggings.

"Why don't you drop that thing?" Thea asked. "I won't mind a shower. I've been wet before."

"No use taking chances."

From the canyon they were unable to watch the sky, since only a strip of the zenith was visible. The flat ledge about the watch-tower was the only level spot large enough for single-stick exercise, and they were still practicing there when, at about four o'clock, a tremendous roll of thunder echoed between the cliffs and the atmosphere suddenly became thick.

Fred thrust the sticks in a cleft in the rock. "We're in for it, Thea. Better make for your cave where there are blankets." He caught her elbow and hurried her along the path before the cliff-houses. They made the half-mile at a quick trot, and as they ran the rocks and the sky and the air between the cliffs turned a turbid green, like the color in a moss agate. When they reached the blanketed rock room, they looked at each other and laughed. Their faces had taken on a greenish pallor. Thea's hair, even, was green.

"Dark as pitch in here," Fred exclaimed as they hurried over the old rock doorstep. "But it's warm. The rocks hold the heat. It's going to be terribly cold outside, all right." He was interrupted by a deafening peal of thunder. "Lord, what an echo! Lucky you don't mind. It's worth watching out there. We needn't come in yet."

The green light grew murkier and murkier. The smaller vegetation was blotted out. The yuccas, the cedars, and *piñons* stood dark and rigid, like bronze. The swallows flew up with sharp, terrified twitterings. Even the quaking asps were still. While Fred and Thea watched from the doorway, the light changed to purple. Clouds of dark vapor, like chlorine gas, began to float down from the head canyon and hung between them and the cliff-houses in the opposite wall. Before they knew it, the wall itself had disappeared. The air was positively venomous-looking and grew colder every minute. The thunder seemed to crash against one cliff, then against the other, and to go shrieking off into the inner canyon.

The moment the rain broke, it beat the vapors down. In the gulf before them the water fell in spouts, and dashed from the high cliffs overhead. It tore aspens and chokecherry bushes out of the ground and left the yuccas hanging by their tough roots. Only the little cedars stood black and unmoved in the torrents that fell from so far above. The rock chamber was full of fine spray from the streams of water that shot over the doorway. Thea crept to the back wall and rolled herself in a blanket, and Fred threw the heavier blankets over her. The wool of the Navajo sheep was soon kindled by the warmth of her body, and was impenetrable to dampness. Her hair, where it hung below the rubber hat, gathered the moisture like a sponge. Fred put on the slicker, tied the sweater about his neck, and settled himself cross-legged beside her. The chamber was so dark that, although he could see the outline of her head and shoulders, he could not see her face. He struck a wax match to light his pipe. As he sheltered it between his hands, it sizzled and sputtered, throwing a yellow flicker over Thea and her blankets.

"You look like a gypsy," he said as he dropped the match. "Any one you'd rather be shut up with than me? No? Sure about that?"

"I think I am. Aren't you cold?"

"Not especially." Fred smoked in silence, listening to the roar of the water outside. "We may not get away from here right away," he remarked.

"I shan't mind. Shall you?"

He laughed grimly and pulled on his pipe. "Do you know where you're at, Miss Thea Kronborg?" he said at last. "You've got me going pretty hard, I suppose you know. I've had a lot of sweethearts, but I've never been so much—engrossed before. What are you going to do about it?" He heard nothing from the blankets. "Are you going to play fair, or is it about my cue to cut away?"

"I'll play fair. I don't see why you want to go."

"What do you want me around for?—to play with?"

Thea struggled up among the blankets. "I want you for everything. I don't know whether I'm what people call in love with you or not. In Moonstone that meant sitting in a hammock with somebody. I don't want to sit in a hammock with you, but I want to do almost everything else. Oh, hundreds of things!"

"If I run away, will you go with me?"

"I don't know. I'll have to think about that. Maybe I would." She freed herself from her wrappings and stood up. "It's not raining so hard now. Hadn't we better start this minute? It will be night before we get to Biltmer's."

Fred struck another match. "It's seven. I don't know how much of the path may be washed away. I don't even know whether I ought to let you try it without a lantern."

Thea went to the doorway and looked out. "There's nothing else to do. The sweater and the slicker will keep me dry, and this will be my chance to find out whether these shoes are really water-tight. They cost a week's salary." She retreated to the back of the cave. "It's getting blacker every minute."

Ottenburg took a brandy flask from his coat pocket. "Better have some of this before we start. Can you take it without water?"

Thea lifted it obediently to her lips. She put on the sweater and Fred helped her to get the clumsy slicker on over it. He buttoned it and fastened the high collar. She could feel that his hands were hurried and clumsy. The coat was too big, and he took off his necktie and belted it in at the waist. While she tucked her hair more securely under the rubber hat he stood in front of her, between her and the gray doorway, without moving.

"Are you ready to go?" she asked carelessly.

"If you are," he spoke quietly, without moving, except to bend his head forward a little.

Thea laughed and put her hands on his shoulders. "You know how to handle me, don't you?" she whispered. For the first time, she kissed him without constraint or embarrassment.

"Thea, Thea, Thea!" Fred whispered her name three times, shaking her a little as if to waken her. It was too dark to see, but he could feel that she was smiling.

When she kissed him she had not hidden her face on his shoulder,—she had risen a little on her toes, and stood straight and free. In that moment when he came close to her actual personality, he felt in her the same expansion that he had noticed at Mrs. Nathanmeyer's. She became freer and stronger under impulses. When she rose to meet him like that, he felt her flash into everything that she had ever suggested to him, as if she filled out her own shadow.

She pushed him away and shot past him out into the rain. "Now for it, Fred," she called back exultantly. The rain was pouring steadily down through the dying gray twilight, and muddy streams were spouting and foaming over the cliff.

Fred caught her and held her back. "Keep behind me, Thea. I don't know about the path. It may be gone altogether. Can't tell what there is under this water."

But the path was older than the white man's Arizona. The rush of water had washed away the dust and stones that lay on the surface, but the rock skeleton of the Indian trail was there, ready for the foot. Where the streams poured down through gullies, there was always a cedar or a *piñon* to cling to. By wading and slipping and climbing, they got along. As they neared the head of the canyon, where the path lifted and rose in steep loops to the surface of the plateau, the climb was more difficult. The earth above had broken away and washed down over the trail, bringing rocks and bushes and even young trees with it. The last ghost of daylight was dying and there was no time to lose. The canyon behind them was already black.

"We've got to go right through the top of this pine tree, Thea. No time to hunt a way around. Give me your hand." After they had crashed through the mass of branches, Fred stopped abruptly. "Gosh, what a hole! Can you jump it? Wait a minute."

He cleared the washout, slipped on the wet rock at the farther side, and caught himself just in time to escape a tumble. "If I could only find something to hold to, I could give you a hand. It's so cursed dark, and there are no trees here where they're needed. Here's something; it's a root. It will hold all right." He braced himself on the rock, gripped the crooked root with one hand and swung himself across toward Thea, holding out his arm. "Good jump! I must say you don't lose your nerve in a tight place. Can you keep at it a little longer? We're almost out. Have to make that next ledge. Put your foot on my knee and catch something to pull by."

Thea went up over his shoulder. "It's hard ground up here," she panted. "Did I wrench your arm when I slipped then? It was a cactus I grabbed, and it startled me."

"Now, one more pull and we're on the level."

They emerged gasping upon the black plateau. In the last five minutes the darkness had solidified and it seemed as if the skies were pouring black water. They could not see where the sky ended or the plain began. The light at the ranch house burned a steady spark through the rain. Fred drew Thea's arm through his and they struck off toward the light. They could not see each other, and the rain at their backs seemed to drive them along. They kept laughing as they stumbled over tufts of grass or stepped into slippery pools. They were delighted with each other and with the adventure which lay behind them.

"I can't even see the whites of your eyes, Thea. But I'd know who was here stepping out with me, anywhere. Part coyote you are, by the feel of you. When you make up your mind to jump, you jump! My gracious, what's the matter with your hand?"

"Cactus spines. Didn't I tell you when I grabbed the cactus? I thought it was a root. Are we going straight?"

"I don't know. Somewhere near it, I think. I'm very comfortable, aren't you? You're warm, except your cheeks. How funny they are when they're wet. Still, you always feel like you. I like this. I could walk to Flagstaff. It's fun, not being able to see anything. I feel surer of you when I can't see you. Will you run away with me?"

Thea laughed. "I won't run far to-night. I'll think about it. Look, Fred, there's somebody coming."

"Henry, with his lantern. Good enough! Halloo! Hallo—o—o!" Fred shouted.

The moving light bobbed toward them. In half an hour Thea was in her big feather bed, drinking hot lentil soup, and almost before the soup was swallowed she was asleep.

VIII

ON the first day of September Fred Ottenburg and Thea Kronborg left Flagstaff by the east-bound express. As the bright morning advanced, they sat alone on the rear platform of the observation car, watching the yellow miles unfold and disappear. With complete content they saw the brilliant, empty country flash by. They were tired of the desert and the dead races, of a world without change or ideas. Fred said he was glad to sit back and let the Santa Fé do the work for a while.

"And where are we going, anyhow?" he added.

"To Chicago, I suppose. Where else would we be going?" Thea hunted for a handkerchief in her handbag.

"I wasn't sure, so I had the trunks checked to Albuquerque. We can recheck there to Chicago, if you like. Why Chicago? You'll never go back to Bowers. Why wouldn't this be a good time to make a run for it? We could take the southern branch at Albuquerque, down to El Paso, and then over into Mexico. We are exceptionally free. Nobody waiting for us anywhere."

Thea sighted along the steel rails that quivered in the light behind them. "I don't see why I couldn't marry you in Chicago, as well as any place," she brought out with some embarrassment.

Fred took the handbag out of her nervous clasp and swung it about on his finger. "You've no particular love for that spot, have you? Besides, as I've told you, my family would make a row. They are an excitable lot. They discuss and argue everlastingly. The only way I can ever put anything through is to go ahead, and convince them afterward."

"Yes; I understand. I don't mind that. I don't want to marry your family. I'm sure you wouldn't want to marry mine. But I don't see why we have to go so far."

"When we get to Winslow, you look about the freight yards and you'll probably see several yellow cars with my name on them. That's why, my dear. When your visiting-card is on every beer bottle, you can't do things quietly. Things get into the papers." As he watched her troubled expression, he grew anxious. He leaned forward on his camp-chair, and kept twirling the handbag between his knees. "Here's a suggestion, Thea," he said presently. "Dismiss it if you don't like it: suppose we go down to Mexico on the chance. You've never seen anything like Mexico City; it will be a lark for you, anyhow. If you change your mind, and don't want to marry me, you can go back to Chicago, and I'll take a steamer from Vera Cruz and go up to New York. When I get to Chicago, you'll be at work, and nobody will ever be the wiser. No reason why we shouldn't both travel in Mexico, is there? You'll be traveling alone. I'll merely tell you the right places to stop, and come to take you driving. I won't put any pressure on you. Have I ever?" He swung the bag toward her and looked up under her hat.

"No, you haven't," she murmured. She was thinking that her own position might be less difficult if he had used what he called pressure. He clearly wished her to take the responsibility.

"You have your own future in the back of your mind all the time," Fred began, "and I have it in mine. I'm not going to try to carry you off, as I might another girl. If you wanted to quit me, I couldn't hold you, no matter how many times you had married me. I don't want to over-persuade you. But I'd like mighty well to get you down to that jolly old city, where everything would please you, and give myself a chance. Then, if you thought you could have a better time with me than without me, I'd try to grab you before you changed your mind. You are not a sentimental person."

Thea drew her veil down over her face. "I think I am, a little; about you," she said quietly. Fred's irony somehow hurt her.

"What's at the bottom of your mind, Thea?" he asked

hurriedly. "I can't tell. Why do you consider it at all, if you're not sure? Why are you here with me now?"

Her face was half-averted. He was thinking that it looked older and more firm—almost hard—under a veil.

"Isn't it possible to do things without having any very clear reason?" she asked slowly. "I have no plan in the back of my mind. Now that I'm with you, I want to be with you; that's all. I can't settle down to being alone again. I am here to-day because I want to be with you to-day." She paused. "One thing, though; if I gave you my word, I'd keep it. And you could hold me, though you don't seem to think so. Maybe I'm not sentimental, but I'm not very light, either. If I went off with you like this, it wouldn't be to amuse myself."

Ottenburg's eyes fell. His lips worked nervously for a moment. "Do you mean that you really care for me, Thea Kronborg?" he asked unsteadily.

"I guess so. It's like anything else. It takes hold of you and you've got to go through with it, even if you're afraid. I was afraid to leave Moonstone, and afraid to leave Harsanyi. But I had to go through with it."

"And are you afraid now?" Fred asked slowly.

"Yes; more than I've ever been. But I don't think I could go back. The past closes up behind one, somehow. One would rather have a new kind of misery. The old kind seems like death or unconsciousness. You can't force your life back into that mould again. No, one can't go back." She rose and stood by the back grating of the platform, her hand on the brass rail.

Fred went to her side. She pushed up her veil and turned her most glowing face to him. Her eyes were wet and there were tears on her lashes, but she was smiling the rare, whole-hearted smile he had seen once or twice before. He looked at her shining eyes, her parted lips, her chin a little lifted. It was as if they were colored by a sunrise he could not see. He put his hand over hers and clasped it with a strength she felt. Her eyelashes trembled, her mouth softened, but her eyes were still brilliant.

"Will you always be like you were down there, if I go with you?" she asked under her breath.

His fingers tightened on hers. "By God, I will!" he muttered.

"That's the only promise I'll ask you for. Now go away for a while and let me think about it. Come back at lunch-time and I'll tell you. Will that do?"

"Anything will do, Thea, if you'll only let me keep an eye on you. The rest of the world doesn't interest me much. You've got me in deep."

Fred dropped her hand and turned away. As he glanced back from the front end of the observation car, he saw that she was still standing there, and any one would have known that she was brooding over something. The earnestness of her head and shoulders had a certain nobility. He stood looking at her for a moment.

When he reached the forward smoking-car, Fred took a seat at the end, where he could shut the other passengers from his sight. He put on his traveling-cap and sat down wearily, keeping his head near the window. "In any case, I shall help her more than I shall hurt her," he kept saying to himself. He admitted that this was not the only motive which impelled him, but it was one of them. "I'll make it my business in life to get her on. There's nothing else I care about so much as seeing her have her chance. She hasn't touched her real force yet. She isn't even aware of it. Lord, don't I know something about them? There isn't one of them that has such a depth to draw from. She'll be one of the great artists of our time. Playing accompaniments for that cheese-faced sneak! I'll get her off to Germany this winter, or take her. She hasn't got any time to waste now. I'll make it up to her, all right."

Ottenburg certainly meant to make it up to her, in so far as he could. His feeling was as generous as strong human feelings are likely to be. The only trouble was, that he was married already, and had been since he was twenty.

His older friends in Chicago, people who had been friends of his family, knew of the unfortunate state of his personal affairs; but they were people whom in the natural course of things Thea Kronborg would scarcely meet. Mrs. Frederick Ottenburg lived in California, at Santa Barbara, where her health was supposed to be better than elsewhere, and her husband lived in Chicago. He visited his wife every winter to reinforce her position, and his devoted mother, although her hatred for her daughter-in-law was scarcely approachable in words, went to Santa Barbara every year to make things look better and to relieve her son.

When Frederick Ottenburg was beginning his junior year at Harvard, he got a letter from Dick Brisbane, a Kansas City boy he knew, telling him that his *fiancée*, Miss Edith Beers, was going to New York to buy her trousseau. She would be at the Holland House, with her aunt and a girl from Kansas City who was to be a bridesmaid, for two weeks or more. If Ottenburg happened to be going down to New York, would he call upon Miss Beers and "show her a good time"?

Fred did happen to be going to New York. He was going down from New Haven, after the Thanksgiving game. He called on Miss Beers and found her, as he that night telegraphed Brisbane, a "ripping beauty, no mistake." He took her and her aunt and her uninteresting friend to the theater and to the opera, and he asked them to lunch with him at the Waldorf. He took no little pains in arranging the luncheon with the head waiter. Miss Beers was the sort of girl with whom a young man liked to seem experienced. She was dark and slender and fiery. She was witty and slangy; said daring things and carried them off with *nonchalance*. Her childish extravagance and contempt for all the serious facts of life could be charged to her father's generosity and his long packing-house purse. Freaks that would have been vulgar and ostentatious in a more simple-minded girl, in Miss Beers seemed whimsical and picturesque. She darted about in magnificent furs and pumps and close-clinging gowns, though that was the day of full skirts. Her hats were large and floppy. When she wriggled out of her mole-skin coat at luncheon, she looked like a slim black weasel. Her satin dress was a mere sheath, so conspicuous by its severity and scantness that everyone in the dining-room stared. She ate nothing but alligator-pear salad and hothouse grapes, drank a little champagne, and took cognac in her coffee. She ridiculed, in the raciest slang, the singers they had heard at the opera the night before, and when her aunt pretended to reprove her, she murmured indifferently, "What's the matter with you, old sport?" She rattled on with a subdued loquaciousness, always keeping her voice low and monotonous, always looking out of the corner of her eye and speaking, as it were, in asides, out of the corner of her mouth. She was scornful of everything,—which became her eyebrows. Her face was mobile and discontented, her eyes quick and black. There was a sort of smouldering fire about her, young Ottenburg thought. She entertained him prodigiously.

After luncheon Miss Beers said she was going uptown to be fitted, and that she would go alone because her aunt made her nervous. When Fred held her coat for her, she murmured, "Thank you, Alphonse," as if she were addressing the waiter. As she stepped into a hansom, with a long stretch of thin silk stocking, she said negligently, over her fur collar, "Better let me take you along and drop you somewhere." He sprang in after her, and she told the driver to go to the Park.

It was a bright winter day, and bitterly cold. Miss Beers asked Fred to tell her about the game at New Haven, and when he did so paid no attention to what he said. She sank back into the hansom and held her muff before her face, lowering it occasionally to utter laconic remarks about the people in the carriages they passed, interrupting Fred's narrative in a disconcerting manner. As they entered the Park he happened to glance under her wide black hat at her black eyes and hair—the muff hid everything else—and discovered that she was crying. To his solicitous inquiry she replied that it "was enough to make you damp, to go and try on dresses to marry a man you weren't keen about."

Further explanations followed. She had thought she was "perfectly cracked" about Brisbane, until she met Fred at the Holland House three days ago. Then she knew she would scratch Brisbane's eyes out if she married him. What was she going to do?

Fred told the driver to keep going. What did she want to do? Well, she didn't know. One had to marry somebody, after all the machinery had been put in motion. Perhaps she might as well scratch Brisbane as anybody else; for scratch she would, if she didn't get what she wanted.

Of course, Fred agreed, one had to marry somebody. And certainly this girl beat anything he had ever been up against before. Again he told the driver to go ahead. Did she mean that she would think of marrying him, by any chance? Of course she did, Alphonse. Hadn't he seen that all over her face three days ago? If he hadn't, he was a snowball.

By this time Fred was beginning to feel sorry for the driver. Miss Beers, however, was compassionless. After a few more turns, Fred suggested tea at the Casino. He was very cold himself and remembering the shining silk hose and pumps, he wondered that the girl was not frozen. As they got out of the hansom, he slipped the driver a bill and told him to have something hot while he waited.

At the tea-table, in a snug glass enclosure, with the steam sputtering in the pipes beside them and a brilliant winter sunset without, they developed their plan. Miss Beers had with her plenty of money, destined for tradesmen, which she was quite willing to divert into other channels—the first excitement of buying a trousseau had worn off, anyway. It was very much like any other shopping. Fred had his allowance and a few hundred he had won on the game. She would meet him to-morrow morning at the Jersey ferry. They could take one of the west-bound Pennsylvania trains and go—anywhere, some place where the laws weren't too fussy.—Fred had not even thought about the laws!—It would be all right with her father; he knew Fred's family.

Now that they were engaged, she thought she would like to drive a little more. They were jerked about in the cab for another hour through the deserted Park. Miss Beers, having removed her hat, reclined upon Fred's shoulder.

The next morning they left Jersey City by the latest fast train out. They had some misadventures, crossed several States before they found a justice obliging enough to marry two persons whose names automatically instigated inquiry. The bride's family were rather pleased with her originality; besides, any one of the Ottenburg boys was clearly a better match than young Brisbane. With Otto Ottenburg, however, the affair went down hard, and to his wife, the once proud Katarina Fürst, such a disappointment was almost unbearable. Her sons had always been clay in her hands, and now the *geliebter Sohn** had escaped her.

Beers, the packer, gave his daughter a house in St. Louis, and Fred went into his father's business. At the end of a year, he was mutely appealing to his mother for sympathy. At the end of two, he was drinking and in open rebellion. He had learned to detest his wife. Her wastefulness and cruelty revolted him. The ignorance and the fatuous conceit which lay behind her grimacing mask of slang and ridicule humiliated him so deeply that he became absolutely reckless. Her grace was only an uneasy wriggle, her audacity was the result of insolence and envy, and her wit was restless spite. As her personal mannerisms grew more and more odious to him, he began to dull his perceptions with champagne. He had it for tea, he drank it with dinner, and during the evening he took enough to insure that he would be well insulated when he got home. This behavior spread alarm among his friends. It was scandalous, and it did not occur among brewers. He was violating the *noblesse oblige** of his guild. His father and his father's partners looked alarmed.

When Fred's mother went to him and with clasped hands entreated an explanation, he told her that the only trouble was that he couldn't hold enough wine to make life endurable, so he was going to get out from under and enlist in the navy. He didn't want anything but the shirt on his back and clean salt air. His mother could look out; he was going to make a scandal.

Mrs. Otto Ottenburg went to Kansas City to see Mr. Beers, and had the satisfaction of telling him that he had brought up his daughter like a savage, *eine Ungebildete**. All the Ottenburgs and all the Beers, and many of their friends, were drawn into the quarrel. It was to public opinion, however and not to his mother's activities, that Fred owed his partial escape from bondage. The cosmopolitan brewing world of St. Louis had conservative standards. The Ottenburgs' friends were not predisposed in favor of the plunging Kansas City set, and they disliked young Fred's wife from the day that she was brought among them. They found her ignorant and ill-bred and insufferably impertinent. When they became aware of how matters were going between her and Fred, they omitted no opportunity to snub her. Young Fred had always been popular, and St. Louis people took up his cause with warmth. Even the younger men, among whom Mrs. Fred tried to draft a following, at first avoided and then ignored her. Her defeat was so conspicuous, her life became such a desert, that she at last consented to accept the house in Santa Barbara which Mrs. Otto Ottenburg had long owned and cherished. This villa, with its luxuriant gardens, was the price of Fred's furlough. His mother was only too glad to offer it in his behalf. As soon as his wife was established in California, Fred was transferred from St. Louis to Chicago.

A divorce was the one thing Edith would never, never, give him. She told him so, and she told his family so, and her father stood behind her. She would enter into no arrangement that might eventually lead to divorce. She had insulted her husband before guests and servants, had scratched his face, thrown hand-mirrors and hairbrushes and nail-scissors at him often enough, but she knew that Fred was hardly the fellow who would go into court and offer that sort of evidence. In her behavior with other men she was discreet.

After Fred went to Chicago, his mother visited him often, and dropped a word to her old friends there, who were already kindly disposed toward the young man. They gossiped as little as was compatible with the interest they felt, undertook to make life agreeable for Fred, and told his story only where they felt it would do good: to girls who seemed to find the young brewer attractive. So far, he had behaved well, and had kept out of entanglements.

Since he was transferred to Chicago, Fred had been abroad several times, and had fallen more and more into the way of going about among young artists,—people with whom personal relations were incidental. With women, and even girls, who had careers to follow, a young man might have pleasant friendships without being regarded as a prospective suitor or lover. Among artists his position was not irregular, because with them his marriageableness was not an issue. His tastes, his enthusiasm, and his agreeable personality made him welcome.

With Thea Kronborg he had allowed himself more liberty than he usually did in his friendships or gallantries with young artists, because she seemed to him distinctly not the marrying kind. She impressed him as equipped to be an artist, and to be nothing else, already directed, concentrated, formed as to mental habit. He was generous and sympathetic, and she was lonely and needed friendship; needed cheerfulness. She had not much power of reaching out toward useful people or useful experiences, did not see opportunities. She had no tact about going after good positions or enlisting the interest of influential persons. She antagonized people rather than conciliated them. He discovered at once that she had a merry side, a robust humor that was deep and hearty, like her laugh, but it slept most of the time under her own doubts and the dullness of her life. She had not what is called a "sense of humor." That is, she had no intellectual humor; no power to enjoy the absurdities of people, no relish of their pretentiousness and inconsistencies—which only depressed her. But her joviality, Fred felt, was an asset, and ought to be developed. He discovered that she was more receptive and more effective under a pleasant stimulus than she was under the gray grind which she considered her salvation. She was still Methodist enough to believe that if a thing were hard and irksome, it must be good for her. And yet, whatever she did well was spontaneous. Under the least glow of excitement, as at Mrs. Nathanmeyer's, he had seen the apprehensive, frowning drudge of Bowers's studio flash into a resourceful and consciously beautiful woman.

His interest in Thea was serious, almost from the first, and so sincere that he felt no distrust of himself. He believed that he knew a great deal more about her possibilities than Bowers knew, and he liked to think that he had given her a stronger hold on life. She had never seen herself or known herself as she did at Mrs. Nathanmeyer's musical evenings. She had been a different girl ever since. He had not anticipated that she would grow more fond of him than his immediate usefulness warranted. He thought he knew the ways of artists, and, as he said, she must have been "at it from her cradle." He had imagined, perhaps, but never really believed, that he would find her waiting for him sometime as he found her waiting on the day he reached the Biltmer ranch. Once he found her so—well, he did not pretend to be anything more or less than a reasonably well-intentioned young man. A lovesick girl or a flirtatious woman he could have handled easily enough. But a personality like that, unconsciously revealing itself for the first time under the exaltation of a personal feeling,—what could one do but watch it? As he used to say to himself, in reckless moments back there in the canyon, "You can't put out a sunrise." He had to watch it, and then he had to share it.

Besides, was he really going to do her any harm? The Lord knew he would marry her if he could! Marriage would be an incident, not an end with her; he was sure of that. If it were not he, it would be some one else; some one who would be a weight about her neck, probably; who would hold her back and beat her down and divert her from the first plunge for which he felt she was gathering all her energies. He meant to help her, and he could not think of another man who would. He went over his unmarried friends, East and West, and he could not think of one who would know what she was driving at—or care. The clever ones were selfish, the kindly ones were stupid.

"Damn it, if she's going to fall in love with somebody, it had better be me than any of the others—of the sort she'd find. Get her tied up with some conceited ass who'd try to make her over, train her like a puppy! Give one of 'em a big nature like that, and he'd be horrified. He wouldn't show his face in the clubs until he'd gone after her and combed her down to conform to some fool idea in his own head—put there by some other woman, too, his first sweetheart or his grandmother or a maiden aunt. At least, I understand her. I know what she needs and where she's bound, and I mean to see that she has a fighting chance."

His own conduct looked crooked, he admitted; but he asked himself whether, between men and women, all ways were not more or less crooked. He believed those which are called straight were the most dangerous of all. They seemed to him, for the most part, to lie between windowless stone walls, and their rectitude had been achieved at the expense of light and air. In their unquestioned regularity lurked every sort of human cruelty and meanness, and every kind of humiliation and suffering. He would rather have any woman he cared for wounded than crushed. He would deceive her not once, he told himself fiercely, but a hundred times, to keep her free.

When Fred went back to the observation car at one o'clock, after the luncheon call, it was empty, and he found Thea alone on the platform. She put out her hand, and met his eyes.

"It's as I said. Things have closed behind me. I can't go back, so I am going on—to Mexico?" She lifted her face with an eager, questioning smile.

Fred met it with a sinking heart. Had he really hoped she would give him another answer? He would have given pretty much anything— But there, that did no good. He could give only what he had. Things were never complete in this world; you had to snatch at them as they came or go without. Nobody could look into her face and draw back, nobody who had any courage. She had courage enough for anything—look at her mouth and chin and eyes! Where did it come from, that light? How could a face, a familiar face, become so the picture of hope, be painted with the very colors of youth's exaltation? She was right; she was not one of those who draw back. Some people get on by avoiding dangers, others by riding through them.

They stood by the railing looking back at the sand levels, both feeling that the train was steaming ahead very fast. Fred's mind was a confusion of images and ideas. Only two things were clear to him: the force of her determination, and the belief that, handicapped as he was, he could do better by her than another man would do. He knew he would always remember her, standing there with that expectant, forward-looking smile, enough to turn the future into summer.

PART V

DR. ARCHIE'S VENTURE

PART V

I

DR. HOWARD ARCHIE had come down to Denver for a meeting of the stockholders in the San Felipe silver mine. It was not absolutely necessary for him to come, but he had no very pressing cases at home. Winter was closing down in Moonstone, and he dreaded the dullness of it. On the 10th day of January, therefore, he was registered at the Brown Palace Hotel. On the morning of the 11th he came down to breakfast to find the streets white and the air thick with snow. A wild northwester was blowing down from the mountains, one of those beautiful storms that wrap Denver in dry, furry snow, and make the city a loadstone to thousands of men in the mountains and on the plains. The brakemen out on their box-cars, the miners up in their diggings, the lonely homesteaders in the sand hills of Yucca and Kit Carson Counties, begin to think of Denver, muffled in snow, full of food and drink and good cheer, and to yearn for her with that admiration which makes her, more than other American cities, an object of sentiment.

Howard Archie was glad he had got in before the storm came. He felt as cheerful as if he had received a legacy that morning, and he greeted the clerk with even greater friendliness than usual when he stopped at the desk for his mail. In the dining-room he found several old friends seated here and there before substantial breakfasts: cattlemen and mining engineers from odd corners of the State, all looking fresh and well pleased with themselves. He had a word with one and another before he sat down at the little table by a window, where the Austrian head waiter stood attentively behind a chair. After his breakfast was put before him, the doctor began to run over his letters. There was one directed in Thea Kronborg's handwriting, forwarded from Moonstone.

He saw with astonishment, as he put another lump of sugar into his cup, that this letter bore a New York postmark. He had known that Thea was in Mexico, traveling with some Chicago people, but New York, to a Denver man, seems much farther away than Mexico City. He put the letter behind his plate, upright against the stem of his water goblet, and looked at it thoughtfully while he drank his second cup of coffee. He had been a little anxious about Thea; she had not written to him for a long while.

As he never got good coffee at home, the doctor always drank three cups for breakfast when he was in Denver. Oscar knew just when to bring him a second pot, fresh and smoking. "And more cream, Oscar, please. You know I like lots of cream," the doctor murmured, as he opened the square envelope, marked in the upper right-hand corner, "Everett House, Union Square." The text of the letter was as follows:—

DEAR DOCTOR ARCHIE:—

I have not written to you for a long time, but it has not been unintentional. I could not write you frankly, and so I would not write at all. I can be frank with you now, but not by letter. It is a great deal to ask, but I wonder if you could come to New York to help me out? I have got into difficulties, and I need your advice. I need your friendship. I am afraid I must even ask you to lend me money, if you can without serious inconvenience. I have to go to Germany to study, and it can't be put off any longer. My voice is ready. Needless to say, I don't want any word of this to reach my family. They are the last people I would turn to, though I love my mother dearly. If you can come, please telegraph me at this hotel. Don't despair of me. I'll make it up to you yet.

                         Your old friend,
                              THEA KRONBORG.

This in a bold, jagged handwriting with a Gothic turn to the letters,—something between a highly sophisticated hand and a very unsophisticated one,—not in the least smooth or flowing.

The doctor bit off the end of a cigar nervously and read the letter through again, fumbling distractedly in his pockets for matches, while the waiter kept trying to call his attention to the box he had just placed before him. At last Oscar came out, as if the idea had just struck him, "Matches, sir?"

"Yes, thank you." The doctor slipped a coin into his palm and rose, crumpling Thea's letter in his hand and thrusting the others into his pocket unopened. He went back to the desk in the lobby and beckoned the clerk, upon whose kindness he threw himself apologetically.

"Harry, I've got to pull out unexpectedly. Call up the Burlington, will you, and ask them to route me to New York the quickest way, and to let us know. Ask for the hour I'll get in. I have to wire."

"Certainly, Dr. Archie. Have it for you in a minute." The young man's pallid, clean-scraped face was all sympathetic interest as he reached for the telephone. Dr. Archie put out his hand and stopped him.

"Wait a minute. Tell me, first, is Captain Harris down yet?"

"No, sir. The Captain hasn't come down yet this morning."

"I'll wait here for him. If I don't happen to catch him, nail him and get me. Thank you, Harry."

The doctor spoke gratefully and turned away. He began to pace the lobby, his hands behind him, watching the bronze elevator doors like a hawk. At last Captain Harris issued from one of them, tall and imposing, wearing a Stetson and fierce mustaches, a fur coat on his arm, a solitaire glittering upon his little finger and another in his black satin ascot. He was one of the grand old bluffers of those good old days. As gullible as a schoolboy, he had managed, with his sharp eye and knowing air and twisted blond mustaches, to pass himself off for an astute financier, and the Denver papers respectfully referred to him as the Rothschild* of Cripple Creek.

Dr. Archie stopped the Captain on his way to breakfast. "Must see you a minute, Captain. Can't wait. Want to sell you some shares in the San Felipe. Got to raise money."

The Captain grandly bestowed his hat upon an eager porter who had already lifted his fur coat tenderly from his arm and stood nursing it. In removing his hat, the Captain exposed a bald, flushed dome, thatched about the ears with yellowish gray hair. "Bad time to sell, doctor. You want to hold on to San Felipe, and buy more. What have you got to raise?"

"Oh, not a great sum. Five or six thousand. I've been buying up close and have run short."

"I see, I see. Well, doctor, you'll have to let me get through that door. I was out last night, and I'm going to get my bacon, if you lose your mine." He clapped Archie on the shoulder and pushed him along in front of him. "Come ahead with me, and we'll talk business."

Dr. Archie attended the Captain and waited while he gave his order, taking the seat the old promoter indicated.

"Now, sir," the Captain turned to him, "you don't want to sell anything. You must be under the impression that I'm one of these damned New England sharks that get their pound of flesh off the widow and orphan. If you're a little short, sign a note and I'll write a check. That's the way gentlemen do business. If you want to put up some San Felipe as collateral, let her go, but I shan't touch a share of it. Pens and ink, please, Oscar,"—he lifted a large forefinger to the Austrian.

The Captain took out his checkbook and a book of blank notes, and adjusted his nose-nippers. He wrote a few words in one book and Archie wrote a few in the other. Then they each tore across perforations and exchanged slips of paper.

"That's the way. Saves office rent," the Captain commented with satisfaction, returning the books to his pocket. "And now, Archie, where are you off to?"

"Got to go East to-night. A deal waiting for me in New York." Dr. Archie rose.

The Captain's face brightened as he saw Oscar approaching with a tray, and he began tucking the corner of his napkin inside his collar, over his ascot. "Don't let them unload anything on you back there, doctor," he said genially, "and don't let them relieve you of anything, either. Don't let them get any Cripple stuff off you. We can manage our own silver out here, and we're going to take it out by the ton, sir!"

The doctor left the dining-room, and after another consultation with the clerk, he wrote his first telegram to Thea:—

Miss Thea Kronborg,
　　　　Everett House, New York.

Will call at your hotel eleven o'clock Friday morning. Glad to come. Thank you.

ARCHIE

He stood and heard the message actually clicked off on the wire, with the feeling that she was hearing the click at the other end. Then he sat down in the lobby and wrote a note to his wife and one to the other doctor in Moonstone. When he at last issued out into the storm, it was with a feeling of elation rather than of anxiety. Whatever was wrong, he could make it right. Her letter had practically said so.

He tramped about the snowy streets, from the bank to the Union Station, where he shoved his money under the grating of the ticket window as if he could not get rid of it fast enough. He had never been in New York, never been farther east than Buffalo. "That's rather a shame," he reflected boyishly as he put the long tickets in his pocket, "for a man nearly forty years old." However, he thought as he walked up toward the club, he was on the whole glad that his first trip had a human interest, that he was going for something, and because he was wanted. He loved holidays. He felt as if he were going to Germany himself. "Queer,"—he went over it with the snow blowing in his face,— "but that sort of thing is more interesting than mines and making your daily bread. It's worth paying out to be in on it,—for a fellow like me. And when it's Thea— Oh, I back her!" he laughed aloud as he burst in at the door of the Athletic Club, powdered with snow.

Archie sat down before the New York papers and ran over the advertisements of hotels, but he was too restless to read. Probably he had better get a new overcoat, and he was not sure about the shape of his collars. "I don't want to look different to her from everybody else there," he mused. "I guess I'll go down and have Van look me over. He'll put me right."

So he plunged out into the snow again and started for his tailor's. When he passed a florist's shop he stopped and looked in at the window, smiling; how naturally pleasant things recalled one another. At the tailor's he kept whistling, "Flow gently, Sweet Afton,"* while Van Dusen advised him, until that resourceful tailor and haberdasher exclaimed, "You must have a date back there, doctor; you behave like a bridegroom," and made him remember that he wasn't one.

Before he let him go, Van put his finger on the Masonic pin* in his client's lapel. "Mustn't wear that, doctor. Very bad form back there."

II

FRED OTTENBURG, smartly dressed for the afternoon, with a long black coat and gaiters, was sitting in the dusty parlor of the Everett House. His manner was not in accord with his personal freshness, the good lines of his clothes, and the shining smoothness of his hair. His attitude was one of deep dejection, and his face, though it had the cool, unimpeachable fairness possible only to a very blond young man, was by no means happy. A page shuffled into the room and looked about. When he made out the dark figure in a shadowy corner, tracing over the carpet pattern with a cane, he droned, "The lady says you can come up, sir."

Fred picked up his hat and gloves and followed the creature, who seemed an aged boy in uniform, through dark corridors that smelled of old carpets. The page knocked at the door of Thea's sitting-room, and then wandered away. Thea came to the door with a telegram in her hand. She asked Ottenburg to come in and pointed to one of the clumsy, sullen-looking chairs that were as thick as they were high. The room was brown with time, dark in spite of two windows that opened on Union Square, with dull curtains and carpet, and heavy, respectable-looking furniture in somber colors. The place was saved from utter dismalness by a coal fire under the black marble mantelpiece,—brilliantly reflected in a long mirror that hung between the two windows. This was the first time Fred had seen the room, and he took it in quickly, as he put down his hat and gloves.

Thea seated herself at the walnut writing-desk, still holding the slip of yellow paper. "Dr. Archie is coming," she said. "He will be here Friday morning."

"Well, that's good, at any rate," her visitor replied with a determined effort at cheerfulness. Then, turning to the fire, he added blankly, "If you want him."

"Of course I want him. I would never have asked such a thing of him if I hadn't wanted him a great deal. It's a very expensive trip." Thea spoke severely. Then she went on, in a milder tone. "He doesn't say anything about the money, but I think his coming means that he can let me have it."

Fred was standing before the mantel, rubbing his hands together nervously. "Probably. You are still determined to call on him?" He sat down tentatively in the chair Thea had indicated. "I don't see why you won't borrow from me, and let him sign with you, for instance. That would constitute a perfectly regular business transaction. I could bring suit against either of you for my money."

Thea turned toward him from the desk. "We won't take that up again, Fred. I should have a different feeling about it if I went on your money. In a way I shall feel freer on Dr. Archie's, and in another way I shall feel more bound. I shall try even harder." She paused. "He is almost like my father," she added irrelevantly.

"Still, he isn't, you know," Fred persisted. "It wouldn't be anything new. I've loaned money to students before, and got it back, too."

"Yes; I know you're generous," Thea hurried over it, "but this will be the best way. He will be here on Friday, did I tell you?"

"I think you mentioned it. That's rather soon. May I smoke?" he took out a small cigarette case. "I suppose you'll be off next week?" he asked as he struck a match.

"Just as soon as I can," she replied with a restless movement of her arms, as if her dark-blue dress were too tight for her. "It seems as if I'd been here forever."

"And yet," the young man mused, "we got in only four days ago. Facts really don't count for much, do they? It's all in the way people feel: even in little things."

Thea winced, but she did not answer him. She put the telegram back in its envelope and placed it carefully in one of the pigeonholes of the desk.

"I suppose," Fred brought out with effort, "that your friend is in your confidence?"

"He always has been. I shall have to tell him about myself. I wish I could without dragging you in."

Fred shook himself. "Don't bother about where you drag me, please," he put in, flushing. "I don't give—" he subsided suddenly.

"I'm afraid," Thea went on gravely, "that he won't understand. He'll be hard on you."

Fred studied the white ash of his cigarette before he flicked it off. "You mean he'll see me as even worse than I am. Yes, I suppose I shall look very low to him: a fifth-rate scoundrel. But that only matters in so far as it hurts his feelings."

Thea sighed. "We'll both look pretty low. And after all, we must really be just about as we shall look to him."

Ottenburg started up and threw his cigarette into the grate. "That I deny. Have you ever been really frank with this preceptor of your childhood, even when you *were* a child? Think a minute, have you? Of course not! From your cradle, as I once told you, you've been 'doing it' on the side, living your own life, admitting to yourself things that would horrify him. You've always deceived him to the extent of letting him think you different from what you are. He couldn't understand then, he can't understand now. So why not spare yourself and him?"

She shook her head. "Of course, I've had my own thoughts. Maybe he has had his, too. But I've never done anything before that he would much mind. I must put myself right with him,—as right as I can,—to begin over. He'll make allowances for me. He always has. But I'm afraid he won't for you."

"Leave that to him and me. I take it you want me to see him?" Fred sat down again and began absently to trace the carpet pattern with his cane. "At the worst," he spoke wanderingly, "I thought you'd perhaps let me go in on the business end of it and invest along with you. You'd put in your talent and ambition and hard work, and I'd put in the money and—well, nobody's good wishes are to be scorned, not even mine. Then, when the thing panned out big, we could share together. Your doctor friend hasn't cared half so much about your future as I have."

"He's cared a good deal. He doesn't know as much about such things as you do. Of course you've been a great deal more help to me than any one else ever has," Thea said quietly. The black clock on the mantel began to strike. She listened to the five strokes and then said, "I'd have liked your helping me eight months ago. But now, you'd simply be keeping me."

"You weren't ready for it eight months ago." Fred leaned back at last in his chair. "You simply weren't ready for it. You were too tired. You were too timid. Your whole tone was too low. You couldn't rise from a chair like that,"—she had started up apprehensively and gone toward the window.—"You were fumbling and awkward. Since then you've come into your personality. You were always locking horns with it before. You were a sullen little drudge eight months ago, afraid of being caught at either looking or moving like yourself. Nobody could tell anything about you. A voice is not an instrument that's found ready-made. A voice is personality. It can be as big as a circus and as common as dirt.— There's good money in that kind, too, but I don't happen to be interested in them.—Nobody could tell much about what you might be able to do, last winter. I divined more than anybody else."

"Yes, I know you did." Thea walked over to the old-fashioned mantel and held her hands down to the glow of the fire. "I owe so much to you, and that's what makes things hard. That's why I have to get away from you altogether. I depend on you for so many things. Oh, I did even last winter in Chicago!" She knelt down by the grate and held her hands closer to the coals. "And one thing leads to another."

Ottenburg watched her as she bent toward the fire. His glance brightened a little. "Anyhow, you couldn't look as you do now, before you knew me. You *were* clumsy. And whatever you do now, you do splendidly. And you can't cry enough to spoil your face for more than ten minutes. It comes right back, in spite of you. It's only since you've known me that you've let yourself be beautiful."

Without rising she turned her face away. Fred went on impetuously. "Oh, you can turn it away from me, Thea; you can take it away from me! All the same—" his spurt died and he fell back. "How can you turn on me so, after all!" he sighed.

"I haven't. But when you arranged with yourself to take me in like that, you couldn't have been thinking very kindly of me. I can't understand how you carried it through, when I was so easy, and all the circumstances were so easy."

Her crouching position by the fire became threatening. Fred got up, and Thea also rose.

"No," he said, "I can't make you see that now. Some time later, perhaps, you will understand better. For one thing, I honestly could not imagine that words, names, meant so much to you." Fred was talking with the desperation of a man who has put himself in the wrong and who yet feels that there was an idea of truth in his conduct. "Suppose that you had married your brakeman and lived with him year after year, caring for him even less than you do for your doctor, or for Harsanyi. I suppose you would have felt quite all right about it, because that relation has a name in good standing. To me, that seems—sickening!" He took a rapid turn about the room and then as Thea remained standing, he rolled one of the elephantine chairs up to the hearth for her.

"Sit down and listen to me for a moment, Thea." He began pacing from the hearthrug to the window and back again, while she sat down compliantly. "Don't you know most of the people in the world are not individuals at all? They never have an individual idea or experience. A lot of girls go to boarding-school together, come out the same season, dance at the same parties, are married off in groups, have their babies at about the same time, send their children to school together, and so the human crop renews itself.

Such women know as much about the reality of the forms they go through as they know about the wars they learn the dates of. They get their most personal experiences out of novels and plays. Everything is second-hand with them. Why, you *couldn't* live like that."

Thea sat looking toward the mantel, her eyes half closed, her chin level, her head set as if she were enduring something. Her hands, very white, lay passive on her dark gown. From the window corner Fred looked at them and at her. He shook his head and flashed an angry, tormented look out into the blue twilight over the Square, through which muffled cries and calls and the clang of car bells came up from the street. He turned again and began to pace the floor, his hands in his pockets.

"Say what you will, Thea Kronborg, you are not that sort of person. You will never sit alone with a pacifier and a novel. You won't subsist on what the old ladies have put into the bottle for you. You will always break through into the realities. That was the first thing Harsanyi found out about you; that you couldn't be kept on the outside. If you'd lived in Moonstone all your life and got on with the discreet brakeman, you'd have had just the same nature. Your children would have been the realities then, probably. If they'd been commonplace, you'd have killed them with driving. You'd have managed some way to live twenty times as much as the people around you."

Fred paused. He sought along the shadowy ceiling and heavy mouldings for words. When he began again, his voice was lower, and at first he spoke with less conviction, though again it grew on him. "Now I knew all this—oh, knew it better than I can ever make you understand! You've been running a handicap. You had no time to lose. I wanted you to have what you need and to get on fast—get through with me, if need be; I counted on that. You've no time to sit round and analyze your conduct or your feelings. Other women give their whole lives to it. They've nothing else to do. Helping a man to get his divorce is a career for them; just the sort of intellectual exercise they like."

Fred dived fiercely into his pockets as if he would rip them out and scatter their contents to the winds. Stopping before her, he took a deep breath and went on again, this time slowly. "All that sort of thing is foreign to you. You'd be nowhere at it. You haven't that kind of mind. The grammatical niceties of conduct are dark to you. You're simple—and poetic." Fred's voice seemed to be wandering about in the thickening dusk. "You won't play much. You won't, perhaps, love many times." He paused. "And you did love me, you know. Your railroad friend would have understood me. I *could* have thrown you back. The reverse was there,—it stared me in the face,—but I couldn't pull it. I let you drive ahead." He threw out his hands. What Thea noticed, oddly enough, was the flash of the firelight on his cuff link. He turned again. "And you'll always drive ahead," he muttered. "It's your way."

There was a long silence. Fred had dropped into a chair. He seemed, after such an explosion, not to have a word left in him. Thea put her hand to the back of her neck and pressed it, as if the muscles there were aching.

"Well," she said at last, "I at least overlook more in you than I do in myself. I am always excusing you to myself. I don't do much else."

"Then why, in Heaven's name, won't you let me be your friend? You make a scoundrel of me, borrowing money from another man to get out of my clutches."

"If I borrow from him, it's to study. Anything I took from you would be different. As I said before, you'd be keeping me."

"Keeping! I like your language. It's pure Moonstone, Thea,— like your point of view. I wonder how long you'll be a Methodist." He turned away bitterly.

"Well, I've never said I wasn't Moonstone, have I? I am, and that's why I want Dr. Archie. I can't see anything so funny about Moonstone, you know." She pushed her chair back a little from the hearth and clasped her hands over her knee, still looking thoughtfully into the red coals. "We always come back to the same thing, Fred. The name, as you call it, makes a difference to me how I feel about myself. You would have acted very differently with a girl of your own kind, and that's why I can't take anything from you now. You've made everything impossible. Being married is one thing and not being married is the other thing, and that's all there is to it. I can't see how you reasoned with yourself, if you took the trouble to reason. You say I was too much alone, and yet what you did was to cut me off more than I ever had been. Now I'm going to try to make good to my friends out there. That's all there is left for me."

"Make good to your friends!" Fred burst out. "What one of them cares as I care, or believes as I believe? I've told you I'll never ask a gracious word from you until I can ask it with all the churches in Christendom at my back."

Thea looked up, and when she saw Fred's face, she thought sadly that he, too, looked as if things were spoiled for him. "If you know me as well as you say you do, Fred," she said slowly, "then you are not being honest with yourself. You know that I can't do things halfway. If you kept me at all—you'd keep me." She dropped her head wearily on her hand and sat with her forehead resting on her fingers.

Fred leaned over her and said just above his breath, "Then, when I get that divorce, you'll take it up with me again? You'll at least let me know, warn me, before there is a serious question of anybody else?"

Without lifting her head, Thea answered him. "Oh, I don't think there will ever be a question of anybody else. Not if I can help it. I suppose I've given you every reason to think there will be,—at once, on shipboard, any time."

Ottenburg drew himself up like a shot. "Stop it, Thea!" he said sharply. "That's one thing you've never done. That's like any common woman." He saw her shoulders lift a little and grow calm. Then he went to the other side of the room and took up his hat and gloves from the sofa. He came back cheerfully. "I didn't drop in to bully you this afternoon. I came to coax you to go out for tea with me somewhere." He waited, but she did not look up or lift her head, still sunk on her hand.

Her handkerchief had fallen. Fred picked it up and put it on her knee, pressing her fingers over it. "Good-night, dear and wonderful," he whispered,—"wonderful and dear! How can you ever get away from me when I will always follow you, through every

wall, through every door, wherever you go." He looked down at
her bent head, and the curve of her neck that was so sad. He
stooped, and with his lips just touched her hair where the firelight
made it ruddiest. "I didn't know I had it in me, Thea. I thought it
was all a fairy tale. I don't know myself any more." He closed his
eyes and breathed deeply. "The salt's all gone out of your hair.
It's full of sun and wind again. I believe it has memories." Again
she heard him take a deep breath. "I could do without you for a
lifetime, if that would give you to yourself. A woman like you
doesn't find herself, alone."

She thrust her free hand up to him. He kissed it softly, as if she
were asleep and he were afraid of waking her. From the door he
turned back irrelevantly. "As to your old friend, Thea, if he's to
be here on Friday, why,"—he snatched out his watch and held it
down to catch the light from the grate,—"he's on the train now!
That ought to cheer you. Good-night." She heard the door close.

III

On Friday afternoon Thea Kronborg was walking excitedly up
and down her sitting-room, which at that hour was flooded by
thin, clear sunshine. Both windows were open, and the fire in the
grate was low, for the day was one of those false springs that
sometimes blow into New York from the sea in the middle of
winter, soft, warm, with a persuasive salty moisture in the air
and a relaxing thaw under foot. Thea was flushed and animated,
and she seemed as restless as the sooty sparrows that chirped and
cheeped distractingly about the windows. She kept looking at the
black clock, and then down into the Square. The room was full of
flowers, and she stopped now and then to arrange them or to
move them into the sunlight. After the bellboy came to announce
a visitor, she took some Roman hyacinths from a glass and stuck
them in the front of her dark-blue dress.

When at last Fred Ottenburg appeared in the doorway, she met
him with an exclamation of pleasure. "I am glad you've come,
Fred. I was afraid you might not get my note, and I wanted to see

you before you see Dr. Archie. He's so nice!" She brought her hands together to emphasize her statement.

"Is he? I'm glad. You see I'm quite out of breath. I didn't wait for the elevator, but ran upstairs. I was so pleased at being sent for." He dropped his hat and overcoat. "Yes, I should say he is nice! I don't seem to recognize all of these," waving his handkerchief about at the flowers.

"Yes, he brought them himself, in a big box. He brought lots with him besides flowers. Oh, lots of things! The old Moonstone feeling,"—Thea moved her hand back and forth in the air, fluttering her fingers,—"the feeling of starting out, early in the morning, to take my lesson."

"And you've had everything out with him?"

"No, I haven't."

"Haven't?" He looked up in consternation.

"No, I haven't!" Thea spoke excitedly, moving about over the sunny patches on the grimy carpet. "I've lied to him, just as you said I had always lied to him, and that's why I'm so happy. I've let him think what he likes to think. Oh, I couldn't do anything else, Fred,"—she shook her head emphatically. "If you'd seen him when he came in, so pleased and excited! You see this is a great adventure for him. From the moment I began to talk to him, he entreated me not to say too much; not to spoil his notion of me. Not in so many words, of course. But if you'd seen his eyes, his face, his kind hands! Oh, no! I couldn't." She took a deep breath, as if with a renewed sense of her narrow escape.

"Then, what did you tell him?" Fred demanded.

Thea sat down on the edge of the sofa and began shutting and opening her hands nervously. "Well, I told him enough, and not too much. I told him all about how good you were to me last winter, getting me engagements and things, and how you had helped me with my work more than anybody. Then I told him about how you sent me down to the ranch when I had no money or anything." She paused and wrinkled her forehead. "And I told him that I wanted to marry you and ran away to Mexico with you, and that I was awfully happy until you told me that you couldn't marry me because—well, I told him why." Thea dropped her eyes and moved the toe of her shoe about restlessly on the carpet.

"And he took it from you, like that?" Fred asked, almost with awe.

"Yes, just like that, and asked no questions. He was hurt; he had some wretched moments. I could see him squirming and squirming and trying to get past it. He kept shutting his eyes and rubbing his forehead. But when I told him that I absolutely knew you wanted to marry me, that you would whenever you could, that seemed to help him a good deal."

"And that satisfied him?" Fred asked wonderingly. He could not quite imagine what kind of person Dr. Archie might be.

"He took me by the shoulders once and asked, oh, in such a frightened way, 'Thea, was he *good* to you, this young man?' When I told him you were, he looked at me again: 'And you care for him a great deal, you believe in him?' Then he seemed satisfied." Thea paused. "You see, he's just tremendously good, and tremendously afraid of things—of some things. Otherwise he would have got rid of Mrs. Archie." She looked up suddenly: "You were right, though; one can't tell people about things they don't know already."

Fred stood in the window, his back to the sunlight, fingering the jonquils. "Yes, you can, my dear. But you must tell it in such a way that they don't know you're telling it, and that they don't know they're hearing it."

Thea smiled past him, out into the air. "I see. It's a secret. Like the sound in the shell."

"What's that?" Fred was watching her and thinking how moving that faraway expression, in her, happened to be. "What did you say?"

She came back. "Oh, something old and Moonstony! I have almost forgotten it myself. But I feel better than I thought I ever could again. I can't wait to be off. Oh, Fred," she sprang up, "I want to get at it!"

As she broke out with this, she threw up her head and lifted herself a little on her toes. Fred colored and looked at her fearfully, hesitatingly. Her eyes, which looked out through the window, were bright—they had no memories. No, she did not remember. That momentary elevation had no associations for her. It was unconscious.

He looked her up and down and laughed and shook his head. "You are just all I want you to be—and that is,—not for me! Don't worry, you'll get at it. You are at it. My God! have you ever, for one moment, been at anything else?"

Thea did not answer him, and clearly she had not heard him. She was watching something out in the thin light of the false spring and its treacherously soft air.

Fred waited a moment. "Are you going to dine with your friend to-night?"

"Yes. He has never been in New York before. He wants to go about. Where shall I tell him to go?"

"Wouldn't it be a better plan, since you wish me to meet him, for you both to dine with me? It would seem only natural and friendly. You'll have to live up a little to his notion of us." Thea seemed to consider the suggestion favorably. "If you wish him to be easy in his mind," Fred went on, "that would help. I think, myself, that we are rather nice together. Put on one of the new dresses you got down there, and let him see how lovely you can be. You owe him some pleasure, after all the trouble he has taken."

Thea laughed, and seemed to find the idea exciting and pleasant. "Oh, very well! I'll do my best. Only don't wear a dress coat, please. He hasn't one, and he's nervous about it."

Fred looked at his watch. "Your monument up there is fast. I'll be here with a cab at eight. I'm anxious to meet him. You've given me the strangest idea of his callow innocence and aged indifference."

She shook her head. "No, he's none of that. He's very good, and he won't admit things. I love him for it. Now as I look back on it, I see that I've always, even when I was little, shielded him."

As she laughed, Fred caught the bright spark in her eye that he knew so well, and held it for a happy instant. Then he blew her a kiss with his finger-tips and fled.

IV

AT nine o'clock that evening our three friends were seated in the balcony of a French restaurant, much gayer and more intimate than any that exists in New York to-day. This old restaurant was built by a lover of pleasure, who knew that to dine gayly human beings must have the reassurance of certain limitations of space and of a certain definite style; that the walls must be near enough to suggest shelter, the ceiling high enough to give the chandeliers a setting. The place was crowded with the kind of people who dine late and well, and Dr. Archie, as he watched the animated groups in the long room below the balcony, found this much the most festive scene he had ever looked out upon. He said to himself, in a jovial mood somewhat sustained by the cheer of the board, that this evening alone was worth his long journey. He followed attentively the orchestra, ensconced at the farther end of the balcony, and told Thea it made him feel "quite musical" to recognize "The Invitation to the Dance" or "The Blue Danube,"* and that he could remember just what kind of day it was when he heard her practicing them at home, and lingered at the gate to listen.

For the first few moments, when he was introduced to young Ottenburg in the parlor of the Everett House, the doctor had been awkward and unbending. But Fred, as his father had often observed, "was not a good mixer for nothing." He had brought Dr. Archie around during the short cab ride, and in an hour they had become old friends. From the moment when the doctor lifted his glass and, looking consciously at Thea, said, "To your success," Fred liked him. He felt his quality; understood his courage in some directions and what Thea called his timidity in others, his unspent and miraculously preserved youthfulness. Men could never impose upon the doctor, he guessed, but women always could. Fred liked, too, the doctor's manner with Thea, his bashful admiration and the little hesitancy by which he betrayed his consciousness of the change in her. It was just this change that, at present, interested Fred more than anything else. That, he felt was his "created value," and it was his best chance for any peace of mind. If that were not real, obvious to an old friend like Archie, then he cut a very poor figure, indeed.

Fred got a good deal, too, out of their talk about Moonstone. From her questions and the doctor's answers he was able to form some conception of the little world that was almost the measure of Thea's experience, the one bit of the human drama that she had followed with sympathy and understanding. As the two ran over the list of their friends, the mere sound of a name seemed to recall volumes to each of them, to indicate mines of knowledge and observation they had in common. At some names they laughed delightedly, at some indulgently and even tenderly.

"You two young people must come out to Moonstone when Thea gets back," the doctor said hospitably.

"Oh, we shall!" Fred caught it up. "I'm keen to know all these people. It is very tantalizing to hear only their names."

"Would they interest an outsider very much, do you think, Dr. Archie?" Thea leaned toward him. "Isn't it only because we've known them since I was little?"

The doctor glanced at her deferentially. Fred had noticed that he seemed a little afraid to look at her squarely—perhaps a trifle embarrassed by a mode of dress to which he was unaccustomed. "Well, you are practically an outsider yourself, Thea, now," he observed smiling. "Oh, I know," he went on quickly in response to her gesture of protest,—"I know you don't change toward your old friends, but you can see us all from a distance now. It's all to your advantage that you can still take your old interest, isn't it, Mr. Ottenburg?"

"That's exactly one of her advantages, Dr. Archie. Nobody can ever take that away from her, and none of us who came later can ever hope to rival Moonstone in the impression we make. Her scale of values will always be the Moonstone scale. And, with an artist, that *is* an advantage." Fred nodded.

Dr. Archie looked at him seriously. "You mean it keeps them from getting affected?"

"Yes; keeps them from getting off the track generally."

While the waiter filled the glasses, Fred pointed out to Thea a big black French barytone who was eating anchovies by their tails at one of the tables below, and the doctor looked about and studied his fellow diners.

"Do you know, Mr. Ottenburg," he said deeply, "these people all look happier to me than our Western people do. Is it simply good manners on their part, or do they get more out of life?"

Fred laughed to Thea above the glass he had just lifted. "Some of them are getting a good deal out of it now, doctor. This is the hour when bench-joy brightens."

Thea chuckled and darted him a quick glance. "Bench-joy! Where did you get that slang?"

"That happens to be very old slang, my dear. Older than Moonstone or the sovereign State of Colorado. Our old friend Mr. Nathanmeyer could tell us why it happens to hit you." He leaned forward and touched Thea's wrist, "See that fur coat just coming in, Thea. It's D'Albert. He's just back from his Western tour. Fine head, hasn't he?"

"To go back," said Dr. Archie; "I insist that people do look happier here. I've noticed it even on the street, and especially in the hotels."

Fred turned to him cheerfully. "New York people live a good deal in the fourth dimension Dr. Archie. It's that you notice in their faces."

The doctor was interested. "The fourth dimension," he repeated slowly; "and is that slang, too?"

"No,"—Fred shook his head,—"that's merely a figure. I mean that life is not quite so personal here as it is in your part of the world. People are more taken up by hobbies, interests that are less subject to reverses than their personal affairs. If you're interested in Thea's voice, for instance, or in voices in general, that interest is just the same, even if your mining stocks go down."

The doctor looked at him narrowly. "You think that's about the principal difference between country people and city people, don't you?"

Fred was a little disconcerted at being followed up so resolutely, and he attempted to dismiss it with a pleasantry. "I've never thought much about it, doctor. But I should say, on the spur of the moment, that that is one of the principal differences between people anywhere. It's the consolation of fellows like me who don't accomplish much. The fourth dimension is not good for business, but we think we have a better time."

Dr. Archie leaned back in his chair. His heavy shoulders were contemplative. "And she," he said slowly; "should you say that she is one of the kind you refer to?" He inclined his head toward the shimmer of the pale-green dress beside him. Thea was leaning, just then, over the balcony rail, her head in the light from the chandeliers below.

"Never, never!" Fred protested. "She's as hard-headed as the worst of you—with a difference."

The doctor sighed. "Yes, with a difference; something that makes a good many revolutions to the second. When she was little I used to feel her head to try to locate it."

Fred laughed. "Did you, though? So you were on the track of it? Oh, it's there! We can't get round it, miss," as Thea looked back inquiringly. "Dr. Archie, there's a fellow townsman of yours I feel a real kinship for." He pressed a cigar upon Dr. Archie and struck a match for him. "Tell me about Spanish Johnny."

The doctor smiled benignantly through the first waves of smoke. "Well, Johnny's an old patient of mine, and he's an old admirer of Thea's. She was born a cosmopolitan, and I expect she learned a good deal from Johnny when she used to run away and go to Mexican Town. We thought it a queer freak then."

The doctor launched into a long story, in which he was often eagerly interrupted or joyously confirmed by Thea, who was drinking her coffee and forcing open the petals of the roses with an ardent and rather rude hand. Fred settled down into enjoying his comprehension of his guests. Thea, watching Dr. Archie and interested in his presentation, was unconsciously impersonating her suave, gold-tinted friend. It was delightful to see her so radiant and responsive again. She had kept her promise about looking her best; when one could so easily get together the colors of an apple branch in early spring, that was not hard to do. Even Dr. Archie felt, each time he looked at her, a fresh consciousness. He recognized the fine texture of her mother's skin, with the difference that, when she reached across the table to give him a bunch of grapes, her arm was not only white, but somehow a little dazzling. She seemed to him taller, and freer in all her movements. She had now a way of taking a deep breath when she was interested, that made her seem very strong, somehow, and brought her at one quite overpoweringly. If he seemed shy, it was not that he was intimidated by her worldly clothes, but that her greater positiveness, her whole augmented self, made him feel that his accustomed manner toward her was inadequate.

Fred, on his part, was reflecting that the awkward position in which he had placed her would not confine or chafe her long. She looked about at other people, at other women, curiously. She was not quite sure of herself, but she was not in the least afraid or apologetic. She seemed to sit there on the edge, emerging from one world into another, taking her bearings, getting an idea of the concerted movement about her, but with absolute self-confidence. So far from shrinking, she expanded. The mere kindly effort to please Dr. Archie was enough to bring her out.

There was much talk of aurae at that time, and Fred mused that every beautiful, every compellingly beautiful woman, had an aura, whether other people did or no. There was, certainly, about the woman he had brought up from Mexico, such an emanation. She existed in more space than she occupied by measurement. The enveloping air about her head and shoulders was subsidized—was more moving than she herself, for in it lived the awakenings, all the first sweetness that life kills in people. One felt in her such a wealth of *Jugendzeit*,* all those flowers of the mind and the blood that bloom and perish by the myriad in the few exhaustless years when the imagination first kindles. It was in watching her as she emerged like this, in being near and not too near, that one got, for a moment, so much that one had lost; among other legendary things the legendary theme of the absolutely magical power of a beautiful woman.

After they had left Thea at her hotel, Dr. Archie admitted to Fred, as they walked up Broadway through the rapidly chilling air, that once before he had seen their young friend flash up into a more potent self, but in a darker mood. It was in his office one night, when she was at home the summer before last. "And then I got the idea," he added simply, "that she would not live like other people: that for better or worse, she had uncommon gifts."

"Oh, we'll see that it's for better, you and I," Fred reassured him. "Won't you come up to my hotel with me? I think we ought to have a long talk."

"Yes, indeed," said Dr. Archie gratefully; "I think we ought."

V

THEA was to sail on Tuesday, at noon, and on Saturday Fred Ottenburg arranged for her passage, while she and Dr. Archie went shopping. With rugs and sea-clothes she was already provided; Fred had got everything of that sort she needed for the voyage up from Vera Cruz. On Sunday afternoon Thea went to see the Harsanyis. When she returned to her hotel, she found a note from Ottenburg, saying that he had called and would come again tomorrow. On Monday morning, while she was at breakfast, Fred came in. She knew by his hurried, distracted air as he entered the dining-room that something had gone wrong. He had just got a telegram from home. His mother had been thrown from her carriage and hurt; a concussion of some sort, and she was unconscious. He was leaving for St. Louis that night on the eleven o'clock train. He had a great deal to attend to during the day. He would come that evening, if he might, and stay with her until train time, while she was doing her packing. Scarcely waiting for her consent, he hurried away.

All day Thea was somewhat cast down. She was sorry for Fred, and she missed the feeling that she was the one person in his mind. He had scarcely looked at her when they exchanged words at the breakfast-table. She felt as if she were set aside, and she did not seem so important even to herself as she had yesterday. Certainly, she reflected, it was high time that she began to take care of herself again. Dr. Archie came for dinner, but she sent him away early, telling him that she would be ready to go to the boat with him at half-past ten the next morning. When she went upstairs, she looked gloomily at the open trunk in her sitting-room, and at the trays piled on the sofa. She stood at the window and watched a quiet snowstorm spending itself over the city. More than anything else falling snow always made her think of Moonstone; of the Kohlers' garden, of Thor's sled, of dressing by lamplight and starting off to school before the paths were broken.

When Fred came, he looked tired, and he took her hand almost without seeing her.

"I'm so sorry, Fred. Have you had any more word?"

"She was still unconscious at four this afternoon. It doesn't look very encouraging." He approached the fire and warmed his hands. He seemed to have contracted, and he had not at all his habitual ease of manner. "Poor mother!" he exclaimed; "nothing like this should have happened to her. She has so much pride of person. She's not at all an old woman, you know. She's never got beyond vigorous and rather dashing middle age." He turned abruptly to Thea and for the first time really looked at her. "How badly things come out! She'd have liked you for a daughter-in-law. Oh, you'd have fought like the devil, but you'd have respected each other." He sank into a chair and thrust his feet out to the fire. "Still," he went on thoughtfully, seeming to address the ceiling, "it might have been bad for you. Our big German houses, our good German cooking—you might have got lost in the upholstery. That substantial comfort might take the temper out of you, dull your edge. Yes," he sighed, "I guess you were meant for the jolt of the breakers."

"I guess I'll get plenty of jolt," Thea murmured, turning to her trunk.

"I'm rather glad I'm not staying over until to-morrow," Fred reflected. "I think it's easier for me to glide out like this. I feel now as if everything were rather casual, anyhow. A thing like that dulls one's feelings."

Thea, standing by her trunk, made no reply. Presently he shook himself and rose. "Want me to put those trays in for you?"

"No, thank you. I'm not ready for them yet."

Fred strolled over to the sofa, lifted a scarf from one of the trays and stood abstractedly drawing it through his fingers. "You've been so kind these last few days, Thea, that I began to hope you might soften a little; that you might ask me to come over and see you this summer."

"If you thought that, you were mistaken," she said slowly. "I've hardened, if anything. But I shan't carry any grudge away with me, if you mean that."

He dropped the scarf. "And there's nothing—nothing at all you'll let me do?"

"Yes, there is one thing, and it's a good deal to ask. If I get knocked out, or never get on, I'd like you to see that Dr. Archie gets his money back. I'm taking three thousand dollars of his."

"Why, of course I shall. You may dismiss that from your mind. How fussy you are about money, Thea. You make such a point of it." He turned sharply and walked to the windows.

Thea sat down in the chair he had quitted. "It's only poor people who feel that way about money, and who are really honest," she said gravely. "Sometimes I think that to be really honest, you must have been so poor that you've been tempted to steal."

"To what?"

"To steal. I used to be, when I first went to Chicago and saw all the things in the big stores there. Never anything big, but little things, the kind I'd never seen before and could never afford. I did take something once, before I knew it."

Fred came toward her. For the first time she had his whole attention, in the degree to which she was accustomed to having it. "Did you? What was it?" he asked with interest.

"A sachet. A little blue silk bag of orris-root powder. There was a whole counterful of them, marked down to fifty cents. I'd never seen any before, and they seemed irresistible. I took one up and wandered about the store with it. Nobody seemed to notice, so I carried it off."

Fred laughed. "Crazy child! Why, your things always smell of orris; is it a penance?"

"No, I love it. But I saw that the firm didn't lose anything by me. I went back and bought it there whenever I had a quarter to spend. I got a lot to take to Arizona. I made it up to them."

"I'll bet you did!" Fred took her hand. "Why didn't I find you that first winter? I'd have loved you just as you came!"

Thea shook her head. "No, you wouldn't, but you might have found me amusing. The Harsanyis said yesterday afternoon that I wore such a funny cape and that my shoes always squeaked. They think I've improved. I told them it was your doing if I had, and then they looked scared."

"Did you sing for Harsanyi?"

"Yes. He thinks I've improved there, too. He said nice things to me. Oh, he was very nice! He agrees with you about my going to Lehmann,* if she'll take me. He came out to the elevator with me, after we had said good-bye. He said something nice out there, too, but he seemed sad."

"What was it that he said?"

"He said, 'When people, serious people, believe in you, they give you some of their best, so—take care of it, Miss Kronborg.' Then he waved his hands and went back."

"If you sang, I wish you had taken me along. Did you sing well?" Fred turned from her and went back to the window. "I wonder when I shall hear you sing again." He picked up a bunch of violets and smelled them. "You know, your leaving me like this—well, it's almost inhuman to be able to do it so kindly and unconditionally."

"I suppose it is. It was almost inhuman to be able to leave home, too,—the last time, when I knew it was for good. But all the same, I cared a great deal more than anybody else did. I lived through it. I have no choice now. No matter how much it breaks me up, I have to go. Do I seem to enjoy it?"

Fred bent over her trunk and picked up something which proved to be a score, clumsily bound. "What's this? Did you ever try to sing this?" He opened it and on the engraved title-page read Wunsch's inscription, "*Einst, O Wunder!*" He looked up sharply at Thea.

"Wunsch gave me that when he went away. I've told you about him, my old teacher in Moonstone. He loved that opera."

Fred went toward the fireplace, the book under his arm, singing softly:—

"*Einst, O Wunder, entblüht auf meinem Grabe,*
  Eine Blume der Asche meines Herzens;

"You have no idea at all where he is, Thea?" He leaned against the mantel and looked down at her.

"No, I wish I had. He may be dead by this time. That was five years ago, and he used himself hard. Mrs. Kohler was always afraid he would die off alone somewhere and be stuck under the prairie. When we last heard of him, he was in Kansas."

"If he were to be found, I'd like to do something for him. I seem to get a good deal of him from this." He opened the book again, where he kept the place with his finger, and scrutinized the purple ink. "How like a German! Had he ever sung the song for you?"

"No. I didn't know where the words were from until once, when Harsanyi sang it for me, I recognized them."

Fred closed the book. "Let me see, what was your noble brakeman's name?"

Thea looked up with surprise. "Ray, Ray Kennedy."

"Ray Kennedy!" he laughed. "It couldn't well have been better! Wunsch and Dr. Archie, and Ray, and I,"—he told them off on his fingers,—"your whistling-posts! You haven't done so badly. We've backed you as we could, some in our weakness and some in our might. In your dark hours—and you'll have them— you may like to remember us." He smiled whimsically and dropped the score into the trunk. "You are taking that with you?"

"Surely I am. I haven't so many keepsakes that I can afford to leave that. I haven't got many that I value so highly."

"That you value so highly?" Fred echoed her gravity playfully. "You are delicious when you fall into your vernacular." He laughed half to himself.

"What's the matter with that? Isn't it perfectly good English?"

"Perfectly good Moonstone, my dear. Like the ready-made clothes that hang in the windows, made to fit everybody and fit nobody, a phrase that can be used on all occasions. Oh,"—he started across the room again,—"that's one of the fine things about your going! You'll be with the right sort of people and you'll learn a good, live, warm German, that will be like yourself. You'll get a new speech full of shades and color like your voice; alive, like your mind. It will be almost like being born again, Thea."

She was not offended. Fred had said such things to her before, and she wanted to learn. In the natural course of things she would never have loved a man from whom she could not learn a great deal.

"Harsanyi said once," she remarked thoughtfully, "that if one became an artist one had to be born again, and that one owed nothing to anybody."

"Exactly. And when I see you again I shall not see you, but your daughter. May I?" He held up his cigarette case questioningly and then began to smoke, taking up again the song which ran in his head:—

> *"Deutlich schimmert auf jedem, Purpurblättchen, Adelaide!"**

"I have half an hour with you yet, and then, exit Fred." He walked about the room, smoking and singing the words under his breath. "You'll like the voyage," he said abruptly. "That first approach to a foreign shore, stealing up on it and finding it— there's nothing like it. It wakes up everything that's asleep in you. You won't mind my writing to some people in Berlin? They'll be nice to you."

"I wish you would." Thea gave a deep sigh. "I wish one could look ahead and see what is coming to one."

"Oh, no!" Fred was smoking nervously; "that would never do. It's the uncertainty that makes one try. You've never had any sort of chance, and now I fancy you'll make it up to yourself. You'll find the way to let yourself out in one long flight."

Thea put her hand on her heart. "And then drop like the rocks we used to throw—anywhere." She left the chair and went over to the sofa, hunting for something in the trunk trays. When she came back she found Fred sitting in her place. "Here are some handkerchiefs of yours. I've kept one or two. They're larger than mine and useful if one has a headache."

"Thank you. How nicely they smell of your things!" He looked at the white squares for a moment and then put them in his pocket. He kept the low chair, and as she stood beside him he took her hands and sat looking intently at them, as if he were examining them for some special purpose, tracing the long round fingers with the tips of his own. "Ordinarily, you know, there are reefs that a man catches to and keeps his nose above water. But this is a case by itself. There seems to be no limit as to how much I can be in love with you. I keep going." He did not lift his eyes from her fingers, which he continued to study with the same fervor. "Every kind of stringed instrument there is plays in your hands, Thea," he whispered, pressing them to his face.

She dropped beside him and slipped into his arms, shutting her eyes and lifting her cheek to his. "Tell me one thing," Fred whispered. "You said that night on the boat, when I first told you, that if you could you would crush it all up in your hands and throw it into the sea. Would you, all those weeks?"

She shook her head.

"Answer me, would you?"

"No, I was angry then. I'm not now. I'd never give them up. Don't make me pay too much." In that embrace they lived over again all the others. When Thea drew away from him, she dropped her face in her hands. "You are good to me," she breathed, "you are!"

Rising to his feet, he put his hands under her elbows and lifted her gently. He drew her toward the door with him. "Get all you can. Be generous with yourself. Don't stop short of splendid things. I want them for you more than I want anything else, more than I want one splendid thing for myself. I can't help feeling that you'll gain, somehow, by my losing so much. That you'll gain the very thing I lose. Take care of her, as Harsanyi said. She's wonderful!" He kissed her and went out of the door without looking back, just as if he were coming again to-morrow.

Thea went quickly into her bedroom. She brought out an armful of muslin things, knelt down, and began to lay them in the trays. Suddenly she stopped, dropped forward and leaned against the open trunk, her head on her arms. The tears fell down on the dark old carpet. It came over her how many people must have said good-bye and been unhappy in that room. Other people, before her time, had hired this room to cry in. Strange rooms and strange streets and faces, how sick at heart they made one! Why was she going so far, when what she wanted was some familiar place to hide in?—the rock house, her little room in Moonstone, her own bed. Oh, how good it would be to lie down in that little bed, to cut the nerve that kept one struggling, that pulled one on and on, to sink into peace there, with all the family safe and happy downstairs. After all, she was a Moonstone girl, one of the preacher's children. Everything else was in Fred's imagination. Why was she called upon to take such chances? Any safe, hum-drum work that did not compromise her would be better. But if she failed now, she would lose her soul. There was nowhere to fall, after one took that step, except into abysses of wretchedness. She knew what abysses, for she could still hear the old man play-ing in the snowstorm, "*Ach, ich habe sie verloren!*" That melody was released in her like a passion of longing. Every nerve in her body thrilled to it. It brought her to her feet, carried her somehow to bed and into troubled sleep.

That night she taught in Moonstone again: she beat her pupils in hideous rages, she kept on beating them. She sang at funerals, and struggled at the piano with Harsanyi. In one dream she was looking into a hand-glass and thinking that she was getting better-looking, when the glass began to grow smaller and smaller and her own reflection to shrink, until she realized that she was looking into Ray Kennedy's eyes, seeing her face in that look of his which she could never forget. All at once the eyes were Fred Ottenburg's, and not Ray's. All night she heard the shrieking of trains, whistling in and out of Moonstone, as she used to hear them in her sleep when they blew shrill in the winter air. But to-night they were terrifying,—the spectral, fated trains that "raced with death," about which the old woman from the depot used to pray.

In the morning she wakened breathless after a struggle with Mrs. Livery Johnson's daughter. She started up with a bound, threw the blankets back and sat on the edge of the bed, her night-dress open, her long braids hanging over her bosom, blinking at the daylight. After all, it was not too late. She was only twenty years old, and the boat sailed at noon. There was still time!

PART VI

KRONBORG

Ten Years Later

PART VI

KRONBORG

I

IT is a glorious winter day. Denver, standing on her high plateau under a thrilling green-blue sky, is masked in snow and glittering with sunlight. The Capitol building is actually in armor, and throws off the shafts of the sun until the beholder is dazzled and the outlines of the building are lost in a blaze of reflected light. The stone terrace is a white field over which fiery reflections dance, and the trees and bushes are faithfully repeated in snow— on every black twig a soft, blurred line of white. From the terrace one looks directly over to where the mountains break in their sharp, familiar lines against the sky. Snow fills the gorges, hangs in scarfs on the great slopes, and on the peaks the fiery sunshine is gathered up as by a burning-glass.

Howard Archie is standing at the window of his private room in the offices of the San Felipe Mining Company, on the sixth floor of the Raton Building, looking off at the mountain glories of his State while he gives dictation to his secretary. He is ten years older than when we saw him last, and emphatically ten years more prosperous. A decade of coming into things has not so much aged him as it has fortified, smoothed, and assured him. His sandy hair and imperial conceal whatever gray they harbor. He has not grown heavier, but more flexible, and his massive shoulders carry fifty years and the control of his great mining interests more lightly than they carried forty years and a country practice. In short, he is one of the friends to whom we feel grateful for having got on in the world, for helping to keep up the general temperature and our own confidence in life. He is an acquaintance that one would hurry to overtake and greet among a hundred. In his warm handshake and generous smile there is the stimulating cordiality of good fellows come into good fortune and eager to pass it on; something that makes one think better of the lottery of life and resolve to try again.

When Archie had finished his morning mail, he turned away from the window and faced his secretary. "Did anything come up yesterday afternoon while I was away, T. B.?"

Thomas Burk turned over the leaf of his calendar. "Governor Alden sent down to say that he wanted to see you before he sends his letter to the Board of Pardons. Asked if you could go over to the State House this morning."

Archie shrugged his shoulders. "I'll think about it."

The young man grinned.

"Anything else?" his chief continued.

T. B. swung round in his chair with a look of interest on his shrewd, clean-shaven face. "Old Jasper Flight was in, Dr. Archie. I never expected to see him alive again. Seems he's tucked away for the winter with a sister who's a housekeeper at the Oxford. He's all crippled up with rheumatism, but as fierce after it as ever. Wants to know if you or the company won't grub-stake him again. Says he's sure of it this time; had located something when the snow shut down on him in December. He wants to crawl out at the first break in the weather, with that same old burro with the split ear. He got somebody to winter the beast for him. He's superstitious about that burro, too; thinks it's divinely guided. You ought to hear the line of talk he put up here yesterday; said when he rode in his carriage, that burro was a-going to ride along with him."

Archie laughed. "Did he leave you his address?"

"He didn't neglect anything," replied the clerk cynically.

"Well, send him a line and tell him to come in again. I like to hear him. Of all the crazy prospectors I've ever known, he's the most interesting, because he's really crazy. It's a religious conviction with him, and with most of 'em it's a gambling fever or pure vagrancy. But Jasper Flight believes that the Almighty keeps the secret of the silver deposits in these hills, and gives it away to the deserving. He's a downright noble figure. Of course I'll stake him! As long as he can crawl out in the spring. He and that burro are a sight together. The beast is nearly as white as Jasper; must be twenty years old."

"If you stake him this time, you won't have to again," said T. B. knowingly. "He'll croak up there, mark my word. Says he never ties the burro at night now, for fear he might be called sudden, and the beast would starve. I guess that animal could eat a lariat rope, all right, and enjoy it."

"I guess if we knew the things those two have eaten, and haven't eaten, in their time, T. B., it would make us vegetarians." The doctor sat down and looked thoughtful. "That's the way for the old man to go. It would be pretty hard luck if he had to die in a hospital. I wish he could turn up something before he cashes in. But his kind seldom do; they're bewitched. Still, there was Stratton. I've been meeting Jasper Flight, and his side meat and tin pans, up in the mountains for years, and I'd miss him. I always halfway believe the fairy tales he spins me. Old Jasper Flight," Archie murmured, as if he liked the name or the picture it called up.

A clerk came in from the outer office and handed Archie a card. He sprang up and exclaimed, "Mr. Ottenburg? Bring him in."

Fred Ottenburg entered, clad in a long, fur-lined coat, holding a checked-cloth hat in his hand, his cheeks and eyes bright with the outdoor cold. The two men met before Archie's desk and their handclasp was longer than friendship prompts except in regions where the blood warms and quickens to meet the dry cold. Under the general keying-up of the altitude, manners take on a heartiness, a vivacity, that is one expression of the half-unconscious excitement which Colorado people miss when they drop into lower strata of air. The heart, we are told, wears out early in that high atmosphere, but while it pumps it sends out no sluggish stream. Our two friends stood gripping each other by the hand and smiling.

"When did you get in, Fred? And what have you come for?" Archie gave him a quizzical glance.

"I've come to find out what you think you're doing out here," the younger man declared emphatically. "I want to get next, I do. When can you see me?"

"Anything on to-night? Then suppose you dine with me. Where can I pick you up at five-thirty?"

"Bixby's office, general freight agent of the Burlington." Ottenburg began to button his overcoat and drew on his gloves. "I've got to have one shot at you before I go, Archie. Didn't I tell you Pinky Alden was a cheap squirt?"

Alden's backer laughed and shook his head. "Oh, he's worse than that, Fred. It isn't polite to mention what he is, outside of the Arabian Nights. I guessed you'd come to rub it into me."

Ottenburg paused, his hand on the doorknob, his high color challenging the doctor's calm. "I'm disgusted with you, Archie, for training with such a pup. A man of your experience!"

"Well, he's been an experience," Archie muttered. "I'm not coy about admitting it, am I?"

Ottenburg flung open the door. "Small credit to you. Even the women are out for capital and corruption, I hear. Your Governor's done more for the United Breweries in six months than I've been able to do in six years. He's the lily-livered sort we're looking for. Good-morning."

That afternoon at five o'clock Dr. Archie emerged from the State House after his talk with Governor Alden, and crossed the terrace under a saffron sky. The snow, beaten hard, was blue in the dusk; a day of blinding sunlight had not even started a thaw. The lights of the city twinkled pale below him in the quivering violet air, and the dome of the State House behind him was still red with the light from the west. Before he got into his car, the doctor paused to look about him at the scene of which he never tired. Archie lived in his own house on Colfax Avenue, where he had roomy grounds and a rose garden and a conservatory. His housekeeping was done by three Japanese boys, devoted and resourceful, who were able to manage Archie's dinner parties, to see that he kept his engagements, and to make visitors who stayed at the house so comfortable that they were always loath to go away.

Archie had never known what comfort was until he became a widower, though with characteristic delicacy, or dishonesty, he insisted upon accrediting his peace of mind to the San Felipe, to Time, to anything but his release from Mrs. Archie.

Mrs. Archie died just before her husband left Moonstone and

came to Denver to live, six years ago. The poor woman's fight against dust was her undoing at last. One summer day when she was rubbing the parlor upholstery with gasoline,—the doctor had often forbidden her to use it on any account, so that was one of the pleasures she seized upon in his absence,—an explosion occurred. Nobody ever knew exactly how it happened, for Mrs. Archie was dead when the neighbors rushed in to save her from the burning house. She must have inhaled the burning gas and died instantly.

Moonstone severity relented toward her somewhat after her death. But even while her old cronies at Mrs. Smiley's millinery store said that it was a terrible thing, they added that nothing but a powerful explosive *could* have killed Mrs. Archie, and that it was only right the doctor should have a chance.

Archie's past was literally destroyed when his wife died. The house burned to the ground, and all those material reminders which have such power over people disappeared in an hour. His mining interests now took him to Denver so often that it seemed better to make his headquarters there. He gave up his practice and left Moonstone for good. Six months afterward, while Dr. Archie was living at the Brown Palace Hotel, the San Felipe mine began to give up that silver hoard which old Captain Harris had always accused it of concealing, and San Felipe headed the list of mining quotations in every daily paper, East and West. In a few years Dr. Archie was a very rich man. His mine was such an important item in the mineral output of the State, and Archie had a hand in so many of the new industries of Colorado and New Mexico, that his political influence was considerable. He had thrown it all, two years ago, to the new reform party, and had brought about the election of a governor of whose conduct he was now heartily ashamed. His friends believed that Archie himself had ambitious political plans.

II

WHEN Ottenburg and his host reached the house on Colfax Avenue, they went directly to the library, a long double room on the second floor which Archie had arranged exactly to his own taste. It was full of books and mounted specimens of wild game, with a big writing-table at either end, stiff, old-fashioned engravings; heavy hangings and deep upholstery.

When one of the Japanese boys brought the cocktails, Fred turned from the fine specimen of peccoray he had been examining and said, "A man is an owl to live in such a place alone, Archie. Why don't you marry? As for me, just because I can't marry, I find the world full of charming, unattached women, any one of whom I could fit up a house for with alacrity."

"You're more knowing than I." Archie spoke politely. "I'm not very wide awake about women. I'd be likely to pick out one of the uncomfortable ones—and there are a few of them, you know." He drank his cocktail and rubbed his hands together in a friendly way. "My friends here have charming wives, and they don't give me a chance to get lonely. They are very kind to me, and I have a great many pleasant friendships."

Fred put down his glass. "Yes, I've always noticed that women have confidence in you. You have the doctor's way of getting next. And you enjoy that kind of thing?"

"The friendship of attractive women? Oh, dear, yes! I depend upon it a great deal."

The butler announced dinner, and the two men went downstairs to the dining-room. Dr. Archie's dinners were always good and well served, and his wines were excellent.

"I saw the Fuel and Iron people to-day," Ottenburg said, looking up from his soup. "Their heart is in the right place. I can't see why in the mischief you ever got mixed up with that reform gang, Archie. You've got nothing to reform out here. The situation has always been as simple as two and two in Colorado; mostly a matter of a friendly understanding."

"Well,"—Archie spoke tolerantly,—"some of the young fellows

seemed to have red-hot convictions, and I thought it was better to let them try their ideas out."

Ottenburg shrugged his shoulders. "A few dull young men who haven't ability enough to play the old game the old way, so they want to put on a new game which doesn't take so much brains and gives away more advertising: that's what your anti-saloon league and vice commission amounts to. They provide notoriety for the fellows who can't distinguish themselves at running a business or practicing law or developing an industry. Here you have a mediocre lawyer with no brains and no practice, trying to get a look-in on something. He comes up with the novel proposition that the prostitute has a hard time of it, puts his picture in the paper, and the first thing you know, he's a celebrity. He gets the rake-off and she's just where she was before. How could you fall for a mouse-trap like Pink Alden, Archie?"

Dr. Archie laughed as he began to carve. "Pink seems to get under your skin. He's not worth talking about. He's gone his limit. People won't read about his blameless life any more. I knew those interviews he gave out would cook him. They were a last resort. I could have stopped him, but by that time I'd come to the conclusion. that I'd let the reformers down. I'm not against a general shaking-up, but the trouble with Pinky's crowd is they never get beyond a general writing-up. We gave them a chance to do something, and they just kept on writing about each other and what temptations they had overcome."

While Archie and his friend were busy with Colorado politics, the impeccable Japanese attended swiftly and intelligently to his duties, and the dinner, as Ottenburg at last remarked, was worthy of more profitable conversation.

"So it is," the doctor admitted. "Well, we'll go upstairs for our coffee and cut this out. Bring up some cognac and arak, Tai," he added as he rose from the table.

They stopped to examine a moose's head on the stairway, and when they reached the library the pine logs in the fireplace had been lighted, and the coffee was bubbling before the hearth. Tai placed two chairs before the fire and brought a tray of cigarettes.

"Bring the cigars in my lower desk drawer, boy," the doctor

directed. "Too much light in here, isn't there, Fred? Light the lamp there on my desk, Tai." He turned off the electric glare and settled himself deep into the chair opposite Ottenburg's.

"To go back to our conversation, doctor," Fred began while he waited for the first steam to blow off his coffee; "why don't you make up your mind to go to Washington? There'd be no fight made against you. I needn't say the United Breweries would back you. There'd be some *kudos* coming to us, too; backing a reform candidate."

Dr. Archie measured his length in his chair and thrust his large boots toward the crackling pitch-pine. He drank his coffee and lit a big black cigar while his guest looked over the assortment of cigarettes on the tray. "You say why don't I," the doctor spoke with the deliberation of a man in the position of having several courses to choose from, "but, on the other hand, why should I?" He puffed away and seemed, through his half-closed eyes, to look down several long roads with the intention of luxuriously rejecting all of them and remaining where he was. "I'm sick of politics. I'm disillusioned about serving my crowd, and I don't particularly want to serve yours. Nothing in it that I particularly want; and a man's not effective in politics unless he wants something for himself, and wants it hard. I can reach my ends by straighter roads. There are plenty of things to keep me busy. We haven't begun to develop our resources in this State; we haven't had a look in on them yet. That's the only thing that isn't fake—making men and machines go, and actually turning out a product."

The doctor poured himself some white cordial and looked over the little glass into the fire with an expression which led Ottenburg to believe that he was getting at something in his own mind. Fred lit a cigarette and let his friend grope for his idea.

"My boys, here," Archie went on, "have got me rather interested in Japan. Think I'll go out there in the spring, and come back the other way, through Siberia. I've always wanted to go to Russia." His eyes still hunted for something in his big fireplace. With a slow turn of his head he brought them back to his guest and fixed them upon him. "Just now, I'm thinking of running on to New York for a few weeks," he ended abruptly.

Ottenburg lifted his chin. "Ah!" he exclaimed, as if he began to see Archie's drift. "Shall you see Thea?"

"Yes." The doctor replenished his cordial glass. "In fact, I suspect I am going exactly *to* see her. I'm getting stale on things here, Fred. Best people in the world and always doing things for me. I'm fond of them, too, but I've been with them too much. I'm getting ill-tempered, and the first thing I know I'll be hurting people's feelings. I snapped Mrs. Dandridge up over the telephone this afternoon when she asked me to go out to Colorado Springs on Sunday to meet some English people who are staying at the Antlers. Very nice of her to want me, and I was as sour as if she'd been trying to work me for something. I've got to get out for a while, to save my reputation."

To this explanation Ottenburg had not paid much attention. He seemed to be looking at a fixed point: the yellow glass eyes of a fine wildcat over one of the bookcases. "You've never heard her at all, have you?" he asked reflectively. "Curious, when this is her second season in New York."

"I was going on last March. Had everything arranged. And then old Cap Harris thought he could drive his car and me through a lamp-post and I was laid up with a compound fracture for two months. So I didn't get to see Thea."

Ottenburg studied the red end of his cigarette attentively. "She might have come out to see you. I remember you covered the distance like a streak when she wanted you."

Archie moved uneasily. "Oh, she couldn't do that. She had to get back to Vienna to work on some new parts for this year. She sailed two days after the New York season closed."

"Well, then she couldn't, of course." Fred smoked his cigarette close and tossed the end into the fire. "I'm tremendously glad you're going now. If you're stale, she'll jack you up. That's one of her specialties. She got a rise out of me last December that lasted me all winter."

"Of course," the doctor apologized, "you know so much more about such things. I'm afraid it will be rather wasted on me. I'm no judge of music."

"Never mind that." The younger man pulled himself up in his

chair. "She gets it across to people who aren't judges. That's just what she does." He relapsed into his former lassitude. "If you were stone deaf, it wouldn't all be wasted. It's a great deal to watch her. Incidentally, you know, she is very beautiful. Photographs give you no idea."

Dr. Archie clasped his large hands under his chin. "Oh, I'm counting on that. I don't suppose her voice will sound natural to me. Probably I wouldn't know it."

Ottenburg smiled. "You'll know it, if you ever knew it. It's the same voice, only more so. You'll know it."

"Did you, in Germany that time, when you wrote me? Seven years ago, now. That must have been at the very beginning."

"Yes, somewhere near the beginning. She sang one of the Rhine daughters."* Fred paused and drew himself up again. "Sure, I knew it from the first note. I'd heard a good many young voices come up out of the Rhine, but, by gracious, I hadn't heard one like that!" He fumbled for another cigarette. "Mahler* was conducting that night. I met him as he was leaving the house and had a word with him. 'Interesting voice you tried out this evening,' I said. He stopped and smiled. 'Miss Kronborg, you mean? Yes, very. She seems to sing for the idea. Unusual in a young singer.' I'd never heard him admit before that a singer could have an idea. She not only had it, but she got it across. The Rhine music, that I'd known since I was a boy, was fresh to me, vocalized for the first time. You realized that she was beginning that long story, adequately, with the end in view. Every phrase she sang was basic. She simply *was* the idea of the Rhine music." Ottenburg rose and stood with his back to the fire. "And at the end, where you don't see the maidens at all, the same thing again: two pretty voices *and* the Rhine voice." Fred snapped his fingers and dropped his hand.

The doctor looked up at him enviously. "You see, all that would be lost on me," he said modestly. "I don't know the dream nor the interpretation thereof. I'm out of it. It's too bad that so few of her old friends can appreciate her."

"Take a try at it," Fred encouraged him. "You'll get in deeper than you can explain to yourself. People with no personal interest do that."

"I suppose," said Archie diffidently, "that college German, gone to seed, wouldn't help me out much. I used to be able to make my German patients understand me."

"Sure it would!" cried Ottenburg heartily. "Don't be above knowing your libretto. That's all very well for musicians, but common mortals like you and me have got to know what she's singing about. Get out your dictionary and go at it as you would at any other proposition. Her diction is beautiful, and if you know the text you'll get a great deal. So long as you're going to hear her, get all that's coming to you. You bet in Germany people know their librettos by heart! You Americans are so afraid of stooping to learn anything."

"I *am* a little ashamed," Archie admitted. "I guess that's the way we mask our general ignorance. However, I'll stoop this time; I'm more ashamed not to be able to follow her. The papers always say she's such a fine actress." He took up the tongs and began to rearrange the logs that had burned through and fallen apart. "I suppose she has changed a great deal?" he asked absently.

"We've all changed, my dear Archie,—she more than most of us. Yes, and no. She's all there, only there's a great deal more of her. I've had only a few words with her in several years. It's better not, when I'm tied up this way. The laws are barbarous, Archie."

"Your wife is—still the same?" the doctor asked sympathetically.

"Absolutely. Hasn't been out of a sanitarium for seven years now. No prospect of her ever being out, and as long as she's there I'm tied hand and foot. What does society get out of such a state of things, I'd like to know, except a tangle of irregularities? If you want to reform, there's an opening for you!"

"It's bad, oh, very bad; I agree with you!" Dr. Archie shook his head. "But there would be complications under another system, too. The whole question of a young man's marrying has looked pretty grave to me for a long while. How have they the courage to keep on doing it? It depresses me now to buy wedding presents." For some time the doctor watched his guest, who was sunk in bitter reflections. "Such things used to go better than they do now, I believe. Seems to me all the married people I knew when I was a boy were happy enough." He paused again and bit the end off a fresh cigar. "You never saw Thea's mother, did you, Ottenburg? That's a pity. Mrs. Kronborg was a fine woman. I've always been afraid Thea made a mistake, not coming home when Mrs. Kronborg was ill, no matter what it cost her."

Ottenburg moved about restlessly. "She couldn't, Archie, she positively couldn't. I felt you never understood that, but I was in Dresden at the time, and though I wasn't seeing much of her, I could size up the situation for myself. It was by just a lucky chance that she got to sing *Elizabeth** that time at the Dresden Opera, a complication of circumstances. If she'd run away for any reason, she might have waited years for such a chance to come again. She gave a wonderful performance and made a great impression. They offered her certain terms; she had to take them and follow it up then and there. In that game you can't lose a single trick. She was ill herself, but she sang. Her mother was ill, and she sang. No, you mustn't hold that against her, Archie. She did the right thing there." Ottenburg drew out his watch. "Hello! I must be traveling. You hear from her regularly?"

"More or less regularly. She was never much of a letter-writer. She tells me about her engagements and contracts, but I know so little about that business that it doesn't mean much to me beyond the figures, which seem very impressive. We've had a good deal of business correspondence, about putting up a stone to her father and mother, and, lately, about her youngest brother, Thor. He is with me now; he drives my car. To-day he's up at the mine."

Ottenburg, who had picked up his overcoat, dropped it. "Drives your car?" he asked incredulously.

"Yes. Thea and I have had a good deal of bother about Thor. We tried a business college, and an engineering school, but it was no good. Thor was born a chauffeur before there were cars to drive. He was never good for anything else; lay around home and collected postage stamps and took bicycles to pieces, waiting for the automobile to be invented. He's just as much a part of a car as the steering-gear. I can't find out whether he likes his job with me or not, or whether he feels any curiosity about his sister. You can't find anything out from a Kronborg nowadays. The mother was different."

Fred plunged into his coat. "Well, it's a queer world, Archie. But you'll think better of it, if you go to New York. Wish I were going with you. I'll drop in on you in the morning at about eleven. I want a word with you about this Interstate Commerce Bill. Good-night."

Dr. Archie saw his guest to the motor which was waiting below, and then went back to his library, where he replenished the fire and sat down for a long smoke. A man of Archie's modest and rather credulous nature develops late, and makes his largest gain between forty and fifty. At thirty, indeed, as we have seen, Archie was a soft-hearted boy under a manly exterior, still whistling to keep up his courage. Prosperity and large responsibilities—above all, getting free of poor Mrs. Archie—had brought out a good deal more than he knew was in him. He was thinking tonight as he sat before the fire, in the comfort he liked so well, that but for lucky chances, and lucky holes in the ground, he would still be a country practitioner, reading his old books by his office lamp. And yet, he was not so fresh and energetic as he ought to be. He was tired of business and of politics. Worse than that, he was tired of the men with whom he had to do and of the women who, as he said, had been kind to him. He felt as if he were still hunting for something, like old Jasper Flight. He knew that this was an unbecoming and ungrateful state of mind, and he reproached himself for it. But he could not help wondering why it was that life, even when it gave so much, after all gave so little. What was it that he had expected and missed? Why was he, more than he was anything else, disappointed?

He fell to looking back over his life and asking himself which years of it he would like to live over again,—just as they had been,—and they were not many. His college years he would live again, gladly. After them there was nothing he would care to repeat until he came to Thea Kronborg. There had been some-thing stirring about those years in Moonstone, when he was a restless young man on the verge of breaking into larger enterprises, and when she was a restless child on the verge of growing up into something unknown. He realized now that she had counted for a great deal more to him than he knew at the time. It was a continuous sort of relationship. He was always on the lookout for her as he went about the town, always vaguely expecting her as he sat in his office at night. He had never asked himself then if it was strange that he should find a child of twelve the most interesting and companionable person in Moonstone. It had seemed a pleasant, natural kind of solicitude. He explained it then by the fact that he had no children of his own. But now, as he looked back at those years, the other interests were faded and inanimate. The thought of them was heavy. But wherever his life had touched Thea Kronborg's, there was still a little warmth left, a little sparkle. Their friendship seemed to run over those discontented years like a leafy pattern; still bright and fresh when the other patterns had faded into the dull background. Their walks and drives and confidences, the night they watched the rabbit in the moon-light,—why were these things stirring to remember? Whenever he thought of them, they were distinctly different from the other memories of his life; always seemed humorous, gay, with a little thrill of anticipation and mystery about them. They came nearer to being tender secrets than any others he possessed. Nearer than anything else they corresponded to what he had hoped to find in the world, and had not found. It came over him now that the unexpected favors of fortune, no matter how dazzling, do not mean very much to us. They may excite or divert us for a time, but when we look back, the only things we cherish are those which in some way met our original want; the desire which formed in us in early youth, undirected, and of its own accord.

III

FOR the first four years after Thea went to Germany things went on as usual with the Kronborg family. Mrs. Kronborg's land in Nebraska increased in value and brought her in a good rental. The family drifted into an easier way of living, half without realizing it, as families will. Then Mr. Kronborg, who had never been ill, died suddenly of cancer of the liver, and after his death Mrs. Kronborg went, as her neighbors said, into a decline. Hearing discouraging reports of her from the physician who had taken over his practice, Dr. Archie went up from Denver to see her. He found her in bed, in the room where he had more than once attended her, a handsome woman of sixty with a body still firm and white, her hair, faded now to a very pale primrose, in two thick braids down her back, her eyes clear and calm. When the doctor arrived, she was sitting up in her bed, knitting. He felt at once how glad she was to see him, but he soon gathered that she had made no determination to get well. She told him, indeed, that she could not very well get along without Mr. Kronborg. The doctor looked at her with astonishment. Was it possible that she could miss the foolish old man so much? He reminded her of her children.

"Yes," she replied; "the children are all very well, but they are not father. We were married young."

The doctor watched her wonderingly as she went on knitting, thinking how much she looked like Thea. The difference was one of degree rather than of kind. The daughter had a compelling enthusiasm, the mother had none. But their framework, their foundation, was very much the same.

In a moment Mrs. Kronborg spoke again. "Have you heard anything from Thea lately?"

During his talk with her, the doctor gathered that what Mrs. Kronborg really wanted was to see her daughter Thea. Lying there day after day, she wanted it calmly and continuously. He told her that, since she felt so, he thought they might ask Thea to come home.

"I've thought a good deal about it," said Mrs. Kronborg slowly. "I hate to interrupt her, now that she's begun to get advancement. I expect she's seen some pretty hard times, though she was never one to complain. Perhaps she'd feel that she would like to come. It would be hard, losing both of us while she's off there."

When Dr. Archie got back to Denver he wrote a long letter to Thea, explaining her mother's condition and how much she wished to see her, and asking Thea to come, if only for a few weeks. Thea had repaid the money she had borrowed from him, and he assured her that if she happened to be short of funds for the journey, she had only to cable him.

A month later he got a frantic sort of reply from Thea. Complications in the opera at Dresden had given her an unhoped-for opportunity to go on in a big part. Before this letter reached the doctor, she would have made her début as *Elizabeth*, in "Tannhauser." She wanted to go to her mother more than she wanted anything else in the world, but, unless she failed,—which she would not,—she absolutely could not leave Dresden for six months. It was not that she chose to stay; she had to stay—or lose everything. The next few months would put her five years ahead, or would put her back so far that it would be of no use to struggle further. As soon as she was free, she would go to Moonstone and take her mother back to Germany with her. Her mother, she was sure, could live for years yet, and she would like German people and German ways, and could be hearing music all the time. Thea said she was writing her mother and begging her to help her one last time; to get strength and to wait for her six months, and then she (Thea) would do everything. Her mother would never have to make an effort again.

Dr. Archie went up to Moonstone at once. He had great confidence in Mrs. Kronborg's power of will, and if Thea's appeal took hold of her enough, he believed she might get better. But when he was shown into the familiar room off the parlor, his heart sank. Mrs. Kronborg was lying serene and fateful on her pillows. On the dresser at the foot of her bed there was a large photograph of Thea in the character in which she was to make her début. Mrs. Kronborg pointed to it.

"Isn't she lovely, doctor? It's nice that she hasn't changed much. I've seen her look like that many a time."

They talked for a while about Thea's good fortune. Mrs. Kronborg had had a cablegram saying, "First performance well received. Great relief." In her letter Thea said; "If you'll only get better, dear mother, there's nothing I can't do. I will make a really great success, if you'll try with me. You shall have everything you want, and we will always be together. I have a little house all picked out where we are to live."

"Bringing up a family is not all it's cracked up to be," said Mrs. Kronborg with a flicker of irony, as she tucked the letter back under her pillow. "The children you don't especially need, you have always with you, like the poor. But the bright ones get away from you. They have their own way to make in the world. Seems like the brighter they are, the farther they go. I used to feel sorry that you had no family, doctor, but maybe you're as well off."

"Thea's plan seems sound to me, Mrs. Kronborg. There's no reason I can see why you shouldn't pull up and live for years yet, under proper care. You'd have the best doctors in the world over there, and it would be wonderful to live with anybody who looks like that." He nodded at the photograph of the young woman who must have been singing "*Dich, theure Halle, grüss' ich wieder*,"* her eyes looking up, her beautiful hands outspread with pleasure.

Mrs. Kronborg laughed quite cheerfully. "Yes, wouldn't it? If father were here, I might rouse myself. But sometimes it's hard to come back. Or if she were in trouble, maybe I could rouse myself."

"But, dear Mrs. Kronborg, she is in trouble," her old friend expostulated. "As she says, she's never needed you as she needs you now. I make my guess that she's never begged anybody to help her before."

Mrs. Kronborg smiled. "Yes, it's pretty of her. But that will pass. When these things happen far away they don't make such a mark; especially if your hands are full and you've duties of your own to think about. My own father died in Nebraska when Gunner was born,—we were living in Iowa then,—and I was sorry, but the baby made it up to me. I was father's favorite, too. That's the way it goes, you see."

The doctor took out Thea's letter to him, and read it over to Mrs. Kronborg. She seemed to listen, and not to listen.

When he finished, she said thoughtfully: "I'd counted on hearing her sing again. But I always took my pleasures as they come. I always enjoyed her singing when she was here about the house.

While she was practicing I often used to leave my work and sit down in a rocker and give myself up to it, the same as if I'd been at an entertainment. I was never one of these housekeepers that let their work drive them to death. And when she had the Mexicans over here, I always took it in. First and last,"—she glanced judicially at the photograph,—"I guess I got about as much out of Thea's voice as anybody will ever get."

"I guess you did!" the doctor assented heartily; "and I got a good deal myself. You remember how she used to sing those Scotch songs for me, and lead us with her head, her hair bobbing?"

"'Flow Gently, Sweet Afton,'—I can hear it now," said Mrs. Kronborg; "and poor father never knew when he sang sharp! He used to say, 'Mother, how do you always know when they make mistakes practicing?'" Mrs. Kronborg chuckled.

Dr. Archie took her hand, still firm like the hand of a young woman. "It was lucky for her that you did know. I always thought she got more from you than from any of her teachers."

"Except Wunsch; he was a real musician," said Mrs. Kronborg respectfully. "I gave her what chance I could, in a crowded house. I kept the other children out of the parlor for her. That was about all I could do. If she wasn't disturbed, she needed no watching. She went after it like a terrier after rats from the first, poor child. She was downright afraid of it. That's why I always encouraged her taking Thor off to outlandish places. When she was out of the house, then she was rid of it."

After they had recalled many pleasant memories together, Mrs. Kronborg said suddenly: "I always understood about her going off without coming to see us that time. Oh, I know! You had to keep your own counsel. You were a good friend to her. I've never forgot that." She patted the doctor's sleeve and went on absently. "There was something she didn't want to tell me, and that's why she didn't come. Something happened when she was with those people in Mexico. I worried for a good while, but I guess she's come out of it all right. She'd had a pretty hard time, scratching along alone like that when she was so young, and my farms in Nebraska were down so low that I couldn't help her none. That's no way to send a girl out. But I guess, whatever there was, she wouldn't be afraid to tell me now." Mrs. Kronborg looked up at the photograph with a smile. "She doesn't look like she was beholding to anybody, does she?"

"She isn't, Mrs. Kronborg. She never has been. That was why she borrowed the money from me."

"Oh, I knew she'd never have sent for you if she'd done anything to shame us. She was always proud." Mrs. Kronborg paused and turned a little on her side. "It's been quite a satisfaction to you and me, doctor, having her voice turn out so fine. The things you hope for don't always turn out like that, by a long sight. As long as old Mrs. Kohler lived, she used always to translate what it said about Thea in the German papers she sent. I could make some of it out myself,—it's not very different from Swedish,—but it pleased the old lady. She left Thea her piece-picture of the burning of Moscow. I've got it put away in moth-balls for her, along with the oboe her grandfather brought from Sweden. I want her to take father's oboe back there some day." Mrs. Kronborg paused a moment and compressed her lips. "But I guess she'll take a finer instrument than that with her, back to Sweden!" she added.

Her tone fairly startled the doctor, it was so vibrating with a fierce, defiant kind of pride he had heard often in Thea's voice. He looked down wonderingly at his old friend and patient. After all, one never knew people to the core. Did she, within her, hide some of that still passion of which her daughter was all-compact?

"That last summer at home wasn't very nice for her," Mrs. Kronborg began as placidly as if the fire had never leaped up in her. "The other children were acting-up because they thought I might make a fuss over her and give her the big-head. We gave her the dare, somehow, the lot of us, because we couldn't understand her changing teachers and all that. That's the trouble about giving the dare to them quiet, unboastful children; you never know how far it'll take 'em. Well, we ought not to complain, doctor; she's given us a good deal to think about."

The next time Dr. Archie came to Moonstone, he came to be a

pall-bearer at Mrs. Kronborg's funeral. When he last looked at her, she was so serene and queenly that he went back to Denver feeling almost as if he had helped to bury Thea Kronborg herself. The handsome head in the coffin seemed to him much more really Thea than did the radiant young woman in the picture, looking about at the Gothic vaultings and greeting the Hall of Song.

IV

ONE bright morning late in February Dr. Archie was breakfasting comfortably at the Waldorf. He had got into Jersey City on an early train, and a red, windy sunrise over the North River had given him a good appetite. He consulted the morning paper while he drank his coffee and saw that "Lohengrin"* was to be sung at the opera that evening. In the list of the artists who would appear was the name "Kronborg." Such abruptness rather startled him. "Kronborg": it was impressive and yet, somehow, disrespectful; somewhat rude and brazen, on the back page of the morning paper. After breakfast he went to the hotel ticket office and asked the girl if she could give him something for "Lohengrin," "near the front." His manner was a trifle awkward and he wondered whether the girl noticed it. Even if she did, of course, she could scarcely suspect. Before the ticket stand he saw a bunch of blue posters announcing the opera casts for the week. There was "Lohengrin," and under it he saw:—

*Elsa von Brabant** . . . Thea Kronborg.

That looked better. The girl gave him a ticket for a seat which she said was excellent. He paid for it and went out to the cab-stand. He mentioned to the driver a number on Riverside Drive and got into a taxi. It would not, of course, be the right thing to call upon Thea when she was going to sing in the evening. He knew that much, thank goodness! Fred Ottenburg had hinted to him that, more than almost anything else, that would put one in wrong.

When he reached the number to which he directed his letters, he dismissed the cab and got out for a walk. The house in which Thea lived was as impersonal as the Waldorf, and quite as large. It was above 116th Street, where the Drive narrows, and in front of it the shelving bank dropped to the North River. As Archie strolled about the paths which traversed this slope, below the street level, the fourteen stories of the apartment hotel rose above him like a perpendicular cliff. He had no idea on which floor Thea lived, but he reflected, as his eye ran over the many windows, that the outlook would be fine from any floor. The forbidding hugeness of the house made him feel as if he had expected to meet Thea in a crowd and had missed her. He did not really believe that she was hidden away behind any of those glittering windows, or that he was to hear her this evening. His walk was curiously uninspiring and unsuggestive. Presently remembering that Ottenburg had encouraged him to study his lesson, he went down to the opera house and bought a libretto. He had even brought his old "Adler's German and English" in his trunk, and after luncheon he settled down in his gilded suite at the Waldorf with a big cigar and the text of "Lohengrin."

The opera was announced for seven-forty-five, but at half-past seven Archie took his seat in the right front of the orchestra circle. He had never been inside the Metropolitan Opera House* before, and the height of the audience room, the rich color, and the sweep of the balconies were not without their effect upon him. He watched the house fill with a growing feeling of expectation. When the steel curtain rose and the men of the orchestra took their places, he felt distinctly nervous. The burst of applause which greeted the conductor keyed him still higher. He found that he had taken off his gloves and twisted them to a string. When the lights went down and the violins began the overture, the place looked larger than ever; a great pit shadowy and solemn. The whole atmosphere, he reflected, was somehow more serious than he had anticipated.

After the curtains were drawn back upon the scene beside the Scheldt, he got readily into the swing of the story. He was so much interested in the bass who sang *King Henry* that he had almost forgotten for what he was waiting so nervously, when the *Herald* began in stentorian tones to summon *Elsa Von Brabant*. Then he began to realize that he was rather frightened. There was a flutter of white at the back of the stage, and women began to come in: two, four, six, eight, but not the right one. It flashed across him that this was something like buck-fever, the paralyzing moment that comes upon a man when his first elk looks at him through the bushes, under its great antlers; the moment when a man's mind is so full of shooting that he forgets the gun in his hand until the buck nods adieu to him from a distant hill.

All at once, before the buck had left him, she was there. Yes, unquestionably it was she. Her eyes were downcast, but the head, the cheeks, the chin—there could be no mistake; she advanced slowly, as if she were walking in her sleep. Some one spoke to her; she only inclined her head. He spoke again, and she bowed her head still lower. Archie had forgotten his libretto, and he had not counted upon these long pauses. He had expected her to appear and sing and reassure him. They seemed to be waiting for her. Did she ever forget? Why in thunder didn't she— She made a sound, a faint one. The people on the stage whispered together and seemed confounded. His nervousness was absurd. She must have done this often before; she knew her bearings. She made another sound, but he could make nothing of it. Then the King sang to her, and Archie began to remember where they were in the story. She came to the front of the stage, lifted her eyes for the first time, clasped her hands and began, "*Einsam in trüben Tagen*".*

Yes, it was exactly like buck-fever. Her face was there, toward the house now, before his eyes, and he positively could not see it. She was singing, at last, and he positively could not hear her. He was conscious of nothing but an uncomfortable dread and a sense of crushing disappointment. He had, after all, missed her. Whatever was there, she was not there—for him.

The King interrupted her. She began again, "*In lichter Waffen Scheine*."* Archie did not know when his buck-fever passed, but presently he found that he was sitting quietly in a darkened house, not listening to but dreaming upon a river of silver sound. He felt apart from the others, drifting alone on the melody, as if he had been alone with it for a long while and had known it all before. His power of attention was not great just then, but in so far as it went he seemed to be looking through an exalted calmness at a beautiful woman from far away, from another sort of life and feeling and understanding than his own, who had in her face something he had known long ago, much brightened and beautified. As a lad he used to believe that the faces of people who died were like that in the next world; the same faces, but shining with the light of a new understanding. No, Ottenburg had not prepared him!

What he felt was admiration and estrangement. The homely reunion, that he had somehow expected, now seemed foolish. Instead of feeling proud that he knew her better than all these people about him, he felt chagrined at his own ingenuousness. For he did not know her better. This woman he had never known; she had somehow devoured his little friend, as the wolf ate up Red Ridinghood. Beautiful, radiant, tender as she was, she chilled his old affection; that sort of feeling was not appropriate. She seemed much, much farther away from him than she had seemed all those years when she was in Germany. The ocean he could cross, but there was something here he could not cross. There was a moment, when she turned to the King and smiled that rare, sunrise smile of her childhood, when he thought she was coming back to him. After the *Herald's* second call for her champion, when she knelt in her impassioned prayer, there was again something familiar, a kind of wild wonder that she had had the power to call up long ago. But she merely reminded him of Thea; this was not the girl herself.

After the tenor came on, the doctor ceased trying to make the woman before him fit into any of his cherished recollections. He took her, in so far as he could, for what she was then and there. When the knight raised the kneeling girl and put his mailed hand on her hair, when she lifted to him a face full of worship and passionate humility, Archie gave up his last reservation. He knew no more about her than did the hundreds around him, who sat in the shadow and looked on, as he looked, some with more understanding, some with less. He knew as much about *Ortrude* or

*Lohengrin** as he knew about *Elsa*—more, because she went further than they, she sustained the legendary beauty of her conception more consistently. Even he could see that. Attitudes, movements, her face, her white arms and fingers, everything was suffused with a rosy tenderness, a warm humility, a gracious and yet—to him—wholly estranging beauty.

During the balcony singing in the second act the doctor's thoughts were as far away from Moonstone as the singer's doubtless were. He had begun, indeed, to feel the exhilaration of getting free from personalities, of being released from his own past as well as from Thea Kronborg's. It was very much, he told himself, like a military funeral, exalting and impersonal. Something old died in one, and out of it something new was born. During the duet with *Ortrude*, and the splendors of the wedding processional, this new feeling grew and grew. At the end of the act there were many curtain calls and *Elsa* acknowledged them, brilliant, gracious, spirited, with her far-breaking smile; but on the whole she was harder and more self-contained before the curtain than she was in the scene behind it. Archie did his part in the applause that greeted her, but it was the new and wonderful he applauded, not the old and dear. His personal, proprietary pride in her was frozen out.

He walked about the house during the *entr'acte*,* and here and there among the people in the foyer he caught the name "Kronborg." On the staircase, in front of the coffee-room, a long-haired youth with a fat face was discoursing to a group of old women about "die Kronborg." Dr. Archie gathered that he had crossed on the boat with her.

After the performance was over, Archie took a taxi and started for Riverside Drive. He meant to see it through to-night. When he entered the reception hall of the hotel before which he had strolled that morning, the hall porter challeged him. He said he was waiting for Miss Kronborg. The porter looked at him suspiciously and asked whether he had an appointment. He answered brazenly that he had. He was not used to being questioned by hall boys. Archie sat first in one tapestry chair and then in another, keeping a sharp eye on the people who came in and went up in the elevators. He walked about and looked at his watch. An hour dragged by. No one had come in from the street now for about twenty minutes, when two women entered, carrying a great many flowers and followed by a tall young man in chauffeur's uniform. Archie advanced toward the taller of the two women, who was veiled and carried her head very firmly. He confronted her just as she reached the elevator. Although he did not stand directly in her way, something in his attitude compelled her to stop. She gave him a piercing, defiant glance through the white scarf that covered her face. Then she lifted her hand and brushed the scarf back from her head. There was still black on her brows and lashes. She was very pale and her face was drawn and deeply lined. She looked, the doctor told himself with a sinking heart, forty years old. Her suspicious, mystified stare cleared slowly.

"Pardon me," the doctor murmured, not knowing just how to address her here before the porters, "I came up from the opera. I merely wanted to say good-night to you."

Without speaking, still looking incredulous, she pushed him into the elevator. She kept her hand on his arm while the cage shot up, and she looked away from him, frowning, as if she were trying to remember or realize something. When the cage stopped, she pushed him out of the elevator through another door, which a maid opened, into a square hall. There she sank down on a chair and looked up at him.

"Why didn't you let me know?" she asked in a hoarse voice.

Archie heard himself laughing the old, embarrassed laugh that seldom happened to him now. "Oh, I wanted to take my chance with you, like anybody else. It's been so long, now!"

She took his hand through her thick glove and her head dropped forward. "Yes, it has been long," she said in the husky voice, "and so much has happened."

"And you are so tired, and I am a clumsy old fellow to break in on you to-night," the doctor added sympathetically. "Forgive me, this time." He bent over and put his hand soothingly on her shoulder. He felt a strong shudder run through her from head to foot.

Still bundled in her fur coat as she was, she threw both arms about him and hugged him. "Oh, Dr. Archie, *Dr. Archie*,"—she shook him,—"don't let me go. Hold on, now you're here," she laughed, breaking away from him at the same moment and sliding out of her fur coat. She left it for the maid to pick up and pushed the doctor into the sitting-room, where she turned on the lights. "Let me *look* at you. Yes; hands, feet, head, shoulders—just the same. You've grown no older. You can't say as much for me, can you?"

She was standing in the middle of the room, in a white silk shirtwaist and a short black velvet skirt, which somehow suggested that they had "cut off her petticoats all round about." She looked distinctly clipped and plucked. Her hair was parted in the middle and done very close to her head, as she had worn it under the wig. She looked like a fugitive, who had escaped from something in clothes caught up at hazard. It flashed across Dr. Archie that she was running away from the other woman down at the opera house, who had used her hardly.

He took a step toward her. "I can't tell a thing in the world about you, Thea—if I may still call you that."

She took hold of the collar of his overcoat. "Yes, call me that. Do: I like to hear it. You frighten me a little, but I expect I frighten you more. I'm always a scarecrow after I sing a long part like that—so high, too." She absently pulled out the handkerchief that protruded from his breast pocket and began to wipe the black paint off her eyebrows and lashes. "I can't take you in much to-night, but I must see you for a little while." She pushed him to a chair. "I shall be more recognizable to-morrow. You mustn't think of me as you see me to-night. Come at four to-morrow afternoon and have tea with me. Can you? That's good."

She sat down in a low chair beside him and leaned forward, drawing her shoulders together. She seemed to him inappropriately young and inappropriately old, shorn of her long tresses at one end and of her long robes at the other.

"How do you happen to be here?" she asked abruptly. "How can you leave a silver mine? I couldn't! Sure nobody'll cheat you? But you can explain everything to-morrow." She paused. "You remember how you sewed me up in a poultice, once? I wish you could to-night. I need a poultice, from top to toe. Something very disagreeable happened down there. You said you were out front? Oh, don't say anything about it. I always know exactly how it goes, unfortunately. I was rotten in the balcony. I never get that. You didn't notice it? Probably not, but I did."

Here the maid appeared at the door and her mistress rose. "My supper? Very well, I'll come. I'd ask you to stay, doctor, but there wouldn't be enough for two. They seldom send up enough for one,"—she spoke bitterly. "I haven't got a sense of you yet,"—turning directly to Archie again. "You haven't been here. You've only announced yourself, and told me you are coming to-morrow. You haven't seen me, either. This is not I. But I'll be here waiting for you to-morrow, my whole works! Good-night, till then." She patted him absently on the sleeve and gave him a little shove toward the door.

V

WHEN Archie got back to his hotel at two o'clock in the morning, he found Fred Ottenburg's card under his door, with a message scribbled across the top: "When you come in, please call up room 811, this hotel." A moment later Fred's voice reached him over the telephone.

"That you, Archie? Won't you come up? I'm having some supper and I'd like company. Late? What does that matter? I won't keep you long."

Archie dropped his overcoat and set out for room 811. He found Ottenburg in the act of touching a match to a chafing-dish, at a table laid for two in his sitting-room. "I'm catering here," he announced cheerfully. "I let the waiter off at midnight, after he'd set me up. You'll have to account for yourself, Archie."

The doctor laughed, pointing to three wine-coolers under the table. "Are you expecting guests?"

"Yes, two." Ottenburg held up two fingers,—"you, and my higher self. He's a thirsty boy, and I don't invite him often. He has been known to give me a headache. Now, where have you been, Archie, until this shocking hour?"

"Bah, you've been banting!" the doctor exclaimed, pulling out his white gloves as he searched for his handkerchief and throwing them into a chair. Ottenburg was in evening clothes and very pointed dress shoes. His white waistcoat, upon which the doctor had fixed a challenging eye, went down straight from the top button, and he wore a camelia. He was conspicuously brushed and trimmed and polished. His smoothly controlled excitement was wholly different from his usual easy cordiality, though he had his face, as well as his figure, well in hand. On the serving-table there was an empty champagne pint and a glass. He had been having a little starter, the doctor told himself, and would probably be running on high gear before he got through. There was even now an air of speed about him.

"Been, Freddy?"—the doctor at last took up his question. "I expect I've been exactly where you have. Why didn't you tell me you were coming on?"

"I wasn't, Archie." Fred lifted the cover of the chafing-dish and stirred the contents. He stood behind the table, holding the lid with his handkerchief. "I had never thought of such a thing. But Landry, a young chap who plays her accompaniments and who keeps an eye out for me, telegraphed me that Madame Rheinecker had gone to Atlantic City with a bad throat, and Thea might have a chance to sing *Elsa*. She has sung it only twice here before, and I missed it in Dresden. So I came on. I got in at four this afternoon and saw you registered, but I thought I wouldn't butt in. How lucky you got here just when she was coming on for this. You couldn't have hit a better time." Ottenburg stirred the contents of the dish faster and put in more sherry. "And where have you been since twelve o'clock, may I ask?"

Archie looked rather self-conscious, as he sat down on a fragile gilt chair that rocked under him, and stretched out his long legs. "Well, if you'll believe me, I had the brutality to go to see her. I wanted to identify her. Couldn't wait."

Ottenburg placed the cover quickly on the chafing-dish and took a step backward. "You did, old sport? My word! None but

the brave deserve the fair. Well,"—he stooped to turn the wine,—
"and how was she?"

"She seemed rather dazed, and pretty well used up. She
seemed disappointed in herself, and said she hadn't done herself
justice in the balcony scene."

"Well, if she didn't, she's not the first. Beastly stuff to sing right
in there; lies just on the 'break' in the voice." Fred pulled a bottle
out of the ice and drew the cork. Lifting his glass he looked
meaningly at Archie. "You know who, doctor. Here goes!" He
drank off his glass with a sigh of satisfaction. After he had turned
the lamp low under the chafing-dish, he remained standing, looking pensively down at the food on the table. "Well, she rather
pulled it off! As a backer, you're a winner, Archie. I congratulate
you." Fred poured himself another glass. "Now you must eat
something, and so must I. Here, get off that bird cage and find a
steady chair. This stuff ought to be rather good; head waiter's
suggestion. Smells all right." He bent over the chafing-dish and
began to serve the contents. "Perfectly innocuous: mushrooms
and truffles and a little crab-meat. And now, on the level, Archie,
how did it hit you?"

Archie turned a frank smile to his friend and shook his head.
"It was all miles beyond me, of course, but it gave me a pulse.
The general excitement got hold of me, I suppose. I like your
wine, Freddy." He put down his glass. "It goes to the spot to-
night. She *was* all right, then? You weren't disappointed?"

"Disappointed? My dear Archie, that's the high voice we
dream of; so pure and yet so virile and human. That combination
hardly ever happens with sopranos." Ottenburg sat down and
turned to the doctor, speaking calmly and trying to dispel his
friend's manifest bewilderment. "You see, Archie, there's the
voice itself, so beautiful and individual, and then there's something else; the thing in it which responds to every shade of
thought and feeling, spontaneously, almost unconsciously. That
color has to be born in a singer, it can't be acquired; lots of
beautiful voices haven't a vestige of it. It's almost like another
gift—the rarest of all. The voice simply is the mind and is the
heart. It can't go wrong in interpretation, because it has in it the

thing that makes all interpretation. That's why you feel so sure of her. After you've listened to her for an hour or so, you aren't afraid of anything. All the little dreads you have with other artists vanish. You lean back and you say to yourself, 'No, *that* voice will never betray.' *Treulich geführt, treulich bewacht.*"*

Archie looked envyingly at Fred's excited, triumphant face. How satisfactory it must be, he thought, to really know what she was doing and not to have to take it on hearsay. He took up his glass with a sigh. "I seem to need a good deal of cooling off to-night. I'd just as lief forget the Reform Party for once.

"Yes, Fred," he went on seriously; "I thought it sounded very beautiful, and I thought she was very beautiful, too. I never imagined she could be as beautiful as that."

"Wasn't she? Every attitude a picture, and always the right kind of picture, full of that legendary, supernatural thing she gets into it. I never heard the prayer sung like that before. That look that came in her eyes; it went right out through the back of the roof. Of course, you get an *Elsa* who can look through walls like that, and visions and Grail-knights happen naturally. She becomes an abbess, that girl, after *Lohengrin* leaves her. She's made to live with ideas and enthusiasms, not with a husband." Fred folded his arms, leaned back in his chair, and began to sing softly:—

> "*In lichter Waffen Scheine,*
> *Ein Ritter nahte da.*"*

"Doesn't she die, then, at the end?" the doctor asked guardedly.

Fred smiled, reaching under the table. "Some *Elsas* do; she didn't. She left me with the distinct impression that she was just beginning. Now, doctor, here's a cold one." He twirled a napkin smoothly about the green glass, the cork gave and slipped out with a soft explosion. "And now we must have another toast. It's up to you, this time."

The doctor watched the agitation in his glass. "The same," he said without lifting his eyes. "That's good enough. I can't raise you."

Fred leaned forward, and looked sharply into his face. "That's the point; how *could* you raise me? Once again!"

"Once again, and always the same!" The doctor put down his glass. "This doesn't seem to produce any symptoms in me to-night." He lit a cigar. "Seriously, Freddy, I wish I knew more about what she's driving at. It makes me jealous, when you are so in it and I'm not."

"In it?" Fred started up. "My God, haven't you seen her this blessed night?—when she'd have kicked any other man down the elevator shaft, if I know her. Leave me something; at least what I can pay my five bucks for."

"Seems to me you get a good deal for your five bucks," said Archie ruefully. "And that, after all, is what she cares about,—what people get."

Fred lit a cigarette, took a puff or two, and then threw it away. He was lounging back in his chair, and his face was pale and drawn hard by that mood of intense concentration which lurks under the sunny shallows of the vineyard. In his voice there was a longer perspective than usual, a slight remoteness. "You see, Archie, it's all very simple, a natural development. It's exactly what Mahler said back there in the beginning, when she sang *Woglinde*.* It's the idea, the basic idea, pulsing behind every bar she sings. She simplifies a character down to the musical idea it's built on, and makes everything conform to that. The people who chatter about her being a great actress don't seem to get the notion of where *she* gets the notion. It all goes back to her original endowment, her tremendous musical talent. Instead of inventing a lot of business and expedients to suggest character, she knows the thing at the root, and lets the musical pattern take care of her. The score pours her into all those lovely postures, makes the light and shadow go over her face, lifts her and drops her. She lies on it, the way she used to lie on the Rhine music. Talk about rhythm!"

The doctor frowned dubiously as a third bottle made its appearance above the cloth. "Aren't you going in rather strong?"

Fred laughed. "No, I'm becoming too sober. You see this is breakfast now; kind of wedding breakfast. I feel rather wedding-ish. I don't mind. You know," he went on as the wine gurgled out,

"I was thinking to-night when they sprung the wedding music, how any fool can have that stuff played over him when he walks up the aisle with some dough-faced little hussy who's hooked him. But it isn't every fellow who can see—well, what we saw tonight. There are compensations in life, Dr. Howard Archie, though they come in disguise. Did you notice her when she came down the stairs? Wonder where she gets that bright-and-morning star look? Carries to the last row of the family circle. I moved about all over the house. I'll tell you a secret, Archie: that carrying power was one of the first things that put me wise. Noticed it down there in Arizona, in the open. That, I said, belongs only to the big ones." Fred got up and began to move rhythmically about the room, his hands in his pockets. The doctor was astonished at his ease and steadiness, for there were slight lapses in his speech. "You see, Archie, *Elsa* isn't a part that's particularly suited to Thea's voice at all, as I see her voice. It's over-lyrical for her. She makes it, but there's nothing in it that fits her like a glove, except, maybe, that long duet in the third act. There, of course,"—he held out his hands as if he were measuring something,—"we know exactly where we are. But wait until they give her a chance at something that lies properly in her voice, and you'll see me rosier than I am to-night."

Archie smoothed the tablecloth with his hand. "I am sure I don't want to see you any rosier, Fred."

Ottenburg threw back his head and laughed. "It's enthusiasm, doctor. It's not the wine. I've got as much inflated as this for a dozen trashy things: brewers' dinners and political orgies. You, too, have your extravagances, Archie. And what I like best in you is this particular enthusiasm, which is not at all practical or sensible, which is downright Quixotic. You are not altogether what you seem, and you have your reservations. Living among the wolves, you have not become one. *Lupibus vivendi non lupus sum.*"*

The doctor seemed embarrassed. "I was just thinking how tired she looked, plucked of all her fine feathers, while we get all the fun. Instead of sitting here carousing, we ought to go solemnly to bed."

"I get your idea." Ottenburg crossed to the window and threw it open. "Fine night outside; a hag of a moon just setting. It begins to smell like morning. After all, Archie, think of the lonely and rather solemn hours we've spent waiting for all this, while she's been—reveling."

Archie lifted his brows. "I somehow didn't get the idea tonight that she revels much."

"I don't mean this sort of thing." Fred turned toward the light and stood with his back to the window. "That," with a nod toward the wine-cooler, "is only a cheap imitation, that any poor stiff-fingered fool can buy and feel his shell grow thinner. But take it from me, no matter what she pays, or how much she may see fit to lie about it, the real, the master revel is hers." He leaned back against the window sill and crossed his arms. "Anybody with all that voice and all that talent and all that beauty, has her hour. Her hour," he went on deliberately, "when she can say 'there it is, at last, *wie im Traum ich*—

> "'As in my dream I dreamed it,
> As in my will it was.'"

He stood silent a moment, twisting the flower from his coat by the stem and staring at the blank wall with haggard abstraction. "Even I can say to-night, Archie," he brought out slowly,

> "'As in my dream I dreamed it,
> As in my will it was.'

Now, doctor, you may leave me. I'm beautifully drunk, but not with anything that ever grew in France."

The doctor rose. Fred tossed his flower out of the window behind him and came toward the door. "I say," he called, "have you a date with anybody?"

The doctor paused, his hand on the knob. "With Thea, you mean? Yes. I'm to go to her at four this afternoon—if you haven't paralyzed me."

"Well, you won't eat me, will you, if I break in and send up my card? She'll probably turn me down cold, but that won't hurt my feelings. If she ducks me, you tell her for me, that to spite me now she'd have to cut off more than she can spare. Good-night, Archie."

VI

IT was late on the morning after the night she sang *Elsa*, when Thea Kronborg stirred uneasily in her bed. The room was darkened by two sets of window shades, and the day outside was thick and cloudy. She turned and tried to recapture unconsciousness, knowing that she would not be able to do so. She dreaded waking stale and disappointed after a great effort. The first thing that came was always the sense of the futility of such endeavor, and of the absurdity of trying too hard. Up to a certain point, say eighty degrees, artistic endeavor could be fat and comfortable, methodical and prudent. But if you went further than that, if you drew yourself up toward ninety degrees, you parted with your defenses and left yourself exposed to mischance. The legend was that in those upper reaches you might be divine; but you were much likelier to be ridiculous. Your public wanted just about eighty degrees; if you gave it more it blew its nose and put a crimp in you. In the morning, especially, it seemed to her very probable that whatever struggled above the good average was not quite sound. Certainly very little of that superfluous ardor, which cost so dear, ever got across the footlights. These misgivings waited to pounce upon her when she wakened. They hovered about her bed like vultures.

She reached under her pillow for her handkerchief, without opening her eyes. She had a shadowy memory that there was to be something unusual, that this day held more disquieting possibilities than days commonly held. There was something she dreaded; what was it? Oh, yes, Dr. Archie was to come at four.

A reality like Dr. Archie, poking up out of the past, reminded one of disappointments and losses, of a freedom that was no more: reminded her of blue, golden mornings long ago, when she used to waken with a burst of joy at recovering her precious self and her precious world; when she never lay on her pillows at eleven o'clock like something the waves had washed up. After all, why had he come? It had been so long, and so much had happened. The things she had lost, he would miss readily enough.

What she had gained, he would scarcely perceive. He, and all that he recalled, lived for her as memories. In sleep, and in hours of illness or exhaustion, she went back to them and held them to her heart. But they were better as memories. They had nothing to do with the struggle that made up her actual life. She felt drearily that she was not flexible enough to be the person her old friend expected her to be, the person she herself wished to be with him.

Thea reached for the bell and rang twice,—a signal to her maid to order her breakfast. She rose and ran up the window shades and turned on the water in her bathroom, glancing into the mirror apprehensively as she passed it. Her bath usually cheered her, even on low mornings like this. Her white bathroom, almost as large as her sleeping-room, she regarded as a refuge. When she turned the key behind her, she left care and vexation on the other side of the door. Neither her maid nor the management nor her letters nor her accompanist could get at her now.

When she pinned her braids about her head, dropped her nightgown and stepped out to begin her Swedish movements, she was a natural creature again, and it was so that she liked herself best. She slid into the tub with anticipation and splashed and tumbled about a good deal. Whatever else she hurried, she never hurried her bath. She used her brushes and sponges and soaps like toys, fairly playing in the water. Her own body was always a cheering sight to her. When she was careworn, when her mind felt old and tired, the freshness of her physical self, her long, firm lines, the smoothness of her skin, reassured her. This morning, because of awakened memories, she looked at herself more carefully than usual, and was not discouraged. While she was in the tub she began to whistle softly the tenor aria, "*Ah! Fuyez, douce image*,"* somehow appropriate to the bath. After a noisy moment under the cold shower, she stepped out on the rug flushed and glowing, threw her arms above her head, and rose on her toes, keeping the elevation as long as she could. When she dropped back on her heels and began to rub herself with the towels, she took up the aria again, and felt quite in the humor for seeing Dr. Archie. After she had returned to her bed, the maid brought her letters and the morning papers with her breakfast.

"Telephone Mr. Landry and ask him if he can come at half-past three, Theresa, and order tea to be brought up at five."

When Howard Archie was admitted to Thea's apartment that afternoon, he was shown into the music-room back of the little reception room. Thea was sitting in a davenport behind the piano, talking to a young man whom she later introduced as her friend Mr. Landry. As she rose, and came to meet him, Archie felt a deep relief, a sudden thankfulness. She no longer looked clipped and plucked, or dazed and fleeing.

Dr. Archie neglected to take account of the young man to whom he was presented. He kept Thea's hands and held her where he met her, taking in the light, lively sweep of her hair, her clear green eyes and her throat that came up strong and dazzlingly white from her green velvet gown. The chin was as lovely as ever, the cheeks as smooth. All the lines of last night had disappeared. Only at the outer corners of her eyes, between the eye and the temple, were the faintest indications of a future attack —mere kitten scratches that playfully hinted where one day the cat would claw her. He studied her without any embarrassment. Last night everything had been awkward; but now, as he held her hands, a kind of harmony came between them, a reëstablishment of confidence.

"After all, Thea,—in spite of all, I still know you," he murmured.

She took his arm and led him up to the young man who was standing beside the piano. "Mr. Landry knows all about you, Dr. Archie. He has known about you for many years." While the two men shook hands she stood between them, drawing them together by her presence and her glances. "When I first went to Germany, Landry was studying there. He used to be good enough to work with me when I could not afford to have an accompanist for more than two hours a day. We got into the way of working together. He is a singer, too, and has his own career to look after, but he still manages to give me some time. I want you to be friends." She smiled from one to the other.

The rooms, Archie noticed, full of last night's flowers, were furnished in light colors, the hotel bleakness of them a little softened by a magnificent Steinway piano, white bookshelves full of books and scores, some drawings of ballet dancers, and the very deep sofa behind the piano.

"Of course," Archie asked apologetically, "you have seen the papers?"

"Very cordial, aren't they? They evidently did not expect as much as I did. *Elsa* is not really in my voice. I can sing the music, but I have to go after it."

"That is exactly," the doctor came out boldly, "what Fred Ottenburg said this morning."

They had remained standing, the three of them, by the piano, where the gray afternoon light was strongest. Thea turned to the doctor with interest. "Is Fred in town? They were from him, then — some flowers that came last night without a card." She indicated the white lilacs on the window sill. "Yes, he would know, certainly," she said thoughtfully. "Why don't we sit down? There will be some tea for you in a minute, Landry. He's very dependent upon it," disapprovingly to Archie. "Now tell me, Doctor, did you really have a good time last night, or were you uncomfortable? Did you feel as if I were trying to hold my hat on by my eyebrows?"

He smiled. "I had all kinds of a time. But I had no feeling of that sort. I couldn't be quite sure that it was you at all. That was why I came up here last night. I felt as if I'd lost you."

She leaned toward him and brushed his sleeve reassuringly. "Then I didn't give you an impression of painful struggle? Landry was singing at Weber and Fields'* last night. He didn't get in until the performance was half over. But I see the *Tribune* man felt that I was working pretty hard. Did you see that notice, Oliver?"

Dr. Archie looked closely at the red-headed young man for the first time, and met his lively brown eyes, full of a droll, confiding sort of humor. Mr. Landry was not prepossessing. He was under-sized and clumsily made, with a red, shiny face and a sharp little nose that looked as if it had been whittled out of wood and was always in the air, on the scent of something. Yet it was this queer little beak, with his eyes, that made his countenance anything of a face at all. From a distance he looked like the grocery-man's delivery boy in a small town. His dress seemed an acknow-ledgment of his grotesqueness: a short coat, like a little boys' roundabout, and a vest fantastically sprigged and dotted, over a lavender shirt.

At the sound of a muffled buzz, Mr. Landry sprang up. "May I answer the telephone for you?" He went to the writing-table and took up the receiver. "Mr. Ottenburg is downstairs," he said, turning to Thea and holding the mouthpiece against his coat.

"Tell him to come up," she replied without hesitation. "How long are you going to be in town, Dr. Archie?"

"Oh, several weeks, if you'll let me stay. I won't hang around and be a burden to you, but I want to try to get educated up to you, though I expect it's late to begin."

Thea rose and touched him lightly on the shoulder. "Well, you'll never be any younger, will you?"

"I'm not so sure about that," the doctor replied gallantly.

The maid appeared at the door and announced Mr. Frederick Ottenburg. Fred came in, very much got up, the doctor reflected, as he watched him bending over Thea's hand. He was still pale and looked somewhat chastened, and the lock of hair that hung down over his forehead was distinctly moist. But his black after-noon coat, his gray tie and gaiters were of a correctness that Dr. Archie could never attain for all the efforts of his faithful slave, Van Deusen, the Denver haberdasher. To be properly up to those tricks, the doctor supposed, you had to learn them young. If he were to buy a silk hat that was the twin of Ottenburg's, it would be shaggy in a week, and he could never carry it as Fred held his.

Ottenburg had greeted Thea in German, and as she replied in the same language, Archie joined Mr. Landry at the window. "You know Mr. Ottenburg, he tells me?"

Mr. Landry's eyes twinkled. "Yes, I regularly follow him about, when he's in town. I would, even if he didn't send me such wonderful Christmas presents: Russian vodka by the half-dozen!"

Thea called to them, "Come, Mr. Ottenburg is calling on all of us. Here's the tea."

The maid opened the door and two waiters from downstairs appeared with covered trays. The tea-table was in the parlor. Thea drew Ottenburg with her and went to inspect it. "Where's the rum? Oh, yes, in that thing! Everything seems to be here, but send up some currant preserves and cream cheese for Mr. Ottenburg. And in about fifteen minutes, bring some fresh toast. That's all, thank you."

For the next few minutes there was a clatter of teacups and responses about sugar. "Landry always takes rum. I'm glad the rest of you don't. I'm sure it's bad." Thea poured the tea standing and got through with it as quickly as possible, as if it were a refreshment snatched between trains. The tea-table and the little room in which it stood seemed to be out of scale with her long step, her long reach, and the energy of her movements. Dr. Archie, standing near her, was pleasantly aware of the animation of her figure. Under the clinging velvet, her body seemed independent and unsubdued.

They drifted, with their plates and cups, back to the music-room. When Thea followed them, Ottenburg put down his tea suddenly. "Aren't you taking anything? Please let me." He started back to the table.

"No, thank you, nothing. I'm going to run over that aria for you presently, to convince you that I can do it. How did the duet go, with Schlag?"

She was standing in the doorway and Fred came up to her: "That you'll never do any better. You've worked your voice into it perfectly. Every *nuance*—wonderful!"

"Think so?" She gave him a sidelong glance and spoke with a certain gruff shyness which did not deceive anybody, and was not meant to deceive. The tone was equivalent to "Keep it up. I like it, but I'm awkward with it."

Fred held her by the door and did keep it up, furiously, for full five minutes. She took it with some confusion, seeming all the while to be hesitating, to be arrested in her course and trying to pass him. But she did not really try to pass, and her color deepened. Fred spoke in German, and Archie caught from her an occasional *Ja? So?* muttered rather than spoken.

When they rejoined Landry and Dr. Archie, Fred took up his tea again. "I see you're singing *Venus* Saturday night. Will they never let you have a chance at *Elizabeth*?"*

She shrugged her shoulders. "Not here. There are so many singers here, and they try us out in such a stingy way. Think of it, last year I came over in October, and it was the first of December before I went on at all! I'm often sorry I left Dresden."

"Still," Fred argued, "Dresden is limited."

"Just so, and I've begun to sigh for those very limitations. In New York everything is impersonal. Your audience never knows its own mind, and its mind is never twice the same. I'd rather sing where the people are pig-headed and throw carrots at you if you don't do it the way they like it. The house here is splendid, and the night audiences are exciting. I hate the matinées; like singing at a *Kaffeklatsch*." She rose and turned on the lights.

"Ah!" Fred exclaimed, "why do you do that? That is a signal that tea is over." He got up and drew out his gloves.

"Not at all. Shall you be here Saturday night?" She sat down on the piano bench and leaned her elbow back on the keyboard. "Necker sings *Elizabeth*. Make Dr. Archie go. Everything she sings is worth hearing."

"But she's failing so. The last time I heard her she had no voice at all. She *is* a poor vocalist!"

Thea cut him off. "She's a great artist, whether she's in voice or not, and she's the only one here. If you want a big voice, you can take my *Ortrude* of last night; that's big enough, and vulgar enough."

Fred laughed and turned away, this time with decision. "I don't want her!" he protested energetically. "I only wanted to get a rise out of you. I like Necker's *Elizabeth* well enough. I like your *Venus* well enough, too."

"It's a beautiful part, and it's often dreadfully sung. It's very hard to sing, of course."

Ottenburg bent over the hand she held out to him. "For an uninvited guest, I've fared very well. You were nice to let me come up. I'd have been terribly cut up if you'd sent me away. May I?" He kissed her hand lightly and backed toward the door, still smiling, and promising to keep an eye on Archie. "He can't be trusted at all, Thea. One of the waiters at Martin's worked a Tourainian hare off on him at luncheon yesterday, for seven twenty-five."

Thea broke into a laugh, the deep one he recognized. "Did he have a ribbon on, this hare? Did they bring him in a gilt cage?"

"No,"—Archie spoke up for himself,—"they brought him in a brown sauce, which was very good. He didn't taste very different from any rabbit."

"Probably came from a push-cart on the East Side." Thea looked at her old friend commiseratingly. "Yes, *do* keep an eye on him, Fred. I had no idea," shaking her head. "Yes, I'll be obliged to you."

"Count on me!" Their eyes met in a gay smile, and Fred bowed himself out.

VII

ON Saturday night Dr. Archie went with Fred Ottenburg to hear "Tannhäuser."* Thea had a rehearsal on Sunday afternoon, but as she was not on the bill again until Wednesday, she promised to dine with Archie and Ottenburg on Monday, if they could make the dinner early.

At a little after eight on Monday evening, the three friends returned to Thea's apartment and seated themselves for an hour of quiet talk.

"I'm sorry we couldn't have had Landry with us to-night," Thea said, "but he's on at Weber and Fields' every night now. You ought to hear him, Dr. Archie. He often sings the old Scotch airs you used to love."

"Why not go down this evening?" Fred suggested hopefully, glancing at his watch. "That is, if you'd like to go. I can telephone and find what time he comes on."

Thea hesitated. "No, I think not. I took a long walk this after-noon and I'm rather tired. I think I can get to sleep early and be so much ahead. I don't mean at once, however," seeing Dr.

Archie's disappointed look. "I always like to hear Landry," she added. "He never had much voice, and it's worn, but there's a sweetness about it, and he sings with such taste."

"Yes, doesn't he? May I?" Fred took out his cigarette case. "It really doesn't bother your throat?"

"A little doesn't. But cigar smoke does. Poor Dr. Archie! Can you do with one of those?"

"I'm learning to like them," the doctor declared, taking one from the case Fred proffered him.

"Landry's the only fellow I know in this country who can do that sort of thing," Fred went on. "Like the best English ballad singers. He can sing even popular stuff by higher lights, as it were."

Thea nodded. "Yes; sometimes I make him sing his most foolish things for me. It's restful, as he does it. That's when I'm homesick, Dr. Archie."

"You knew him in Germany, Thea?" Dr. Archie had quietly abandoned his cigarette as a comfortless article. "When you first went over?"

"Yes. He was a good friend to a green girl. He helped me with my German and my music and my general discouragement. Seemed to care more about my getting on than about himself. He had no money, either. An old aunt had loaned him a little to study on.—Will you answer that, Fred?"

Fred caught up the telephone and stopped the buzz while Thea went on talking to Dr. Archie about Landry. Telling some one to hold the wire, he presently put down the instrument and approached Thea with a startled expression on his face.

"It's the management," he said quietly. "Gloeckler has broken down: fainting fits. Madame Rheinecker is in Atlantic City and Schramm is singing in Philadelphia tonight. They want to know whether you can come down and finish *Sieglinde*."*

"What time is it?"

"Eight fifty-five. The first act is just over. They can hold the curtain twenty-five minutes."

Thea did not move. "Twenty-five and thirty-five makes sixty," she muttered. "Tell them I'll come if they hold the curtain till I am in the dressing-room. Say I'll have to wear her costumes, and the dresser must have everything ready. Then call a taxi, please."

Thea had not changed her position since he first interrupted her, but she had grown pale and was opening and shutting her hands rapidly. She looked, Fred thought, terrified. He half turned toward the telephone, but hung on one foot.

"Have you ever sung the part?" he asked.

"No, but I've rehearsed it. That's all right. Get the cab." Still she made no move. She merely turned perfectly blank eyes to Dr. Archie and said absently, "It's curious, but just at this minute I can't remember a bar of 'Walküre'* after the first act. And I let my maid go out." She sprang up and beckoned Archie without so much, he felt sure, as knowing who he was. "Come with me." She went quickly into her sleeping-chamber and threw open a door into a trunk-room. "See that white trunk? It's not locked. It's full of wigs, in boxes. Look until you find one marked 'Ring 2.' Bring it quick!" While she directed him, she threw open a square trunk and began tossing out shoes of every shape and color.

Ottenburg appeared at the door. "Can I help you?"

She threw him some white sandals with long laces and silk stockings pinned to them. "Put those in something, and then go to the piano and give me a few measures in there—you know." She was behaving somewhat like a cyclone now, and while she wrenched open drawers and closet doors, Ottenburg got to the piano as quickly as possible and began to herald the reappearance of the Volsung pair, trusting to memory.

In a few moments Thea came out enveloped in her long fur coat with a scarf over her head and knitted woolen gloves on her hands. Her glassy eye took in the fact that Fred was playing from memory, and even in her distracted state, a faint smile flickered over her colorless lips. She stretched out a woolly hand, "The score, please. Behind you, there."

Dr. Archie followed with a canvas box and a satchel. As they went through the hall, the men caught up their hats and coats. They left the music-room, Fred noticed, just seven minutes after he got the telephone message. In the elevator Thea said in that husky whisper which had so perplexed Dr. Archie when he first heard it, "Tell the driver he must do it in twenty minutes, less if he can. He must leave the light on in the cab. I can do a good deal in twenty minutes. If only you hadn't made me eat—— Damn that duck!" she broke out bitterly; "why did you?"

"Wish I had it back! But it won't bother you, to-night. You need strength," he pleaded consolingly.

But she only muttered angrily under her breath, "Idiot, idiot!"

Ottenburg shot ahead and instructed the driver, while the doctor put Thea into the cab and shut the door. She did not speak to either of them again. As the driver scrambled into his seat she opened the score and fixed her eyes upon it. Her face, in the white light, looked as bleak as a stone quarry.

As her cab slid away, Ottenburg shoved Archie into a second taxi that waited by the curb. "We'd better trail her," he explained. "There might be a hold-up of some kind." As the cab whizzed off he broke into an eruption of profanity.

"What's the matter, Fred?" the doctor asked. He was a good deal dazed by the rapid evolutions of the last ten minutes.

"Matter enough!" Fred growled, buttoning his overcoat with a shiver. "What a way to sing a part for the first time! That duck really is on my conscience. It will be a wonder if she can do anything but quack! Scrambling on in the middle of a performance like this, with no rehearsal! The stuff she has to sing in there is a fright—rhythm, pitch,—and terribly difficult intervals."

"She looked frightened," Dr. Archie said thoughtfully, "but I thought she looked—determined."

Fred sniffed. "Oh, determined! That's the kind of rough deal that makes savages of singers. Here's a part she's worked on and got ready for for years, and now they give her a chance to go on and butcher it. Goodness knows when she's looked at the score last, or whether she can use the business she's studied with this cast. Necker's singing *Brünnhilde*;* she may help her, if it's not one of her sore nights."

"Is she sore at Thea?" Dr. Archie asked wonderingly.

"My dear man, Necker's sore at everything. She's breaking up; too early; just when she ought to be at her best. There's one story that she is struggling under some serious malady, another that she learned a bad method at the Prague Conservatory and has ruined her organ. She's the sorest thing in the world. If she weathers this winter through, it'll be her last. She's paying for it with the last rags of her voice. And then—" Fred whistled softly.

"Well, what then?"

"Then our girl may come in for some of it. It's dog eat dog, in this game as in every other."

The cab stopped and Fred and Dr. Archie hurried to the box office. The Monday-night house was sold out. They bought standing room and entered the auditorium just as the press representative of the house was thanking the audience for their patience and telling them that although Madame Gloeckler was too ill to sing, Miss Kronborg had kindly consented to finish her part. This announcement was met with vehement applause from the upper circles of the house.

"She has her—constituents," Dr. Archie murmured.

"Yes, up there, where they're young and hungry. These people down here have dined too well. They won't mind, however. They like fires and accidents and *divertissements*. Two *Sieglindes* are more unusual than one, so they'll be satisfied."

After the final disappearance of the mother of Siegfried, Ottenburg and the doctor slipped out through the crowd and left the house. Near the stage entrance Fred found the driver who had brought Thea down. He dismissed him and got a larger car. He and Archie waited on the sidewalk, and when Kronborg came out alone they gathered her into the cab and sprang in after her.

Thea sank back into a corner of the back seat and yawned. "Well, I got through, eh?" Her tone was reassuring. "On the whole, I think I've given you gentlemen a pretty lively evening, for one who has no social accomplishments."

"Rather! There was something like a popular uprising at the end of the second act. Archie and I couldn't keep it up as long as the rest of them did. A howl like that ought to show the management which way the wind is blowing. You probably know you were magnificent."

"I thought it went pretty well," she spoke impartially. "I was rather smart to catch his tempo there, at the beginning of the first recitative, when he came in too soon, don't you think? It's tricky in there, without a rehearsal. Oh, I was all right! He took that syncopation too fast in the beginning. Some singers take it fast there—think it sounds more impassioned. That's one way!" She sniffed, and Fred shot a mirthful glance at Archie. Her boastfulness would have been childish in a schoolboy. In the light of what she had done, of the strain they had lived through during the last two hours, it made one laugh,—almost cry. She went on, robustly: "And I didn't feel my dinner, really, Fred. I am hungry again, I'm ashamed to say,—and I forgot to order anything at my hotel."

Fred put his hand on the door. "Where to? You must have food."

"Do you know any quiet place, where I won't be stared at? I've still got make-up on."

"I do. Nice English chop-house on Forty-fourth Street. Nobody there at night but theater people after the show, and a few bachelors." He opened the door and spoke to the driver.

As the car turned, Thea reached across to the front seat and drew Dr. Archie's handkerchief out of his breast pocket.

"This comes to me naturally," she said, rubbing her cheeks and eyebrows. "When I was little I always loved your handkerchiefs because they were silk and smelled of Cologne water. I think they must have been the only really clean handkerchiefs in Moonstone. You were always wiping my face with them, when you met me out in the dust, I remember. Did I never have any?"

"I think you'd nearly always used yours up on your baby brother."

Thea sighed. "Yes, Thor had such a way of getting messy. You say he's a good chauffeur?" She closed her eyes for a moment as if they were tired. Suddenly she looked up. "Isn't it funny, how we travel in circles? Here you are, still getting me clean, and Fred is still feeding me. I would have died of starvation at that boarding-house on Indiana Avenue if he hadn't taken me out to the Buckingham and filled me up once in a while. What a cavern I was to fill, too. The waiters used to look astonished. I'm still singing on that food."

Fred alighted and gave Thea his arm as they crossed the icy sidewalk. They were taken upstairs in an antiquated lift and found the cheerful chop-room half full of supper parties. An English company playing at the Empire had just come in. The waiters, in red waistcoats, were hurrying about. Fred got a table at the back of the room, in a corner, and urged his waiter to get the oysters on at once.

"Takes a few minutes to open them, sir," the man expostulated.

"Yes, but make it as few as possible, and bring the lady's first. Then grilled chops with kidneys, and salad."

Thea began eating celery stalks at once, from the base to the foliage. "Necker said something nice to me to-night. You might have thought the management would say something, but not they." She looked at Fred from under her blackened lashes. "It *was* a stunt, to jump in and sing that second act without rehearsal. It doesn't sing itself."

Ottenburg was watching her brilliant eyes and her face. She was much handsomer than she had been early in the evening. Excitement of this sort enriched her. It was only under such excitement, he reflected, that she was entirely illuminated, or wholly present. At other times there was something a little cold and empty, like a big room with no people in it. Even in her most genial moods there was a shadow of restlessness, as if she were waiting for something and were exercising the virtue of patience. During dinner she had been as kind as she knew how to be, to him and to Archie, and had given them as much of herself as she could. But, clearly, she knew only one way of being really kind, from the core of her heart out; and there was but one way in which she could give herself to people largely and gladly, spontaneously. Even as a girl she had been at her best in vigorous effort, he remembered; physical effort, when there was no other kind at hand. She could be expansive only in explosions. Old Nathanmeyer had seen it. In the very first song Fred had ever heard her sing, she had unconsciously declared it.

Thea Kronborg turned suddenly from her talk with Archie and peered suspiciously into the corner where Ottenburg sat with folded arms, observing her. "What's the matter with you, Fred? I'm afraid of you when you're quiet,—fortunately you almost never are. What are you thinking about?"

"I was wondering how you got right with the orchestra so quickly, there at first. I had a flash of terror," he replied easily.

She bolted her last oyster and ducked her head. "So had I! I don't know how I did catch it. Desperation, I suppose; same way the Indian babies swim when they're thrown into the river. I *had* to. Now it's over, I'm glad I had to. I learned a whole lot to-night."

Archie, who usually felt that it behooved him to be silent during such discussions, was encouraged by her geniality to venture, "I don't see how you can learn anything in such a turmoil; or how you can keep your mind on it, for that matter."

Thea glanced about the room and suddenly put her hand up to her hair. "Mercy, I've no hat on! Why didn't you tell me? And I seem to be wearing a rumpled dinner dress, with all this paint on my face! I must look like something you picked up on Second Avenue. I hope there are no Colorado reformers about, Dr. Archie. What a dreadful old pair these people must be thinking you! Well, I had to eat." She sniffed the savor of the grill as the waiter uncovered it. "Yes, draught beer, please. No, thank you, Fred, *no* champagne.—To go back to your question, Dr. Archie, you can believe I keep my mind on it. That's the whole trick, in so far as stage experience goes; keeping right there every second. If I think of anything else for a flash, I'm done for. But at the same time, one can take things in—with another part of your brain, maybe. It's different from what you get in study, more practical and conclusive. There are some things you learn best in calm, and some in storm. You learn the delivery of a part only before an audience."

"Heaven help us," gasped Ottenburg. "Weren't you hungry, though! It's beautiful to see you eat."

"Glad you like it. Of course I'm hungry. Are you staying over for 'Rheingold' Friday afternoon?"

"My dear Thea,"—Fred lit a cigarette,—"I'm a serious business man now. I have to sell beer. I'm due in Chicago on

Wednesday. I'd come back to hear you, but *Fricka** is not an alluring part."

"Then you've never heard it well done." She spoke up hotly. "Fat German woman scolding her husband, eh? That's not my idea. Wait till you hear my *Fricka*. It's a beautiful part." Thea leaned forward on the table and touched Archie's arm. "You remember, Dr. Archie, how my mother always wore her hair, parted in the middle and done low on her neck behind, so you got the shape of her head and such a calm, white forehead? I wear mine like that for *Fricka*. A little more coronet effect, built up a little higher at the sides, but the idea's the same. I think you'll notice it." She turned to Ottenburg reproachfully: "It's noble music, Fred, from the first measure. There's nothing lovelier than the *wonniger Hausrath*.* It's all such comprehensive sort of music—fateful. Of course, *Fricka knows*," Thea ended quietly.

Fred sighed. "There, you've spoiled my itinerary. Now I'll have to come back, of course. Archie, you'd better get busy about seats to-morrow."

"I can get you box seats, somewhere. I know nobody here, and I never ask for any." Thea began hunting among her wraps. "Oh, how funny! I've only these short woolen gloves, and no sleeves. Put on my coat first. Those English people can't make out where you got your lady, she's so made up of contradictions." She rose laughing and plunged her arms into the coat Dr. Archie held for her. As she settled herself into it and buttoned it under her chin, she gave him an old signal with her eyelid. "I'd like to sing another part tonight. This is the sort of evening I fancy, when there's something to do. Let me see: I have to sing in 'Trovatore'* Wednesday night, and there are rehearsals for the 'Ring' every day this week. Consider me dead until Saturday, Dr. Archie. I invite you both to dine with me on Saturday night, the day after 'Rheingold.' And Fred must leave early, for I want to talk to you alone. You've been here nearly a week, and I haven't had a serious word with you. *Tak for mad*,* Fred, as the Norwegians say."

VIII

THE "Ring of the Niebelungs" was to be given at the Metropolitan on four successive Friday afternoons. After the first of these performances, Fred Ottenburg went home with Landry for tea. Landry was one of the few public entertainers who own real estate in New York. He lived in a little three-story brick house on Jane Street, in Greenwich Village, which had been left to him by the same aunt who paid for his musical education.

Landry was born, and spent the first fifteen years of his life, on a rocky Connecticut farm not far from Cos Cob. His father was an ignorant, violent man, a bungling farmer and a brutal husband. The farmhouse, dilapidated and damp, stood in a hollow beside a marshy pond. Oliver had worked hard while he lived at home, although he was never clean or warm in winter and had wretched food all the year round. His spare, dry figure, his prominent larynx, and the peculiar red of his face and hands belonged to the chore-boy he had never outgrown. It was as if the farm, knowing he would escape from it as early as he could, had ground its mark on him deep. When he was fifteen Oliver ran away and went to live with his Catholic aunt, on Jane Street, whom his mother was never allowed to visit. The priest of St. Joseph's Parish discovered that he had a voice.

Landry had an affection for the house on Jane Street, where he had first learned what cleanliness and order and courtesy were. When his aunt died he had the place done over, got an Irish housekeeper, and lived there with a great many beautiful things he had collected. His living expenses were never large, but he could not restrain himself from buying graceful and useless objects. He was a collector for much the same reason that he was a Catholic, and he was a Catholic chiefly because his father used to sit in the kitchen and read aloud to his hired men disgusting "exposures" of the Roman Church, enjoying equally the hideous stories and the outrage to his wife's feelings.

At first Landry bought books; then rugs, drawings, china. He had a beautiful collection of old French and Spanish fans. He kept them in an escritoire he had brought from Spain, but there were always a few of them lying about in his sitting-room.

While Landry and his guest were waiting for the tea to be brought, Ottenburg took up one of these fans from the low marble mantel-shelf and opened it in the firelight. One side was painted with a pearly sky and floating clouds. On the other was a formal garden where an elegant shepherdess with a mask and crook was fleeing on high heels from a satin-coated shepherd.

"You ought not to keep these things about, like this, Oliver. The dust from your grate must get at them."

"It does, but I get them to enjoy them, not to have them. They're pleasant to glance at and to play with at odd times like this, when one is waiting for tea or something."

Fred smiled. The idea of Landry stretched out before his fire playing with his fans, amused him. Mrs. McGinnis brought the tea and put it before the hearth: old teacups that were velvety to the touch and a pot-bellied silver cream pitcher of an Early Georgian pattern, which was always brought, though Landry took rum.

Fred drank his tea walking about, examining Landry's sumptuous writing-table in the alcove and the Boucher drawing in red chalk over the mantel. "I don't see how you can stand this place without a heroine. It would give me a raging thirst for gallantries."

Landry was helping himself to a second cup of tea. "Works quite the other way with me. It consoles me for the lack of her. It's just feminine enough to be pleasant to return to. Not any more tea? Then sit down and play for me. I'm always playing for other people, and I never have a chance to sit here quietly and listen."

Ottenburg opened the piano and began softly to boom forth the shadowy introduction to the opera they had just heard. "Will that do?" he asked jokingly. "I can't seem to get it out of my head."

"Oh, excellently! Thea told me it was quite wonderful, the way you can do Wagner scores on the piano. So few people can give one any idea of the music. Go ahead, as long as you like. I can smoke, too." Landry flattened himself out on his cushions and abandoned himself to ease with the circumstance of one who has never grown quite accustomed to ease.

Ottenburg played on, as he happened to remember. He understood now why Thea wished him to hear her in "Rheingold." It had been clear to him as soon as *Fricka* rose from sleep and looked out over the young world, stretching one white arm toward the new Götterburg* shining on the heights. "*Wotan! Gemahl! erwache!*"* She was pure Scandinavian, this *Fricka*: "Swedish summer"! he remembered old Mr. Nathanmeyer's phrase. She had wished him to see her because she had a distinct kind of loveliness for this part, a shining beauty like the light of sunset on distant sails. She seemed to take on the look of immortal loveliness, the youth of the golden apples, the shining body and the shining mind. *Fricka* had been a jealous spouse to him for so long that he had forgot she meant wisdom before she meant domestic order, and that, in any event, she was always a goddess. The *Fricka* of that afternoon was so clear and sunny, so nobly conceived, that she made a whole atmosphere about herself and quite redeemed from shabbiness the helplessness and unscrupulousness of the gods. Her reproaches to *Wotan* were the pleadings of a tempered mind, a consistent sense of beauty. In the long silences of her part, her shining presence was a visible complement to the discussion of the orchestra. As the themes which were to help in weaving the drama to its end first came vaguely upon the ear, one saw their import and tendency in the face of this clearest-visioned of the gods.

In the scene between *Fricka* and *Wotan*, Ottenburg stopped. "I can't seem to get the voices, in there."

Landry chuckled. "Don't try. I know it well enough. I expect I've been over that with her a thousand times. I was playing for her almost every day when she was first working on it. When she begins with a part she's hard to work with: so slow you'd think she was stupid if you didn't know her. Of course she blames it all on her accompanist. It goes on like that for weeks sometimes. This did. She kept shaking her head and staring and looking gloomy. All at once, she got her line—it usually comes suddenly, after stretches of not getting anywhere at all—and after that it kept changing and clearing. As she worked her voice into it, it got more and more of that 'gold' quality that makes her *Fricka* so different."

Fred began *Fricka's* first aria again. "It's certainly different. Curious how she does it. Such a beautiful idea, out of a part that's always been so ungrateful. She's a lovely thing, but she was never so beautiful as that, really. Nobody is." He repeated the loveliest phrase. "How does she manage it, Landry? You've worked with her."

Landry drew cherishingly on the last cigarette he meant to permit himself before singing. "Oh, it's a question of a big personality—and all that goes with it. Brains, of course. Imagination, of course. But the important thing is that she was born full of color, with a rich personality. That's a gift of the gods, like a fine nose. You have it, or you haven't. Against it, intelligence and musicianship and habits of industry don't count at all. Singers are a conventional race. When Thea was studying in Berlin the other girls were mortally afraid of her. She has a pretty rough hand with women, dull ones, and she could be rude, too! The girls used to call her *die Wölfin*."*

Fred thrust his hands into his pockets and leaned back against the piano. "Of course, even a stupid woman could get effects with such machinery: such a voice and body and face. But they couldn't possibly belong to a stupid woman, could they?"

Landry shook his head. "It's personality; that's as near as you can come to it. That's what constitutes real equipment. What she does is interesting because she does it. Even the things she discards are suggestive. I regret some of them. Her conceptions are colored in so many different ways. You've heard her *Elizabeth*? Wonderful, isn't it? She was working on that part years ago when her mother was ill. I could see her anxiety and grief getting more and more into the part. The last act is heart-breaking. It's as homely as a country prayer meeting: might be any lonely woman getting ready to die. It's full of the thing every plain creature finds out for himself, but that never gets written down. It's unconscious memory, maybe; inherited memory, like folk-music. I call it personality."

Fred laughed, and turning to the piano began coaxing the *Fricka* music again. "Call it anything you like, my boy. I have a name for it myself, but I shan't tell you." He looked over his shoulder at Landry, stretched out by the fire. "You have a great time watching her, don't you?"

"Oh, yes!" replied Landry simply. "I'm not interested in much that goes on in New York. Now, if you'll excuse me, I'll have to dress." He rose with a reluctant sigh. "Can I get you anything? Some whiskey?"

"Thank you, no. I'll amuse myself here. I don't often get a chance at a good piano when I'm away from home. You haven't had this one long, have you? Action's a bit stiff. I say," he stopped Landry in the doorway, "has Thea ever been down here?"

Landry turned back. "Yes. She came several times when I had erysipelas. I was a nice mess, with two nurses. She brought down some inside window-boxes, planted with crocuses and things. Very cheering, only I couldn't see them or her."

"Didn't she like your place?"

"She thought she did, but I fancy it was a good deal cluttered up for her taste. I could hear her pacing about like something in a cage. She pushed the piano back against the wall and the chairs into corners, and she broke my amber elephant." Landry took a yellow object some four inches high from one of his low book-cases. "You can see where his leg is glued on,—a souvenir. Yes, he's lemon amber, very fine."

Landry disappeared behind the curtains and in a moment Fred heard the wheeze of an atomizer. He put the amber elephant on the piano beside him and seemed to get a great deal of amusement out of the beast.

IX

WHEN Archie and Ottenburg dined with Thea on Saturday evening, they were served downstairs in the hotel dining-room, but they were to have their coffee in her own apartment. As they were going up in the elevator after dinner, Fred turned suddenly to

Thea. "And why, please, did you break Landry's amber elephant?"

She looked guilty and began to laugh. "Hasn't he got over that yet? I didn't really mean to break it. I was perhaps careless. His things are so over-petted that I was tempted to be careless with a lot of them."

"How can you be so heartless, when they're all he has in the world?"

"He has me. I'm a great deal of diversion for him; all he needs. There," she said as she opened the door into her own hall, "I shouldn't have said that before the elevator boy."

"Even an elevator boy couldn't make a scandal about Oliver. He's such a catnip man."

Dr. Archie laughed, but Thea, who seemed suddenly to have thought of something annoying, repeated blankly, "Catnip man?"

"Yes, he lives on catnip, and rum tea. But he's not the only one. You are like an eccentric old woman I know in Boston, who goes about in the spring feeding catnip to street cats. You dispense it to a lot of fellows. Your pull seems to be more with men than with women, you know; with seasoned men, about my age, or older. Even on Friday afternoon I kept running into them, old boys I hadn't seen for years, thin at the part and thick at the girth, until I stood still in the draft and held my hair on. They're always there; I hear them talking about you in the smoking-room. Probably we don't get to the point of apprehending anything good until we're about forty. Then, in the light of what is going, and of what, God help us! is coming, we arrive at understanding."

"I don't see why people go to the opera, anyway,—serious people." She spoke discontentedly. "I suppose they get something, or think they do. Here's the coffee. There, please," she directed the waiter. Going to the table she began to pour the coffee, standing. She wore a white dress trimmed with crystals which had rattled a good deal during dinner, as all her movements had been impatient and nervous, and she had twisted the dark velvet rose at her girdle until it looked rumpled and weary. She poured the coffee as if it were a ceremony in which she did not believe. "Can you make anything of Fred's nonsense, Dr. Archie?" she asked, as he came to take his cup.

Fred approached her. "My nonsense is all right. The same brand has gone with you before. It's you who won't be jollied. What's the matter? You have something on your mind."

"I've a good deal. Too much to be an agreeable hostess." She turned quickly away from the coffee and sat down on the piano bench, facing the two men. "For one thing, there's a change in the cast for Friday afternoon. They're going to let me sing *Sieglinde*." Her frown did not conceal the pleasure with which she made this announcement.

"Are you going to keep us dangling about here forever, Thea? Archie and I are supposed to have other things to do." Fred looked at her with an excitement quite as apparent as her own.

"Here I've been ready to sing *Sieglinde* for two years, kept in torment, and now it comes off within two weeks, just when I want to be seeing something of Dr. Archie. I don't know what their plans are down there. After Friday they may let me cool for several weeks, and they may rush me. I suppose it depends somewhat on how things go Friday afternoon."

"Oh, they'll go fast enough! That's better suited to your voice than anything you've sung here. That gives you every opportunity I've waited for." Ottenburg crossed the room and standing beside her began to play "*Du bist der Lenz*."*

With a violent movement Thea caught his wrists and pushed his hands away from the keys.

"Fred, can't you be serious? A thousand things may happen between this and Friday to put me out. Something will happen. If that part were sung well, as well as it ought to be, it would be one of the most beautiful things in the world. That's why it never is sung right, and never will be." She clenched her hands and opened them despairingly, looking out of the open window. "It's inaccessibly beautiful!" she brought out sharply.

Fred and Dr. Archie watched her. In a moment she turned back to them. "It's impossible to sing a part like that well for the first time, except for the sort who will never sing it any better. Everything hangs on that first night, and that's bound to be bad.

There you are," she shrugged impatiently. "For one thing, they change the cast at the eleventh hour and then rehearse the life out of me."

Ottenburg put down his cup with exaggerated care. "Still, you really want to do it, you know."

"Want to?" she repeated indignantly; "of course I want to! If this were only next Thursday night— But between now and Friday I'll do nothing but fret away my strength. Oh, I'm not saying I don't need the rehearsals! But I don't need them strung out through a week. That system's well enough for phlegmatic singers; it only drains me. Every single feature of operatic routine is detrimental to me. I usually go on like a horse that's been fixed to lose a race. I have to work hard to do my worst, let alone my best. I wish you could hear me sing well, once," she turned to Fred defiantly; "I have, a few times in my life, when there was nothing to gain by it."

Fred approached her again and held out his hand. "I recall my instructions, and now I'll leave you to fight it out with Archie. He can't possibly represent managerial stupidity to you as I seem to have a gift for doing."

As he smiled down at her, his good humor, his good wishes, his understanding, embarrassed her and recalled her to herself. She kept her seat, still holding his hand. "All the same, Fred, isn't it too bad, that there are so many things—" She broke off with a shake of the head.

"My dear girl, if I could bridge over the agony between now and Friday for you— But you know the rules of the game; why torment yourself? You saw the other night that you had the part under your thumb. Now walk, sleep, play with Archie, keep your tiger hungry, and she'll spring all right on Friday. I'll be there to see her, and there'll be more than I, I suspect. Harsanyi's on the *Wilhelm der Grosse*; gets in on Thursday."

"Harsanyi?" Thea's eye lighted. "I haven't seen him for years. We always miss each other." She paused, hesitating. "Yes, I should like that. But he'll be busy, maybe?"

"He gives his first concert at Carnegie Hall, week after next. Better send him a box if you can."

"Yes, I'll manage it." Thea took his hand again. "Oh, I should like that, Fred!" she added impulsively. "Even if I were put out, he'd get the idea!"—she threw back her head,—"for there is an idea!"

"Which won't penetrate here," he tapped his brow and began to laugh. "You are an ungrateful huzzy, *comme les autres!*"*

Thea detained him as he turned away. She pulled a flower out of a bouquet on the piano and absently drew the stem through the lapel of his coat. "I shall be walking in the Park to-morrow afternoon, on the reservoir path, between four and five, if you care to join me. You know that after Harsanyi I'd rather please you than anyone else. You know a lot, but he knows even more than you."

"Thank you. Don't try to analyze it. *Schlafen Sie wohl!*"* he kissed her fingers and waved from the door, closing it behind him.

"He's the right sort, Thea." Dr. Archie looked warmly after his disappearing friend. "I've always hoped you'd make it up with Fred."

"Well, haven't I? Oh, marry him, you mean! Perhaps it may come about, some day. Just at present he's not in the marriage market any more than I am, is he?"

"No, I suppose not. It's a damned shame that a man like Ottenburg should be tied up as he is, wasting all the best years of his life. A woman with general paresis ought to be legally dead."

"Don't let us talk about Fred's wife, please. He had no business to get into such a mess, and he had no business to stay in it. He's always been a softy where women were concerned."

"Most of us are, I'm afraid," Dr. Archie admitted meekly.

"Too much light in here, isn't there? Tires one's eyes. The stage lights are hard on mine." Thea began turning them out. "We'll leave the little one, over the piano." She sank down by Archie on the deep sofa. "We two have so much to talk about that we keep away from it altogether; have you noticed? We don't even nibble the edges. I wish we had Landry here to-night to play for us. He's very comforting."

"I'm afraid you don't have enough personal life, outside your work, Thea." The doctor looked at her anxiously.

She smiled at him with her eyes half closed. "My dear doctor, I don't have any. Your work becomes your personal life. You are not much good until it does. It's like being woven into a big web. You can't pull away, because all your little tendrils are woven into the picture. It takes you up, and uses you, and spins you out; and that is your life. Not much else can happen to you."

"Didn't you think of marrying, several years ago?"

"You mean Nordquist? Yes; but I changed my mind. We had been singing a good deal together. He's a splendid creature."

"Were you much in love with him, Thea?" the doctor asked hopefully.

She smiled again. "I don't think I know just what that expression means. I've never been able to find out. I think I was in love with you when I was little, but not with any one since then. There are a great many ways of caring for people. It's not, after all, a simple state, like measles or tonsilitis. Nordquist is a taking sort of man. He and I were out in a rowboat once in a terrible storm. The lake was fed by glaciers,—ice water,—and we couldn't have swum a stroke if the boat had filled. If we hadn't both been strong and kept our heads, we'd have gone down. We pulled for every ounce there was in us, and we just got off with our lives. We were always being thrown together like that, under some kind of pressure. Yes, for a while I thought he would make everything right." She paused and sank back, resting her head on a cushion, pressing her eyelids down with her fingers. "You see," she went on abruptly, "he had a wife and two children. He hadn't lived with her for several years, but when she heard that he wanted to marry again, she began to make trouble. He earned a good deal of money, but he was careless and always wretchedly in debt. He came to me one day and told me he thought his wife would settle for a hundred thousand marks and consent to a divorce. I got very angry and sent him away. Next day he came back and said he thought she'd take fifty thousand."

Dr. Archie drew away from her, to the end of the sofa. "Good God, Thea,"— He ran his handkerchief over his forehead. "What sort of people—" He stopped and shook his head.

Thea rose and stood beside him, her hand on his shoulder.

"That's exactly how it struck me," she said quietly. "Oh, we have things in common, things that go away back, under everything. You understand, of course. Nordquist didn't. He thought I wasn't willing to part with the money. I couldn't let myself buy him from Fru Nordquist, and he couldn't see why. He had always thought I was close about money, so he attributed it to that. I am careful,"—she ran her arm through Archie's and when he rose began to walk about the room with him. "I can't be careless with money. I began the world on six hundred dollars, and it was the price of a man's life. Ray Kennedy had worked hard and been sober and denied himself, and when he died he had six hundred dollars to show for it. I always measure things by that six hundred dollars, just as I measure high buildings by the Moonstone standpipe. There are standards we can't get away from."

Dr. Archie took her hand. "I don't believe we should be any happier if we did get away from them. I think it gives you some of your poise, having that anchor. You look," glancing down at her head and shoulders, "sometimes so like your mother."

"Thank you. You couldn't say anything nicer to me than that. On Friday afternoon, didn't you think?"

"Yes, but at other times, too. I love to see it. Do you know what I thought about that first night when I heard you sing? I kept remembering the night I took care of you when you had pneumonia, when you were ten years old. You were a terribly sick child, and I was a country doctor without much experience. There were no oxygen tanks about then. You pretty nearly slipped away from me. If you had—"

Thea dropped her head on his shoulder. "I'd have saved myself and you a lot of trouble, wouldn't I? Dear Dr. Archie!" she murmured.

"As for me, life would have been a pretty bleak stretch, with you left out." The doctor took one of the crystal pendants that hung from her shoulder and looked into it thoughtfully. "I guess I'm a romantic old fellow, underneath. And you've always been my romance. Those years when you were growing up were my happiest. When I dream about you, I always see you as a little girl."

They paused by the open window. "Do you? Nearly all my dreams, except those about breaking down on the stage or missing trains, are about Moonstone. You tell me the old house has been pulled down, but it stands in my mind, every stick and timber. In my sleep I go all about it, and look in the right drawers and cupboards for everything. I often dream that I'm hunting for my rubbers in that pile of overshoes that was always under the hatrack in the hall. I pick up every overshoe and know whose it is, but I can't find my own. Then the school bell begins to ring and I begin to cry. That's the house I rest in when I'm tired. All the old furniture and the worn spots in the carpet—it rests my mind to go over them."

They were looking out of the window. Thea kept his arm. Down on the river four battleships were anchored in line, brilliantly lighted, and launches were coming and going, bringing the men ashore. A searchlight from one of the ironclads was playing on the great headland up the river, where it makes its first resolute turn. Overhead the night-blue sky was intense and clear.

"There's so much that I want to tell you," she said at last, "and it's hard to explain. My life is full of jealousies and disappointments, you know. You get to hating people who do contemptible work and who get on just as well as you do. There are many disappointments in my profession, and bitter, bitter contempts!" Her face hardened, and looked much older. "If you love the good thing vitally, enough to give up for it all that one must give up for it, then you must hate the cheap thing just as hard. I tell you, there is such a thing as creative hate! A contempt that drives you through fire, makes you risk everything and lose everything, makes you a long sight better than you ever knew you could be." As she glanced at Dr. Archie's face, Thea stopped short and turned her own face away. Her eyes followed the path of the searchlight up the river and rested upon the illumined headland.

"You see," she went on more calmly, "voices are accidental things. You find plenty of good voices in common women, with common minds and common hearts. Look at that woman who sang *Ortrude* with me last week. She's new here and the people are wild about her. 'Such a beautiful volume of tone!' they say. I give you my word she's as stupid as an owl and as coarse as a pig, and any one who knows anything about singing would see that in an instant. Yet she's quite as popular as Necker, who's a great artist. How can I get much satisfaction out of the enthusiasm of a house that likes her atrociously bad performance at the same time that it pretends to like mine? If they like her, then they ought to hiss me off the stage.. We stand for things that are irreconcilable, absolutely. You can't try to do things right and not despise the people who do them wrong. How can I be indifferent? If that doesn't matter, then nothing matters. Well, sometimes I've come home as I did the other night when you first saw me, so full of bitterness that it was as if my mind were full of daggers. And I've gone to sleep and wakened up in the Kohlers' garden, with the pigeons and the white rabbits, so happy! And that saves me." She sat down on the piano bench. Archie thought she had forgotten all about him, until she called his name. Her voice was soft now, and wonderfully sweet. It seemed to come from somewhere deep within her, there were such strong vibrations in it. "You see, Dr. Archie, what one really strives for in art is not the sort of thing you are likely to find when you drop in for a performance at the opera. What one strives for is so far away, so deep, so beautiful" —she lifted her shoulders with a long breath, folded her hands in her lap and sat looking at him with a resignation that made her face noble,—"that there's nothing one can say about it, Dr. Archie."

Without knowing very well what it was all about, Archie was passionately stirred for her. "I've always believed in you, Thea; always believed," he muttered.

She smiled and closed her eyes. "They save me: the old things, things like the Kohlers' garden. They are in everything I do."

"In what you sing, you mean?"

"Yes. Not in any direct way,"—she spoke hurriedly,—"the light, the color, the feeling. Most of all the feeling. It comes in when I'm working on a part, like the smell of a garden coming in at the window. I try all the new things, and then go back to the old. Perhaps my feelings were stronger then. A child's attitude toward everything is an artist's attitude. I am more or less of an artist now, but then I was nothing else. When I went with you to Chicago that first time, I carried with me the essentials, the foundation of all I do now. The point to which I could go was scratched in me then. I haven't reached it yet, by a long way."

Archie had a swift flash of memory. Pictures passed before him. "You mean," he asked wonderingly, "that you knew then that you were so gifted?"

Thea looked up at him and smiled. "Oh, I didn't know anything! Not enough to ask you for my trunk when I needed it. But you see, when I set out from Moonstone with you, I had had a rich, romantic past. I had lived a long, eventful life, and an artist's life, every hour of it. Wagner says, in his most beautiful opera, that art is only a way of remembering youth. And the older we grow the more precious it seems to us, and the more richly we can present that memory. When we've got it all out,—the last, the finest thrill of it, the brightest hope of it,"—she lifted her hand above her head and dropped it,—"then we stop. We do nothing but repeat after that. The stream has reached the level of its source. That's our measure."

There was a long, warm silence. Thea was looking hard at the floor, as if she were seeing down through years and years, and her old friend stood watching her bent head. His look was one with which he used to watch her long ago, and which, even in thinking about her, had become a habit of his face. It was full of solicitude, and a kind of secret gratitude, as if to thank her for some inexpressible pleasure of the heart. Thea turned presently toward the piano and began softly to waken an old air:—*

"Ca' the yowes to the knowes,
Ca' them where the heather grows,
Ca' them where the burnie rowes,
   My bonnie dear-ie."

Archie sat down and shaded his eyes with his hand. She turned her head and spoke to him over her shoulder. "Come on, you know the words better than I. That's right."

"We'll gae down by Clouden's side,
Through the hazels spreading wide,
O'er the waves that sweetly glide,
   To the moon sae clearly.
Ghaist nor bogle shalt thou fear,
Thou'rt to love and Heav'n sae dear,
Nocht of ill may come thee near,
   My bonnie dear-ie!"

"We can get on without Landry. Let's try it again, I have all the words now. Then we'll have 'Sweet Afton.' Come: '*Ca' the yowes to the knowes*'—"

X

OTTENBURG dismissed his taxicab at the 91st Street entrance of the Park and floundered across the drive through a wild spring snowstorm. When he reached the reservoir path he saw Thea ahead of him, walking rapidly against the wind. Except for that one figure, the path was deserted. A flock of gulls were hovering over the reservoir, seeming bewildered by the driving currents of snow that whirled above the black water and then disappeared within it. When he had almost overtaken Thea, Fred called to her, and she turned and waited for him with her back to the wind. Her hair and furs were powdered with snowflakes, and she looked like some rich-pelted animal, with warm blood, that had run in out of the woods. Fred laughed as he took her hand.

"No use asking how you do. You surely needn't feel much anxiety about Friday, when you can look like this."

She moved close to the iron fence to make room for him beside her, and faced the wind again. "Oh, I'm *well* enough, in so far as that goes. But I'm not lucky about stage appearances. I'm easily upset, and the most perverse things happen."

"What's the matter? Do you still get nervous?"

"Of course I do. I don't mind nerves so much as getting numbed," Thea muttered, sheltering her face for a moment with her muff. "I'm under a spell, you know, hoo-dooed. It's the thing

I *want* to do that I can never do. Any other effects I can get easily enough."

"Yes, you get effects, and not only with your voice. That's where you have it over all the rest of them; you're as much at home on the stage as you were down in Panther Canyon—as if you'd just been let out of a cage. Didn't you get some of your ideas down there?"

Thea nodded. "Oh, yes! For heroic parts, at least. Out of the rocks, out of the dead people. You mean the idea of standing up under things, don't you, meeting catastrophe? No fussiness. Seems to me they must have been a reserved, somber people, with only a muscular language, all their movements for a purpose; simple, strong, as if they were dealing with fate bare-handed." She put her gloved fingers on Fred's arm. "I don't know how I can ever thank you enough. I don't know if I'd ever have got anywhere without Panther Canyon. How did you know that was the one thing to do for me? It's the sort of thing nobody ever helps one to, in this world. One can learn how to sing, but no singing teacher can give anybody what I got down there. How did you know?"

"I didn't know. Anything else would have done as well. It was your creative hour. I knew you were getting a lot, but I didn't realize how much."

Thea walked on in silence. She seemed to be thinking.

"Do you know what they really taught me?" she came out suddenly. "They taught me the inevitable hardness of human life. No artist gets far who doesn't know that. And you can't know it with your mind. You have to realize it in your body, somehow; deep. It's an animal sort of feeling. I sometimes think it's the strongest of all. Do you know what I'm driving at?"

"I think so. Even your audiences feel it, vaguely: that you've sometime or other faced things that make you different."

Thea turned her back to the wind, wiping away the snow that clung to her brows and lashes. "Ugh!" she exclaimed; "no matter how long a breath you have, the storm has a longer. I haven't signed for next season, yet, Fred. I'm holding out for a big contract: forty performances. Necker won't be able to do much next winter. It's going to be one of those between seasons; the old singers are too old, and the new ones are too new. They might as well risk me as anybody. So I want good terms. The next five or six years are going to be my best."

"You'll get what you demand, if you are uncompromising. I'm safe in congratulating you now."

Thea laughed. "It's a little early. I may not get it at all. They don't seem to be breaking their necks to meet me. I can go back to Dresden."

As they turned the curve and walked westward they got the wind from the side, and talking was easier.

Fred lowered his collar and shook the snow from his shoulders. "Oh, I don't mean on the contract particularly. I congratulate you on what you can do, Thea, and on all that lies behind what you do. On the life that's led up to it, and on being able to care so much. That, after all, is the unusual thing."

She looked at him sharply, with a certain apprehension. "Care? Why shouldn't I care? If I didn't, I'd be in a bad way. What else have I got?" She stopped with a challenging interrogation, but Ottenburg did not reply. "You mean," she persisted, "that you don't care as much as you used to?"

"I care about your success, of course." Fred fell into a slower pace. Thea felt at once that he was talking seriously and had dropped the tone of half-ironical exaggeration he had used with her of late years. "And I'm grateful to you for what you demand from yourself, when you might get off so easily. You demand more and more all the time, and you'll do more and more. One is grateful to anybody for that; it makes life in general a little less sordid. But as a matter of fact, I'm not much interested in how anybody sings anything."

"That's too bad of you, when I'm just beginning to see what is worth doing, and how I want to do it!" Thea spoke in an injured tone.

"That's what I congratulate you on. That's the great difference between your kind and the rest of us. It's how long you're able to keep it up that tells the story. When you needed enthusiasm from the outside, I was able to give it to you. Now you must let me withdraw."

"I'm not tying you, am I?" she flashed out. "But withdraw to what? What do you want?"

Fred shrugged. "I might ask you, What have I got? I want things that wouldn't interest you; that you probably wouldn't understand. For one thing, I want a son to bring up."

"I can understand that. It seems to me reasonable. Have you also found somebody you want to marry?"

"Not particularly." They turned another curve, which brought the wind to their backs, and they walked on in comparative calm, with the snow blowing past them. "It's not your fault, Thea, but I've had you too much in my mind. I've not given myself a fair chance in other directions. I was in Rome when you and Nordquist were there. If that had kept up, it might have cured me."

"It might have cured a good many things," remarked Thea grimly.

Fred nodded sympathetically and went on. "In my library in St. Louis, over the fireplace, I have a property spear I had copied from one in Venice,—oh, years ago, after you first went abroad, while you were studying. You'll probably be singing *Brünnhilde* pretty soon now, and I'll send it on to you, if I may. You can take it and its history for what they're worth. But I'm nearly forty years old, and I've served my turn. You've done what I hoped for you, what I was honestly willing to lose you for—then. I'm older now, and I think I was an ass. I wouldn't do it again if I had the chance, not much! But I'm not sorry. It takes a great many people to make one—*Brünnhilde*."

Thea stopped by the fence and looked over into the black choppiness on which the snowflakes fell and disappeared with magical rapidity. Her face was both angry and troubled. "So you really feel I've been ungrateful. I thought you sent me out to get something. I didn't know you wanted me to bring in something easy. I thought you wanted something—" She took a deep breath and shrugged her shoulders. "But there! nobody on God's earth wants it, *really!* If one other person wanted it,"—she thrust her hand out before him and clenched it,—"my God, what I could do!"

Fred laughed dismally. "Even in my ashes I feel myself pushing you! How can anybody help it? My dear girl, can't you see that anybody else who wanted it as you do would be your rival, your deadliest danger? Can't you see that it's your great good fortune that other people can't care about it so much?"

But Thea seemed not to take in his protest at all. She went on vindicating herself. "It's taken me a long while to do anything, of course, and I've only begun to see daylight. But anything good is—expensive. It hasn't seemed long. I've always felt responsible to you."

Fred looked at her face intently, through the veil of snowflakes, and shook his head. "To me? You are a truthful woman, and you don't mean to lie to me. But after the one responsibility you do feel, I doubt if you've enough left to feel responsible to God! Still, if you've ever in an idle hour fooled yourself with thinking I had anything to do with it, Heaven knows I'm grateful."

"Even if I'd married Nordquist," Thea went on, turning down the path again, "there would have been something left out. There always is. In a way, I've always been married to you. I'm not very flexible; never was and never shall be. You caught me young. I could never have that over again. One can't, after one begins to know anything. But I look back on it. My life hasn't been a gay one, any more than yours. If I shut things out from you, you shut them out from me. We've been a help and a hindrance to each other. I guess it's always that way, the good and the bad all mixed up. There's only one thing that's all beautiful—and always beautiful! That's why my interest keeps up."

"Yes, I know." Fred looked sidewise at the outline of her head against the thickening atmosphere. "And you give one the impression that that is enough. I've gradually, gradually given you up."

"See, the lights are coming out." Thea pointed to where they flickered, flashes of violet through the gray tree-tops. Lower down the globes along the drives were becoming a pale lemon color. "Yes, I don't see why anybody wants to marry an artist, anyhow. I remember Ray Kennedy used to say he didn't see how any woman could marry a gambler, for she would only be marrying what the game left." She shook her shoulders impatiently. "Who marries who is a small matter, after all. But I hope I can bring back your interest in my work. You've cared longer and more than anybody else, and I'd like to have somebody human to make a report to once in a while. You can send me your spear. I'll do my best. If you're not interested, I'll do my best anyhow. I've only a few friends, but I can lose every one of them, if it has to be. I learned how to lose when my mother died.—We must hurry now. My taxi must be waiting."

The blue light about them was growing deeper and darker, and the falling snow and the faint trees had become violet. To the south, over Broadway, there was an orange reflection in the clouds. Motors and carriage lights flashed by on the drive below the reservoir path, and the air was strident with horns and shrieks from the whistles of the mounted policemen.

Fred gave Thea his arm as they descended from the embankment. "I guess you'll never manage to lose me or Archie, Thea. You do pick up queer ones. But loving you is a heroic discipline. It wears a man out. Tell me one thing: could I have kept you, once, if I'd put on every screw?"

Thea hurried him along, talking rapidly, as if to get it over. "You might have kept me in misery for a while, perhaps. I don't know. I have to think well of myself, to work. You could have made it hard. I'm not ungrateful. I was a difficult proposition to deal with. I understand now, of course. Since you didn't tell me the truth in the beginning, you couldn't very well turn back after I'd set my head. At least, if you'd been the sort who could, you wouldn't have had to,—for I'd not have cared a button for that sort, even then." She stopped beside a car that waited at the curb and gave him her hand. "There. We part friends?"

Fred looked at her. "You know. Ten years."

"I'm not ungrateful," Thea repeated as she got into her cab.

"Yes," she reflected, as the taxi cut into the Park carriage road, "we don't get fairy tales in this world, and he has, after all, cared more and longer than anybody else." It was dark outside now, and the light from the lamps along the drive flashed into the cab. The snowflakes hovered like swarms of white bees about the globes.

Thea sat motionless in one corner staring out of the window at the cab lights that wove in and out among the trees, all seeming to be bent upon joyous courses. Taxicabs were still new in New York, and the theme of popular minstrelsy. Landry had sung her a ditty he heard in some theater on Third Avenue, about

> "But there passed him a bright-eyed taxi
> With the girl of his heart inside."

Almost inaudibly Thea began to hum the air, though she was thinking of something serious, something that had touched her deeply. At the beginning of the season, when she was not singing often, she had gone one afternoon to hear Paderewski's* recital. In front of her sat an old German couple, evidently poor people who had made sacrifices to pay for their excellent seats. Their intelligent enjoyment of the music, and their friendliness with each other, had interested her more than anything on the programme. When the pianist began a lovely melody in the first movement of the Beethoven D minor sonata, the old lady put out her plump hand and touched her husband's sleeve and they looked at each other in recognition. They both wore glasses, but such a look! Like forget-me-nots, and so full of happy recollections. Thea wanted to put her arms around them and ask them how they had been able to keep a feeling like that, like a nosegay in a glass of water.

XI

DR. ARCHIE saw nothing of Thea during the following week. After several fruitless efforts, he succeeded in getting a word with her over the telephone, but she sounded so distracted and driven that he was glad to say goodnight and hang up the instrument. There were, she told him, rehearsals not only for "Walküre," but also for "Götterdämmerung,"* in which she was to sing *Waltraute** two weeks later.

On Thursday afternoon Thea got home late, after an exhausting rehearsal. She was in no happy frame of mind. Madame Necker, who had been very gracious to her that night when she went on to complete Gloeckler's performance of *Sieglinde*, had, since Thea was cast to sing the part instead of Gloeckler in the production of the "Ring," been chilly and disapproving, distinctly hostile. Thea had always felt that she and Necker stood for the same sort of endeavor, and that Necker recognized it and had a cordial feeling for her. In Germany she had several times sung *Brangaena** to Necker's *Isolde*,* and the older artist had let her know that she thought she sang it beautifully. It was a bitter disappointment to find that the approval of so honest an artist as Necker could not stand the test of any significant recognition by the management. Madame Necker was forty, and her voice was failing just when her powers were at their height. Every fresh young voice was an enemy, and this one was accompanied by gifts which she could not fail to recognize.

Thea had her dinner sent up to her apartment, and it was a very poor one. She tasted the soup and then indignantly put on her wraps to go out and hunt a dinner. As she was going to the elevator, she had to admit that she was behaving foolishly. She took off her hat and coat and ordered another dinner. When it arrived, it was no better than the first. There was even a burnt match under the milk toast. She had a sore throat, which made swallowing painful and boded ill for the morrow. Although she had been speaking in whispers all day to save her throat, she now perversely summoned the housekeeper and demanded an account of some laundry that had been lost. The housekeeper was indifferent and impertinent, and Thea got angry and scolded violently. She knew it was very bad for her to get into a rage just before bedtime, and after the housekeeper left she realized that for ten dollars' worth of underclothing she had been unfitting herself for a performance which might eventually mean many thousands. The best thing now was to stop reproaching herself for her lack of sense, but she was too tired to control her thoughts.

While she was undressing—Thérèse was brushing out her *Sieglinde* wig in the trunk-room—she went on chiding herself bitterly. "And how am I ever going to get to sleep in this state?" she kept asking herself. "If I don't sleep, I'll be perfectly worthless to-morrow. I'll go down there to-morrow and make a fool of myself. If I'd let that laundry alone with whatever nigger has stolen it— *Why* did I undertake to reform the management of this hotel tonight? After to-morrow I could pack up and leave the place. There's the Phillamon—I liked the rooms there better, anyhow—and the Umberto—" She began going over the advantages and disadvantages of different apartment hotels. Suddenly she checked herself. "What *am* I doing this for? I can't move into another hotel to-night. I'll keep this up till morning. I shan't sleep a wink."

Should she take a hot bath, or shouldn't she? Sometimes it relaxed her, and sometimes it roused her and fairly put her beside herself. Between the conviction that she must sleep and the fear that she couldn't, she hung paralyzed. When she looked at her bed, she shrank from it in every nerve. She was much more afraid of it than she had ever been of the stage of any opera house. It yawned before her like the sunken road at Waterloo.

She rushed into her bathroom and locked the door. She would risk the bath, and defer the encounter with the bed a little longer. She lay in the bath half an hour. The warmth of the water penetrated to her bones, induced pleasant reflections and a feeling of well-being. It was very nice to have Dr. Archie in New York, after all, and to see him get so much satisfaction out of the little companionship she was able to give him. She liked people who got on, and who became more interesting as they grew older. There was Fred; he was much more interesting now than he had been at thirty. He was intelligent about music, and he must be very intelligent in his business, or he would not be at the head of the Brewers' Trust. She respected that kind of intelligence and success. Any success was good. She herself had made a good start, at any rate, and now, if she could get to sleep— Yes, they were all more interesting than they used to be. Look at Harsanyi, who had been so long retarded; what a place he had made for himself in Vienna. If she could get to sleep, she would show him something to-morrow that he would understand.

She got quickly into bed and moved about freely between the sheets. Yes, she was warm all over. A cold, dry breeze was coming in from the river, thank goodness! She tried to think about her little rock house and the Arizona sun and the blue sky. But that led to memories which were still too disturbing. She turned on her side, closed her eyes, and tried an old device.

She entered her father's front door, hung her hat and coat on the rack, and stopped in the parlor to warm her hands at the stove. Then she went out through the dining-room, where the boys were getting their lessons at the long table; through the sitting-room, where Thor was asleep in his cot bed, his dress and stocking hanging on a chair. In the kitchen she stopped for her lantern and her hot brick. She hurried up the back stairs and through the windy loft to her own glacial room. The illusion was marred only by the consciousness that she ought to brush her teeth before she went to bed, and that she never used to do it. Why—? The water was frozen solid in the pitcher, so she got over that. Once between the red blankets there was a short, fierce battle with the cold; then, warmer—warmer. She could hear her father shaking down the hard-coal burner for the night, and the wind rushing and banging down the village street. The boughs of the cottonwood, hard as bone, rattled against her gable. The bed grew softer and warmer. Everybody was warm and well down-stairs. The sprawling old house had gathered them all in, like a hen, and had settled down over its brood. They were all warm in her father's house. Softer and softer. She was asleep. She slept ten hours without turning over. From sleep like that, one awakes in shining armor.

On Friday afternoon there was an inspiring audience; there was not an empty chair in the house. Ottenburg and Dr. Archie had seats in the orchestra circle, got from a ticket broker. Landry had not been able to get a seat, so he roamed about in the back of the house, where he usually stood when he dropped in after his own turn in vaudeville was over. He was there so often and at such irregular hours that the ushers thought he was a singer's husband, or had something to do with the electrical plant.

Harsanyi and his wife were in a box, near the stage, in the second circle. Mrs. Harsanyi's hair was noticeably gray, but her face was fuller and handsomer than in those early years of struggle, and she was beautifully dressed. Harsanyi himself had changed very little. He had put on his best afternoon coat in honor of his pupil, and wore a pearl in his black ascot. His hair was longer and more bushy than he used to wear it, and there was now one gray lock on the right side. He had always been an elegant figure, even when he went about in shabby clothes and was crushed with work. Before the curtain rose he was restless and nervous, and kept looking at his watch and wishing he had got a few more letters off before he left his hotel. He had not been in New York since the advent of the taxicab, and had allowed himself too much time. His wife knew that he was afraid of being disappointed this afternoon. He did not often go to the opera because the stupid things that singers did vexed him so, and it always put him in a rage if the conductor held the tempo or in any way accommodated the score to the singer.

When the lights went out and the violins began to quaver their long D against the rude figure of the basses, Mrs. Harsanyi saw her husband's fingers fluttering on his knee in a rapid tattoo. At the moment when *Sieglinde* entered from the side door, she leaned toward him and whispered in his ear, "Oh, the lovely creature!" But he made no response, either by voice or gesture. Throughout the first scene he sat sunk in his chair, his head forward and his one yellow eye rolling restlessly and shining like a tiger's in the dark. His eye followed *Sieglinde* about the stage like a satellite, and as she sat at the table listening to *Siegmund's* long narrative, it never left her. When she prepared the sleeping draught and disappeared after *Hunding*,* Harsanyi bowed his head still lower and put his hand over his eye to rest it. The tenor,—a young man who sang with great vigor, went on:—

> *"Wälse! Wälse!*
> *Wo ist dein Schwert?"**

Harsanyi smiled, but he did not look forth again until *Sieglinde* reappeared. She went through the story of her shameful bridal feast and into the Walhall' music, which she always sang so nobly, and the entrance of the one-eyed stranger:—

> *"Mir allein*
> *Weckte das Auge."**

Mrs. Harsanyi glanced at her husband, wondering whether the singer on the stage could not feel his commanding glance. On came the *crescendo*:—

> *"Was je ich verlor,*
> *Was je ich beweint*
> *Wär mir gewonnen."*

> (All that I have lost,
> All that I have mourned,
> Would I then have won.)

Harsanyi touched his wife's arm softly.

Seated in the moonlight, the *Volsung* pair began their loving inspection of each other's beauties, and the music born of murmuring sound passed into her face, as the old poet said,—and into her body as well. Into one lovely attitude after another the music swept her, love impelled her. And the voice gave out all that was best in it. Like the spring, indeed, it blossomed into memories and prophecies, it recounted and it foretold, as she sang the story of her friendless life, and of how the thing which was truly herself, "bright as the day, rose to the surface" when in the hostile world she for the first time beheld her Friend. Fervently she rose into the hardier feeling of action and daring, the pride in herostrength and hero-blood, until in a splendid burst, tall and shining like a Victory, she christened him:—

> *"Siegmund—*
> *So nenn ich dich!"**

Her impatience for the sword swelled with her anticipation of his act, and throwing her arms above her head, she fairly tore a sword out of the empty air for him, before *Nothung** had left the tree. *In höchster Trunkenheit*,* indeed, she burst out with the flaming cry of their kinship: "If you are *Siegmund*, I am

Sieglinde!" Laughing, singing, bounding, exulting,—with their passion and their sword,—the *Volsungs* ran out into the spring night.

As the curtain fell, Harsanyi turned to his wife. "At last," he sighed, "somebody with *enough!* Enough voice and talent and beauty, enough physical power. And such a noble, noble style!"

"I can scarcely believe it, Andor. I can see her now, that clumsy girl, hunched up over your piano. I can see her shoulders. She always seemed to labor so with her back. And I shall never forget that night when you found her voice."

The audience kept up its clamor until, after many reappearances with the tenor, Kronborg came before the curtain alone. The house met her with a roar, a greeting that was almost savage in its fierceness. The singer's eyes, sweeping the house, rested for a moment on Harsanyi, and she waved her long sleeve toward his box.

"She *ought* to be pleased that you are here," said Mrs. Harsanyi. "I wonder if she knows how much she owes to you."

"She owes me nothing," replied her husband quickly. "She paid her way. She always gave something back, even then."

"I remember you said once that she would do nothing common," said Mrs. Harsanyi thoughtfully.

"Just so. She might fail, die, get lost in the pack. But if she achieved, it would be nothing common. There are people whom one can trust for that. There is one way in which they will never fail." Harsanyi retired into his own reflections.

After the second act Fred Ottenburg brought Archie to the Harsanyis' box and introduced him as an old friend of Miss Kronborg. The head of a musical publishing house joined them, bringing with him a journalist and the president of a German singing society. The conversation was chiefly about the new *Sieglinde*. Mrs. Harsanyi was gracious and enthusiastic, her husband nervous and uncommunicative. He smiled mechanically, and politely answered questions addressed to him. "Yes, quite so." "Oh, certainly." Every one, of course, said very usual things with great conviction. Mrs. Harsanyi was used to hearing and uttering the commonplaces which such occasions demanded.

When her husband withdrew into the shadow, she covered his retreat by her sympathy and cordiality. In reply to a direct question from Ottenburg, Harsanyi said, flinching, "*Isolde?* Yes, why not? She will sing all the great rôles, I should think."

The chorus director said something about "dramatic temperament." The journalist insisted that it was "explosive force," "projecting power."

Ottenburg turned to Harsanyi. "What is it, Mr. Harsanyi? Miss Kronborg says if there is anything in her, you are the man who can say what it is."

The journalist scented copy and was eager. "Yes, Harsanyi. You know all about her. What's her secret?"

Harsanyi rumpled his hair irritably and shrugged his shoulders. "Her secret? It is every artist's secret,"—he waved his hand,—"passion. That is all. It is an open secret, and perfectly safe. Like heroism, it is inimitable in cheap materials."

The lights went out. Fred and Archie left the box as the second act came on.

Artistic growth is, more than it is anything else, a refining of the sense of truthfulness. The stupid believe that to be truthful is easy; only the artist, the great artist, knows how difficult it is. That afternoon nothing new came to Thea Kronborg, no enlightenment, no inspiration. She merely came into full possession of things she had been refining and perfecting for so long. Her inhibitions chanced to be fewer than usual, and, within herself, she entered into the inheritance that she herself had laid up, into the fullness of the faith she had kept before she knew its name or its meaning.

Often when she sang, the best she had was unavailable; she could not break through to it, and every sort of distraction and mischance came between it and her. But this afternoon the closed roads opened, the gates dropped. What she had so often tried to reach, lay under her hand. She had only to touch an idea to make it live.

While she was on the stage she was conscious that every movement was the right movement, that her body was absolutely the instrument of her idea. Not for nothing had she kept it so severely, kept it filled with such energy and fire. All that deep-rooted vitality flowered in her voice, her face, in her very finger-tips. She felt like a tree bursting into bloom. And her voice was as flexible as her body; equal to any demand, capable of every *nuance*. With the sense of its perfect companionship, its entire trustworthiness, she had been able to throw herself into the dramatic exigencies of the part, everything in her at its best and everything working together.

The third act came on, and the afternoon slipped by. Thea Kronborg's friends, old and new, seated about the house on different floors and levels, enjoyed her triumph according to their natures. There was one there, whom nobody knew, who perhaps got greater pleasure out of that afternoon than Harsanyi himself. Up in the top gallery a gray-haired little Mexican, withered and bright as a string of peppers beside a 'dobe door, kept praying and cursing under his breath, beating on the brass railing and shouting "Bravó! Bravó!" until he was repressed by his neighbors.

He happened to be there because a Mexican band was to be a feature of Barnum and Bailey's circus that year. One of the managers of the show had traveled about the Southwest, signing up a lot of Mexican musicians at low wages, and had brought them to New York. Among them was Spanish Johnny. After Mrs. Tellamantez died, Johnny abandoned his trade and went out with his mandolin to pick up a living for one. His irregularities had become his regular mode of life.

When Thea Kronborg came out of the stage entrance on Fortieth Street, the sky was still flaming with the last rays of the sun that was sinking off behind the North River. A little crowd of people was lingering about the door—musicians from the orchestra who were waiting for their comrades, curious young men, and some poorly dressed girls who were hoping to get a glimpse of the singer. She bowed graciously to the group, through her veil, but she did not look to the right or left as she crossed the sidewalk to her cab. Had she lifted her eyes an instant and glanced out through her white scarf, she must have seen the only man in the crowd who had removed his hat when she emerged, and who stood with it crushed up in his hand. And she would have known him, changed as he was. His lustrous black hair was full of gray, and his face was a good deal worn by the *extasi*, so that it seemed to have shrunk away from his shining eyes and teeth and left them too prominent. But she would have known him. She passed so near that he could have touched her, and he did not put on his hat until her taxi had snorted away. Then he walked down Broadway with his hands in his overcoat pockets, wearing a smile which embraced all the stream of life that passed him and the lighted towers that rose into the limpid blue of the evening sky. If the singer, going home exhausted in her cab, was wondering what was the good of it all, that smile, could she have seen it, would have answered her. It is the only commensurate answer.

Here we must leave Thea Kronborg. From this time on the story of her life is the story of her achievement. The growth of an artist is an intellectual and spiritual development which can scarcely be followed in a personal narrative. This story attempts to deal only with the simple and concrete beginnings which color and accent an artist's work, and to give some account of how a Moonstone girl found her way out of a vague, easy-going world into a life of disciplined endeavor. Any account of the loyalty of young hearts to some exalted ideal, and the passion with which they strive, will always, in some of us, rekindle generous emotions.

EPILOGUE

EPILOGUE

MOONSTONE again, in the year 1909. The Methodists are giving an ice-cream sociable in the grove about the new court-house. It is a warm summer night of full moon. The paper lanterns which hang among the trees are foolish toys, only dimming, in little lurid circles, the great softness of the lunar light that floods the blue heavens and the high plateau. To the east the sand hills shine white as of old, but the empire of the sand is gradually diminishing. The grass grows thicker over the dunes than it used to, and the streets of the town are harder and firmer than they were twenty-five years ago. The old inhabitants will tell you that sand-storms are infrequent now, that the wind blows less persistently in the spring and plays a milder tune. Cultivation has modified the soil and the climate, as it modifies human life.

The people seated about under the cottonwoods are much smarter than the Methodists we used to know. The interior of the new Methodist Church looks like a theater, with a sloping floor, and as the congregation proudly say, "opera chairs." The matrons who attend to serving the refreshments to-night look younger for their years than did the women of Mrs. Kronborg's time, and the children all look like city children. The little boys wear "Buster Browns" and the little girls Russian blouses. The country child, in made-overs and cut-downs, seems to have vanished from the face of the earth.

At one of the tables, with her Dutch-cut twin boys, sits a fair-haired, dimpled matron who was once Lily Fisher. Her husband is president of the new bank, and she "goes East for her summers," a practice which causes envy and discontent among her neighbors. The twins are well-behaved children, biddable, meek, neat about their clothes, and always mindful of the proprieties they have learned at summer hotels. While they are eating their ice-cream and trying not to twist the spoon in their mouths, a little shriek of laughter breaks from an adjacent table. The twins look up. There sits a spry little old spinster whom they know well.

She has a long chin, a long nose, and she is dressed like a young girl, with a pink sash and a lace garden hat with pink rosebuds. She is surrounded by a crowd of boys,—loose and lanky, short and thick,—who are joking with her roughly, but not unkindly.

"Mamma," one of the twins comes out in a shrill treble, "why is Tillie Kronborg always talking about a thousand dollars?"

The boys, hearing this question, break into a roar of laughter, the women titter behind their paper napkins, and even from Tillie there is a little shriek of appreciation. The observing child's remark had made every one suddenly realize that Tillie never stopped talking about that particular sum of money. In the spring, when she went to buy early strawberries, and was told that they were thirty cents a box, she was sure to remind the grocer that though her name was Kronborg she didn't get a thousand dollars a night. In the autumn, when she went to buy her coal for the winter, she expressed amazement at the price quoted her, and told the dealer he must have got her mixed up with her niece to think she could pay such a sum. When she was making her Christmas presents, she never failed to ask the women who came into her shop what you *could* make for anybody who got a thousand dollars a night. When the Denver papers announced that Thea Kronborg had married Frederick Ottenburg, the head of the Brewers' Trust, Moonstone people expected that Tillie's vain-gloriousness would take another form. But Tillie had hoped that Thea would marry a title, and she did not boast much about Ottenburg,—at least not until after her memorable trip to Kansas City to hear Thea sing.

Tillie is the last Kronborg left in Moonstone. She lives alone in a little house with a green yard, and keeps a fancy-work and millinery store. Her business methods are informal, and she would never come out even at the end of the year, if she did not receive a draft for a good round sum from her niece at Christmas time. The arrival of this draft always renews the discussion as to what Thea would do for her aunt if she really did the right thing. Most of the Moonstone people think Thea ought to take Tillie to New York and keep her as a companion. While they are feeling sorry for Tillie because she does not live at the Plaza, Tillie is trying not to hurt their feelings by showing too plainly how much she realizes the superiority of her position. She tries to be modest when she complains to the postmaster that her New York paper is more than three days late. It means enough, surely, on the face of it, that she is the only person in Moonstone who takes a New York paper or who has any reason for taking one. A foolish young girl, Tillie lived in the splendid sorrows of "Wanda" and "Strathmore";* a foolish old girl, she lives in her niece's triumphs. As she often says, she just missed going on the stage herself.

That night after the sociable, as Tillie tripped home with a crowd of noisy boys and girls, she was perhaps a shade troubled. The twin's question rather lingered in her ears. Did she, perhaps, insist too much on that thousand dollars? Surely, people didn't for a minute think it was the money she cared about? As for that, Tillie tossed her head, she didn't care a rap. They must understand that this money was different.

When the laughing little group that brought her home had gone weaving down the sidewalk through the leafy shadows and had disappeared, Tillie brought out a rocking chair and sat down on her porch. On glorious, soft summer nights like this, when the moon is opulent and full, the day submerged and forgotten, she loves to sit there behind her rose-vine and let her fancy wander where it will. If you chanced to be passing down that Moonstone street and saw that alert white figure rocking there behind the screen of roses and lingering late into the night, you might feel sorry for her, and how mistaken you would be! Tillie lives in a little magic world, full of secret satisfactions. Thea Kronborg has given much noble pleasure to a world that needs all it can get, but to no individual has she given more than to her queer old aunt in Moonstone. The legend of Kronborg, the artist, fills Tillie's life; she feels rich and exalted in it. What delightful things happen in her mind as she sits there rocking! She goes back to those early days of sand and sun, when Thea was a child and Tillie was herself, so it seems to her, "young." When she used to hurry to church to hear Mr. Kronborg's wonderful sermons, and when Thea used to stand up by the organ of a bright Sunday morning and sing "Come, Ye Disconsolate." Or she thinks about that wonderful time when the Metropolitan Opera Company sang a week's engagement in Kansas City, and Thea sent for her and had her stay with her at the Coates House and go to every performance at Convention Hall. Thea let Tillie go through her costume trunks and try on her wigs and jewels. And the kindness of Mr. Ottenburg! When Thea dined in her own room, he went down to dinner with Tillie, and never looked bored or absent-minded when she chattered. He took her to the hall the first time Thea sang there, and sat in the box with her and helped her through "Lohengrin." After the first act, when Tillie turned tearful eyes to him and burst out, "I don't care, she always seemed grand like that, even when she was a girl. I expect I'm crazy, but she just seems to me full of all them old times!"—Ottenburg was so sympathetic and patted her hand and said, "But that's just what she is, full of the old times, and you are a wise woman to see it." Yes, he said that to her. Tillie often wondered how she had been able to bear it when Thea came down the stairs in the wedding robe embroidered in silver, with a train so long it took six women to carry it.

Tillie had lived fifty-odd years for that week, but she got it, and no miracle was ever more miraculous than that. When she used to be working in the fields on her father's Minnesota farm, she couldn't help believing that she would some day have to do with the "wonderful," though her chances for it had then looked so slender.

The morning after the sociable, Tillie, curled up in bed, was roused by the rattle of the milk cart down the street. Then a neighbor boy came down the sidewalk outside her window, singing "Casey Jones" as if he hadn't a care in the world. By this time Tillie was wide awake. The twin's question, and the subsequent laughter, came back with a faint twinge. Tillie knew she was short-sighted about facts, but this time— Why, there were her scrap-books, full of newspaper and magazine articles about Thea, and half-tone cuts, snap-shots of her on land and sea, and photographs of her in all her parts. There, in her parlor, was the phonograph that had come from Mr. Ottenburg last June, on

Thea's birthday; she had only to go in there and turn it on, and let Thea speak for herself. Tillie finished brushing her white hair and laughed as she gave it a smart turn and brought it into her usual French twist. If Moonstone doubted, she had evidence enough: in black and white, in figures and photographs, evidence in hair lines on metal disks. For one who had so often seen two and two as making six, who had so often stretched a point, added a touch, in the good game of trying to make the world brighter than it is, there was positive bliss in having such deep foundations of support. She need never tremble in secret lest she might some-time stretch a point in Thea's favor.—Oh, the comfort, to a soul too zealous, of having at last a rose so red it could not be further painted, a lily so truly auriferous that no amount of gilding could exceed the fact!

Tillie hurried from her bedroom, threw open the doors and windows, and let the morning breeze blow through her little house.

In two minutes a cob fire was roaring in her kitchen stove, in five she had set the table. At her household work Tillie was always bursting out with shrill snatches of song, and as suddenly stop-ping, right in the middle of a phrase, as if she had been struck dumb. She emerged upon the back porch with one of these bursts, and bent down to get her butter and cream out of the ice-box. The cat was purring on the bench and the morning-glories were thrusting their purple trumpets in through the lattice-work in a friendly way. They reminded Tillie that while she was wait-ing for the coffee to boil she could get some flowers for her breakfast table. She looked out uncertainly at a bush of sweet-briar that grew at the edge of her yard, off across the long grass and the tomato vines. The front porch, to be sure, was dripping with crimson ramblers that ought to be cut for the good of the vines; but never the rose in the hand for Tillie! She caught up the kitchen shears and off she dashed through grass and drenching dew. Snip, snip; the short-stemmed sweet-briars, salmon-pink and golden-hearted, with their unique and inimitable woody perfume, fell into her apron.

After she put the eggs and toast on the table, Tillie took last

Sunday's New York paper from the rack beside the cupboard and sat down, with it for company. In the Sunday paper there was always a page about singers, even in summer, and that week the musical page began with a sympathetic account of Madame Kronborg's first performance of *Isolde* in London. At the end of the notice, there was a short paragraph about her having sung for the King* at Buckingham Palace and having been presented with a jewel by His Majesty.

Singing for the King; but Goodness! she was always doing things like that! Tillie tossed her head. All through breakfast she kept sticking her sharp nose down into the glass of sweet-briar, with the old incredible lightness of heart, like a child's balloon tugging at its string. She had always insisted, against all evidence, that life was full of fairy tales, and it was! She had been feeling a little down, perhaps, and Thea had answered her, from so far. From a common person, now, if you were troubled, you might get a letter. But Thea almost never wrote letters. She answered every one, friends and foes alike, in one way, her own way, her only way. Once more Tillie has to remind herself that it is all true, and is not something she has "made up." Like all romancers, she is a little terrified at seeing one of her wildest conceits admitted by the hard-headed world. If our dream comes true, we are almost afraid to believe it; for that is the best of all good fortune, and nothing better can happen to any of us.

When the people on Sylvester Street tire of Tillie's stories, she goes over to the east part of town, where her legends are always welcome. The humbler people of Moonstone still live there. The same little houses sit under the cottonwoods; the men smoke their pipes in the front doorways, and the women do their washing in the back yard. The older women remember Thea, and how she used to come kicking her express wagon along the sidewalk, steering by the tongue and holding Thor in her lap. Not much happens in that part of town, and the people have long memories. A boy grew up on one of those streets who went to Omaha and built up a great business, and is now very rich. Moonstone people always speak of him and Thea together, as examples of Moonstone enterprise. They do, however, talk oftener of Thea. A voice has even a wider appeal than a fortune. It is the one gift that all creatures would possess if they could. Dreary Maggie Evans, dead nearly twenty years, is still remembered because Thea sang at her funeral "after she had studied in Chicago."

However much they may smile at her, the old inhabitants would miss Tillie. Her stories give them something to talk about and to conjecture about, cut off as they are from the restless currents of the world. The many naked little sandbars which lie beneath Venice and the mainland, in the seemingly stagnant water of the lagoons, are made habitable and wholesome only because, every night, a foot and a half of tide creeps in from the sea and winds its fresh brine up through all that network of shining waterways. So, into all the little settlements of quiet people, tidings of what their boys and girls are doing in the world bring real refreshment; bring to the old, memories, and to the young, dreams.

APPENDIX

The Appendix that follows prints Cather's Preface to the revised edition of *The Song of the Lark* in the 1937 Autograph Edition of her novels (see Note on the Text). It reflects the principles of novelistic form that she developed after writing *O Pioneers!* (1913), *The Song of the Lark* (1915), and *My Ántonia* (1918). These principles are most clearly expressed in her 1922 essay 'The Novel Démeublé' (*The New Republic*, April 1922; repr. Willa Cather, *Not Under Forty* (New York, 1936)), in which she developed her theory of 'the unfurnished novel' whose highest qualities are evident in 'Whatever is felt upon the page without being specifically named there . . . the inexplicable presence of the thing not named, . . . the overtone divined by the ear but not heard by it, the verbal mood, the emotional aura of the fact or the thing or the deed.' Though some aspects of 'The Novel Démeublé' are pertinent to the original version of *The Song of the Lark*, it can hardly be called 'unfurnished', a term more applicable to Cather's novels of the 1920s, especially *A Lost Lady* (1923), *The Professor's House* (1925), and *My Mortal Enemy* (1926). Nevertheless the Preface provides crucial information for interpreting the text.

PREFACE

THE SONG OF THE LARK was written in the years 1914 and 1915. The title of the book is unfortunate; many readers take it for granted that the 'lark song' refers to the vocal accomplishments of the heroine, which is altogether a mistake. Her song was not of the skylark order. The book was named for a rather second-rate French painting in the Chicago Art Institute; a picture in which a little peasant girl, on her way to work in the fields at early morning, stops and looks up to listen to a lark. The title was meant to suggest a young girl's awakening to something beautiful. I wanted to call the story 'Artist's Youth,' but my publisher discouraged me, wisely enough.

The chief fault of the book is that it describes a descending curve; the life of a successful artist in the full tide of achievement is not so interesting as the life of a talented young girl 'fighting her way,' as we say. Success is never so interesting as struggle—not even to the successful, not even to the most mercenary forms of ambition.

The life of nearly every artist who succeeds in the true sense (succeeds in delivering himself completely to his art) is more or less like Wilde's story, 'The Portrait of Dorian Grey.'* As Thea Kronborg is more and more released into the dramatic and musical possibilities of her profession, as her artistic life grows fuller and richer, it becomes more interesting to her than her own life. As the gallery of her musical impersonations grows in number and beauty, as that perplexing thing called 'style' (which is a singer's very self) becomes more direct and simple and noble, the Thea Kronborg who is behind the imperishable daughters of music becomes somewhat dry and preoccupied. Her human life is made up of exacting engagements and dull business detail, of shifts to evade an idle, gaping world which is determined that no artist shall ever do his best. Her artistic life is the only one in which she is happy, or free, or even very real. It is the reverse of Wilde's story; the harassed, susceptible human creature comes and goes, subject to colds, brokers, dressmakers, managers. But the free creature, who retains her youth and beauty and warm imagination, is kept shut up in the closet, along with the scores and wigs.

The interesting and important fact that, in an artist of the type I chose, personal life becomes paler as the imaginative life becomes richer, does not, however, excuse my story for becoming paler. The story set out to tell of an artist's awakening and struggle; her floundering escape from a smug, domestic, self-satisfied provincial world of utter ignorance. It should have been content to do that. I should have disregarded conventional design and stopped where my first conception stopped, telling the latter part of the story by suggestion merely. What I cared about, and still care about, was the girl's escape; the play of blind chance, the way in which commonplace occurrences fell together to liberate her from commonness. She seemed wholly at the mercy of accident; but to persons of her vitality and honesty, fortunate accidents will always happen.

WILLA CATHER

NEW BRUNSWICK, CANADA
July 16, 1932

EXPLANATORY NOTES

1   *The Song of the Lark*: title of a painting by French artist Jules Breton (1827–1906). See Cather's Preface to the revised 1937 Autograph Edition (Appendix, p. 416).

    'It . . . Juan': poem (1851) by Austrian Romantic poet Nicolaus Lenau (1802–50), which provided the inspiration for Richard Strauss's orchestral piece (1889) of the same name.

2   *To Isabelle McClung*: Cather met McClung (1877–1938), a devotee of the arts and a member of a prominent and wealthy Pittsburgh family, in 1899. Their intimate friendship (Cather lived with McClung's family from 1901 to 1906) was crucial to the establishment of her literary career.

    On . . . be: the dedicatory poem is by Cather.

7   *Napoleon III*: Louis Napoleon Bonaparte (1808–73), president (1848–52) and later emperor (1852–70) of France.

9   *Fay Templeton*: enormously popular American singer and comedienne (1865–1939) best known for her performances in light operas and musical extravaganzas.

    troche: a medicated lozenge.

10   *Thea*: in Greek, a goddess.

12   *Brussels carpet*: a type of machine-made carpet characterized by colourful patterns; in a modest household like the Kronborgs', a prized possession.

    Czerny's 'Daily Studies': Karl Czerny (1791–1857), Austrian pianist known for his technical studies of the piano.

15   *sovereign State of Colorado*: Colorado was admitted to the United States in 1876; thus, the novel takes place after this date.

    tower of Babel: Babel was an ancient city in the land of Shinar in which a tower intended to reach heaven was begun.

16   *Malaga grapes*: very sweet grapes imported from Málaga, Spain; particularly before mass transport of perishable foods, an elegant luxury item.

    Professor Wunsch: the music teacher's name means 'wish' or 'desire'; see Part I, Ch. XI.

17   *Chihuahua*: a state in northern Mexico.

    'My . . . good-night': *Childe Harold's Pilgrimage*, I. xiii. 1.

    'There . . . revelry': *Childe Harold's Pilgrimage*, III. xxi. 1.

    Thor: in Scandinavian mythology, the god of thunder.

22   *fairy tale*: Hans Christian Andersen's *The Snow Queen*.

25 *Jenny Lind*: Swedish soprano (1820–87), sang opera in Europe, later a concert and oratorio performer; toured the USA (1850–2) with great success under P. T. Barnum's management; called 'the Swedish nightingale' because of the range and quality of her voice.

27 *'Morgen'*: 'Morning' or 'Good morning'.

'Weiter . . . Immer . . . Schön!': 'forward . . . always . . . fine!'

'Ein . . . vier': 'One, two, three, four'.

'Invitation . . . Dance': Karl Maria von Weber's 'Rondo brillant' in D flat major, opus 65, for piano (1819).

28 *'Lente . . . equi'*: Ovid, *Amores* I. xiii. 40.

Napoleon's . . . Moscow: the turning point in French emperor Napoleon I's (1769–1821) campaign to conquer Europe occurred when he was forced to retreat from Moscow in 1812.

Murat: Joachim Murat (1767–1815), cavalry commander and Marshal of France under Napoleon I.

29 *'Come . . . Disconsolate'*: hymn (1816) by the Irish poet Thomas Moore, set to a German tune.

38 *'A Distinguished . . . Paris'*: Balzac's *Un grand homme de Province à Paris* (1839).

40 *'La Golandrina'*: 'The Swallow'.

41 *'Mi testa! . . . Muchacha!'*: 'My head! . . . The fever! . . . The little girl!'

La Junta, Albuquerque, Chihuahua: locations moving south from Colorado to New Mexico to Mexico.

48 *Robert Ingersoll*: famous American orator and lawyer (1833–99); widely read lecturer who questioned the tenets of Christian belief.

'The Age of Reason': defence of deism (1794–6) by Thomas Paine, English political radical and pamphleteer.

49 *'nada'*: 'nothing'.

'Ultimo Amor': 'Most Recent Love'.

'Fluvia de Oro': roughly, 'River of Gold'; Cather's Spanish is not exact.

'Noches de Algeria': 'Nights in Algeria'.

50 *Forty-niners*: colloquial reference to the large numbers of adventurers who swelled the California population between the discovery of gold (January 1848) and the end of 1849.

Mormons: the overland trek (1846–8) of the Mormons (Church of Jesus Christ of Latter-day Saints) from Illinois to the Great Salt Lake passed over the Laramie Plain.

51 *'Westward . . . way'*: first line of last stanza of George Berkeley's poem 'On the Prospect of Planting Arts and Learning in America' (1752).

Greaser: disparaging slang for a Mexican; someone with oily skin.

53 *Greely's party*: Adolphus Greely (1844–1935) led a US expedition to the Arctic (1881) to establish an international meteorological station; though its members performed many notable feats of exploration, all but seven of the twenty-five died of exposure, starvation, or drowning.

55 *W.C.T.U.*: Women's Christian Temperance Union, founded at Cleveland, Ohio (1874) as a result of the temperance crusade spreading through the Middle West; campaigned for legislation prohibiting the sale of liquor and harmful drugs, for the abolishment of prostitution, and for a single standard of sexual purity.

eyes . . . Mariner's: '"By thy long gray beard and glittering eye | Now wherefore stopp'st thou me?"' Samuel Taylor Coleridge, 'The Rime of the Ancient Mariner', i. i. 4 (1798).

'with . . . motion': slight misquotation from 'The Rime of the Ancient Mariner', v. xxi. 4. The correct wording is 'with a short uneasy motion'.

56 *'Ballade . . . Reinecke*: Carl Reinecke (1824–1910), German pianist, teacher, conductor, and composer.

57 *'Selections . . . Erminie'*: popular comic opera by Edward Jacobowski, with libretto by Claxson Bellamy and Harry Paulton, first produced in London in 1885 and on Broadway in 1886.

'The . . . Boy': lurid and melodramatic poem (1834), frequently used for recitations, in which the speaker kills himself rather than be taken prisoner by the Russians; written by Ann Sophia Winterbotham Stephens (1810–86), magazine editor and prolific writer of thrillers and historical romances.

Progressive Eucre Club: club formed to play eucre, a card game popular around the turn of the century.

'Beloved . . . Night': probably the popular song 'Beloved, It Is Morn' by English composer and singer Florence Aylward (1895), the last verse of which begins, 'Beloved, it is night, it is night!'

claqueurs: literally, hired applauders, though these are probably Kennedy's friends and colleagues.

McCook: large town in south-west Nebraska; here Cather perhaps inadvertently reveals that 'Moonstone' is based on Red Cloud, Nebraska, *c.*100 miles east of McCook.

'Thy . . . I': song (1884) 'for low voice' by Michael Walton to words by Edward Oxenford.

58 *'Rock . . . me'*: first line of 'Rock of Ages', well-known hymn, words by A. M. Toplady (1776) set to music by Thomas Hastings (1832).

'She . . . heart': from 'Home, Sweet Home', the heroine's nostalgic song in *Ciari; or, The Maid of Milan*, opera by Henry Bishop with libretto by J. H. Payne, produced and published at London, 1823.

'*When . . Watched*': most likely the hymn 'While Shepherds Watched Their Flocks By Night', various musical settings, words by Nahum Tate (*c.*1703) based on the Gospel according to St Luke.

59 '*Musical Memories*' . . . *Haweis*: *My Musical Memories* by Hugh Reginald Haweis (1839–1901) went through at least four editions between 1884 and 1892 and was later expanded as *My Musical Life*, which also reached at least four editions. The book featured Wagner and the Ring Cycle; see Part V, 'Kronborg'.

61 '*Among . . . Breakers*': *Among the Breakers; A Drama, in Two Acts* (1872) by George M. Baker (1832–90), author of plays designed for amateur production.

'*The . . .1812*': *The Veteran of 1812, or, Kesiah and the Scout. A Romantic Military Drama in Five Acts* (1883) by T. Trask Woodward.

intrigante: schemer.

62 '*The . . . Shiloh*': probably *The Drummer Boy; or, The Battle-Field of Shiloh, A new military allegory in five acts and accompanying tableaux, Arranged from incidents of the late war, and respectfully dedicated to the Grand Army of the Republic* (1868) by Samuel J. Muscroft.

supers: short for 'supernumeraries': in theatrical parlance, individuals employed in addition to the regular company, who appear on stage but do not speak.

63 '*Just . . . Mother*': Civil War song (1863) by American composer George Frederick Root.

64 *Leipsic*: English spelling of Leipzig, commercial and industrial city in Saxony and hub of German book and music publishing; a major European cultural centre whose musical reputation reached its peak in the nineteenth and early twentieth centuries. Reinecke (see n. to p. 56 above) conducted and taught there, 1860–1902.

Gluck's 'Orpheus': *Orfeo ed Eurydice* (1762), Italian opera composed by Christoph Willibald von Gluck (1714–87).

'*Aber ja!*': 'But yes; of course!'

65 '*rhythmus*': rhythm.

'*vom . . . mir*': 'Follow the score, accompany me'.

'*Ach . . . dahin*': 'Ah, I have lost her, | All my happiness is gone'.

'*Noch einmal*': 'Once more; over again'.

'*Schön*': 'Beautiful'.

'*Euridice . . . bin!*': 'Woe that I am on Earth!' from Orpheus' lament, Act III.

'*Only . . . good*': Wunsch is probably remembering the celebrated contralto Pauline Viardot (1821–1910), daughter of Spanish tenor Manuel García and principal singer of the Paris Opera, whose some 150 performances (1859–62) in the title role of Berlioz's edition of Gluck's *Orfeo* were acclaimed for reaching tragic heights rarely seen on the stage. Viardot was particularly esteemed by intellectuals, whose appreciation for her artistry and dramatic skill was greater than that of the general public.

66   *'künst-ler-isch'*: 'artistic'.

67   *Hasenpfeffer*: spicy rabbit stew.

68   *Jacob*: literally, Jacob; figuratively, an ordinary fellow.

69   *und . . . weiter*: and so forth.

     Lieder: literally, songs; the word is applied to a distinctive type of solo vocal composition that came into being during the Romantic period, in which the poetic text is as important as the music.

     'Im . . . Mann!': Heinrich Heine, 'Lyrisches Intermezzo' (1822–3), No. 45.

71   *'der . . . Phantasie'*: spirit, imagination.

     'Aber . . . Fräulein!': 'But not American girls!'

     'Märchen': fairy tales.

     'in . . . Kunst!': 'in the heart, in the heart, and without this there is no art, there is no art!'

78   *Brown . . . Hotel*: luxury hotel completed in 1892, shortly after mineral strikes in the nearby mountains ignited Denver's growth.

     Flint's Physiology: probably *The Physiology of man; Designed to represent the existing state of physiological science as applied to the functions of the human body* by Austin Flint, jun., 5 vols. (1836–75).

     Dr. Oliver Wendell Holmes: Holmes (1809–94) was a leading figure among the Boston Brahmins and on the Harvard University faculty, a physician, author, and lecturer who wrote about medicine from both humanistic and scientific perspectives in poems, essays, novels, and clinical papers.

79   *Waverley Novels*: series of thirty-two historical novels and tales by Sir Walter Scott (1771–1832), named after the first novel in the series (1814).

     Constance de Beverley: a nun in Sir Walter Scott's dramatic poem 'Marmion' (1808) who is put to death by the religious authorities after she breaks her vows for Lord Marmion (who abandons her). Eventually, the papers she leaves behind help bring Marmion to justice.

     Duchesse de Langeais: protagonist of the novel *La Duchesse de Langeais* (1833–4), part of Balzac's *Comédie humaine*, a scheming Parisian socialite and *femme fatale* who ends her days in a convent.

     Robert Burns: foremost Scottish poet (1756–96), wrote lyrical, narrative, and satiric poems in the vernacular, many of them set to old Scottish tunes.

82   *picador*: mounted assistant to a matador.

83   *'Mein Gott'*: 'My God!'

     'das Mistbeet!': 'the hotbed!'

'*Wieder!*': 'again!'

'*Die ... Bäume!*': 'The trees!'

'*Der ... Himmel*': 'The dovecote! righteous heaven!'

85 *Fuszreise*: walking tour.

   Einst ... Wunder!: opening of the third stanza of 'Adelaide' by German poet Friedrich von Matthisson (1767–1831), which Beethoven set to music (op. 46). Though a sentimental love poem, its third verse can be read as a comment on the relationship between broken-down teacher and promising pupil: 'Some day, a miracle! A marvel! my grave shall bear a flower, | From its ashes my heart shall yield a blossom, | Brightly gleaming, brightly gleaming'. The poem begins, 'Lonely wanders thy friend ...'.

86 '*Leben ... Kind!*': farewell, farewell, my child!

92 '*tree-diagramming system*': method of analysing sentences by dividing them into trunk, branch, and twig (main clause, dependent clause, modifier). Probably also a dig at Lucius Sherman, chairman of the English Department at the University of Nebraska during Cather's years there (1891–5), who was known for his 'scientific' method of examining literature, which involved word-counts, charts, diagrams, formulae, and equations. Cather chafed under his arid pedantry and missed no opportunity, then or later, to satirize his methods.

   '*Thanatopsis,*' ... '*Immortality*': blank-verse poem by William Cullen Bryant on the subject of death (1817–21); Shakespeare, *Hamlet*, III. i. 56 ff.; Cato's speech on immortality from Joseph Addison's 1713 play *Cato* (V. i), based on the life of Cato the Younger (95–46 BC).

95 *padre*: father.

96 *Maggie ... Barefoot*': Augustus Waldauer's *Little Barefoot: a domestic drama in five acts* was translated from the German and published in an acting edition by Samuel French of New York in 1863. Maggie (Margaret Julia) Mitchell (1832–1918) was acclaimed for the seeming artlessness and sincerity of her portrayals. Touring across the USA in both male and female roles, her greatest success was in *Fanchon, the Cricket*, a dramatization by Waldauer of George Sand's story 'La Petite Fadette', which she performed for thirty years.

98 '*The Odalisque*': harem slave girl.

99 *Ray even ... English than ever*: this passage was removed from the English edition of the novel at the request of John Murray, Cather's British publisher.

   Mrs. ... Wales: Lillie Langtry (1852–1929), known as the Jersey Lily (she came from Jersey in the Channel Islands), one of the first English society women to go on the stage, made her debut in London in 1881 after her husband's financial failure. She first toured the USA in 1882. A success with the public but never taken seriously by the critics, she was noted for her great beauty and her liaison with Albert Edward, Prince of Wales (1841–1910), Queen Victoria's eldest son, who eventually (1901–10) became King of England. Oscar Wilde wrote *Lady Windermere's Fan* for her and Langtry, Texas, is named after her.

99   *Y.M.C.A.*: Young Men's Christian Association.

102   *Cliff . . . Chelly*: Canyon de Chelly, in northeast Arizona, contains the ruins of several hundred prehistoric Indian villages, most of them built between AD 350 and 1300, which are characterized by spectacular cliff dwellings whose inhabitants may be the ancestors of present-day Pueblo Indians. It became a national monument in 1931.

105   *'batched'*: lived a bachelor's life.

109   *'the youth . . . bore'*: 'A youth who bore, 'mid snow and ice, | A banner with the strange device, Excelsior!' from Henry Wadsworth Longfellow's 'Excelsior' (1841), Latin for 'higher'.

113   *'fascinator'*: a scarf of crochet work, lace, etc., narrowing toward the ends, worn as a woman's head covering.

114   *Doxology*: expression of praise to God.

     Jules Verne: French novelist (1828–1905) who achieved great popularity by combining adventure and popular science in books such as *Voyage au centre de la terre* (1864).

115   *'Anna Karenina'*: realistic novel (1874–7) of a tragic, adulterous love affair by Russian author Leo Tolstoy (1828–1910).

     Korsunsky: the director of the ball depicted in Part I, ch. 22 of *Anna Karenina*.

117   *dossier*: record, file.

118   *Naaman . . . Rimmon*: see 2 Kgs. 5: 1–19.

121   *Same . . . surrender*: *'le mot de Cambronne'*, the word—*'merde'*, an impolite synonym for 'excrement'—supposedly uttered by Pierre Jacques Etienne Cambronne (1770–1842), one of Napoleon's generals at Waterloo, in response to an English demand for surrender.

122   *'The . . . Awakened'*: Cather may have in mind either Pre-Raphaelite painter William Holman Hunt's (1827–1910) famous painting *The Awakening Conscience* (1854), which depicts a fallen woman's conversion from sin and rejection of her cynical lover, or another British painting by James Sant (1820–1916), entitled *The Soul's Awakening*, which portrays a young woman wearing an exalted expression and pressing an open book to her heart. In any case, the association of purity with womanhood was a tenet of Victorian thinking .

123   *Mary Anderson*: celebrated American actress, born 1859 in Sacramento, died 1940 in England. Major roles included Rosalind in *As You Like It*, the dual roles of Hermione and Perdita in *The Winter's Tale* (an historical first), Juliet in *Romeo and Juliet*, Julia in James Sheridan Knowles' *The Hunchback*, the title role in Richard Lalor Shiels' *Evadne, or, The Statue*

and Pauline in *The Lady of Lyons, or Love and Pride*, by Edward Bulwer Lytton. Though her acting style, which was old-fashioned and classical rather than realistic, did not receive much critical approval, the reviewers were always impressed with her voice, which was unusually full, deep, and melodious, and she was consistently popular with the public, who called her 'our Mary'.

124 *old Dumas*: Alexandre Dumas, *père*, French novelist (1802–70). Cather quotes this passage again in her 1922 essay, 'The Novel Démeublé' ('The Unfurnished Novel'), where the elder Dumas is singled out for recognizing the difference between the novel as art and as journalism.

Romanticists: artists participating in the Romantic movement in European literature, art, and music that began toward the end of the eighteenth century as rebellion against Classicism; Romanticism emphasized imagination and emotion over reason, intellect, and artistic convention. In France some important writers associated with the movement were Alphonse de Lamartine, Victor Hugo, Alfred de Musset, Alfred de Vigny, Théophile Gautier, George Sand (pen name of Amandine Aurore Lucile Dupin, Baronne Dudevant), Stendhal (pen name of Henri Beyle), Charles Augustin Sainte-Beuve and Prosper Mérimée, in addition to Dumas *père*.

144 *Jephthah's . . . Absalom*: Judges, ch. 11, tells of Jephthah's pledge to God, which accidentally led to the sacrifice of his daughter and only child; Rizpah was Saul's concubine, who held watch over her dead sons on Mt. Gibeah (2 Sam. 3: 7, 21: 8–11); King David's lament for his son Absalom is described in 2 Sam. 18–19.

Homestead Act: the Homestead Act of 1862 provided for the free transfer of a quarter section (160 acres) of unoccupied public land to each homesteader after five years of residence and improvement. Most of Cather's pioneer characters are homesteaders.

146 *'The . . . Magdalene'*: Mary Magdalene appears in the New Testament as a demoniac healed by Jesus, as a watcher at the Cross, as an attendant at Jesus's burial, and as one of those who found the tomb empty (Matt. 27, 28, Mark 15, 16, Luke 8, 24, Josh. 19, 20). She is generally associated with the repentant prostitute who anointed Jesus's feet (Luke 7)

148 *'Gute . . . Morgen'*: 'Good night, good morning'.

Naples . . . Caesar: famous bust of Caesar (*c*.100–44 BC) in the Museo Nazionale, Naples, Italy. Considered one of the most accurate renderings of Caesar, the colossal head, approx. 3′ high, emphasizes his power and authority without altering his physical peculiarities.

149 *Caesar's 'Commentaries'*: the *Commentarii di Bello Gallico* or *Commentaries on the Gallic War* (*c*.58–44 BC), Julius Caesar's seven-volume history of the Gallic Wars, is considered a model of clear, concise Latin and historical accuracy and has been read by generations of students, Cather among them.

149 *Kaffeeklatsch*: social gathering for informal conversation at which coffee is served.

151 *Sängerfest*: choral festival.

152 *Kinderszenen*: *Scenes of Childhood* (1838), thirteen short pieces for solo piano by Robert Schumann.

154 *cantabile*: songlike and flowing in style.

    Christian . . . Destruction: in John Bunyan's prose allegory *The Pilgrim's Progress from This World to That Which Is to Come* (1678, 1684), Christian flees the City of Destruction in order to avoid the destruction of himself, his family, and his town as prophesied in the Bible.

156 *gaucheries*: instances of awkward or embarrassing behaviour.

159 *Theodore Thomas*: American conductor, born Germany (1835–1905), came to the USA at 10, originally a violinist, conducted both the New York Philharmonic and his own orchestra, eventually becoming permanent conductor of the newly founded Chicago Symphony Orchestra, a post he held until his death. Thomas had a major impact on the development of musical taste in the USA.

161 *chaise longue*: couch, day-bed.

162 *'The . . . Nine'*: originally an English hymn by Sir John Frederick Bridge of a text by Elizabeth Cecilia Clefane, but this is probably the popular gospel hymn setting composed by American Evangelistic singer, composer, and hymnbook compiler Ira David Sankey (1840–1908).

163 *entre-chat*: ballet step in which the legs cross before and behind each other while the dancer is in the air.

    pianissimo: very softly.

165 *'Die Lorelei'*: song by Franz Liszt based on a poem by Heine, about a siren who lures sailors on the Rhine to shipwreck.

166 *'Ich . . . bin'*: 'I don't know what it means that I am so sad'.

167 *'Und . . . gethan'*: 'And the Lorelei has done this with her singing'.

    diminuendo: gradually getting softer.

169 *Art Institute*: founded by a small group of artists in 1866 as the Chicago Academy of Fine Arts, the Institute, which is world-famous for its collections, is housed on Michigan Avenue in an Italian Renaissance building constructed for the World's Columbian Exposition in 1893 and has two life-size bronze lions flanking the steps to the front entrance.

170 *Barbizon School*: informal school of French landscape painting (*c.*1830–70) whose name derives from the village of Barbizon, near the forest of Fontainebleau; Jean Baptiste Camille Corot was one of its members.

    the Sunday Inter-Ocean: alternative name of the *Chicago Record-Herald*, newspaper published daily 1901–14.

171 *Dying . . . 'Childe Harold'*: reproduction of the statue *The Dying Gaul*,

familiarly known as *The Dying Gladiator*, originally part of a group of Greek bronzes (*c.*240–200 BC) commemorating their defeat of the Gauls, later reproduced in marble for the Romans (Capitoline Museum, Rome) and widely copied in the nineteenth century. Byron describes the dying gladiator in Book IV, stanzas 140–1 of 'Childe Harold's Pilgrimage': 'he is gone, | Ere ceased the inhuman shout which hailed the wretch who won. | He heard it, but he heeded not—his eyes | Were with his heart, and that was far away; . . . where his rude hut by the Danube lay'.

Venus di Milo: semi-nude marble statue (*c.*200 BC) of Aphrodite, the Greek goddess of love, beauty, and fertility, portrayed with Classical features and in a relaxed, twisting upright stance, originally at Melos, now in the Louvre, Paris, and widely copied in the nineteenth century.

Apollo Belvedere: copy of a statue of Apollo, second only to Zeus in the Greek hierarchy and god of light, order, beauty, and youth. Reproductions in varied sizes of a Roman marble copy now in the Vatican Museum, Rome (the Greek original is lost) were widely displayed in public and private settings during the eighteenth and nineteenth centuries.

great . . . name: probably a copy of Andrea del Verrocchio's *Equestrian Monument of Bartolommeo Colleoni* (*c.*1483–8, bronze, height approx. 13', Venice), which depicts the army commander who commissioned the monument as a looming embodiment of forceful dominance, lip contemptuously curled, and seated upon a robust, active horse.

Gérôme . . . Grief: Jean Léon Gérôme, French artist, painted *La Douleur du Pacha* in 1882 to illustrate a poem by Victor Hugo; the Art Institute of Chicago acquired the painting in 1898.

173 *Dvorak's . . . World'*: Antonín Dvořák (1841–1904), Bohemian composer, spent 1892–5 in New York as head of the National Conservatory, during which period he wrote his E minor symphony 'From the New World' (op. 95, 1893), generally referred to as his 5th symphony, while staying at the Bohemian settlement at Spillville, Iowa; the symphony makes great use of American folk music.

Largo: the second movement of Dvořák's symphony; *largo* means in a slow, dignified fashion.

'*Rhinegold*': *Das Rheingold* (1869), first of four sequential operas in German composer Richard Wagner's (1813–83) cycle of musical dramas, *Der Ring des Nibelungen*, based on the *Nibelungenlied*, a medieval German epic drawing on legend and folklore. References to Wagner, the dominant figure in late nineteenth-century opera, abound in Cather's works.

rainbow bridge: in the last scene of *Das Rheingold* the gods enter Valhalla over a rainbow bridging the Rhine while the Rhinemaidens lament and the river sings.

178 *Rathskeller*: restaurant.

178 *Henrietta Sontag*: German operatic soprano (1805–54) of international fame who performed in the USA in 1852.

194 '*Rosa de Noche*': rose of night. Cather heard the Mexican youth Julio (see Introduction p. xiii) sing this three-stanza love song (in which the contralto singer compares herself to the rose of night, the dry winds of day, and the fading stars) on her crucial first trip to the Southwest (see Chronology, p. xxx), and included her English translation of it in a letter to Elizabeth Shepley Sergeant (Pierpont Morgan Library, NY).

195 *serenata*: strictly speaking, music sung and played at night.

196 *Torreon*: one of the leading commercial centres in northern Mexico.
     simpatico: congenial.

199 '*a Paraíso*': 'in paradise'.
     casa: house, home.
     '*Hace frio!*': 'It's cold!'

200 *El Parreño*: the title refers to a person from Parral, a city near the southern border of Chihuahua that was familiar to US citizens as the locus of Mexican revolutionary Pancho Villa. Cather may be implying that Johnny Tellamantez is from Parral; see note to p. 41 above. The last two lines should be translated as 'And he told me as penitence | To kiss your little mouth' and in Spanish should be: 'Anoche me confesé | Con un padre carmelita | Y me de penitencia | Que besara tu boquita' .

201 '*Trovatore*': *Il trovatore* (The Troubadour), enormously popular four-act opera (1853) by Giuseppe Verdi (1813–1901). Johnny and his friends are probably singing from the much-loved 'Anvil Chorus', which was commonly anthologized during the period.

202 '*Ach, wunderschön!*': 'ah, beautiful!'
     Lucia: *Lucia di Lammermoor* (1835), opera by Italian composer Gaetano Donizetti (1797–1848) with libretto by Salvatore Cammarano based on Sir Walter Scott's novel *The Bride of Lammermoor*. The famous sextet is from Act 2.
     '*Horch!*': 'Listen!'

207 *Pauline Hall*: popular American actress, dancer, and singer (1860–1919) who performed for over forty years and travelled throughout the country, from 1892 with her own company. The New York production of *Erminie*, in which she took the leading role, ran for 800 performances.
     Clara Morris or Modjeska: Tillie Kronborg's incorrect rendering of Helena Modjeska (1844–1909), Polish actress admired for her intelligence, dignity, and charm who achieved fame in the USA, especially in plays by Shakespeare and Ibsen, and who toured throughout the country with Otis Skinner and Maurice Barrymore. Cather met Modjeska in 1898 and made her a character in *My Mortal Enemy* (1926).

209 '*He . . . all*': second stanza of 'My Dear and Only Love' by James Graham, Marquess of Montrose (1612–50).

219 *'Rejoice Greatly'*: 'Rejoice greatly, O daughter of Zion', soprano aria from George Frideric Handel's oratorio *The Messiah*.

223 *'On . . . Pens'*: 'On Mighty Pens Uplifted Soars', aria from Franz Joseph Haydn's oratorio *The Creation*.

  fakir: also spelt *fakeer*; from the Arabic, a performer of tricks or miracles; a wonder-worker.

226 *'Dans . . . a-lar ———mes!'*: 'During our alarms!' From the last stanza of Charles Gounod's popular setting (1853) of the religious song, which requires a series of high notes.

  crescendo: increasing in tone, i.e., gradually getting louder.

229 *Bayreuth*: city in the German state of Bavaria, from 1872 Wagner's adopted city and the site of his theatre, which remained the hub of his music after his death (1883).

  'I. . . Liveth': soprano aria from Handel's *Messiah*.

231 *'Gioconda'*: *La Gioconda*, opera by Amilcare Ponchielli first produced in 1876 and based on a play by Victor Hugo.

  Grieg: Edvard Grieg (1843–1907), Norwegian composer particularly famous for his piano concerto, whose work is often based upon peasant musical idioms.

232 *Prize Song*: courtship song that wins the singing contest—and the bride—at the end of Wagner's comic opera *Die Meistersinger von Nürnberg* (*The Mastersingers of Nuremberg*) (1867).

  Turnverein . . . Turners: gymnastic or athletic clubs popular among German-Americans during the late nineteenth and early twentieth centuries, especially in the Midwest; gymnasts or athletes.

234 *Worth gowns*: Charles Frederick Worth (1825–95), an English designer who settled in Paris, founded the House of Worth, and was the leading arbiter of women's styles for over a generation.

236 *Nietzsche club*: reading clubs (*Vereine*) devoted to cultural topics were common among Germans and German-Americans around the turn of the century. German philosopher Friedrich Nietzsche (1844–1900), later known primarily for his theory of the Superman, was much in vogue among sophisticated intellectuals before the First World War, when he was read as part of a vitalist, new-generation philosophy, especially by young people.

  Rousseaus: Théodore Rousseau (1812–1867), French painter and member of the Barbizon school.

  painting . . . world: probably Edouard Manet's *La Chanteuse de Rues* or *The Street Singer* (1862), which depicts a woman in a grey dress holding a guitar and eating from a bunch of cherries; now in the Boston Museum of Fine Arts.

238 *'gnädige Frau'*: sympathetic lady.

239 *St. John's Day*: feast of the nativity of St John the Baptist, often referred
     to as midsummer day (it occurs around the summer solstice) and thus
     associated with love and lovers by way of ancient fertility rites.

242 *Francis Thompson*: British poet and essayist (1859–1907).

244 *'The . . . Sonata'*: novel by Leo Tolstoy (1889) told as the confession of an
     insane man who murdered his wife in a fit of jealousy; the title is a
     reference to Beethoven's Kreutzer Sonata for piano and violin, played in
     the novel by the wife and her male friend.

247 *Panther Canyon*: actually Walnut Canyon in north-central Arizona near
     Flagstaff, whose major feature is cliff dwellings cut into a 400′ canyon.
     Occupied by peoples probably related to today's Pueblo Indians *c.*1000–
     1200, it became a National Monument in 1915.

251 *piñons*: pine trees.

271 *Zorn etchings*: Anders Zorn was a Swedish painter, etcher, and sculptor
     (1860–1920) whose genre and landscape scenes enjoyed great popularity.

285 *geliebter Sohn*: beloved son.

     noblesse oblige: literally, nobility obliges; more generally the concept that
     persons of high social rank have an obligation to behave in a principled
     fashion.

     eine Ungebildete: one who is ill-bred, uneducated.

295 *Rothschild*: an allusion to the great wealth of the famous international
     banking family.

298 *'Flow . . . Afton'*: song with words by Robert Burns to an old Scottish
     tune.

     Masonic pin: pin worn by member of the secret fraternal order of Free
     and Accepted Masons, familiarly known as Freemasons. Members,
     all male, are typically organized into lodges. Masonic teachings enjoin
     morality, chastity, obedience to the higher law of the land, and belief in a
     higher being. Dissemination from England and Scotland to the USA
     began in the early eighteenth century. Around the turn of the century,
     as the USA underwent urbanization, Masonic lodges were particularly
     associated with provincial small-town life, hence Van Dusen's remark.

310 *'The . . . Danube'*: the most popular of the 400 Viennese waltzes of
     Johann Strauss jun.

314 *Jugendzeit*: youth.

318 *Lehmann*: soprano Lilli Lehmann (1848–1929), one of Bayreuth's leading
     singers, famous in Wagner roles on both sides of the Atlantic (she per-
     formed for almost forty years) but also highly versatile, and an outstand-
     ing singing teacher.

320 *'Deutlich . . . Adelaide!'*: 'Brightly gleaming on every purple petal,
     Adelaide!'

336 *Rhine daughters*: the Rhinemaidens in *Das Rheingold*.

Mahler: Gustav Mahler (1860–1911), Austrian composer and conductor, who after conducting at opera houses in Budapest, Hamburg, and Vienna conducted at the Metropolitan Opera in New York (1908–10), where his performance standards became legendary.

338 *Elizabeth*: the heroine of Wagner's opera *Tannhäuser* (1845).

343 *'Dich . . . wieder'*: 'Dear hall, I greet you again'; Elizabeth's song in *Tannhäuser*.

346 *'Lohengrin'*: romantic opera by Wagner (1850).

Elsa von Brabant: the heroine of *Lohengrin*.

347 *Metropolitan Opera House*: at the time of the novel, located on Broadway between 30th and 40th streets in a building designed by J. C. Cady that had opened in 1883.

348 *'Einsam . . . Tagen'*: 'Lonely in days of sadness', opening of Elsa's first song, sometimes referred to as 'Elsa's Dream' (Act 1, scene 2).

'In . . . Scheine': 'In light and shining armour', a phrase from the same song .

350 *Ortrude . . . Lohengrin*: Ortrud or Ortrude is an evil sorceress with whom Elsa sings a duet; Lohengrin, the hero of the opera, is a knight of the Holy Grail.

entr'acte: intermission.

356 *'Treulich . . . bewacht'*: 'faithfully guided, faithfully guarded'; Fred is combining two different lines from the bridal chorus (Act 3, scene 1).

'In . . . da': 'In light and shining armour | A knight approaches'.

357 *Woglinde*: the particular Rhinemaiden whom Thea portrayed in *Das Rheingold*.

358 *'Lupibus . . . sum'*: roughly, 'Although I live with the wolves I am not a wolf'. Cather has invented this epigrammatic saying. 'Lupibus' should be lupis and 'vivendi' cannot be made to construe in this context.

361 *aria . . . image'*: 'Ah, begone, sweet vision', from the Chevalier's song of renunciation, Act 3 of Jules Massenet's opera *Manon* (1884).

363 *Weber and Fields'*: Broadway music hall, opened and managed from 1896–1904 by the popular burlesque comedy team of Joseph Weber (1867–1942) and Lew Fields (1867–1941).

366 *Venus . . . Elizabeth*: in Wagner's opera *Tannhäuser* Venus is the would-be seductress while Elizabeth epitomizes the ideal.

367 *Tannhäuser*: Wagner's 1845 opera is based on the life of the thirteenth century German minstrel Tannhäuser, whose adventurous wanderings became the stuff of legend.

368 *Sieglinde*: important soprano role in Wagner's *Die Walküre*.

369 *'Walküre'*: *Die Walküre*, the second opera in Wagner's Ring Cycle, first produced in 1870, concerns the reunion of and love between Siegmund

and Sieglinde, brother and sister who are the offspring of a mortal mother and Wotan, the chief of the gods.

370 *Brünnhilde*: one of the Valkyries who escort the souls of slain warriors to Valhalla; a pivotal character in the last three parts of the Ring Cycle, who in *Die Walküre* is punished by Wotan for protecting Siegfried.

375 *Fricka*: goddess of marriage and wife of Wotan in the Ring Cycle.

'wonniger Hausrath': 'blissful household', an allusion to Fricka's scene 2 aria in *Das Rheingold*.

'Trovatore': Thea's would be the leading role of Leonora, a noble lady-in-waiting at the court of Aragon. This is the opera from which Thea sang with Johnny Tellamantez at the dance in Mexico Town; see note to p. 201.

'Tak for mad': 'Thanks for dinner'.

378 *Götterburg*: Valhalla.

'Wotan! . . . erwache!': 'Wotan! Husband! awake!'

379 *die Wölfin*: she-wolf.

382 *'Du . . . Lenz'*: 'You are the spring', Sieglinde's response to Siegmund in their love duet, Act 1, *Die Walküre*.

384 *'comme les autres!'*: 'like the others'.

'Schlafen . . . wohl!': 'Sleep well!'

389 *old air*: by Robert Burns.

396 *Paderewski*: Ignace Jan Paderewski (1860–1941), Polish pianist, composer, and statesman. Popular worldwide for his playing, he made many concert tours in the USA.

'Götterdämmerung': twilight of the gods or day of doom resulting in the destruction of the universe; title of the fourth work (1876) in Wagner's Ring Cycle.

Waltraute: the Valkyrie in *Götterdämmerung* who warns Brünnhilde of disasters that will occur if she refuses to relinquish the ring given to her by Siegfried.

397 *Brangaena*: Isolde's attendant in Wagner's *Tristan und Isolde* (1865).

Isolde: Irish princess, wife of King Marke, who falls in love with Tristan.

400 *Hunding*: Sieglinde's husband.

'Wälse . . . Schwert': 'Wälse! Wälse! | Where is thy sword?'

401 *'Mir . . . Auge'*: 'For me only | the eye awakened'. The one-eyed stranger is Wotan.

'Siegmund . . . dich': 'Siegmund— | So I name thee!'

Nothung: name of the sword that Wotan has driven into a tree; roughly, 'Needful'.

In höchster Trunkenheit: in highest intoxication.

411 *'Wanda'* ... *'Strathmore'*: titles of novels by 'sensation' novelist Marie Louise de la Ramée (1839–1908), who wrote under the pseudonym 'Ouida'.

414 *the King*: King Edward VII.

417 *'The Portrait of Dorian Grey'*: the correct title of Oscar Wilde's 1891 novel is *The Picture of Dorian Gray*.

*The
Oxford
World's
Classics
Website*

www.worldsclassics.co.uk

- Information about new titles
- Explore the full range of Oxford World's Classics
- Links to other literary sites and the main OUP webpage
- Imaginative competitions, with bookish prizes
- Peruse *Compass*, the Oxford World's Classics magazine
- Articles by editors
- Extracts from Introductions
- A forum for discussion and feedback on the series
- Special information for teachers and lecturers

www.worldsclassics.co.uk

American Literature

British and Irish Literature

Children's Literature

Classics and Ancient Literature

Colonial Literature

Eastern Literature

European Literature

History

Medieval Literature

Oxford English Drama

Poetry

Philosophy

Politics

Religion

The Oxford Shakespeare

A complete list of Oxford Paperbacks, including Oxford World's Classics, OPUS, Past Masters, Oxford Authors, Oxford Shakespeare, Oxford Drama, and Oxford Paperback Reference, is available in the UK from the Academic Division Publicity Department, Oxford University Press, Great Clarendon Street, Oxford OX2 6DP.

In the USA, complete lists are available from the Paperbacks Marketing Manager, Oxford University Press, 198 Madison Avenue, New York, NY 10016.

Oxford Paperbacks are available from all good bookshops. In case of difficulty, customers in the UK can order direct from Oxford University Press Bookshop, Freepost, 116 High Street, Oxford OX1 4BR, enclosing full payment. Please add 10 per cent of published price for postage and packing.